ANOTHER GREEN WORLD

ANOTHER GREEN WORLD

RICHARD GRANT

ALFRED A. KNOPF NEW YORK 2006

THIS IS A BORZOI BOOK
PUBLISHED BY ALFRED A. KNOPF

Copyright © 2006 by Richard Grant

Library of Congress Cataloging-in-Publication Data
Grant, Richard, [date].
    Another green world / Richard Grant.—1st ed.
       p.   cm.
    ISBN 0-307-26359-2
    1. World War, 1939–1945—Europe—Fiction. 2. Americans—
Europe—Fiction. 3. World War, 1939–1945—Underground
movements—Fiction. 4. World War, 1939–1945—Poland—Fiction.
5. World War, 1939–1945—Yugoslavia—Fiction. 6. Auschwitz
(Concentration camp)—Fiction. I. Title.
    PS3557.R268A86 2006
813'.54—dc22   2005057930

Manufactured in the United States of America
First Edition

When I look back today,
the image of a romantic
and also a cruel and ruthless world
rises before me.

—Albert Speer

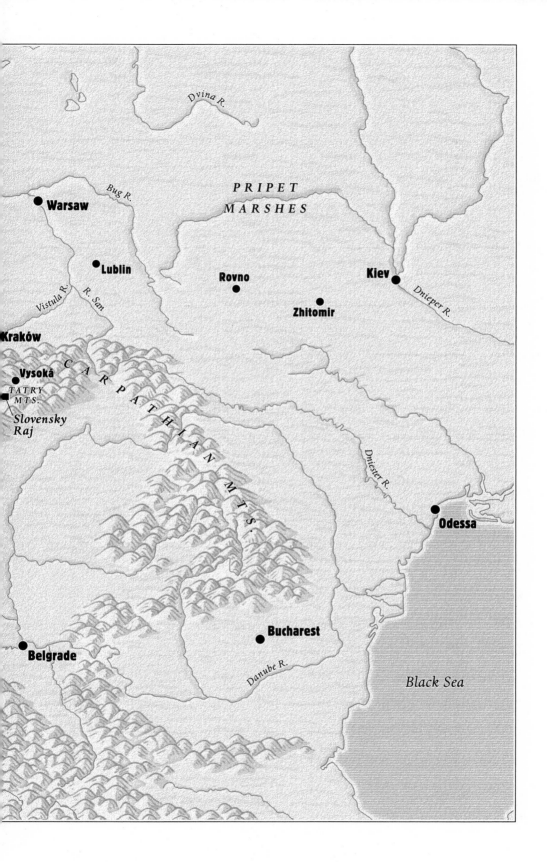

ANOTHER GREEN WORLD

VYSOKÁ, HIGH TATRY

The boy arrived nameless and barefoot. They reckoned he could get by without shoes a while longer, until a suitable pair could be stolen. But names, they had plenty of those, more names than people to wear them. So they began calling him Shlomo, or Solomon, because once there had been a Shlomo whom everybody had liked—when he got killed in an ambush, they blew up a supply train in his honor—and because the boy's lidless, owl-like stare gave him a look of preternatural wisdom. Nobody cared that he must have been called something else. The past meant nothing to these hungry, half-crazed heroes, and few of them expected to know a future. They were like birds shot in flight who would not survive the long, thrilling plummet to the ground.

Meanwhile there was a world to love: mountain lakes that shone black and bottomless like the eyes of a god; sunlight as hard as ice shards; slow-motion waterfalls; a tang of smoke in the upper air; pointed trees and naked, bronze-toned rock; and beyond, unrolling in yellow and green, the vast plain of Northern Europe, like a primed canvas on which generals painted their wars.

Nobody knew where the boy had come from, and he seemed unable to tell them. Certainly he had traveled far because his feet were bleeding from the journey. He was undersized, like everyone who had grown up in the ghettos and the camps, and might have been any age from eight to twenty. He stared at them and at the black spruces and the pitiless blue sky. His eyes drank the world in and gave nothing back. For all you could tell, he was blind. For all you could tell, he was gripped by visions, searing glimpses of eternity. Whatever the truth was, he was not disposed to share it.

He had come, they supposed, seeking the great man, the guerrilla chief, wily and stouthearted, who gave hope to what few of his people remained. The great fighter, so people said, struck at the *niemcy,* the dogs—that is, the Germans—on roads and in forests and in their own well-patrolled lairs. He fought them by night and by daylight, using whatever weapons were available, including his own hands. He had never been beaten, never outsmarted, never caught. The more fervent members of his cult swore he had killed a man with his eyes alone. For years the *niemcy* had hunted him, snarling at his heels like a pack of ravening wolves, yet he had slipped out of their jaws. And still the contest dragged on, the ritual chase, even as hunters and hunted were together dying off.

How much of this legend the boy might have heard was beyond knowing. He sat patiently at the center of the camp, not too close to the fire, not too far away, barely responding when people spoke to him, accepting what food they had to offer with no more than a nod of thanks. He ate like an animal, gnawing and grunting.

A week passed or more—there was little point keeping track, unless a rendezvous or a timed detonator was in question—before the great fighter returned from a mission deep into Poland. He came alone, slipping into the mountain hold so quietly that the sentries might as well have been asleep. Somehow, despite the dark, he noticed the boy straight off. He gave him a look that some described as thoughtful and others as distracted while moving quickly through the camp, summoning this one and that one—only his closest deputies, those he had chosen to run things when he was absent and, in the course of things, dead—and leading them to a small hut near a cold, whispering stream. Later it was said that a sheet of paper had been passed among them. Tallow light flickered briefly and went out. The fighter's shadow fell once more by moonlight.

The boy did not flinch and offered no greeting when the great man stepped closer to the campfire, lowered himself before it and held his hands out, palms open, like a supplicant, or a prisoner demonstrating his harmlessness. He ignored the boy, or seemed to, though they sat barely a stride apart. The rest of the band looked on from a respectful distance, none wishing to disturb their weary leader or to interrupt the rapt observances of the hollow-eyed, wasted boy. They remembered meeting the great man themselves for the first time, after everything one had heard. The surprise of it—how small he was, how physically insignificant: short-legged, long-necked, all joints and no muscle, perhaps even, though no one dared say it, the least bit stoop-shouldered. And that face . . . well. Could this truly be the famous warrior, hated and feared by the Nazis, whose deeds were celebrated around a thousand fires in the outlands of Mitteleuropa?

Such thoughts might have run through the mind of the boy called Shlomo. Or they might not. His empty eyes betrayed nothing, only stared with a perfect equipoise known best to the already-dead. Then suddenly—all who were there remembered such an instant—the great man turned to look at him.

The boy's eyes stretched even wider than before. But he didn't blink; bravely he met the terrible gaze that, so legend held, could kill you as surely as a bullet. Thus they remained, until the hero did something odd with his mouth, or his nose, maybe his ears—you couldn't say exactly what—and the boy responded just as they all had, each in turn.

High on a mountain in a land once called Czechoslovakia, claimed by at least three factions in this war that would go on forever, a boy who wore lightly the name of a king blinked his eyes—those eyes that had watched from the forest while his family was murdered one by one, little Mirka first and Papi last—and with no warning at all, least of all to himself, he began to laugh.

His laughter was high and wild. There was relief in it and a kind of delirium. It rose like smoke on the chilling breeze, and before it faded, the great fighter had taken the boy into his arms and continued to hold him, wordless, as if the two of them had slipped out of the war, out of time itself.

And so in the dark heart of Europe, a lost boy tasted peace.

But what peace could there be for the fighter?

THE DISTRICT

Ingo Miller, the man whose life she was about to ruin, ran a beer-and-schnitzel joint north of Dupont Circle. He lived in a flat upstairs and, so far as anyone knew, rarely set foot off the premises. But this intelligence, like the rest of her private dossier on *Miller, I.,* though extensive, might have been years out of date. So to make certain—and, let's be honest, to buy a little more time—she dispatched a pair of typists armed with a petty-cash disbursement on what some office wag promptly dubbed a Daring Mission Behind Republican Lines. Their report, presented three days later, was dishearteningly clear: Outside his restaurant, the subject had no life worth speaking of. He was making, it seemed, his last stand there, besieged on every side by the twentieth century. If she meant to play Red Death to his barricaded prince, that was the place to do it.

And so it happened that Martina Panich, sometime Roosevelt pom-pom girl and lately leaker-in-chief to the United States War Refugee Board, despite her misgivings—too many to count—and after having killed as much of the day as feasible in her tiny office at Treasury, which she shared with an elderly percolator, set off walking north on Connecticut Avenue shortly after three o'clock, the very worst part of the afternoon. She kept to the shady side—Ingo would appreciate that, no metaphor was too much for him—but Washington heat, like destiny, has a way of finding you. By the time she reached M she felt wrung out, slick with sweat and . . . would you say *abject*? Or did that have to do with your slot in the post-Depression economy?

Either way: at such a moment, second thoughts naturally arose. Martina had agonized over this little stroll uptown for a solid week—truly, she had thought of nothing else. In the end it was unavoidable. She no more wanted to burst in on Ingo's well-ordered universe than to parachute into occupied Belgium. But these days, you do what you have to do. War, as they say, is war.

Yes, and turnips are turnips. The sharp reply—what did it mean?—came in her grandmother's voice, pungently accented, straight out of some shtetl on the rump side of the Pale. It bucked her up. It restored her to her usual condition of chronic, poorly suppressed outrage.

Martina stepped dangerously in front of a bright purple truck from Ridgewell's Catering—even in wartime, the machinery of government runs on hors d'oeuvres and double bourbons—before arriving safely twelve strides later at the Circle proper, a small park that anchored the eastern end of Embassy Row. She waded through pigeons, a boisterous flotilla of navy boys on furlough, chattery secretaries out to lunch from nearby offices, and a jetsam of newspapers, cigarette packs and sandwich wrappers cast up by the human tide on the steps of the old French fountain, its waters greenish, its once-white marble yellowed by auto exhaust. Dutifully she registered the sights and sounds (a siren's whine, a well-dressed wino who believed himself a Justice of the Supreme Court and, to the west, a shoulder of charcoal-gray cloud above the weary lindens of P Street), but her mind remained stubbornly elsewhere. Not on the war— that was too vast to think about, you simply navigated within it—nor on her father's mother, who had died, thank heaven, without fuss in New Jersey. Nor finally on Ingo, quite. Though he was connected, like Martina herself, to this unnamed thing, this risen corpse of their mutual past.

A few paces ahead, just off the sidewalk, a sailor opened his mouth to make fresh. But taking a second look—Martina was older than he'd thought, with a certain expression on her face—he changed his mind and sat staring mumly from his spot on the brown beaten grass, taking in, as she marched by, her proletarian hairdo, her unglamorous low-heeled shoes, and the handbag, tall and sturdy as a valise, she clutched tightly against an antebellum linen blouse that might once have been stylish, now laundered and reworn to within one thread of its life. *These government dames,* he would be thinking. *They'll chew you up as soon as look at you.*

He would be right. Martina left the Circle and proceeded northward on Connecticut. The rumble of a trolley, like bombs falling on a movie screen, rose from the depths of the underground station somewhere beneath her feet. She squared her shoulders. Almost there now—a matter of steps. Her jaw muscles flexed. She was ready to chew up Ingo Miller, her oldest and dearest friend.

★   ★   ★

Before the war (how many sentences began that way) Ingo had owned a *Bierskeller* called the Hessian House. Today he owned an old-world restaurant and lounge called the Rusty Ring. It was the same place—the only changes were the sign out front and, on the menu, certain concessions to wartime food rationing. The same heavy door still crouched at the bottom of the same four concrete steps. The same lace panel—no longer "German"—was strung across the plate-glass window. And somewhere within, proprietarily brooding, changeless, and, in fact, an avowed enemy of change, the same Ingo.

Martina did not pause at the door. In the long, narrow, dimly lit front room she made like a regular patron, trooping up the well-worn path toward the distant mirrored twinkling of the bar. Tables stood mostly empty beneath their starched white cloths. Two guys who looked like wire-service reporters, ties loose and jackets slung over an extra chair, eye-balled her from a corner. Near the center of the room a blue-haired, regal-looking woman brandished a cigarette in a long holder, aiming rather than smoking it, dancing with her head alone to the schmaltz oozing out of the old Victor phonograph. Trust Ingo not to install a jukebox. On the other hand, who'd drop a nickel to hear this stuff?

Inside as out, the place was the same as ever. Maybe old-timers found it comforting. But Ingo had lost his most loyal and free-spending customers—this Martina knew for a fact—back in '41, when the German embassy around the corner on Mass Ave closed shop. Before that, Nazi money had paid for the forest-green carpet and the simulated log fire and other dubious improvements. Martina suspected, and Ingo never explicitly denied, that the row of pictures along the side walls—cheap reproductions of nineteenth-century landscapes of the German Romantic school, mounted in flashy gilt—had begun life as a series of travel posters, shorn now of their inspirational slogans. *American cousins—your Homeland beckons you! See what's doing in the New Europe!* It was to vomit.

She reached the screen of potted greenery that separated the dining room from the lounge. These plants, she believed, had been dying from lack of daylight for the better part of a decade. Even in the final act, nothing here happened quickly. *Twilight of the Palms,* a tragic opera in four parts. Ingo Miller, baritone, sings the part of the Jolly Innkeeper.

Martina parted the fronds. And there he stood: an unmovable eminence, not fat but fleshy, a redoubt of *idées fixes,* safe in his usual spot behind the taps. Ingo's in his cellar, all's right with the world. His yellow hair might be a bit thinner than when she saw him last—*but hey, Marty, we're neither one of us getting any younger.* The difference was, Martina might have hit thirty-five not long ago, but Ingo had been forty his whole life.

Spotting her, he faltered briefly in his routine swabbing of the varnished, glowing surface of the bar, then quickly recovered, slapped the bar rag back in its usual place across his shoulder and broke into a smile. "Look what the cat dragged in," he said cheerfully. "Another bomb-throwing New Dealer."

She affected not to hear. In their history of intramural conflict, politics was only one of several fields on which they'd skirmished. The first shot had been fired in their sandbox days, growing up two doors apart in Brookland, a leafy neighborhood on the northeastern edge of the city. Ingo once tried to yank off her hated pigtails. Martina struck back a few days later under a backyard sprinkler, attempting, with blunt nursery scissors, to excise his penis. How little really had changed. Yet beneath it all she loved him dearly, and she supposed he must love her back; the symmetry of their antagonism seemed to require that.

You couldn't give an inch, though. Martina stepped up to the bar, splaying her fingers on the shiny wood like a predator clawing onto his turf. The effect was diminished by the state of her nails—battered by file drawers, chewed during tense committee hearings, unpainted and, let's face it, unfeminine.

"Can I get you something?" Ingo said placidly, staring through blue and blameless Boy Scout eyes. "Something cold to drink? A bone to gnaw?"

From stage left, a chuckle. Martina whipped her head around to glare at the culprit, a small man in a cheap suit, half hidden behind his newspaper. She held the look until he retreated into the sports pages of the *Washington Herald*—among the District's warring dailies, the only one Martina actually found objectionable. Mission accomplished, she panned in the opposite direction, making certain no trouble would issue from that flank. The face there she vaguely recognized, sallow and gaunt, sweating into a stiff Arrow collar. A would-be war profiteer, she imagined, who'd underestimated both the complexity and the small-town insularity of the place now styling itself Capital of the Free World.

"Ingo," she said, even before her eyes had swung back. "I need to talk to you."

"You know, Marty, I've just put in one of those new *telephones*." Leaning slightly over the bar, his voice chummy, letting you in on a little joke. "It's amazing how well they work. You don't have to shout or anything. People *dial your number,* and you can make plans to meet when it's *mutually convenient.*"

Surprise, however, was a crucial element of her plan. Catch the enemy on the ground, swoop in with the sun at your back; a quick strafing run, customers looking on; then later, in private, the bombshell. "Ingo, I need to talk to you." Pause, emphasis, timing. "Now."

"Why don't you have a seat, Marty?" He indicated an empty bar stool, then a booth along the wall: lady's choice. "I'll have Bernie bring you something. You like those cream tortes, don't you?"

"It's about Isaac," she said.

He didn't react. But that, she thought, was just his talent for impassivity, a protective trick that had become a habit and finally a character trait. The bomb was away, and the pair of them stood there watching it fall.

"You remember Isaac?" Not a question. A goad.

Ingo sighed. He pulled the bar rag off his shoulder, folded it, laid it carefully down. Watching him, Martina caught a glimpse of herself, tensely posed in the wide mirror between bottles of liquor. Her skin looked yellow in this light, the cheeks hollow, a warning flash in those dark eyes. Given the proper sort of hat, she was all ready for Halloween.

"Let's go upstairs," Ingo said wearily.

She knew the way. Around the bar, down the little hall past the restrooms, through a swinging door to the kitchen, Ingo close on her heels. From there, a staircase at the rear of the building, near the alley door. En route, she managed a brief hello to Vernon, Ingo's longtime chef.

"We don't see much of you these days, Miss Panich." Vernon paused to wipe perspiration from a wrinkled brown forehead.

"Official duties," suggested Ingo, nudging her from behind. "Affairs of state. There's a war on, even Treasury's got wind of it."

"Guten tag, Bernie," she called doggedly to the waiter, a more recent arrival, delivered from a chamber ensemble in Vienna via a long boat ride out of Lisbon. Little Bernd Fildermann gave a quick, silent bow, as though still not quite sure of his welcome here.

And with no further ceremony Martina allowed herself to be hustled up the stairs.

How many years has Ingo been living here? And still the place looks like he hasn't settled in. The rooms feel vacant, airless, as if the windows haven't been opened since the Coolidge administration (it is just possible they have not), and the furnishings might have been chosen by some long-dead aunt. Only the distinctive sag of an armchair, recognizably similar in shape to a certain present-day bottom, hints at current habitation. Beside it, a three-legged table holds a reading lamp and one slender volume, hardbound, jacketless. Ever hopeful, Martina lifts the cover. *Love Poems of August von Platen (1796–1835)*. Ex libris Dead Auntie.

"Okay, Marty." Ingo rounded the damask corner of a love seat and drew up with arms folded, countenance grim. "Spill."

She drew a breath. From this point forward, everything hung on how he would react.

"You know what I do for a living," she began.

"Move paper from one basket to another, I should think, like everyone else down there." Quickly he raised a hand, forestalling her. "Wait, yes, I know—you've been in the papers. Something to do with displaced persons, liberated prisoners, that kind of thing."

"That *kind* of thing. But it goes well beyond that. May I sit?"

"Please."

She settled into his armchair—was that an act of covert aggression?—gripping the big handbag by its clasp. "The truth is, Ingo, and I'm saying this off the record, the Board is more or less a personal undertaking of Henry Morgenthau's. He strongly believes"—hastening here, ignoring Ingo's *de rigueur* grimace at the name of the Secretary, her boss, a notorious bleeding heart and, incidentally, the only Jew in FDR's cabinet—"believes very strongly that the United States has a moral obligation toward the victims of Nazi racial policies."

"Nazi, racial, policies." Ingo pronounced the words with elaborate care, as if weighing each on his tongue. "Sounds like a euphemism."

"You could say that. In plain language, we're talking about murder. Murder on an unprecedented scale."

"I thought the term for that was *war*."

"I'm not talking about the war, Ingo. This isn't soldiers killing other soldiers. What I'm talking about—what's *happening* over there is . . ."

While she groped for words, Ingo lowered himself to the love seat with a noisy exhalation, coming to rest in conspicuous discomfort. "I should think, Marty, in your position, with your access to classified reports and whatnot, you'd have developed a more skeptical attitude toward that sort of overblown rhetoric. It's normal in warfare, isn't it, to accuse the other side of atrocities, war crimes, all that? Keeps the blood hot, pumps up support on the home front. 'Why We Fight,' as revealed to Frank Capra. Gives us all a chance to take part. They also serve who sit and preach."

"This isn't propaganda, Ingo."

"I'm not saying we're as bad as *they* are. Don't think I'm saying that."

"I know what you're saying. Just—listen to me."

He made a little show of impatience, tapping his toes, glancing at his watch. Somehow, in her laying of plans, she had pictured him sitting here like an attentive schoolboy while she explained the facts of life in a brisk, no-questions-till-I'm-done-please voice—that voice employed to such good effect by a series of interchangeable nuns while she and Ingo sat side by side, *backs quite straight, children, thank you,* at Francis Xavier Elementary. *In a land like ours, boys and girls, only very far away, bad men are taking all the little Jewish children and putting them on trains, and making them breathe bad air, and then burning them.* But now she could see how Ingo would take that—roughly the same as the press and the War Department and the key people on the Hill were taking it. Only more so. It was not, she had come to think, a matter of disbelief. It was an incapacity to imagine. Like you couldn't imagine a sky full of swirling yellow blobs until Van Gogh painted one for you. Then *voilà,* of course, I see it now. How marvelous! How frightful! Surely not *all* of them.

All of them—but how to spell that out for Ingo, the instinctual unbeliever? *The Nazis are artists, true geniuses, and their medium is immorality.* No: the only way forward was the most brutal and direct, a blow to the heart.

"You're right." She fixed him in a particular kind of stare: Oh, you poor, uninformed civilian. "I do have access to classified reports—look, I've brought a few along. Care to join me in breaking the law?"

She thought she saw his shoulders twitch. Unclasping the handbag—a bit of improvisation here, yielding to a sudden impulse toward violence—she tipped it upside down. A blizzard of daily briefing sheets, memoranda, transcripts, petitions, press clippings, statistical abstracts, railway timetables and fourth-layer carbons on onionskin stormed down, entombing Platen, spilling over onto the drab Edwardian rug.

For seconds the two of them sat there, joined in a state of mild astonishment. Ingo shook his head. "When I said *spill,* Marty . . ."

A giggle escaped her. Like an ear-pop, a sudden equalizing of pressure. It seemed to her that Ingo was struggling to conceal a smile.

"God," she said, "I'm sorry. I didn't mean—"

He waved it off. No need for apologies between old pals, right? "I get the impression, Marty, that you feel you need to *demonstrate* something to me. I wonder why."

Not I wonder *what.*

With the practiced eye of a bureaucrat, she parsed the seeming chaos of paperwork. Daintily she plucked up this and this and that, shuffled them together and pressed them on Ingo in the order she deemed most likely to persuade. A State Department circular, DISTRIBUTION LIMITED, three pages dense with columns and numbers, drafted by an expert in Slavic languages not eager to share his trade secrets. A map of the Carpathian Mountains, Count Dracula's old stomping grounds. A crumpled photo spread from an Australian Socialist weekly, *The Anvil*, cheaply printed, brittle to the touch. Last, deceptively slight, a square of brown paper just larger than needed to roll a cigarette. Ingo accepted the pile incuriously.

"What you're looking at"—she fingered the topmost sheet—"is our best recent tally of resistance organizations in Central Europe. First column name, second column numerical strength—that's a guess, of course—and third operational status. 'A' means fully active, 'I' is for intelligence services only, 'S' for groups devoted primarily to sabotage—you get the idea. 'NI' means no information available."

"A lot of NIs, aren't there."

"Small wonder. You'll notice they tend to coincide with the groups whose strength is given at less than twenty. What happens usually is, these smaller outfits get rounded up and shot. Or they may simply be out of contact. Our information isn't perfect. A lot of it comes via the British, who may or may not be sharing everything they know."

"I thought we were on the same side."

Martina flashed him the look one reserves for the hopelessly naïve. "You'll notice toward the end, something called the Zydowska Organizacja Bojowa or ZOB. That's the Jewish Fighting Organization."

Ingo glanced down. "Another NI."

She resisted the urge, which his air of kingly indifference provoked in her, to throw the handbag at him. "The ZOB was formed in the ghettos during the early stages of occupation. There were plenty of people around to fight in those days, but mostly they took a wait-and-see attitude: you know, maybe we can get through this, there've been pogroms before, we always manage to survive." She shrugged, *what can you do*, recognizing in the gesture her grandmother again. "Now the wait-and-see is over, only there's nobody left to do the fighting."

She paused long enough for Ingo to ask a question, the simplest one: Why? But he didn't—people never did. It was odd, but she knew the pattern by now. Like a blind spot, into which, at one blink, a whole race had vanished. Ingo continued to stare at the page on which the ZOB still enjoyed a hypothetic existence.

"So the next thing there, the map, shows roughly the distribution of resistance forces, principal areas of German anti-partisan operations,

Underground safe zones. The Xs mark recent major engagements. Of course the situation is highly fluid. And I should add, our intelligence, such as it is, is always out of date. What you've got there reflects our best guess at how things stood about six weeks ago. Since then, Tito has swallowed a bigger chunk of Yugoslavia. German strength in Slovakia is building up as the line shifts west. And as of last month, the Red Army has liberated a whole sweep of Poland."

Ingo tightened his lips. "Wouldn't the appropriate term be reconquered?"

"Sure, I get it. They're Communists, so everything they do is evil. Even if it contributes to an Allied victory." She regretted saying this immediately. Escaping into the briar patch of squabbling would suit Ingo fine. By way of atonement she surrendered the armchair and joined Ingo on the love seat, squeezing in all chummy-like.

"There in red," she went on more calmly, pointing at a squiggle that snaked like a garden hose through the mountains on the Czech-Polish frontier, "you can see where the ZOB *might* be operating, assuming it still exists. The main concentration, near Warsaw, was wiped out last autumn. Survivors trickled east into the Pripet Marshes and merged with the Ukrainian Jewish Brigade, under the direct control of Moscow. But a local band or two might be left down here."

She gave him a moment to absorb this. The wicked Reds are over *there;* don't worry about them, they're not even on the map. While down *here,* God willing, is the ZOB. "And in fact, if you look at this newspaper clipping, you'll see evidence that a small resistance group, whose leader, at least, is a Jew, has been active in recent months in exactly this region."

Ingo examined the photo spread as though it were printed in some unfamiliar language. Which in a sense it was: the language of class struggle, Nazism as a terminal case of Late Capitalism, the war as the death rattle of an oppressive world order, all pitched with a broad Australian accent. The story recounted the exploits of workers and peasants waging a secret war of liberation. Grainy photographs showed ruined bridges, a train lying half on its side, tiny figures waving sticks—could they be rifles?—from atop the caboose, smoke rising in a black funnel from what was purported to be a Wehrmacht ammunition depot. Pride of place belonged to a deep-lens shot of someone identified as "the revered commander of this valiant cadre of proletarian fighters." The photo had been magnified well beyond the limits of fidelity; it could have been anyone, anything, man or woman, golem, clotheshorse, melting snowman in jacket and cap. Beneath it, a caption: "Known as the Little Fox, this is the only known likeness of a nameless revolutionary hero."

Ingo said, "Bit of trouble with that syntax, don't you think?" but this struck Martina as weak cover. He couldn't drag his eyes off the picture. Some arresting quality there, though you couldn't quite put a finger on it. Was it the cock of the head, the hint of an insolent stare? The slouch in the shoulders? Something, not quite heroic . . . inspiring, perhaps. Or lucky—at least that. Lucky for now. In the long run, almost certainly doomed. And the revolutionary hero knows it. You can tell, somehow—he knows, he doesn't care. The fight goes on if only for the hell of it. I resist, therefore I am. The world has grown dark, the sun of Weimar has long set, but the nameless fighter pretends not to have noticed. Just one more inning, Ma, come on, we're not even hungry.

Ingo glanced up. "Are you trying to tell me," he said calmly enough, as though it wouldn't have mattered either way, "that this Little Fox actually is Isaac?" There was no need to say more. The picture was nobody they knew, nobody they could know. It was a Rorschach splatter: feel free to project whatever you like on it, just don't expect Ingo to play along.

"But look," she told him.

"Look at what?"

"In your hand."

He was still holding the scrap of brown paper, covered densely with a dark, semi-legible scrawl. What's *this* now?

"It came clipped to the tear sheet," she said, as if that explained everything. The note was not signed.

Ingo read it out, one phrase at a time, as he deciphered them. "'Thought this story might interest you. If so, there is a'—what's this word?—'sequel. From the same source,' comma, 'smuggled over the wire not long ago. Looks authentic to me. You be the judge.' Now an address. '2200 First Street SW.' Not a nice part of town, is it? 'No phone there, just go. You're looking for'—I can't make this out."

"'Vava,' I think it says."

"Really? Oh, I see it. 'Vava. And be sure—'" He squinted a moment longer, making certain. Slowly he raised his head. "'Be sure to take Ingo. She'll only talk to both of you.'"

Martina looked away; the tension was all she could bear. She felt his gaze, steady and contemplative, moving from the paper in his hand to her own averted face, the handbag, the mess on the floor. A blurred and grainy photograph. Putting it together; weighing one thing against another.

"Even if you're right," he said at last, "even *if*—what can we do, other than hope and pray? The war will be over soon. By Christmas, they're saying. Why did you come here, Marty? What do you want from me?"

His voice did not match his words. She turned to face him. His eyes were wide, almost imploring.

Ka-boom, she thought. The bomb had found its target. Ingo Miller, the last isolationist, was about to go to war.

BUZZARDS POINT

Damn him, Ingo thought.

He hauled himself leadenly up the four steps to Connecticut Avenue and for half a minute stood tuning his senses to the rhythms of the city, the afternoon dragging toward a muggy evening, the jostle of pedestrians and steady crawl of traffic uptown. You could never find a cab at this time of day but Ingo guessed it didn't hurt to try.

Four steps. Roughly the depth, so he had read, of a regulation foxhole. The war was less than five years old—three if you counted from when the Yanks came in—yet Ingo's mind, like everyone's, was cluttered with its ephemera. He could open a map and point to Lidice, Coventry, Sebastopol, Saint-Lô. He could tick off the leaders of the Nazi regime and rank them in order of loathsomeness. He knew what an MG-42 was, which army used it, what its shells did when they entered human flesh. Yet he had never *felt* the war, not in a personal way, as a tug in his own well-fed gut, a looming cloud in his future. Never until now.

Isaac. A name, and then the rest: puppet limbs, sarcastic smile, faint and ever-receding voice. *See you next time, pal.* Suddenly a presence—real, unsettling, troublesome as ever, nosing into Ingo's life. His timing characteristically bad. Like a ghost from an unconnected lifetime, the vanished world of youth.

The taxi, a late-model Nash bearing the livery of Earnest's Hackney Service, idled in front of a hydrant at the corner of R, the driver pulling on a cigarette. Ingo had not yet reached the stage at which he would wonder whether such a thing were altogether plausible. Was the cab a timely coincidence or an epiphenomenon, a ripple on the surface that hinted at some dangerous current beneath? Safe on his home turf, protected by a shiny plating of summer sweat, Ingo merely flagged the driver, semaphoring with one finger: *Hang on just a minute.* The cabbie favored him with a nod and a smile made memorable by ghastly yellow teeth.

He found Marty in the kitchen, distracting Vernon from the preparation of *Hühnchenwurst,* a spicy sausage of the chef's own invention made from unrationed chicken trucked in every Saturday by farmers from the Eastern Shore. Thank God Edna, the night waitress, had agreed to come in three hours early. Skinny and tall, with scarlet nails, she was laughing at something Marty had said. At a look from Vernon—head tilting quickly toward Ingo—the kitchen fell quiet. Except for Marty, whose laughter had not really ceased since the 1932 election.

Out on the street, the cabbie flicked away his cigarette and slapped the Nash in gear. Without waiting for instructions he eased forward into traffic. Didn't bat an eye when Ingo read out the address. Perhaps in his job you developed a higher threshold of alarm.

When he spoke, his accent conjured some godforsaken hamlet in the Balkans. "Been another hot one, yes?"

Ingo saw no ground for comment. The weather was Sodomic. But he liked to think it separated real Washingtonians from the other kind, the *arrivistes,* salesmen and budding bureaucrats, illiterate Appalachians on the construction sites and transient junior officers awaiting assignment, a human goulash from all known corners of the world and a few as yet uncharted.

The cabbie at least had been here long enough to manage a rapid zigzag down one-way streets, then to turn south on Seventeenth toward the river. Traffic was thick as usual near Constitution Hall, where the Daughters of the American Revolution had forbidden Marian Anderson to sing on that summer evening five years back, on account of her being colored. She had sung instead on the Monument grounds, coming up on your left, before a crowd of eighty thousand, including Negro families with tiny children gotten up in their Sunday best, hearing an operatic singer for the first time in their lives. *"O beautiful for spacious skies,"* Miss Anderson had sung, and later, *"Nobody knows the trouble I've seen."*

You couldn't hold that concert today if you wanted to. The Mall was littered along its entire length with tempos, cheap and ugly two-story buildings designed to last for the duration and not one pay period longer, accommodating government agencies that hadn't existed eighteen months ago—the War Refugee Board being a case in point.

"So," said the cabbie, "you hear the one about the guy who falls in the Potomac?"

His English, accent aside, was as good as the next man's. Ingo knew the joke, which was making the rounds. But Marty said no, apparently unable to cut this off at the pass.

"Okay, so there's this guy who falls in the Potomac, right? And he's drowning, he's going down for the third time. And this pedestrian crossing the Fourteenth Street Bridge, he looks down and yells, 'Hey, buddy, where do you live?' The drowning guy shouts a street number. So right away the pedestrian jumps in a cab. 'Take me to this address,' he says. They dash over to the other side of town, and he runs up to the poor guy's apartment and tells the landlord he wants to rent the place. 'Sorry,' the landlord tells him. 'That apartment has just been taken.' 'But that's impossible!' says the guy. 'The fellow who lived here, I just saw him drowning in the Potomac River!' 'That's right,' the landlord tells him. 'But the dame who pushed him off the bridge beat you over here.'"

Marty by this time had lapsed into an empty gaze out the window—one of her cloudy moods had come upon her—so it fell to Ingo to offer an adequate chuckle.

The cabbie explained loudly, "The point being, in this town you cannot find a decent place to live."

"Yeah, I get that," said Ingo.

"It's the truth, too."

The driver—Timo, according to a permit taped on the dash—spun hard left onto Independence, following the Potomac downstream. The scenery was more of the same: tempos, traffic, peanut vendors, newsboys flogging the *Evening Star*, soldiers and sailors and WAVES and WACs who all looked in somewhat of a daze, as if they'd just dropped out of the sky from Kansas. There were cops on horseback and MPs in jeeps, people who looked foreign, people who looked lost, people who didn't look like anything at all. Americans. Such as they were.

"Okay, then," Timo muttered, hooking a right onto South Capitol. It might have been a warning: Gird thy loins. The neighborhood here had long been a favorite of Farm Service Bureau photographers, yielding thousands of trite and disheartening shots in which, as a backdrop, you see the gleaming white, neoclassical Rotunda, and in the foreground scenes out of *Uncle Tom's Cabin*—downtrodden darkies in a squalid dooryard, farm animals optional; mothers with empty eyes holding babies who look dead; a tar-paper alley shack bursting with shoeless children—all inevitably captioned, "In the shadow of the Capitol . . ." Notwithstanding, Ingo thought, that shadows fall on the *north* side. Where the slums aren't so picturesquely dreadful.

First Street began with tenements and quickly devolved to empty lots and heavily padlocked warehouses before dead-ending at the riverfront—weed-grown, strewn with beer bottles and those cardboard squares you play the numbers on. Just shy of the embankment, Timo slapped the Nash into neutral and gave them a yellow smile.

"Twenty-two hundred," he said cheerfully. "That would be right about here."

Ingo cased the block. There was no physical evidence that they had reached their destination or that there was any destination to be reached. A barnlike structure of corrugated steel stood on their right, an unintended hedge of mulberry and bamboo on their left, while straight ahead, maybe thirty paces off, the Anacostia slithered by, flat and dirty and slow. There must be some mistake.

But Marty was halfway out the door, and Ingo could hardly permit a woman, even her, to traipse around unescorted in a place like this. So he clambered out and leaned back through the passenger-side window, handing the cabbie the payment due plus a liberal gratuity. "Say, buddy, how about sticking around awhile?"

With a quick nod, Timo killed the ignition.

Ingo glanced up and down the desolate block. "Will you be okay out here?"

In a move too quick to follow, Timo lifted from someplace low a cutdown Louisville Slugger, cored like an apple, its center fitted with a black iron dowel. Self-defense, Ingo guessed, was a knack you picked up early in Balkan hamlets. Timo clicked on the radio, which was airing a jingle on behalf of a downtown jeweler.

> "You don't need cash," says Mr. Tash.
> "If you'll take a chance on romance,
>   I'll take a chance on you!"

"Look." Marty stood before a gap in the mulberries, where a wooden sign had been long overtaken by the endemic rot of the waterfront. Her fingers ran over the chipped and faded lettering. "I think it says 'Buzzards Point Yacht Club.'"

From what he could see, it might as easily have read *Buzz off, you shlub.* But Marty had already slipped through the shadowy opening, and so, with a final glance at the cab, Ingo followed, as he always had done, feeling little of curiosity, still less of hopefulness—only a dumb, stoic resolve to prevent Marty, despite her unstinting efforts toward that end, from getting them both killed.

*   *   *

Inarguably, there were watercraft. A small number of which, mainly turn-of-the-century motor launches, might have passed for yachts. But in the harsh, orange-tinted glare of late afternoon, what Ingo chiefly beheld was a dirty boatyard with three sagging piers and an armada of leaky hulks including one rusted inland tug, a pair of Maryland skipjacks, a side-trawler with a permanent starboard list, a demasted ketch and, most preposterously, an ancient steam-driven tour boat whose patriotic paint job had peeled down to dry-blood primer, clotheslines heavy with drab, shapeless laundry running between its stanchions—the thing looked like a set from the *Our Gang* serial, bobbing on a sullen tide. Away from the shoreline, tucked in a little grove of trees-of-heaven, stood a squarish cinder block building the size of a garage—what do you bet they call this the Clubhouse?—in front of which a Coca-Cola machine gleamed fire-engine-red under a canvas awning on a patio of broken Mexican tile. No question, the place had atmosphere. And something more: Ingo finally realized that each dilapidated boat was inhabited, by men and women, feral-looking children, aged and infirm relations, sinister-looking cats and at least one large, exotically feathered parrot. These were not casual day-sailors but long-term residents. Whatever the Yacht Club might once have hoped to be, it had become a floating tenement.

Marty greeted the first person she met, an elderly woman whose skin had faded to no color at all, rocking in a deck chair that was not intended to rock, with the unprefaced declaration, "We're looking for Vava."

The old lady studied her, in no rush to reply. "Another one now, is it? Well, you'll find Vava down to the end of the second pier. Likely you'll be waking her up. Never seen such a one for napping. Think she hadn't slept in a month of Sundays."

Crossing the boatyard, Ingo felt in an animal way that he was entering alien territory; his nostrils flared at an unknown, perhaps predatory musk. The second pier seemed in no worse shape than the first or third. Halfway along it, a sawed-off metal drum resting on bricks gave forth licking flames, greasy smoke and the heavenly smell of roasting fish. Ingo caught himself relaxing—wherever food was, he was at home. The multicolored children scampering around the fire smiled up at him with round brilliant eyes. The water lapped and gurgled below. He heard Marty exchanging introductions with someone down the pier, but only faintly, as though the voices were muffled by a very thick fog.

"Ingo," she called sharply.

With a couple of kids at his heels, he walked down to where she and a tall woman of striking aspect—a Siberian princess, he thought—stood at opposite ends of a short gangplank.

"Ingo, this is *Vaw*-va," drawing out the difficult vowel. "She's been living here since February. I was just telling her I wish she'd gotten in touch before now!"

A manic tang in her voice. She was as lost as he was, Ingo realized, just as estranged from her native milieu. But while that struck him as a reason to hang back, in Marty evidently it provoked a temperamental urge to plunge onward. The two women regarded him as though something were expected on his part. He could not think what.

"I am so happy to meet you," Vava said at last, though she didn't sound happy. "Won't you both come aboard?"

The gangplank led at an acute angle down to the deck of a vessel so beat-up and salt-grimed that you expected to find Bogie leering sarcastically from the helm. A sliding hatch stood open, and Vava waved them into a claustrophobic cabin with parallel benches flanking a table. Ingo could barely squeeze in, and having done so found himself wedged into an alcove, braced against the rocking of the boat. It was not unpleasant. Marty clambered on hands and knees, a tomboy again, into the seat opposite, followed more gracefully by Vava, whom at last Ingo felt he could decently stare at.

She was attractive—beautiful, possibly—in an exotic, Eurasian fashion. Her hair was darker than blond but not quite brown, her eyes brilliant amber. He fixed her age somewhere in the mid-twenties; that is, a good decade younger than himself.

"Sammy spoke often," she said, "about the two of you."

Sammy? Ingo riffled a mental card file—had he ever known a Sammy? But Marty beamed as if in total comprehension. Yet that's how she would look under any conditions: nose to the wind, wearing her best cocktail-party smile.

Vava's eyes darted at them like she had let slip a small secret. Unimportant, but still secret. For several moments then the three of them sat waiting. For what, it wasn't clear, though Ingo guessed there had to be a story—an over-engineered, Hemingway-esque story with a two-ton theme bolted on. You couldn't just launch into one of those.

Sure enough, Vava pivoted gracefully, extracting from an eye-level cabinet a bottle of plum brandy and a trio of tumblers. Generous cupfuls all around. Ingo went along with it. As the first sip reached the back of his throat, he felt—what was the word?—thrust, bodily, viscerally, into a remembered mental state. Another place, a different decade. A land where people drank sweet potent liquors and lay half-clothed in the sunlight, a time when ideas burst around you like mortar shells. Was it Germany in the Twenties? Or only the other side of the looking-glass, a dimensionless world where Isaac lingered, a blur in a grainy photograph, smiling from under his peasant's cap?

Ingo's eyes refocused to find Vava staring into them, studiously, as if reading his thoughts. She may well have been, as the next thing out of her mouth was, "Shall I tell you how I met Isaac?"

No need to answer. She spoke in a soft, extravagantly accented and sometimes grammatically off-key voice. First a rapid autobiography: born near Vilna and educated in Leningrad, where she lived in the artisans' quarter, Dostoyevsky's old St. Petersburg. At school she joined the Young Pioneers, dumped Dostoyevsky for Marx, attended Comsomol rallies. Shortly before graduation, her first trip abroad to a peace conference in Warsaw, where she was to represent Lithuanian Youth. Here the story grew more exact, the camera pulling in to capture detail.

"It was March. By train we rode, taking the worst seats, in solidarity with the working class. People came from all of Europe. It was cold there—colder than Russia, I thought, but perhaps it is always cold in foreign cities. The gathering was a disappointment, not so big as had been promised, the organizers were sorry. A bad time of year for traveling, they said. But there was another reason. Some of the Western comrades whispered to us—late at night this happened, in little cafés where people read poetry and drafted manifestos and got drunk—they whispered, 'We are worried about this Stalin. We wonder, has the Revolution been betrayed?' Of course on the other side, people shouted back, 'But look at Germany, there is Hitler who wants to destroy us! Everywhere are revanchists and traitors! In hard times, one can only be hard oneself!'"

She shrugged away those old debates, leaving you to guess which side she had taken. "Already it was 1936, everyone knew about the purges. In Warsaw and other places too, Prague, Paris, Istanbul, were living writers and painters who had fled Russia. Sometimes these people were also made to vanish. But our group leader quoted Malinkovsky: The individual counts for nothing. Our duty, in the vanguard, is to think not for ourselves but for the masses at large."

Ingo felt his stomach tighten and opened his mouth, perhaps to argue, though with whom? Malinkovsky? Martina shot him a fierce warning glance that Vava did not appear to notice.

"From a table in the shadows, a voice spoke out: 'When I try to think for the masses, it only gives me a headache.' Most of this was in bad Russian but the word for headache was Yiddish, kopvey. I knew some Yiddish because I came from Vilna, where lived many Jews. Somebody laughed and then somebody else, soon the whole room was laughing. I became angry. This was a provocation, someone was trying to embarrass our group leader. I wanted to know, who is this agitator? But the café was dark, I couldn't tell who had spoken. So I thought, I will remember this voice. Then I will know him, when we meet again.

"And so it happened. The day after, or the next—the rally went four days in all—I heard this voice again, now in daytime, near the main hall. It was not a Polish voice, I thought. But also not the voice of a Jew, such as I had known. And the agitator, when finally I . . . confronted, yes? Confronted him. He did not look as I expected. Not so young as the voice sounded, perhaps no student at all. Shorter, also. With quite red hair and I would say a comical face."

Vava's expression changed. Had she offended her guests with this description of their friend? She had not.

"I was angry still. But the agitator only smiled. You know, a good comrade, happy to see you, that kind of smile. And he said—"

Ingo caught his breath. As though, if he kept absolutely quiet, he might hear that voice for himself. Indeed Vava had the phrasing, the intonation, down cold.

"'Me and some friends are making a movie. Kind of a political movie. Want to be in it?'"

Vava paused here, frowning, seemingly still puzzled by what happened next. She had not said yes. Nonetheless she consented to leave the hall with this red-haired stranger. *Movie* she knew to be an American word; could the agitator be American? This would explain . . . well, perhaps nothing. They rode a streetcar to a different part of the city, like the workers' quarter in Leningrad, dark and populous, crouched beside a frozen river, fires burning in the street. They entered a building that was like a church but empty of pews, from whose tall ceiling hung stage lights and a tangle of wiring. At first Vava saw no other people, only a brightly illuminated corner where a make-believe cottage stood propped on wooden braces. Along a second wall someone had built a tiny forest with real tree boughs, winter-naked, nailed into fantastic configurations and trimmed out with paper scissored into rough ovals. The forest did not look credible at all, though the cottage was not so bad. "It's not *supposed* to be real," the agitator explained. "It's a *folk tale*, get it?"

Ingo's profession had made him an expert listener. He probed Vava's story for tiny cracks. What language was the stranger speaking—bad Russian still? Why were the lights on with no one around? Do they really make movies in Warsaw? In the end, loose threads and all, there was no denying the ring of plausibility. "So this movie," he said mildly, circling back to a point that had struck him as out of character. "It was political, you say?"

"Isaac said it was." Her voice as diffident as his own. "But you know, he said many things."

Ingo nodded and immediately felt disloyal. In any case it was less than half true: Isaac said many things, yes, but he left a far greater number unspoken. And after these many years it was chiefly the uncertainties, the silences, that remained.

"Isaac never had a political bone in his body," Marty said, typically loud and indecorous. "That was one of the things that drove you crazy about him. There he was in the middle of it, but everything seemed to blow right past him."

Vava smiled indulgently. "By 1936," she said, "there were in Europe not many Jews lacking a political bone."

Marty sat back, abashed. Her expression grew pensive. "Warsaw," she said. "He was living in Warsaw? How long did he stay there, I wonder? I hope he had the sense to get out in time."

"Well, obviously he got out *in time*," Ingo said impatiently. "He's still alive, isn't he? At least if that picture—"

"You know it's him."

"I don't know much of anything," he said glumly, feeling this to be all too globally true.

Vava held the two of them in a passive and impenetrable gaze.

Ingo turned to glare at her. "And another thing. Who the hell is Sammy?"

"Sammy is . . ." She seemed genuinely perplexed. "Sammy told me you were old friends, you surely would remember. From Germany, that time . . ."

Marty laid a hand on Ingo's arm and said, in the tone of someone breaking really bad news, "Sammy is Butler. You know, Butler?"

"Oh, good God."

The last person Ingo wanted to hear of again—as in, ever—was Samuel Butler Randolph III: trust-fund Trotskyite, victim of vintage-champagne-poisoning and sometime intimate of the young Miss Martina Panich.

"Butler wrote that newspaper piece," Marty explained. "And the note with this address in it."

Ingo grimly nodded. *Thought this story might interest you. If so, there's a sequel.* "What's the sequel?" he asked.

Vava was no more than momentarily puzzled. Which stood to reason: if this was some kind of trick, she would be in on it.

"You know," she said, her voice smooth and soft, "Isaac had a number of unfortunate experiences. Back in the Thirties and also earlier, perhaps. Unexpected turns of fate he viewed as personal betrayals. He takes such things very much to heart. Too much so, I think. For a time I felt he was becoming, in the Freudian sense, a paranoiac. Though looking back . . . well. He is alive, no? When so many, so very many, are not. And this perhaps makes his paranoia to seem now more like a painful sort of realism. But however that may be, the result is also that he became completely distrustful. Or almost completely. Not one hundred percent, but anyway ninety-nine."

"Ninety-nine," Marty parroted, as if this figure were scientifically exact, a proven constant.

"And just how," said Ingo, "does this concern Butler?"

Vava would allow herself to be neither ruffled nor hurried. "When the war broke out, we found ourselves on different sides of the Molotov line. Sammy and I were at the time working around Lublin, in the East, organizing cells in anticipation of an eventual German attack. Isaac was somewhere west of Kracόw—I believe he has family there. So we found ourselves in the Soviet zone when he was trapped on the German side. For a time we managed to stay in contact. Isaac became affiliated with the ZOB, and Sammy, as an American journalist, was able to travel back and forth, sometimes even to the West. He got from Isaac some good stories which were helpful in his career. Though knowing Isaac, I always wondered . . ."

Ingo coughed to cover what had begun as a chuckle. He entertained for a moment the crazed notion that Isaac was hiding somewhere on board, eavesdropping through a porthole, waiting to astonish them by popping out. This was succeeded by a wave of terrible aloneness.

"Then of course came 1941, and the Germans were in Riga within the first week of their offensive. Now it was I who was caught on the wrong side. Butler flashed his press credentials and his passport and perhaps a little money, and the Germans allowed him to board a ship for Stockholm. He journeyed from there to Moscow and arranged through a certain organization for me to be moved first south to Odessa, and later, by a roundabout route, to Istanbul. I am keeping the story short. It was really quite an ordeal. Naturally, after that we lost touch with Isaac. Later we heard that the entire ZOB had been annihilated, so we more or less gave up hope for him.

"Sammy found a new career as a front-line correspondent. At one time, so he told me, he was the only American journalist traveling with the Red Army. From what I have seen since coming here, I believe that may be correct.

"And so things stood. Until one day, Isaac, who was truly alive, happened to find himself in possession of a very important, very sensitive document."

Ingo almost laughed—probably just a nervous reaction that even Isaac wouldn't have taken amiss. There was no need to ask how such a document might have fallen into those nimble, ever-reaching hands.

"Now there was a problem," Vava went on. "Several problems, in fact. What to do with this piece of paper. For it was too important simply to discard. And implied by this, whom to trust with news of its discovery. Finally, how to communicate this news, once the matter was decided. A chain of problems to be solved. And so Isaac took them one by one. What to do: well, the document must be delivered to the West. How to make contact: here it seems that Sammy came to mind, with his knowledge of that world and his access to many channels of communication—and, it must be said, his hunger for the big scoop. Lastly, whom to trust. For Isaac, this would have been a most serious matter. The most difficult."

She seemed to be addressing chiefly Ingo, except he wasn't entirely paying attention. Something had gripped him, some constriction of consciousness that was moment by moment tightening its hold. The symptoms had started some while back, quietly, but by now they were growing acute. Perhaps it was no more than plum brandy on a changing tide. "Excuse me," he managed to say, "I think maybe I need some air."

He tried to stand but he was caught between the table and the bulkhead. The bile seemed to surge in his gut, and he felt an awful, unreasoning panic. Damn him, he thought. Fifteen years of nothing, and now this. Right back to where we left off.

"Feeling better?" asked Martina, her tone none too gentle.

"I'm fine." Ingo's voice, in his own ears, sounded as forlorn as the bell-buoy clanging far down the river.

Vava said, "Can I get you something?"

He shook his head, though it was probably too dark for them to see.

They stood on the sagging pier. The Washington Monument, blacked out against the fantasy of a German air raid, was faintly visible, mirrored in the river, like a giant candle jutting into the smoky western sky.

"Would somebody," he said, addressing the night at large, "be kind enough to tell me what the hell is going on?"

It was Vava who replied. "Please understand, I have no wish to bring you memories that might be . . . not comfortable. Except there is something I need to tell you, a message. And it is necessary that you believe. Sammy told me this especially. 'You will have a hard time convincing Ingo. He doesn't accept new ideas readily. Part of him still lives in Schiller's age, rebelling against the fucking steam engine.'"

She spoke with a newcomer's ingenuousness. Maybe in Slavic tongues *fucking* was not considered rude. As a critique of Ingo's personality this was hardly new ground—he was the definitive revanchist, and proudly so—but damn it, was there no limit to Butler's cheek? "Why not just give me the message," he said. "Leave the credulity part to me."

The fire in the metal drum had burned down to coals, and in this faintly ominous light Vava's features shifted eastward, settling on their more elemental Asian side. The change deprived her of any definite aspect of age or even gender—which rather suited that protean, eerily modulable voice.

"You must know," she said, "I am the third person to have carried this message. Like those before me I pass it on as accurately as I can. If there is an error, it can only be a minor one, and that chance must be accepted— the message comes from a place where words are dangerous and certain words even worse."

This was becoming, Ingo thought, a fairy tale. An old German *Märchen*, secrets twinkling in the darkness like elfin gold. *Speak the name, Princess, and your beloved need not die.* He shrugged. "Okay," he said, "shoot."

"The message begins, *We never thought they'd put it in writing.*"

As before, it wasn't Vava's voice but an uncanny simulacrum, a distant but recognizable echo like some shortwave signal from the other side of the world.

"*But they always put it in writing. They can't resist. The pig farmer has got to lord it over his pals. So here you go—a memo to Protector, Bohemia and Moravia, signed HH. 'Der Führer hat mir befohlen, die Juden auszurotten.' It's the real thing, I guarantee it.*"

Ingo tried to interrupt. The spectral presence of another being on the pier was so compelling that he wanted to speak back to it. But Vava continued heedless, as though it were Ingo whose reality was debatable.

"*But I can't take it across myself—people need me here. And I don't trust anybody, I mean anybody. Not with this. You've got to come over and get it. But send Ingo, that's my only condition. Ingo I'll trust.*"

Vava paused. Now a P.S., he thought. One last tap to drive the nail home.

"And make it quick—it's getting cold in this damn haystack."

For a while Ingo gazed into the undead cinders. When he raised his head, both women were staring at him, as though awaiting a verdict. What did they expect—tears, laughter, trembling excitement? Whatever it was, he did not intend to provide it.

Marty said, "What does it mean?"

In a mechanical voice Ingo translated the German part—*The Führer has ordered me,* and here some hesitation over the verb, *to destroy,* or perhaps *to eradicate, the Jews*—giving the statement no particular emphasis, as indeed it seemed to demand none. But even in his own thoughts he had no wish to dwell on the last part, the coded signature. Cold in the haystack.

"For God's sake!" Marty was getting worked up; he could feel it in the dark. "Does it sound legit? I mean, do you think it sounds like Isaac?"

Think was not the word for what Ingo was doing. Martina's words, along with others, words from long ago, German jumbled with English, faces, footsteps, hiking songs, a distant landscape, blood staining rock, summer dying in the arms of September. *Do you think it sounds like Isaac?*

Well, you know, now that you ask, I rather think it does. For their bene-fit, he shrugged. "That's impossible to say."

"He's lying," Martina told Vava, one girl to another, "you can hear it in his voice. He's a terrible actor. Well"—she drew a long breath—"this is big, that's for sure. Really big. Isaac's right not to keep this to himself."

She paced. You could practically hear her brain bubbling.

"I know what you're thinking, Marty, and I simply can't believe it." Ingo spoke with the serenity of a man who knows that his opinion, right or wrong, is not worth a tinker's dam.

"What are you going to do?" asked Vava, like the straight man in a vaudeville act.

"There's nothing we *can* do," Ingo said. Still the innocent after all these years. "Unless I'm mistaken, they've got some kind of war going on over there."

Marty spun to face him. "I am so sick of hearing people say that," she said. "Shucks, ma'am, I'm sorry, but we've got this here war to deal with. When that's over, maybe we'll have time to worry about a bunch of Jews."

Ingo made the necessary effort to keep his voice calm. "That's not what I'm saying, as you well know. I'm merely pointing out that, under the circumstances, there's no sense even talking about this any further. There's a limit to what's possible, Marty, even for you."

He waited for her to argue. Instead, after an interval of silence, she told him, "There was a time when you wouldn't have said that. There was a time when *nothing* was impossible. Remember?"

Yes, I remember, he could have replied; that would've been easy enough. But he didn't believe it. Because to remember, to truly know again, and feel again, how things had been—could your mind withstand that? Could your heart? No, it could not. And so he refused to think any more about Isaac: his message, his whereabouts, his fate, his face, his voice. None of it.

It was therefore strange indeed that when Marty prodded him—"You do remember, don't you?"—he heard himself saying yes.

Yes, damn it, I do.

LIBERATED UKRAINE

For Butler, a trip to Front Headquarters was like coming home—notwithstanding Wolfe's dictum that you can never do that again. In the field, where he traveled with a Red Army forward reconnaissance company, he was perpetually the innocent abroad: living rough and taking unnecessary risks to prove his manhood, bathing rarely, letting his beard grow, drinking the stuff that passed for coffee and the deadlier stuff that passed for vodka, clacking through the fraught hours on a special Remington modified to cough out Cyrillic characters and submitting the product to the vagaries of Soviet censorship and subsequent transmission to a baker's dozen leftist broadsheets, whose errant stringer he was. After a few weeks of this he was more than ready to retreat to more congenial environs.

At Headquarters, Butler could relax. He could sleep late and shave with real soap, sip cognac and chat brightly in any of the three or, on a good night, five languages at his disposal. He could opine loudly without fear of provoking violence. He could, if it suited him, stand up and leave the room, the tent or the bombed-out cellar to indulge in golden minutes of privacy. In short, he could return to his truest self, if only for a couple of days.

It didn't matter that Front Headquarters was forever moving from place to place. Nor that the front commander changed from time to time, nor that the whole army might be dissolved, reconstituted and renamed. Yesterday's Voronezh Front, under Vatutin, became today's 4th Ukrainian under Petrov—broadly speaking, a wash. Above all it didn't matter that a tall, broad-shouldered Yank, striding confidently in his sheepskin boots and Astrakhan coat, would never be mistaken for a native of this godfor-

saken steppe. For in the end Front HQ was Butler's home, if he had ever
had one.

He loved the place. He loved its surreal mélange of martial order and
mad improvisation. He admired its tectonic clash of cultural types, soldiers and support staff and camp followers from all corners of the
Eurasian landmass. He marveled at the Brobdingnagian logistics, the
trainloads of paper churned out daily, the reservoir of alcohol drained
each night, the crush of comrades old and new, many of them women,
most of them young, all in the mood for adventure. You couldn't ask for a
finer or more fitting home for the likes of Samuel Butler Randolph III. And
it was there for him, always, in one place or another, as long as the war
should last, whenever he could shake himself loose from the gruesome
monotony of the line.

Butler's first order of business, as soon as he lowered himself from the
cab of the mail truck he'd hitched a ride on, was to orient himself to this
latest place at which Headquarters had come to rest. It was a town or small
city—impossible to judge in its present condition—that the Russians called
Rownje. The Nazis had called it Rovno and made it the center of SS and
police operations in Reichskommisariat Ukraine. As such, it was safely distant from the official, army-run occupation authority in Zhitomir, for the
boches liked to segregate military from "political" operations. The left
hand, doling out ration coupons, might plausibly assert ignorance that the
right hand was machine-gunning several thousand naked, shivering and
sobbing women and children lined up before a ditch outside Melitopol.
Division of labor: one of the higher refinements of Late Capitalism.

On this metal-gray autumn afternoon, Rownje was a treeless, blasted
ruin. The *boches* left little standing during their long retreat. And in towns
like this, from which the Waffen-SS had decamped, the destruction was
especially thorough and sometimes, in a twisted way, poetic. Take the
local Orthodox cathedral, a roughly cube-shaped and brightly painted
structure, circa 1700. It had survived a civil war followed by a generation of
compulsory atheism, and its walls of thick sandstone had withstood the
initial, rather perfunctory Nazi sacking of the town; yet some thoughtful
artillery officer, in the midst of the German withdrawal, had paused on the
road west to Brody, turned his guns around, dialed in a series of correc-
tions and—despite a critical shortage of ammunition—blown apart the
bright blue onion of the cathedral dome. Now the building stood like a
very symbol of the strange beast that was the USSR: hulking, battered,
maimed and desecrated but nonetheless mighty impressive, stubbornly
unwilling to die.

Butler set off in that direction, passing unhurriedly through the narrow, rubble-filled lanes without pausing to ask directions or study the hastily stenciled placards affixed to such walls as still stood—often plastered over earlier, Gothic street markers—giving directions to this or that administrative branch or subordinate command. He trusted his homing instincts, knowing from experience that the most interesting places in this floating, half-real city—the bathhouses, the senior officers' brothel, the improvised labyrinths of the NKVD—would have no street address. They would simply be there, secret places in the ruins, opening before you like Aladdin's cave so long as you knew the magic words.

Butler knew them all. He always had. The key to both his success as a journalist and his failure as a novelist, it made things happen easily and rather too quickly, rendering him congenitally restless.

A block short of the cathedral stood the old public library, a post-Leninist artifact. Its upper stories had been blown apart and its books, of course, long since reduced to ashes. But a row of Willys utility vehicles—jeeps to everyone but the Reds—stood like horses tethered outside a saloon, and two duty drivers sat smoking near a doorway, to which a path through the rubble had been cleared. A stone pediment that once held a statue of some proletarian hero now propped up a sign identifying this as the Foreign Press Liaison Office—Butler's nominal destination.

He recognized one of the drivers, a crusty old fellow from Murmansk. "Enjoying the weather?" he called from several paces off, stepping carefully between bricks and uncollected shell casings and mortar crushed as fine as talc. One thing he hated about places like this was the likelihood of treading on the odd, unidentifiable bit of human remains. He sometimes wished the Red Army would acquire, along with other spoils of victory, the Wehrmacht's fastidiousness. You overrun a town, you press-gang civilian survivors or, if none exist, employ POWs to tidy up the streets; within forty-eight hours, everything is clean enough for the Herr General's mistress to promenade through.

"Better here than home," the old Russian called back. "They'll be having a foot of snow up there by now."

The other driver, a teenager missing most of his left arm, gave a dutiful smirk. Butler wondered if this boy was a victim of battle or of some routine industrial mishap or else—a slight but real possibility—a shirker who'd gotten drunk and chopped his own arm off to avoid being thrown into the line. All manner of social detritus seemed to collect around the Foreign Press Liaison Office, which was convenient for the reporters: a surfeit of willing, if dubious, sources of news from the front, rumors from

Moscow, predictions for the coming offensive, rosters and diagrams showing the order of battle, colorful accounts of partisan raids in Baltic outlands or Carpathian foothills, lurid reports of German atrocities, and
statistics ranging from enemies captured to this year's better-than-
expected harvest of rapeseed. Too easy, even by Butler's standards. Most of
his colleagues spent their days mooning around HQ like a brood of hung-
over vultures. They seldom ventured into the field, and why should they?
Nobody back in Peoria would know any better, and few anywhere would
care.

As far as Yanks were concerned, the war was happening in Okinawa, the
Hurtgen Forest, the Arno Line. It was a story of heroism and sacrifice, a
clash of Hollywood-ready field commanders—Butler's money was on
Jimmy Stewart to play Patton, facing Gable as a rakish Rommel—and,
at its core, a morality play. Eisenhower tossed the word *crusade* about
and nobody thought to question him, for the myth of holy knights versus
infidels—or the Allies as cavalry, Nazis as savage redskins—fit so snugly in
the American *Weltanschauung*.

Never mind that in the big picture, skirmishes in Western Europe barely
counted as a sideshow. That the forces engaged there numbered only a
fraction of those in the East. When five divisions hit the beach on D-Day,
the world held its breath; one hundred and twenty Red Army divisions were
now pointed right at Berlin alone, in just one sector of a six-thousand-
kilometer front, stretching from the Gulf of Finland to the Caspian Sea.
But such details were so numbing that the world switched off the radio. And
never mind that for Germans, the fight with the Anglo-American alliance
was a quarrel among cousins—a distasteful business, but one in which
honor must be preserved—whereas the fight with the subhuman Bolsheviks was nothing less than a *Schicksalskampf*, a struggle for destiny, into
which the whole ruthless fury of an evil regime had been thrown. The truth
of the matter, as Butler's colleagues understood, was that nobody back
home wanted to know what was happening here. The good folks in Peoria
wanted to open their Sunday paper and read about courage and triumph,
not horror and bestiality. They wanted a happy ending and a big-screen
kiss in the last reel—not some blood-drenched Wagnerian opera, corpses
strewn all over the stage, closing on a brazen and dissonant final chord.

And really, whose job was it to disappoint them? It wasn't the task of a
working reporter to explain that this war was no Christian morality play,
but rather a pagan saga—the story of Ragnarok, the last battle, twilight of
the gods, death of the old world order. That was the business of historians,
Butler supposed, or of poets; people working calmly in quiet rooms.

From somewhere in the wastes of Rownje, an explosion went off like the thump of distant fireworks. Cleaning up UXBs, a nice job for the *shtraf* brigades. The one-armed driver—stabbed by guilt?—cocked his head toward the sound, then faced Butler with the sharp, appraising gaze of the bloody-minded opportunist. A character type not prominent in *War and Peace* but well represented in, say, Gogol's *Dead Souls*. Well, so are we all, thought Butler—that is the kind of war it is.

"Say, did you hear they found the place where the Gestapo did their interrogations?" the man said. "And outside, executions. It's an old tsarist mansion with high walls all around. I could get you in there. You'd have an exclusive."

The older one from Murmansk shook his head. "Sammy here's a front-line man. He likes to write about real soldiers, real fighting, not these other things, the torture, the occupation."

Butler smiled and turned away, wondering why Russians liked to call him Sammy. Maybe they felt it sounded American. Inside the ruined library, officious young women behind a folding table proffered travel directions, commissary vouchers, clean linen, first-aid kits, Russian phrase books containing the latest official jargon, a newly commissioned hagiography of Comrade Stalin and the latest tidings from the major Red Army commands. *XVII Army, 2 Bielorussian Front, commanded by Comrade General I. Shretsev, sends its greetings to patriots everywhere and proudly declares the liberation of Vitebsk.* Butler knew a couple of these good Communist ladies in a vague, genial way. As he stood blinking his eyes, adjusting to the interior gloom, a Georgian brunette sporting a red beret and sergeant's insignia gave a little cry of recognition.

"Comrade Sammy! Here, we are holding several items of post for you. Packages from abroad." Flashing a smile, she ducked into an alcove screened by a panel of brightly dyed Azerbaijani cotton.

Butler glanced around the room. On one wall, over disintegrating plaster, a notice board displayed recent press clippings, accounts of the Red Army's progress in rolling back the German aggressors, and a *Pravda* tract by Ehrenburg, the Rimbaud of hot-blooded propaganda. ("One cannot bear the Germans, these fish-eyed oafs; one cannot live while these gray-green slugs are alive. Kill them all and dig them into the earth.") Stacked on the concrete floor, a jumble of Western publications ranging from months-old copies of *Look* and the *Saturday Evening Post* through cheaply printed Maquis broadsheets to last week's *Stars and Stripes*, its cover glumly adorned with Mauldin dogfaces. The only comfortable chairs in sight had been claimed by a pair of earnest Indochinese and a drunken Brit, who was known, for reasons Butler had never learned, as the Reaper. The latter gave him a quick, collegial nod.

From the screened alcove tottered a pile of cardboard boxes, followed by the lady sergeant, struggling to postpone the inevitable collapse.

"Let me help you, tovarich," said Butler, springing forward. His arms briefly tangled with hers, and a few boxes clunked to the floor.

"I'm so sorry." The sergeant was lightly panting.

Butler studied the line of perspiration at her temple, running down skin as dark and fine as polished wood. "Nothing to worry about," he said softly in passable Russian. "I'm sure anything valuable will already have been stolen."

She giggled, met his eyes, flushed becomingly.

"Why don't we just set it all down over here," Butler suggested, edging them into a corner, "and we shall see what we've got. Maybe I can shed some of this stuff right now."

One of the larger packages, postmarked Washington, D.C., held half-pound bags of unground A&P coffee beans, a dozen cartons of Lucky Strikes, a stack of phonograph records and several pairs of extra-sheer nylon stockings.

"These are . . . for you?" the lady sergeant asked, switching to broken English and charmingly failing to mask her open-mouthed wonder.

"No, they're for you," said Butler, pressing the nylons into her hands. "A gift from the people of the United States."

The sergeant stared at him, then broke into a laugh. "Ah, the well-known American largesse," she said, reverting to the polished, Ballet Russe elocution native to Leningrad. Foreign Press Liaison ranks were weighted toward politically reliable university students with a flair for languages.

"Here," Butler said, reaching into the folds of his expensive overcoat, the sort senior Party types got to wear. "I have some stories here that need to be filed, but I expect to be occupied all afternoon. I wonder, if you get a few minutes?"

The sergeant nodded, brisk and businesslike, stacking the sheaf of papers atop the nylons—interrelated clauses of a wordless contract—and regarding Butler with a certain expectancy, wondering if there was more.

There was. Butler quickly inventoried the stack of parcels, culling this or that item for immediate use, stacking the rest against the wall. Soon the pockets discreetly sewn into his coat lining were filled. He smiled at the sergeant, giving her the hapless shrug of a man comically overwhelmed.

"Would it be possible to have the rest of these items shipped forward?

I'm with the 104th Guards, Special Reconnaissance, near Przemysl. Perhaps if someone is driving out in the next day or two . . ."

"Of course, comrade. I will see what can be arranged. Will you be checking in again today?"

"I'll be tied up," said Butler in colloquial English, which everyone knew from the movies. "Got to catch up with the folks back home."

"And home is . . . Washington, D.C.?"

Butler shook his head and smiled.

No sign announced the place he was looking for. The place had no name, and neither did the man who waited there.

Puak, he was called: a Russian word meaning spider. It was not a name but a mask, a fitting image; as *Stalin,* for example, meant steel, and *Füchschen* meant little fox. His position vis-à-vis the 4th Ukrainian Front was undefined and, for all Butler knew, nonexistent. To say he was Moscow's man in Rownje—a typical correspondent's formula—meant nothing, because Moscow, in such a context, might mean any number of things: the Stavka, the Chekha, the NKVD, or any of the rival power blocs within these shadowy organizations. Unquestionably Puak had been sent here by certain higher powers, but who those powers were and what their ultimate motives might be remained as mysterious as the man's true identity.

Butler chuckled when he saw the dull brass plaque engraved with what the casual eye would take for a street number, 1965. In truth this was no address but rather a date: the glorious year, just two decades hence, when—according to a prophecy attributed to Felix Dzerzhinsky—world Capitalism would have breathed its last and the enlightened rule of the proletariat would reach from pole to pole.

Fixing the date there struck some as pessimistic and others as starry-eyed, but to Butler it seemed about right. Today was 1944, and Nazism would surely be destroyed within the year. There would follow a time of upheaval and hardship in Europe—the sort of messy, confusing, and expensive situation from which Americans always strive to extract themselves. They had abandoned Europe in the Twenties and would do so again, Butler was certain, in the Fifties. With the Yanks out, the Soviets would soon be running the show. The old empires would be dismantled, and former colonial subjects—accounting for the bulk of the world's population—would look to the USSR as the great liberating power, a beacon of hope and a model for the future. The United States, thus isolated, would hold out a while longer as a privileged island of revanchism, secure between its shining seas. But that game couldn't go on forever. In the absence of global markets to exploit, America would fall victim to the greed, decadence and hedonism of its own elite. It would die of consumption. As to *when* this would occur, well, 1965 was as good a guess as any.

He stood for a minute outside the building where the brass plaque hung, too small to have been a house, more likely a shop or storefront. For some reason, the notion of a cobbler's workshop came to mind—an echo, perhaps, of one queerly affecting story among the thousands about the *Rattenkrieg* at Stalingrad. Most of these were pure fiction, but the tale of the shoemaker's son turned spy was sufficiently quirky and human-scale that it might actually have happened. And true or not, it would have appealed to Puak.

So it was with no small delight that Butler stepped over a freshly swept threshold into a room that looters had cleared of everything except a long workbench bearing a couple of decades' worth of small hammer marks and the dull black sheen of shoe wax. A man who looked like a Lower East Side cop sat at one end of the bench, calmly twirling an old-fashioned billy club like the ones the Tsar's police had wielded against factory workers on the streets of St. Petersburg. Here, in a town where you could pick up automatic firearms off the sidewalk, this object seemed wonderfully quaint, until Butler looked more closely at the thick, blond-haired man whose narrowed eyes and taut shoulders suggested a readiness to demonstrate the weapon's efficacy on your skull.

"Excuse me, comrade," Butler said politely. "I hope I'm not disturbing you. I was looking for—"

The blond man pointed a thumb toward a doorway at the rear of the shop.

"Thank you, comrade."

Butler ducked, as he often needed to do in these Eastern towns, and stepped through to a dim, low-ceilinged chamber that must have served as the old cobbler's living quarters. A small tile stove in one corner gave off a cozy warmth. A paraffin lamp burned yellow-white beneath its muslin shade, casting a glow of evening over scrubbed wooden walls, wide floorboards, lace curtains and a single scarlet geranium blooming in a rusty jar whose scrollwork proclaimed a fine brand of Finnish sweets, a treat someone must have fetched home long ago, before the Revolution, from a trip abroad.

The small, wraithlike man sitting alone in the room had chosen the largest chair in the darkest corner, as though to further diminish himself.

Butler had to step around the small table bearing the lamp to get a look at him, and even then his form remained indistinct.

Puak was fine-boned and amber-skinned, with Asiatic features. He looked physically weak but morally fierce. If someone had told you his real name was Khan, as in Genghis, you would have believed it. Or, just as readily, you would have believed he was a first cousin of Sri Aurobindo, the Indian mystic. There was an unworldliness about him, yet those dark eyes could belong only to a man who has seen the world down to its writhing, molten core. He sat in perfect stillness, as if this visitor were not fully present or real to him.

Butler never knew how to start. He turned his head, soaking up the room's homey, proletarian charm. "Nice place you've found here," he said, playing the oblivious American. "Pretty flowers. You could forget there's a war on."

"Oh, no," said Puak quickly. His voice was musical and perhaps, just detectably, effeminate. "I'm afraid nothing could ever make me do that." He motioned to a chair near the lamp.

Butler sat down but kept his posture erect. It was much too early to relax.

"And how are things at the front?" Puak said mildly.

A maddening question, in that it could be pointless small talk or a booby trap. "The front has been static the past few weeks," Butler replied guardedly, "since the summer offensive. Straightening out the line, bringing up supplies. Sending reconnaissance teams over. Grabbing sentries to interrogate. Building up for the next push, which ought to carry us right across the old prewar border."

"Carry *us*," Puak said, his tone neutral, academic. "Have you lost your journalistic objectivity?"

Butler felt more at ease now, settling into the dialectic. "Perfect objectivity is an ideal," he said, "like perfect justice. We strive for it. Under true Socialism, we may achieve it. But at the present stage of history, 'objectivity' too often serves as a code word for apathy. Or worse, a shield to defend the status quo. If one makes a correct appraisal of the world situation, then he is obliged to take sides. He must align himself with the people, the workers, in their struggle. But in taking sides, he drops the pose that most people call objectivity, when in fact they mean something like noninvolvement, or detachment, maybe indifference. So if you suggest that I've lost my objectivity as a journalist, then I would agree. In this qualified sense."

Puak nodded. He might or might not have been impressed by Butler's analysis, or have cared. "I don't suppose you've tried that line of reasoning on your editors."

Butler smiled and shrugged. "There are editors and editors. The people I write for appreciate my point of view."

"Do you have much of an audience in America?"

From anyone else, this would have constituted a wise-ass remark. With Puak you never knew.

"Even in America," said Butler, "there is a progressive press. A small one, mostly centered around New York and Chicago. Some of Roosevelt's people—the circle around Eleanor—openly sympathize. That's one tactic they've found to dampen the revolutionary impulses of the people. They encourage weak forms of social-democratic thought and institute harmless measures like the WPA. Keep the progressives inside the tent pissing out, as the saying goes."

Puak nodded. He knew the expression. "Rather like the SPD in Weimar Germany," he said in the same mild tone, and let the idea hang there.

"To an extent. You can never draw exact parallels between the American system and European parliamentary rule. But yes: you could say the Sozialdemokratische Partei Deutschlands was an effective tool for blocking the rise of a truly proletarian movement in Germany. Better to give the people a fraction of what they deserve than nothing at all. Co-opt the opinion-makers, as FDR has done with artists and writers. God knows they come cheap."

"Which is why the Kommunist Partei Deutschland considered the SPD its most dangerous opponent, correct? Rather than the Hitler party?"

"Nach Hitler, kommen wir," said Butler, repeating a slogan heard frequently during the 1932 election, the last in republican Germany. After Hitler, we shall come. "Sure—if you give the people a genuine tyrant, a thoroughly evil man, they'll see the battle lines more clearly. They'll have no stomach for liberal compromise."

Puak knitted his slender fingers and bent forward slightly, nearer the light. "And how well would you say that policy has worked, so far?"

Butler's mouth was already open when he perceived the trap. Puak was inviting him either to declare the Communist Party to have been wrong, or else to applaud the outcome of its strategy: the undermining of a democratic regime and the rise of Nazism, with all that had followed. He shook his head. "If history could be lived backward, any corporal could be a field marshal. We were speaking of America, a totally different proposition. The Democratic Party might resemble the SPD in some ways, but the Republicans are not Nazis. You'll never get a Hitler in America. Adolf at least knows his history. He's evil on a heroic scale. In America you get Senator Bilbo, with his bill to ship the Negroes back to Africa. You get Father Coughlin, shrieking from his pulpit over the radio. And Henry Ford, spending millions to print his anti-Semitic tracts. You get kooks. Wealthy kooks, some of them. Influential kooks, even powerful kooks. But too greedy and self-absorbed to be truly dangerous."

Puak only stared, as though sizing up the depth and breadth of Butler's personal ideology. "I wonder," he said finally, "how well in touch with America you are these days. The real America, not your progressive editors. People at their jobs, in the movie theaters, sitting at home in front of their radios."

Butler shrugged. "I'm still a Yank." From his mouth, it did not sound altogether convincing.

"Any news from over there?" Puak asked blandly. "Any information from your contacts in Washington?"

A peculiar phrase, thought Butler, *contacts in Washington*, for a lover and a pair of longtime friends. More than peculiar, bloodless—and maybe that was the point. Slowly he nodded. "Yes. I've had a letter from Vava, written just after she met with . . . the other two. The man and the woman. Then a shorter note, more recent. The woman had dropped by. She told Vava things are in motion, a plan has been hatched, they've identified a source of funding and volunteers are signing on. No further details. Vava didn't think it safe to press her."

Puak let out a long breath, which might have signaled disappointment, though Butler doubted it. He took it as a given that the Spider had already learned the contents of these letters much as he learned everything else, through a thousand eyes and ears. Butler therefore drew secret pleasure from springing his little surprise.

"I've also gotten a letter from Ingo. It came straight to me at the front— must've gotten redirected somehow." This was as close as he dared come to saying what he believed, that Puak was having his mail opened. "Ingo Miller, you know, he's the—"

"Thank you, I know who Ingo Miller is."

Puak's tone was curt but his eyes danced with what seemed to Butler a kind of hunger.

"Here"—he groped in the Astrakhan coat—"I've got it right here."

Puak waited coolly, hands folded about each other like the ends of a silken cord.

"The thing about Ingo," said Butler, uncrinkling a thin sheet of stationery, "is that he's always making himself out to be a regular, rough-and-tumble fellow. A plain talker. Inside, he's more of a . . . a brooder, among other things. But listen to this." He read it straight, in English, which Puak spoke as well as anyone, with a tendency toward classical, Johnsonian sentence structure. "'Dear Butler, At first I was surprised when Marty told me it was you. Then when I thought about it I wasn't surprised at all. When did you start writing for Australian newspapers? Anyway, it sounds as if you've found your spot.' New paragraph. 'I've agreed, for the time being, to go along with this. But I would like to be sure of two things. One, it's really Isaac we're talking about. Two, this whole thing isn't some wacky stunt of yours, a fool-the-dumb-capitalists kind of thing. I don't know why you would do this, but you have to admit, it sounds like you, no offense intended.' New paragraph, and the writing changes, as if the next bit were written later. I suspect he'd had a drink in the interim. 'You and I never really hit it off in the old days, but at least I remember you as being an honorable man at heart who did not mean to hurt people. Which did not stop you from doing it, of course. Speaking of which, Marty says hi. Please write back and give me some kind of assurance on the two points above. And especially, please level with me if there's anything you know beyond what Vava told us—who, by the by, calls you Sammy. Does this mean you have dropped the literary pose?' He ends there. Signed, 'Your old pal.'"

Butler looked up to find Puak smiling, though just perceptibly so. Perhaps he was amused by Ingo's epistolary style.

"So then," he said after a long pause, "your friend doubts you."

"He doubts, full stop. That's Ingo."

Puak flexed the fingers of one hand. "Well. I suppose you must write back."

Was this a thought or a command? "Yes, of course," said Butler. "But telling him what, I wonder?"

Puak's mouth puckered in thought. "It is a curious thing. Your friend seems not to like you very much. Yet he considers you a man of honor. He believes you are concealing something, yet he asks you to, as he says, level with him. There are paradoxes here. But we are no strangers to paradox, are we? Especially where the human heart is concerned."

Butler felt it an oblique compliment to be included in Puak's *we*. He nodded, uncertainly.

In a quick, catlike move, Puak stood up and took a step in Butler's direction. "These people are our partners. Our teammates. We are stepping onto the same field, from our different directions. We are chasing the same ball. The same rules govern our play—chief among them, that a bullet is the ultimate referee."

In the faint glow of the paraffin lamp, Puak's eyes gleamed like onyx, and his skin had the dry, slightly roughened texture of handmade paper. He looked very old. A revered elder comrade; a man who had stood shoulder-to-shoulder with Lenin. Who had passed beyond any question of trust or allegiance, simply by having survived. Who now lived a pure, ascetic existence, devoid of ego, lacking even a name, his whole being and essence devoted to the Cause.

He raised a finger. "Let them know everything. Don't tell them. But let them come to understand."

"Everything. You mean—"

"That the document in question, the memo signed by Heinrich Himmler, is more than a mere piece of evidence. That it is a decisive weapon in the coming struggle. That the Soviet Union intends to acquire it at all costs. That we are using the Americans just as we have used the partisans, as means to an end. That we do not care a damn about any of the people concerned. Not the Little Fox, not your Washington friends, not the local Underground chiefs. Not even ourselves as individuals."

Butler frowned. "But we have to care a bit, don't we? At least enough to keep everyone alive until the operation is over. I mean, some of these people . . . Ingo Miller for instance. Isaac the Fox. They're kind of vital to pulling this off, aren't they?"

Puak stared straight into Butler's eyes and, with a smile of infinite compassion, shook his head. "It is not permitted to believe that. I'm sorry, but as Marxists we may not believe that any single human being matters so terribly much. All our science, our understanding of history, tells us otherwise. Life is an aggregate process. History is syncretic. Evolution does not occur at isolated locations but across the whole living field—and this remains true whether we are speaking of an organism or an entire society, a sociohistoric system. What matters is only the whole. Not the part. The body, not the cell. Humankind, not this or that ephemeral personality."

He turned suddenly away, leaving behind a palpable silence. Butler felt awkward, having heard this deeply felt protestation of faith from an old man fully aware of his mortality, and straining for transcendence. He smiled. "I'm not sure how I feel myself about being an ephemeral personality."

Puak nodded, his expression kind. "It gets easier with age, I suppose." He moved back to his chair. "Now listen carefully. I will tell you how this thing must be done."

★　　★　　★

A desiccating wind arrived overnight from the east, off the steppe, and did nothing to lighten Butler's pensive mood, nor did a ceiling of clouds the color of a battleship. He awoke tangled in garishly colored blankets in a tent that belonged to one Madame Ladoshka, a camp follower who passed herself off as a Gypsy and earned a respectable livelihood telling the fortunes of soldiers young enough to be her sons.

Butler happened to know she was a Jewess from Minsk, and that before the war she had been a stage actress. When German tanks appeared one morning in 1941, she gathered her few possessions and began walking east. But the Wehrmacht was also moving east, making for Smolensk, so Ladoshka turned south into the Pripet Marshes—a propitious turn, in most respects. Soon she found herself living in a community of partisans run on the principle of a *kolkhoz,* a collective farm. The chairman was an older man who'd fought with the Whites in the Civil War. He fell in love with Ladoshka and treated her tenderly until he was caught in an ambush by the SS, tortured for a couple of days, and left hanging at a crossroads. Ladoshka thus came into possession of his belongings, which chiefly amounted to a large round tent of the type used by Kurdish nomads. She had opened the tent to other women left stranded by the war. But a tentful of women in the middle of a swamp is not a long-term solution to life's problems, so when Marshal Rokossovsky's forces reached Mozyr in the great advance after Stalingrad, Ladoshka rolled up her household and joined the Red Army on its westward march.

Some of the others had come along and now supported themselves as prostitutes. Ladoshka, declaring she had no energy for that kind of thing, taught herself tricks with cards. The most important of these, she confided to Butler one night outside Kiev, was to reveal the Two of Hearts and solemnly aver that the young soldier's beloved would remain faithful to him always. It was an easy trick to learn, though she found it harder to master the concomitant art of dispassion. When the boys' eyes filled with tears, Ladoshka (who had never been a mother) wanted to take them into her arms like babies. But that would have been unprofessional.

She was still asleep, snoring lightly, her face lost in a tangle of gold necklaces and black hair, when Butler slipped out of the tent and onto the hard barren ground at the outskirts of Rownje. All the little gifts from America—the coffee; the cigarettes; the costume jewelry, for Ladoshka; the novels by Steinbeck and Dos Passos, for Puak—had been handed out. All the necessary contacts had been made or reestablished, stories filed, toasts offered and drunk to. No needful thing remained undone. Ordinarily Butler would have savored a few days' respite from the line. But this morning he felt anxious, unable to relax, like a farmer with one eye on the calendar, feeling winter edging up on him.

He walked toward the center of town, using the damaged cathedral as a reference point. The thought of winter—the fierce and unforgiving Russian version that was coming all too soon—fed his jittery mood. He tried to figure the day's date but could get no closer than the latter part of September. Or was it October already? But then, nobody relied on dates anymore. Time was reckoned by geography. *Outside Kiev. At the outskirts of Rownje.* It wasn't only Butler. He could remember a thousand conversations in which someone said, "I've known him since Vinnitsa." Or, "He got killed some time ago, before Kharkov." "First or second Kharkov?" "Third. When our side finally won."

Didn't Wagner have something to say about this? In *Parsifal,* Butler thought. *Du siehst, mein Sohn, zum Raum wird hier die Zeit.* You see, my son, here time becomes space. Something to do with the strange land of the Grail. But then, for Germans, that old dream of conquering the East was something of a Grail quest, wasn't it?

Here time becomes space. Place-names floating in a sea of years—a notion more Buddhist than Marxist. And so was the manner in which cities, like transmigrating souls, shuffled off the mortal coil of names and populations and national affiliations only to be reincarnated in quite different forms. Thus Lodz, formerly of Poland, had been reborn as Litzmannstadt, East Prussia. Lwow, a Ukrainian rail center, became Lemberg in the German province of Galizien, identical except for its striking dearth of Jews. Brno, a Czech town noted for its university and its arms plant, became Brünn, in the Reich Protectorate of Bohemia and Moravia, Reinhard Heydrich presiding; and though its university was shut down, the arms plant was going strong.

Nations themselves were no more permanent: Poland, at present, did not exist. Its eastern provinces were part of the Soviet Union, its western half annexed by the Greater German Reich; the rump in between was called the Generalgouvernement, a land with no name and no future, by Hitler's personal decree.

And now the wheel of history was running in reverse. The ancient fortress-city of Königsberg had lately become Chojna. Soon Danzig would be Gdansk, and if things played out as Butler expected, Berlin itself would be known as Karl-Marx-Stadt, the bustling hub of a new Soviet Socialist Republic.

Reckoning time by cities, Butler was half a year past Dnepropetrovsk but probably still a few months short of Prague. He had always wanted to see Prague. He hoped there would be something left of it.

Cheered by anticipation, he rounded a corner onto the main avenue, where the rubble had been sufficiently bulldozed to allow the passage of an armored column while still permitting foot and motorbike and Cossack pony traffic along the berm. The scene resembled a bazaar. Black marketeers had set up their stalls next to open-air clinics where Red Army medical corpsmen treated the local populace for scurvy, skin rashes, gonorrhea, gunshot wounds, infestations of lice, infected lacerations, gangrene following kitchen-table amputations, broken noses, jaws and limbs, among other side effects of the recent German occupancy. On all sides, courtesans of many ethnic types brazenly plied their trade. Newly arrived conscripts gathered in huddles, their weapons and ammo belts dangling awkwardly from shoulders that looked too thin to hold them. Battle-weary veterans sat in the shelter of crumbled buildings, eyeing the whole scene with blank-faced indifference, dragging deeply on horrid *makhorka* cigarettes made from Turkish stems and leaf stalks rolled in brownish, fast-burning Russian newsprint.

All the while, only a few feet away, a convoy of trucks rumbled through, waved along by a traffic control officer who called out vehicle ID numbers to an NCO jotting unhurriedly on a clipboard. The trucks were mostly American-made, interspersed with domestic models of varying types, some of impressive antiquity, along with the occasional tractor tugging a farm wagon, half a dozen horse-drawn carts and one noisy half-track manned by Mongolians in crisp parade dress. A supply run, Butler surmised, headed out to some depleted and shot-up field command. The long logistics tail that so often wags the fighting dog.

He waited for a break in traffic, then trotted over to where the old public library stood, a ruin among other ruins. Half a block off, he saw the helpful sergeant from Foreign Press Liaison standing at the edge of the road in conversation with a short man wearing a uniform Butler didn't recognize. The Russians had not shaken off their Petrine fondness for uniforms—tokens of class in a classless society.

The sergeant seemed to experience that telepathic tingle that comes from being watched; it took her a moment to find him in the crowd, then she smiled and pumped her arm. "Comrade Sammy!"

Butler raised a hand in greeting. She called again, but the words were lost in the growl of a passing truck.

"You've come just in time," she said as he approached. The uniformed man stood nearby, seemingly forgotten. "Transports are just leaving for your sector. All your parcels are loaded. Everything is arranged."

Butler acknowledged this with a nod. Then he sensed that she expected something more, and he added, "Thank you, tovarich. The packages are important to me. I knew I could entrust them to you."

This appeared to satisfy her. Still, it bothered Butler that his customary ease in such dealings—the effortless flow of compliments, the lighthearted flirting, the whole shtick—momentarily had failed him. Was it a symptom of having been too long at the front, or too long away from it?

"We have just made some tea," the sergeant told him, unable to keep a note of hopefulness out of her voice. "If you would care to—"

"No. Thank you, I'm just . . ." Butler shrugged. He didn't know what he just was. He needed a change, but didn't know what kind. The thought of Ladoshka, tangled amid her bedclothes, filled him with unaccountable despondency. He barely remembered to say goodbye before turning back to the jostling, noisome, disorderly yet somehow purposeful street, crowded with comrades who didn't seem to care where they were going, so long as they'd find Germans to kill when they got there.

The other end of town was a tidier quarter where the devastation was less thorough and the Front's Operations Center had set up shop. Less of the black-market Mardi Gras here, more of the sober business of winning a war. Lower-grade officers scurried about on urgent assignments while their superiors clustered along sunny, well-swept patches of sidewalk swapping secrets and smoking *papirosi*.

Butler thought of approaching one of these groups, introducing himself and conducting an impromptu interview—*Highly placed Red Army sources have told this reporter*—but as he was stepping into the street, a truck veered around a corner and nearly ended his journalistic career on the spot.

He yanked himself back, heart pounding at the near miss. The truck squealed to a stop. From the driver's-side window, a dozen meters up the road, a head emerged, surmounted by a crimson bandanna. Instead of making an apology, the man yelled: "Quick! Get into the truck! Comrade, hurry!"

The head disappeared. On the opposite side of the cab, the passenger door popped open. Butler was caught between anger and an instinct more fundamental to his character: curiosity. He circled to peer through the open door at the driver, who was gesturing frantically.

"Jump in now, or it will be too late!"

Butler placed the man's accent somewhere in the Caucasus. He boarded the truck, a late-model Lend-Lease Studebaker, and silently recorded this subtle indication of status: Studebakers were the most highly regarded of Yankee vehicles, for their tenacity in the awful mud of autumn and the truly unnavigable mud of spring. The driver hit the gas as soon as Butler's foot cleared the road, the door jerking shut from the force of acceleration.

"Thank you, comrade!" the man said, grinding through the gears.

Butler gave him a once-over. He was on the large side, though shorter and more heavily made than Butler. His hair was black under the bandanna, and he wore a swooping, Cossack-style mustache. His clothing comprised a motley of unmatched uniform parts. The topmost layer was a hard-worn, oft-mended infantryman's jacket. At his collar he wore a major's pin, and on his sleeve a patch identifying him as a sniper—a special decoration issued during the most vicious stage of the street fighting in Stalingrad, when the nation's attention had been seized by the daring exploits—some real, mostly imagined—of men and women scrabbling like rats through the burning, dying city, picking off Fascists one by one.

Only after recognizing the patch could Butler identify the object on the seat next to him, strapped carefully in place as if it were a third passenger. Just longer than a baseball bat, it was padded with rags and stuffed into a leather satchel shaped like a slender, battered golf bag. Clearly a cherished personal possession, and Butler could guess what.

The driver caught him looking. His mouth curled in what might pass for a smile. "I'm called Seryoshka."

Butler nodded: a nom de guerre, he thought. "I'm Sammy. I'm a journalist—a war correspondent."

The man's hard stare was, perhaps, a commentary on Butler's accent.

"What's the rush?" Butler asked.

"You'll see."

The truck slowed. By now they had retraced Butler's own route and were nearing the Orthodox cathedral.

"See that man up there?" said Seryoshka.

"The one in the Uncle Joe suit?"

This drew a chuckle. Stalin, like Hitler, was famous for his modesty in personal attire. The thin fellow by the road ahead wore a simple, unmarked gray tunic over black trousers, exactly the sort of man-of-the-people costume preferred by those who were anything but.

Seryoshka chuckled. "That's my politruk." He pronounced the slang term for a political officer with distaste—the only way, Butler supposed, of pronouncing it. "We've been reassigned together, the two of us. Old comrades, you know?" He eased the truck to a halt, abeam of the officer in question.

"Ah, Comrade Major," said the *politruk,* smiling cheerlessly, showing large and well-tended teeth. He glanced at his watch. "I was wondering when you would come."

"Unavoidable delay, comrade," said Seryoshka. "There's been a change in plans. I've been assigned to escort this foreign reporter. A Westerner, writes for the most important papers. *New York Post, Chicago Star.* A real VIP. Doesn't speak a word of Russian. Needs a full-time minder."

"I see." The man looked doubtful. But whatever his doubts may have been, he wasn't eager to voice them in front of a Western journalist.

"I checked at the dispatch office," Seryoshka went on, "and they say there's another truck headed out later. Sometime after three. Wait here, they said."

The *politruk* narrowed his eyes. Butler supposed such men always suspect they're being lied to. Seryoshka gave him a big grin, and he responded by waving him off, resignedly. Seryoshka had won a round, but the fight would continue.

"Ha!" he exulted, once they were safely away. "That was a good one. You have my gratitude, comrade. Look in the map box there, you'll find something to celebrate with. Which way are you headed? I can drop you, if you like. There's plenty of petrol."

"Right up to the line," Butler told him.

"Yes?" Seryoshka eyed him with new interest, taking his eyes for what seemed an imprudently long time off the pitted, washed-out road. "Which part of the line?"

"The sharp edge," said Butler. For some reason, he felt compelled to prove himself to this hardened survivor of Stalingrad, with his sniper's rifle cradled in the seat between them. "Special Reconnaissance Company, 104th Guards Division."

Seryoshka gave a loud, unexpected laugh. "So that's the sharp edge, is it? That's good. That's very good."

Butler couldn't decide what to make of this boisterous Cossack. He just sat there, waiting, as the truck bounced crazily along. Soon Rownje was behind them. Ahead lay an empty and devastated countryside—and beyond that, destiny in all its dark splendor.

"Perhaps you can tell me, comrade," said Seryoshka, breaking a long interval of silence, "what 'special reconnaissance' means. I've been wondering for a while now."

"You have? Might I ask why?"

The Cossack offered him a wry, side-of-the-mouth smile. "It's my new assignment. Me and that asshole back there, we're both headed up to join this unit of yours. This Special Reconnaissance Company. I have been given to understand . . ."

Butler noted the shift to more formal, academy-grade locution. Seryoshka held his gaze, and there was no mistaking the intelligence in that open, unblinking stare.

". . . that something interesting is about to happen in your sector. Some unusual operation. I was told nothing definite. Only that my particular talents—that's how they put it, *your particular talents*—might be useful there. I wonder what you can tell me about that."

Butler said evenly, "I guess it depends what your particular talents are."

Seryoshka looked thoughtful for a moment, then he laughed. "You know, I've never met an American."

"What makes you think I'm American?" Butler felt a shiver of paranoia. It occurred to him, belatedly, how improbable this meeting had been. The pair of them, bound for the same spot on a four-hundred-kilometer front. And both winding up in the same Studebaker cab.

"What else could you be?" said Seryoshka. "Dressed like that. Talking such abysmal Russian. And doing it with such damned self-assurance—like everybody else ought to talk that way, too." He shook his head. "You're American, all right."

Butler nodded. Not at what Seryoshka was saying—he didn't care that his Russian was no good—but because he had struck an agreement with himself: not to care, nor even to wonder, if this encounter was in fact a setup, and Seryoshka some kind of agent assigned to keep an eye on him. What difference did it make? The individual does not matter. The operation will go forward. The plan is set, the stars aligned.

Seryoshka's next question caught him in this odd, fatalistic state of mind; otherwise he wouldn't have answered as he did.

"Tell me—what's an American doing in such a godforsaken place?" This without looking over, while manhandling the truck through a rough stretch of road. "Why aren't you with Koniev or Zhukov, heading for Berlin? You must be on to some story, eh? A real *scoop.*"

Seryoshka used the English word, and Butler responded in that language, so alien here, so starkly literal, devoid of nuance and subtlety. "It's a scoop, all right," he said. "Bunch of innocent Yanks lured into a complicated plot by an old friend—not a loyal friend, just an old one. They get ambushed, robbed, and, I don't know, probably left for dead. But that's okay. That's swell. They're only ephemeral personalities. We're all good Marxists, so we don't care about that. We understand history. We know what's what."

Seryoshka throttled the truck down and turned to gaze at him with an air of melancholy so profound that it seemed a species of wisdom. "Open the map box," he said. "I think we could both use a little something."

He spoke the sort of English—careless with consonants, but every article properly inserted—taught at the larger Russian universities and other, more selective institutions. Quite different from the minimally functional English they crammed into you at service academies.

In the map box, Butler found a bottle of decent but not first-rate vodka and a single tin mug. "Did Puak send you?" he asked, pouring the mug two-thirds full.

"Who is Spider?" asked Seryoshka. He seemed genuinely puzzled. It proved nothing.

Butler raised the mug. "To the great struggle."

"Bugger that," laughed the Cossack. "To coming out alive."

EASTERN SHORE

It was Ingo himself, they would recall, who thought of bringing Timo in. The cabdriver—a Serb, as it turned out—came to mind during a meeting of the small group of conspirators known as the Search Committee (Marty loved making up names like this) when some out-of-towners voiced a desire to meet in restaurants where they wouldn't risk being glimpsed by the press. Such places existed, mostly in neighborhoods you'd have trouble whistling up a cab to fetch you out of. Unbidden to Ingo came the image of a sawed-off Louisville Slugger, then the rough, swarthy hand that gripped it, and finally the stenciled logo of Earnest's Hackney Service. A number was rung, a taxi conjured from the depths of Foggy Bottom, and after a staggering luncheon laid on by a barbecue specialist on an avenue that dare not speak its name, Timo delivered everyone back to hearth, home and hotel in seemly fashion. The modest expense was put down to Logistics.

Not long afterward, a need arose that was in certain respects analogous. Marty popped in to the Rusty Ring one evening to announce a Major Breakthrough. It involved money; it involved powerful backers; unfortunately, it also involved an overnight drive to Ontario.

"The one in Canada?" Ingo asked helplessly.

Yes, that one. And so, some thirty-six blurry hours later, Ingo found himself staring at a stark, unpeopled, coldly beautiful landscape from the window of a limousine normally used for hauling war brides in haste around the District. Timo manned the wheel, a marvel of tireless competence. Their destination was an RCMP training camp on loan to the British Secret Intelligence Service, which had used it earlier in the war to train resistance operatives.

"Not the most convenient spot for a meeting, is it?" said Ingo.

"That's the whole point. These are Hollywood people, Ingo. If you make things too easy, they don't take you seriously."

He didn't get it, but that didn't seem to matter. The camp was patrolled by rough-looking lads in trench coats. Marty flashed a *laissez-passer* and the limo bumped up a long drive to a shambling timbered structure whose parking lot was crowded with luxury motorcars. Inside, beneath rough-sawn beams and mounted antlers, a table was draped in baize and set for twenty-four. At each place stood a water glass, a fountain pen and a stiff-bound sheaf labeled OPERATION SMOKING GUN. Around it, the lavishly costumed all-male cast hovered as though awaiting some cue, which presently came with the entrance of an *éminence grise*, a man of such obvious importance that, in lieu of speaking, he took his place at the head of the table and nodded curtly to a thirtyish factotum. This fellow, one Ari Glasser, thanked everyone for coming, singling out some of the more important guests for a personal welcome—including "Miss Martina Panich, joining us today on behalf of the Roosevelt administration in a strictly off-the-record capacity," which seemed to impress the movers and shakers around the table. He then declared, "Now we must speak of what Mr. Churchill has rightly called a crime so terrible, it does not even have a name."

Ingo had heard it before, or so he thought. But a few minutes into his spiel, Glasser yielded the floor to a wild-eyed, gangly man, "the well-known Rabbi Harvey Grabsteen of Agudas Israel Worldwide," who started talking even while struggling to disentangle himself from his chair. Where Glasser had been polished, Grabsteen was all jagged edges. His voice was high-pitched and quavering; thick veins throbbed at his temples; his whole being radiated moral outrage. And he didn't mince words: Ingo tried to stop listening after a detailed account of SS troopers swinging tiny children by their feet so as to smash their skulls against a railway carriage. It came as a relief to everyone, surely, when the *éminence* cleared his throat and said simply, "Rabbi, what can we do?"

At which point, Glasser gave Marty a discreet little nod.

"If you'll just take a look at the documents in front of you," she said, all businesslike, "I think you'll find we've put together a workable proposition. Now we're calling this Smoking Gun because, until now, the one thing that's eluded us . . ."

Looking back, Ingo was amazed at how easy it had been, though he doubted whether Marty would see it like that. Her part in the affair had left her untypically exhausted; she slept for most of the long ride back to D.C.

*   *   *

By summer's end, what began as a wild-eyed scheme and developed into a closely held plot had become a full-blown hush-hush operation. And since an *operation* requires a center—someplace grander than Ingo's digs on Connecticut Avenue, please—a new and discreet one had been found for it. The original conspirators, joined now by an agglomeration of mappers, trainers, bagmen, financiers, arms suppliers, cooks (no bottle washers), politically committed and currently out-of-contract Hollywood personalities, a golf-cart-load of attorneys, one butcher (no baker, unless you counted Ingo), one cheeky dentist, the howling mad Rabbi Grabsteen and, with a view toward the rough business ahead, a small army of extras, had betaken themselves to a chicken farm allegedly owned by a cousin, or something, of Vernon, the Rusty Ring's conniving chef, in the boggy tidal country across the bay from Annapolis.

They called themselves the Varian Fry Brigade. Another of Marty's unhelpful names, though this one evidently meant something to somebody, if nothing to Ingo. But then what did, during that confusing time? The whole of life had turned upside down or inside out or whichever happened when you began to think the unthinkable and, worse, believe the incredible: that they were really going ahead with this.

In the beginning he figured it was safe to play along. After all, there was zero chance Marty's woolly-headed scheme would bear fruit. Sure, mount a safari to Darkest Europe, why not? Go wading up some godforsaken, Gestapo-patrolled creek looking for our old pal Isaac—did you hear he's a big warrior chief these days? Receive his jolly tidings—*the horror*—and then sail into the sunset while savages in their Death's Head costumes fling poisoned spears at the boat. No problem, Miss Panich, and by the by, how do you take your martini—four to one, or are you a philistine?

The trouble with thinking like this, as he did for a few weeks in August—the Last Days of Innocence, revisited—was that, like many a losing general, Ingo had failed in his appreciation of the enemy. He hadn't allowed for Marty's grim determination, which must come from her mother's Anglo-Catholic side, or, more fatally, for all the favors and phone numbers and political IOUs she'd hoarded over the years. As everyone knew, these New Dealers were in bed with the very worst people—indeed, many of them were the very worst people themselves—and as with birds of a feather, no sooner had Marty tossed a few crumbs in the air than the whole flock of them took wing: sculptors and scriptwriters, trade unionists and deodorant heiresses and orthodontists, soothsayers of the Commodities Exchange and matinee heroes reputed to be homosexual. Ingo by now was lost in his own metaphorizing but that was the general idea.

True disaster struck, he had concluded, when the phone rang late one night and a butter-smooth voice murmured gently in his ear.

"I'm trying to reach Marty Panich. This is Ari Glasser speaking, hope I'm not disturbing you."

He wouldn't have been, except that it was eleven p.m. in California, hence an hour indecent to calculate in Ingo's bedroom in Washington.

"A mutual friend gave me this number," the silky voice ran on. "Is she there by any chance?"

Perhaps it was the fellow's use of the familiar *Marty,* to which Ingo felt singularly entitled. Perhaps it was the hour of night. In any case, and to his lasting regret, he did not do what he ought to have done—*Sorry to hit you with this, pal, but Miss Panich, she dead*—and instead, out of dumb nosiness, hung on the line. Which in turn gave Glasser a chance to speak, which was like giving Houdini a little wiggle room. Because the next thing Ingo knew, Ari had charmed out of him not just Martina's address but also that of the Ring and of "a decent place to camp out in that town of yours." (Ingo named the Hay-Adams on the misplaced assumption it would bankrupt the oozy bastard.) By lunchtime two days hence, Ingo found himself watching helplessly as Bernie Fildermann delivered a plate of *warmer Kartoffelsalad,* bacon chunks and all, to table 3, the big one by the plate-glass window, where he lingered a while chatting about Vienna, which Mr. Glasser seemed to know quite well. He claimed to have attended a performance of the chamber ensemble in which little Bernie had played—splendid, moving, fantastic!—and who knew, perhaps he wasn't lying. Bernie spent the rest of the afternoon floating in bliss an inch above the carpet, as if borne aloft on the wings of Mozart.

In the fullness of time, even Ingo found much about Glasser to admire. It took some learning, but he came to understand how the man's sunny, skin-deep charm might be put to uses infinitely more noble than stitching together a film production deal. Once while chatting up Ingo—a protracted campaign he waged with stout heart, as he would for "any friend of Marty's"—he seemed to receive an unfathomable flash of insight, whereupon he switched in mid-sentence from English to German, not the slurry Wiener variety but a clean, literary *Hochdeutsch* suitable for quoting

Schiller. Then to Ingo's astonishment he did quote Schiller, and moreover so easily that the words fit the context like a chamois glove. Meanwhile, across the room, the mad rabbi was arguing with the proprietress of the chicken farm, a willful gal named Charleva, over the condition of her long, washed-out driveway, which impeded delivery of heavy cargo ambiguously labeled *For Trans-shipment/Matériel*.

"But we give you *money*," Grabsteen shouted, his arms flopping about as though longing for their straitjacket. "We give you *money* and you do *what* with it? Spend it on extra mud?"

Catching Ingo's eye, Glasser gave him a smile—a marvel of nuance and complexity, like a Burgundy aged to perfection—and purred, "Nimmer, das glaubt mir, erscheinen die Götter, nimmer allein!" Believe me, never do the gods appear alone: a more fervent variation on the theme of taking the good with the bad.

The good, or god, that came attached to Harvey Grabsteen took the form of fervid ideological zeal. He hated Nazis with every strand of his being. He had hated them yesterday, he would hate them tomorrow. The fact of their existence, sharing the atmosphere with the rest of us, was to him a personal affront. Desperate to give expression to these feelings, he had latched on to Agudas Israel, a radical Zionist organization whose entire membership he personally constituted in a strategically located patch of southern California. Agudas had spent the war years lobbying hard in every capital of the West, espousing among other radical notions the suggestion that rail lines leading to known death camps be bombed, news of German racial atrocities broadcast, and, most ludicrously, a company of armed volunteers, commanded by Jewish veterans of the First World War, recruited. To what end, no responsible official could imagine, unless it was just the inarticulate urge to *do something, damn it*. But all such proposals, no matter what form they took or what intelligence supported them, had been in vain.

For how, pray tell, could this lunatic group succeed where such responsible bodies as the American Jewish Committee, touting more moderate and sensible ideas (Mr. Roosevelt could give a *speech*, couldn't he?), had been courteously but definitively rebuffed? (No, sorry, he cannot.) The complete response of the American government to date had been the creation of the War Refugee Board, a savvy executive conjuration that, in one stroke, mollified Henry Morgenthau and got that hothead, Martina What's-her-name, safely out of the White House to someplace Eleanor couldn't find her.

Yet behold what the gods have wrought. Here stands Harvey Grabsteen, the soul of disrepute, yelling at a colored chicken farmer, who sensibly ignores him, while a film star with both money and time to burn dangles a wrist in the face of a Great War noncom roughly the size of a Brahma bull, and Ari Glasser, noted Hollywood impresario, purrs Schiller into the ear of a humble barkeep from the sheltered lanes of Brookland who, in blatant disregard of Aristotle's law of *probabilitas,* has somehow become the star of the show.

Happen? Is it really going to happen? Dear Lord, please, I beg you, show me how to stop it.

In late September the weather turned cooler and very dry. By the third week of October the fallen leaves, dry as parchment, presented a serious danger to the three dozen extras who were poised to launch yet another humiliating mission in their make-believe war. You couldn't move without setting off a racket, and the trainees, so-called, had some moving to do.

Realism, they called this. The objective was a low ridge maybe three hundred meters ahead. You could make it out as a row of dark pines against the gray sky. The problems here were (a) you had to get there quickly and (b) undetected, despite certain complications known to include, but perhaps not limited to, (c) hounds and (d) machine guns. The machine guns might not be loaded, though the NCOs claimed otherwise; Ingo wouldn't know about that. But he didn't guess you could unload a hound dog. Vernon claimed they'd been trained by his Uncle Leon to detect white people by their scent.

"I guess that makes Jews safe," quipped a little guy named Stu—a dentist, hence *ex officio* the Varian Fry Brigade's medical officer. Being a dentist did not make him by any stretch the most unlikely or ill-suited trainee in D Squad, which was a dumping ground for the aged, the slow, the timid and the maladroit—in short, for those would-be guerrillas deemed least likely to survive by the troika of Great War sergeants running the show. The fitter candidates—though even here you were speaking in relative terms—had been divvied up like sandlot ball teams between squads A and B. There was no C. Evidently the higher-class letters wanted a bit of space between themselves and these uncouth combatants. To make things worse, in radio chatter, for the sake of unambiguous communication A became "Alpha" and B "Bravo," whereas the lowly D could do no better than "Dog." It was like living on the wrong side of the tracks; after a while, Ingo found, you began to acquire a sort of outlaw pride.

The three veterans of the last war were known among the lower ranks as Three Guys Named Moe and, insofar as possible, avoided. Ingo guessed this wouldn't be so easy in Slovakia.

If only, he thought, I had a snowball's chance of washing out.

But that was unthinkable: Ingo was in for the whole nine yards. No matter how badly he screwed up, the Moes only rode him harder.

"Get down there," growled the largest and toughest of the three, designated One Moe or, in honor of the rifle, M-1. (The man's real name, Ingo happened to know, was Vincent Bloom.) "I'm gonna be timing you. When I say go, you haul your ashes out of here—you've got about forty-five seconds till the shitstorm commences."

Stu, crouching next to Ingo in the shallow trench, gave a moan he might have picked up from his patients back in St. Louis. Ingo didn't think it was worth the trouble. Go ahead, he thought. Loose the damned dogs of war. Get it over with.

"Go!" barked M-1, staring with malevolent voracity at a battle-scarred Timex.

Ingo scrabbled forward, his weapon—a Schmeisser MP-40, like a shorter and uglier tommy gun—cradled between his forearms, as far from his face as he could get it. His elbows and knees banged the gritty, rust-colored dirt of southern Maryland. Leaves crackled around him as the rest of the squad kicked off. The racket must have been audible clear across the empty ground ahead, a half-drained marsh filled with cattails and sword-leaf sedge, interspersed with alder and islandlike clumps of river birch, whose bare limbs and peeling copper bark made them look plague-stricken. This godforsaken place was said to resemble the countryside of Lower Silesia. Ingo, who had been to Silesia, remembered it differently.

Off to the right, not far away, came the baying of bloodhounds.

"This is kinda like Boy Scouts," muttered Stu behind him, sardonically. "Only ten times worse."

As with all Stu's banal comments, Ingo found this both annoying and welcome, as it provided some distraction from the misery at hand.

"Were you ever a Boy Scout?" Stu was scuttling like a crab, trying to overtake Ingo, who could move pretty fast when he was scared enough.

"Shh," Ingo hissed. "Yes, I was."

That was more or less the truth—though Ingo's memory of scouting was probably so far from Stu's as to represent a wholly different experience. To his own way of thinking he had never been a Boy Scout, not really, even though he'd spent much of his youth hiking and camping and learning survival tricks cheek-by-jowl with those who were. Wearing the same olive-drab shorts, the same red-and-yellow bandanna. It had marked, he supposed, the start of his long, undistinguished career as an impersonator. Culminating in his present role: a German-American barkeep pretending to be a Jewish partisan, frightened of his own weapon, wallowing through Chesapeake bottomland, hunted by white-hating hounds. Point man of Dog Squad. Having no end of fun.

Afterward, as always, they gathered for an ordeal formally known as the Post-Operation Brief, more familiarly as a chalk talk. These sessions took place in a shed originally built to house farm machinery, with no heat and little shelter from the autumn wind. Two of the Moes were present, along with all twelve members of D Squad and someone Ingo had never seen before—a morose-looking man, somewhere in his forties, with a week's worth of gray and black stubble. His chambray work clothes didn't look right on him. He had been accorded the honor of a wooden packing crate to sit on, while the Moes stood on either side of a dusty slateboard and the trainees hunched dirty and tired on the packed earthen floor of the barn.

The scrawnier of the Moes—Eat Moe they called him, from the Louis Jordan song—began with a general review of the "tactical situation" and ended with a summary verdict on the squad's performance: You guys would be Ralston's Doberman Chow by this time. He then settled into a meticulous accounting of how the assignment ought to have been carried out, noting point by point, with reference to unreadable chalk diagrams, how the squad's actions had strayed from the recommended course. Now and then he would point to a trainee and announce, "Right there, the Krauts woulda been on you like a cheap suit," or "Congratulations—you just won a free ride in a cattle car."

Through all of this, the morose visitor sat seemingly indifferent. He crossed and uncrossed his legs, and cast a single long, slow glance around the room, lingering nowhere, as though nothing he saw was worth a second look.

Eventually Eat Moe ran out of bad things to say. He singled out a couple of trainees for qualified praise, then made an exaggerated shrug. "The rest of you guys, what can I tell ya? We'll be posting the final roster in the next couple days. I hope you ain't got your hearts set on an expenses-paid holiday in the Old Country."

Now a shuffle, as the squad sensed the end of another chalk talk. But One Moe stepped forward and growled in his no-BS voice, "Hold your water, gentlemen. There's somebody here you want to meet."

The gloomy-looking man showed no more interest than before. He shifted wearily on the packing crate as the big man went on:

"We've been joined today by Captain Aristotle. The captain has come all the way from Hungary, enemy-occupied territory, to give us the benefit of his expertise as we prepare for this mission. I know you'll all be interested in what he has to say."

The man rose slowly to his feet. Ingo found both name and rank implausible: the man looked less like a soldier than a weary grocer—not even the owner of the store, maybe the guy who comes in after hours to stock the shelves—and scarcely called to mind the philosopher, except maybe by his bone-weary *gravitas*. But then he began to speak, in a voice that did not match his body or any other, a voice so ancient and hollow it might have risen from a crypt, and somehow you could not keep from listening.

"The Germans know they have lost this war." His English was clear, accented just enough to lend him an air of worldly sophistication. "They have lost the conquered lands, their source of strategic materials. Their power is spent, their soldiers are too old or too young and are fighting without enough bullets, their tanks are running out of petrol, their General Staff is discredited, the Gestapo is hanging people from lampposts. In the battlefield, they have reverted to the tactics of the Great War. They are dying in place, all across the front. Russian spearheads have penetrated German territory, and the Western allies are nearing the Rhine."

Weltschmerz, thought Ingo. World-pain: one of those mental states for which only Germans have a name. And this poor Joe has got a bad case of it.

"There can be no clearer signal that the war is lost, and that the army knows the war is lost, than the attempt on Hitler's life three months ago. While they were winning, the gentlemen of the Wehrmacht, the von Thises and von Thats from the old aristocratic families, were happy to avert their eyes while the bullyboys stomped all over the continent, looting and murdering and swaggering like drunken oafs. Now the generals have experienced a remarkable change of heart. They have observed that the war cannot be won. And suddenly their eyes are open to the crimes of the state they serve. This government must be replaced, they have decided, with one that can make peace, a government with whom the Western powers will deign to negotiate. A government led by decent, civilized men. Indeed, consisting of men very like themselves. So let us get rid of this vulgar little Austrian and put an end to this silly quarrel before anything really unpleasant happens—such as a Bolshevik horde overrunning all the great capitals of Middle Europe.

"But you see, here the generals have made an error, these men from the choicest bloodlines. They believe the war is over simply because the outcome is no longer in doubt. In the great game of war, as these men learned it reading Clausewitz at Lichterfelde, in a room overlooking the parade ground, one does not carry things past the point of futility. One shoves the little pewter flag-holders about the map, until such time as the result is determined. Then one shakes hands 'round the table and goes upstairs to change for the *Abendessen*. That is how war is fought, or so the members of the General Staff like to think."

Aristotle paused—not for breath, Ingo thought. Rather to give his audience time to absorb what he was telling them. No grocer's stockboy, this one. More like a professor of history. Or a shabby aristocrat who reads history for pleasure, alone in his book-lined study, a poor Hungarian relation of those same Wehrmacht generals he's talking about.

"But this war has never been like that. It has never been the kind of war fought across a map table. Yes, there have been classic encirclements, stolen marches, cavalry charges and the rest of the Lichterfelde repertoire. But this war has never been a struggle for territory, never a duel of opposing field commanders. This is a Hassenkrieg, a war of hatred, and it belongs to a much more venerable tradition—the history of tribal enmity, Huns against the Visigoths, Saxons against the Gauls, each side seeking nothing less than the total destruction of the other. Militarily, one cannot understand this war by studying the campaigns of Bismarck or Napoleon, as they like to do at General Staff College. No, one needs to look back to Frederick Barbarossa, the era of the Crusades, when the struggle was not truly won until the last infidel had been slain, and his family with him, and the village he was born in razed, and his cattle slaughtered, his fields laid waste, the scrolls of his heretic creed thrown into the flames and his head stuck on a pike as a warning to others. And only then, when from every tree waves the cross—the holy cross or the hooked cross, take your pick— only then can victory be declared."

Aristotle turned his head, as though he heard something, a call from on high. "But by the same token, defeat cannot be acknowledged either. The True Faith is not dead as long as a single believer still holds the sacred banner aloft. The struggle must continue. Perhaps there is time to slay an infidel or two. A few heathen screeds might yet be stuffed into the mouths of heretics. There may be fields left to burn, or children to dismember in front of their parents. If so, to carry on the fight is a sacred obligation."

He gave them a slow nod. "Yes: this is the nature of the Hate War. It is hard reality, and at the same time something out of old German myth.

The dark romance of the cross-bearers, the Teutonic Knights. I feel it is important that you understand this, even if the gentlemen of the Wehrmacht do not, or pretend not to. Because you will not be fighting the Wehrmacht if you go over there. The Wehrmacht is busy with the Russians. No, you will be fighting the holy warriors themselves—the SS, the blood-sworn defenders of the faith. Bearers of the hooked cross, which they call the swastika. I have been fighting these men for many years now, and have learned a thing or two about them. Perhaps I can teach you something, those of you who still wish to go. Or perhaps you will decide not to go after all, once you hear what I have to say."

Behind Ingo, Stu shifted noisily, his ammo bandoliers clanking against the entrenching tool on his back. "This guy's a million laughs," he muttered. To Ingo, it sounded like a cry of despair.

There was no getting it out of your head for a while—neither the introduction nor the graphic details that followed. Which made the hoo-rah planned for that night even more ridiculous.

Ingo slumped in a bentwood chair on the lawn behind a stucco-sided bungalow, the kind people used to order back in the Twenties from Sears, Roebuck. Your house arrived on a flatbed truck, a neat pile of precut and numbered pieces, complete with assembly manual. This style of home-building was popular with colored folks especially, because you could gather a whole neighborhood—or a big extended family like Vernon's—and knock the thing together in a week or two, no need to hire carpenters. Ingo had seen bungalows like this one, standing two decades or longer, that from the outside looked fine but on the inside were still awaiting such finishing touches as electrical wiring and a flush toilet.

Unlike those, this Craftsman-style house and its matching, well-kept outbuildings showed all the little signs of prosperity, from fresh cream-yellow paint to a stoop of poured concrete, that accrued to successful farmers in a time of food rationing. Ingo wasn't sure how Charleva had managed this with her husband away in the Artillery Corps. He supposed that the chickens, delivered to the city each Saturday, were part of it. But there were other parts, such as the regular coming and going of local people, white as well as colored, paying cash for fresh eggs and butter and home-canned preserves. He couldn't help wondering what had impelled Charleva to offer up the farm's wide tracts of fallow land and scrubby, cut-over woodlots for the training of three dozen strangers in the art of guerrilla warfare. If it was an act of patriotism, surely it was one of the oddest he'd ever heard of.

But he didn't want to wonder about that just now. He preferred to think of nothing—or, failing that, about the smell of roasting veal and hickory embers that filled the big yard and overwhelmed, thank God, the smell of penned livestock. He had dragged his chair close enough to feel the warmth of the long-smoldering fire. Half a dozen children played touch football nearby while the real thing, Redskins vs. Eagles, was broadcast from Griffith Stadium, the announcer's voice belting out of a big console set up on the side porch. He was neither following the game, exactly, nor ignoring it. He was brooding, like the hens in the low, sprawling barn across the field, camouflaged by eight-foot stalks of joe-pye weed.

From where he sat, he could see the rest of the Brigade gathered around a long table where deviled eggs, potato salad, Coca-Cola and beer had been laid out on a checkered cloth. A big outdoor roast like this would be an occasion, regardless. But today's was downright surreal, not least because of the species of animal charring in the pit.

The whole thing had been arranged, on the sly and at long distance from California, by Ari Glasser, with covert assistance on the ground from Vernon and his Uncle Leon. Besides breeding hounds that hated white people, Leon also was the most esteemed hog-roaster in Queen Anne's County, if not on the whole Eastern Shore—so Vernon claimed. In summer you had to book him weeks ahead, though things did slow down after Labor Day.

The pit had been dug yesterday morning, while the squads were on maneuver, and the fire laid around nightfall in order that the coals would be ready at dawn. And only after that, when Ari arrived late in the evening, breathless from a cross-country flight and a taxi ride that must have seemed just as long and even more dangerous, did it occur to him that roast pig might not be the perfect feast to cap off these particular five weeks of unparalleled chaos and misery.

"What was I thinking?" Glasser was said to have said.

Leon viewed the situation as a professional challenge, and the two men spent hours in the middle of the night driving along the muddy shores of the Chesapeake in an aged Ford he'd rigged out with a special bed for hauling slaughtered animals and kitchen implements and confidential ingredients from job to job. As Ari told it, Leon had finally pulled into a run-down place owned by a friend of his, declaring, "It comes to my mind that we could make do with a fatted calf."

Hence the carcass that now hissed and popped and gave off fragrant smoke within spitting distance of Ingo's cold feet. Seven hours in the fire, it had turned black all over, with red splotches from the secret seasoning slathered on at intervals by Leon, or by Vernon acting as his deputy. Ari had stood for a good deal of that time nearby, nursing a cola, transfixed. You don't see much of this kind of thing in Hollywood, Ingo supposed. He wondered how often, after tonight, the roasted-calf motif would crop up in coming feature films. Maybe some biblical costume drama, *East of Gomorrah* . . . but then a pang somewhere near the heart nearly doubled him over.

He had broken a personal taboo. He had thought about the future, allowing his mind to drift past the fourth quarter of the current Redskins game. It was something he'd been drilling himself not to do, just as his thirty-odd companions, now gathered around the deviled eggs like apostles at the Last Barbecue, had drilled themselves to crawl through mud and shoot automatic weapons and defecate outdoors like real honest-to-God guerrillas.

For his own part, Ingo could not believe the war would be won or lost by his failings as a Scout. On the other hand, he could easily believe that he personally would die of dread if he allowed his thoughts to range unchecked for a single moment.

"It sounds like a close one," someone nearby said.

Ingo started, then recognized Timo. "Close one?"

"The game," said the driver, with a flash of bad teeth. "The Eagles are up by seven but haven't scored in a while. They got the talent, no question. I just think maybe the Skins got more staying power."

Ingo nodded, trying to focus on football, generally a safe topic. The rules were clear and, at least where the formidable Skins were concerned, the outcome seldom in doubt. But win or lose—in marked contrast to the war in Europe, despite predictions to the contrary—the whole shebang really would be over by Christmas.

"I would like to offer a toast," said Ari Glasser, raising his can of National Bohemian just as an annoying jingle for the very product came floating from the radio on the porch. Ingo missed the first part of whatever Ari was toasting to, listening instead to the chipper advertising ensemble. What did these people do when they weren't singing fifteen-second oratorios?

National Beer, National Beer,
You'll like the taste of National Beer.

And while we're singing, we're proud to say,
It's brewed on the shores
Of the Chesapeake Bay.

Glasser concluded, "The Varian Fry Brigade!"

There were murmurs and laughter and, from out in the field, a bit of yelling when one team of kids scored a touchdown against the other.

"What did he say?" Ingo whispered to Martina, who was standing beside him.

She rolled her eyes. "I knew you weren't listening. You never listen. This whole thing is a joke to you, isn't it?"

"No. It isn't a joke."

"A lark, then. A little camping trip. Something to get you out of that city you hate so much."

"I don't hate the District. I was born there."

Glasser was still talking, thanking people. Leon, for such a fine job with this calf. Timo, for ferrying all these supplies out from Washington. Rabbi Grabsteen, for kindly being with us today. And of course Miss Charleva, for allowing us all to join her on this beautiful farm. Without her, none of this . . .

"Who *was* this Varian Fry?" Ingo said, loud enough to drive Glasser's voice out of his head.

"You've never heard of Varian Fry." There was triumph in her voice, of the I-knew-it sort.

By this time people nearby, tipsy and in the mood to be entertained, were turning to catch the latest episode of the Marty & Ingo Show. He was aware of them but didn't mind; he was happy enough to play the straight man. "You'll tell me though, won't you?" he said pleasantly.

"Varian Fry was *just* the greatest American hero of the whole beginning of the war, that's all. He was the only person—back when everybody else was sitting on their thumbs, and you Republicans were frantic about keeping us out of Europe—Varian Fry actually *went* over to France, which the Germans had already occupied, and got to work smuggling people across the border. He saved over a thousand before Pétain's thugs threw him out."

From the eavesdroppers, an excited murmur, probably less over Martina's capsule bio than from hearing someone branded a Republican. Fighting words, in this crowd. Ingo scowled at the faces around him—his comrades, if you could believe it. "Varian," he said thoughtfully, to deepen the scandal. "Sounds like a woman's name, doesn't it?"

He didn't provoke the reaction he was hoping for. For an instant he looked around at the others, into their hopeful, earnest, well-intentioned faces, and felt something like pity that quickly changed into something like panic. These people aren't guerrillas, he thought. No more than I am. They're desk warriors—assistant professors, accountants, a salesman or two. A dress designer from Wilkes-Barre. A futures analyst from Chicago. Christ, a *bartender from Dupont Circle*. We're nothing but a bunch of saps, and we're about to get ourselves killed.

"Wasn't it Varian Fry," said one of the saps, a skinny prelaw student named Eddie Lubovich, practically a kid—"who rescued Marc Chagall?"

"And Hannah Arendt," said somebody else.

"There," said Martina. "You see?"

Ingo shrugged. He had no idea who Hannah Arendt was. Marc Chagall he understood to be some kind of painter—but why would a painter need rescuing? "You folks enjoy yourselves," he said, aping his own occupational geniality, then turned away and wandered over toward the porch, where the announcer was shouting about a *great* play, a really *swell* play, we've got a whole new ball game on our hands now, without a clue as to what had happened or who stood to gain by it.

"Excuse me, Mr. Miller?" said a youthful voice.

Ingo turned to find himself looking slightly upward into the wide brown eyes, almost calflike, of Eddie, who was holding a can of National Boh in either hand. He offered one to Ingo. "You look like you've had a rough day."

"Do I?" Ingo accepted the beer, wondering what Eddie was seeing. Today had been no worse than any other.

The kid didn't answer. He might have been half drunk already, or only excited. Ingo tried to remember being excited—as opposed to, for instance, sick with fear. He watched the boy slurp down his beer, marveling at the clear, sharp light in his eyes, the skin drawn tautly around his temples.

Eddie looked back, his gaze direct and guileless. "Could I ask you something, Mr. Miller?" he said, in a voice that still betrayed the croak of adolescence.

"Call me Ingo. Fire away."

"How did a guy like you . . . I mean, how did you in particular get caught up in all this?"

"All what?" Ingo looked around, pretending to be mystified, then patted Eddie on the shoulder. You could feel the bones right through the wool campus pullover, navy blue with an orange V on the chest. "Never mind. It's kind of a—"

"Long story, sure. It's none of my business, anyway."

"That's not what I was going to say." Ingo shook his head. "Not a long story. Too short, maybe. Over much too soon." He hesitated. "Or, I don't know—maybe not. Maybe it's still going on."

A strange feeling came over him, as if he, not Eddie, were standing there half drunk, light streaming out of his eyes.

"I'm not sure I can explain it now. It's not that I've forgotten—I can remember every bit of it—only I'm not sure it would make sense anymore, if someone tried to retell it. The world has changed so much, it's like the definitions have shifted around. Back then, everything was so different. And I do mean everything."

Eddie gave an uncertain laugh. "The good old days, eh?"

Ingo shook his head. "This is more than nostalgia. And the old days weren't all good. They were just . . . you felt more alive then, somehow. Die goldenen zwanziger Jahre—the Golden Twenties, that's what we called them. That last summer before the Depression. The end of the Free Youth Movement, though I guess you wouldn't have heard of that. Anyhow, there we were—kids from all over—on this beautiful mountain, the Höhe Meissner. It was huge. It was history, that's what everybody was saying. The second Youth Summit. All of us so young, and the world so round, and the future hanging there like you could just reach out and grab it. And then—" He shrugged. "Kommt die Morgensonne, zerfliesst's wie eitel Schaum."

Eddie smiled politely. "I'm afraid you've lost me there, Mr. Miller. I don't speak any German. Other than Blitzkrieg and Sieg heil."

Ingo shook his head. "Why should you? There's nothing left of all that now. But there was a time . . ." He stared hard at Eddie, determined not to be misunderstood. "There was a time, a genuine part of history, and part of our lives, when anything you could think of was possible. You could be whoever, whatever you wanted to be. We all believed that—every one of us there on the Höhe Meissner. And that damn mountain was the center of the world."

HÖHE MEISSNER

What surprised Martina more than anything—possibly excepting the naked gymnasts—was that Ingo had agreed to come in the first place.

If he hadn't, her parents would never have allowed her to go. Sorry, only one Atlantic crossing per family per century. But enter a nonrelated variable and suddenly the equation doesn't hold. Martina couldn't imagine how they expected *Ingo* to keep her safe. Lob spitballs at stray icebergs? Ask mashers politely to leave her alone? But somehow the notion of his trailing along, a familiar and comforting figure from her earliest childhood, had reassured the ma and papa. She started packing that same afternoon.

She supposed it was Ingo himself. The dullness of him. Always with the books or the toy soldiers or the model boats. Those stupid boats! Cork and balsa wood contraptions he would float in trenches specially dug in the backyard, filled with water lugged in buckets. The vividness of the memory surprised her. Martina seldom missed, or even thought about, her childhood. She was glad she'd woken up and joined the Jazz Age—that she hadn't remained stuck in time like poor Ingo, with his Sunday-school clothes and his knapsack full of poetry.

"Just don't go acting like someone from Scott Fitzgerald," her mother had said. As though speaking of a place, some perilous den of sophistication, rather than a fashionable young author.

"Yeah, I'd make a great flapper, wouldn't I, Ma? With these hips?"

Her mother rolled her eyes, pretending to be scandalized while enjoying the banter. "These days, nobody wants to look like what they are. The girls want to look like boys. The boys want to look like Al Capone. I suppose gangsters want to look like . . . I don't know, priests."

"*Girl* priests."

"Oh, you. I was reading just the other day, maybe in *Collier's,* about some men over there someplace"—waving a hand, *over there* meaning Europe, where everyone had completely lost their minds—"who've started going around barefoot, dressed in old rags or what-have-you, traipsing from town to town singing and dancing and begging for food, like something out of the Middle Ages."

"That's old news, Ma. They've been doing that since back in the Teens. We read about it in Contemporary Cultural Studies."

"Back in the Teens! Ancient history, you're saying. Heavens, the world must be spinning faster nowadays."

"It is, Ma. That's the whole point."

"All the more need to be careful, then. You're only twenty."

"Thank *heavens* Ingo Miller will be there." Mocking the overbearing *Hausfrau.* "Now *there's* a fine young man. Goes to church, helps little ladies across the street—a regular Eagle Scout."

Her mother couldn't help but laugh, then quickly atoned. "That's not nice at all! Poor Ingo."

"Sure, Ma. It's what you sound like, though."

But that made it all the more puzzling that Ingo should've agreed to tag along.

He tended to scoff nowadays at what he deemed Martina's, quote, modern ideas, unquote. Especially the ones that could be put down, even remotely, to Anthropology, her most recently declared major. (The last had been Drama, and before that, fleetingly, Psychology.) Her sudden, all-absorbing fascination with this or that culture, her craving for some exotic cuisine, her abrupt changes in musical taste or style of dress . . . you could see how that kind of thing might seem faddish to someone like Ingo, who was still listening to scratchy recordings of the Vienna Philharmonic playing *The Blue Danube.*

"Even Stravinsky likes ragtime," she'd told him, showing off a new snippet of knowledge.

"Stravinsky—isn't he the fellow who caused a riot with his pagan dance piece? The one where the prima ballerina gets burned alive?"

Martina hadn't believed him; but on the other hand she wasn't a hundred percent certain he was wrong. Ingo, though pigheaded, was usually well informed. He knew about the Youth Movement, for instance. She expected him to write it off as modern nonsense, but instead he'd listened calmly for a while, eyes lifted reluctantly from his book—something thick, with a title suspiciously French—then responded simply, "Yes, I know about that."

"You know about what?"

"About the Jugendbewegung. Everyone should. It's a notable prewar development. It's where this craze for the guitar comes from. And for hiking and camping, all that Baden-Powell business. Among other things."

As usual, she had neither fully believed him nor dared to voice her doubts. Ingo was majoring in History with a minor in Music. Which meant, as she saw it, that he dealt primarily in Fact, secondarily in Interpretation, with a touch of Feeling thrown in rarely. So she stuck to her artfully planned sales pitch, culminating in an invitation to join her this coming summer on a journey overseas, and Ingo let her go on trotting out her little knowledge, that well-known dangerous commodity.

She laid it out for him much like her Con-Cult professor—a handsome young Swiss with a pointed accent and Freudian goatee—had explained it for her class. The Youth Movement began as a reaction of Wilhelmine teenagers against the sterile, materialistic lives and bourgeois values of their parents—or something to that effect. In the beginning it comprised loosely organized bands that gathered on weekends for daylong jaunts through the countryside, fleeing the ugly, industrialized, polluted and decadent cities for a cleaner, more authentic and aesthetically satisfying realm of woods and fields, hills and streams, towering cliffs and deep, mist-veiled gorges.

"How very up-to-date," Ingo put in. "As though the Romantics weren't doing that a hundred and fifty years ago."

But it hadn't ended there. At times Martina found that you had to grit your teeth and soldier onward. It hadn't ended with hiking clubs and Saturday outings in the Black Forest. Soon the youth groups joined up, the leaders drafted manifestos and the German flair for organization asserted itself. Local chapters of the leading group, the Wandervogel, sprang up at several universities; membership grew and diversified; the outings became longer, more frequent and better planned; and after a decade or so, what had begun as a spontaneous, inchoate phenomenon began to take on a distinctive style, an identity. It became, as her professor rather grandly had declared, for the first time ever, an authentic voice of youth.

Having now acquired a voice, Youth cast about for something to say with it. Bit by bit the movement, or rather the various branches of this sprawling phenomenon, took up such causes as vegetarianism, universal education, agrarian reform, sexual equality, ecumenism, folk music, the freedom to choose one's own career—

"Tell me," Ingo interrupted, "have they discovered FKK yet? Free-Body Culture? Naked swimming and sunbathing—the body as a temple of beauty, nudity equals nature equals health? That'll be next. With Germans, that's always the next thing."

A decade into the new century—Martina pressed on—the Movement entered a kind of adolescence. The early, innocent days yielded to a period of greater complexity but also greater promise. The original groups spawned factions and subfactions that not infrequently found themselves at odds. Magazines started up, flourished for a time and ceased publication. The movement songbook, the *Zupfgeigenhansl*, sold hundreds of thousands of copies. A new vocabulary, including such stirring terms as *Jugendkultur*, Youth Culture, entered the vernacular. Wandervogel-style clothing—loose, functional, pseudo-peasant garb of roughly woven cotton—gained popularity. Even the new musical fashion, which rejected the stylized complexity of "art music" in favor of a simpler, more direct and participatory manner of performance, attained remarkable currency in the land of Wagner and Beethoven.

"Sure," said Ingo, "and an ensemble called Duke Ellington's Jungle Band has reared its head in the land of John Philip Sousa. Your point, please?"

Martina was almost there. By the eve of the Great War, the Movement had grown to encompass every facet of modern European life. Its membership ranged from evangelical young Lutherans through occult-minded Anthroposophists to "neo-heathens," Wotanists, adherents of worldwide Socialism, readers of Nordic runes, defenders of *völkisch* nationalism, advocates of "racial hygiene," and even a faction advocating full civil liberties for homosexuals.

"For heaven's sake, Marty," complained Ingo, the prude, who seemed to have gone a little pink around the ears.

At last, in the summer of 1913, all these disparate groups came together for a Youth Summit, literally on a mountaintop: someplace outside Kassel in central Germany. Kids from everywhere held meetings and gymnastic competitions and made speeches and staged late-night singing contests, made more speeches and who knows *what else* they did—giving the prude a little wink—and at the end of it all they ratified an official declaration stating the shared ideals and aspirations of Free Youth.

But the summit—you have to understand this—wasn't about meetings and agendas. It was about *being there*. Imagine! Tens of thousands of young people, from all over Europe. Germans and Czechs and Austrians and Poles and Danes, even a few White Russians. The Boy Scouts had sent a delegation from England. There were smaller numbers of French, Swedes,

Lithuanians, Italians. In the end, this gathering, formally known as the *Jugendtag*, turned out to be so much bigger than anyone had anticipated, and coverage in the mainstream press so minimal, that nobody really knew how many kids had been there, where they'd come from or what manner of things had happened outside the published agenda. Legends abounded. But all anyone could say for sure was that some amazing alchemical fusion of massed, unsupervised youth had taken place.

"That's wonderful," said Ingo, "really wonderful. So you didn't actually have a point after all."

When he picked up his book again, she reached over and batted it out of his hand. *"They're doing it all again,"* she blurted. "A second Youth Summit. This summer. Same place, same mountain. Middle of August. I want you to come with me. Please, Ingo. I *have* to be there—it's once in a lifetime— and I need somebody to travel with. Somebody my parents trust. Will you at least *think* about it?"

Ingo said nothing at first. He got a smug look on his face, that aggravating little smile. I know something you don't know, the look said. Then he gathered up his books.

Always with the books. Stacks of them, by writers Martina had never heard of. *The Immoralist,* André Gide. *Der Tod in Venedig,* Thomas Mann. *Cities of the Plain,* Marcel Proust. *Demian,* Hermann Hesse. Some of them were not even translated. Ingo seemed to prefer this, apparently thinking it made him look mysterious. As if there were anything about him that Martina hadn't known for a long, long time.

"Okay, Marty," he said at last, the stack of books balanced in his arms, "I'll go. You can tell your mom."

Simple as that. Simple, yet impossible to figure. Martina was still amazed, when she thought about it. But she didn't have a lot of time to think just now, here on top of the Höhe Meissner, with the summer sun in her hair, uncounted hordes of young people swarming around her, life exploding into brilliance and color like fireworks on the Fourth of July.

As for Ingo, he must have wandered off somewhere. That's what you do here, Martina supposed. You wander. The term *Wandervogel,* before it was applied to free-spirited teenagers, had something to do with birds in flight. The image was apt, she thought—right down to all this weird, bright, colorful plumage.

She peered around from the safety of her beach blanket, her little rectangular patch of middle-class America amid the dark woods and flowery meads of the Old World. The German countryside looked more or less how she'd imagined it from the Brothers Grimm. Overhead, the twisty limbs of ancient towering oaks stretched out like a giant's arms reaching to snatch you. Sunlight fell soft and golden through the boughs to dance on coralbells and lady's slippers. Great weathered rocks hunched like trolls, draped in hoary lichen. On three sides the forest pressed in, mysterious and dark, with little footpaths winding off into the shadows, forbidding yet seductive. On the fourth, you could gaze across a meadow dotted with scarlet poppies and blue cornflowers, and beyond, over a damp green vale, to the roofs and steeples of a perfect, fairy-tale village in the distance, a thousand feet below.

And everywhere between, in field and woods, sprawling in the grass, strolling down the paths, nestled among rocks and trees and wildflowers, were the laughing, heedless, golden-haired children of Hamelin Town, lured away by some wily Piper, lost forever to their families, disporting themselves now in a magical mountain land

> Where waters gushed and fruit-trees grew,
> And flowers put forth a fairer hue,
> And everything was strange and new

But that, Ingo was quick to point out, was Browning. "And Browning"—raising a finger to emphasize this point—"was English. Whereas the Grimms, who spent some time around here, were German. Which is why"—and he again flashed that annoying, I-know-a-secret smile—"everything's so much darker in the Grimm version. Look around you. This is where a lot of the old stories come from. The Grimms hiked around the countryside listening to the old people. The real Hamelin is just up the road—as close as Baltimore, back home. And east of here, around Jena, that's where—"

"Oh, be quiet, Ingo."

This spoken with no malice, like turning the radio down. Still, after that he had wandered off on his own, and Martina reminded herself that, all fancy aside, this was not make-believe. It was real, immediate, touchable. Anyhow, these kids were too old for the Pied Piper, weren't they? A good half of them were of college age, like her and Ingo. And there were grown-ups, too—veterans, she guessed, of 1913, ambling about with a dazed look, as though wondering what, exactly, they had wrought.

They had wrought, Martina thought, something marvelous. She'd never seen kids like these. You never would, in the States. Some of them wore traditional costumes, picture-book stuff—boys in *Lederhosen,* girls in

Dirndl. A group of high school boys calling themselves the New Templar Knights had fashioned medieval-looking tunics and loosely woven skull-caps. Another, the Deutsche Jungenschaft von 1 November, wore blowzy, sky-blue shirts and pants so short Martina turned her head away the first time they trooped by, thinking they were walking around in their under-wear. Most commonly, though, the kids wore whatever caught their fancy. If a girl felt like wearing a bright scarlet blouse, its tails billowing over a pair of men's hiking pants, then she did: easy as that. If a boy felt comfort-able in a one-piece homespun garment like a nightshirt, dyed bright yellow and gathered at the waist with a leather cord—hey, why not? There were kids dressed like peasants from Prussia and kids dressed like mad alchemists from Prague. Girls with their hair cropped close enough to risk sunburn, boys with golden locks tumbling over bare shoulders, muscles rippling on their chests, like dancers in some exotic, manly ballet. One little cluster of friends was dressed all in black, their faces powdered, like walk-ons out of Bram Stoker. Half a dozen girls flitted by in flimsy, diaphanous dresses so thin their breasts showed through—wood-nymphs, Martina supposed. And then, of course, the naked gymnasts; but she still hadn't come to terms with *that.*

You had also, naturally, any number of people in plain, ordinary clothes—like Martina—but somehow you didn't notice them. And after a while, you didn't want to be one. You wanted to be fearless, wild and gay, to look and act as nobody ever had before. What you wanted, ultimately, was to be *here,* exclusively, to forget every other place else you'd ever been and every day you'd spent elsewhere. You wanted to take your place among the runaways from Hamelin, to float up in the mountain air and dance upon the wind.

Which was more or less what people were doing. Music was every-where—sprightly tunes from guitars and flutes and tambourines and a hundred clear voices—and nothing in the world was easier or more natu-ral than to throw your head back and lift your arms and twirl and run and leap to the rhythms and the melodies that wafted on every breeze. You breathed in the music and were nourished. You drank in air that left you intoxicated. You felt the colors like soft, supple textures caressing your eyes. And the sunshine, soft and luxurious sunshine that fell only on Old World mountains, you wore like a second set of clothes. Or even, for some people, and more by the hour, a first.

Oh, where was Ingo?

Martina felt she was going a little crazy, and her German—mostly hand-me-down Yiddish—wouldn't take her very far. Forget about conversation;

she couldn't even read the damn program book, a document the size of the *Saturday Evening Post*. She had studied its illustrations, pen-and-ink work by an artist called Fidus, and had scanned the tables listing hours and names and *Themen* and *Orten*, whatever those were. If she understood correctly, a discussion was coming up soon on *die Judenfrage im Jugendbewegung:* the Jewish Question in the Youth Movement, though as Ingo had explained, this could also mean the Jewish Problem. Problem or question? They are not the same at all. Except perhaps to people with a very strong need for certainty.

Without Ingo, she couldn't make up her mind—it helped so much to have someone to disagree with. She had hoped to catch the Jewish thing, which would be something to tell her father about, something to placate him. *It's part of your heritage. You ought to take an interest.* In theory she agreed; but what was so darned interesting, when you got right down to it? Religions, tribal affiliations, outmoded nation-states—this stuff had as little relevance to the Jazz Age, the era of improvisation and synthesis, as those quaint Templar Knight costumes. You could read all about it in Spengler, if you cared to. Everybody was reading *The Decline of the West* this year, except for Martina, who didn't have time to read, and Ingo, who disapproved.

She sighed. If he didn't show, she'd leave the Germans to sort out their own Jewish Question. Without Ingo she wouldn't understand a word, which was the story of her and Judaism to begin with. She liked listening to her grandmother's stories—her favorite being the girl with the magic broom—when the old lady mangled them into English. But once you got past the folktales and into Torah scrolls and mumbling in Hebrew and the womenfolk left at home, lighting the Shabbas candle . . . for Martina's money, you could keep it. All that *Alte Land*-ish stuff she was happy to leave to Ingo, who wore his German-Americanness like other people wore hair: hyphenated right down the middle.

Setting aside the program book, she began leafing through an old issue of *McCall's* she'd found abandoned in a train station, one of the half-dozen they'd trooped through in towns that grew progressively smaller, lugging their clothes and bedding and Ingo's old pup tent, changing from modern trains to aged carriages tugged slowly by huffing steam engines through too much picturesque scenery, until at last they reached the Kaufunger Wald Naturpark and joined dozens of other kids, detraining at the same place, to complete the journey on foot. A regular pilgrimage, blisters and all.

The *McCall's* featured last year's fashions and an article about how to invest on margin in the booming stock market—Martina couldn't have cared less—but at least, thank God, it was in plain American English. Her eyes roamed peacefully among the paragraphs. For July, the air was cool, and the sun felt good where it touched her. She might have dozed off for a moment or two—reading ladies' magazines often had that effect—when she felt a body flopping down on the blanket beside her.

"Where in the world have you—"

But instead of Ingo, it was a total stranger—a boy, maybe a couple years younger than herself. Bright red hair and a face full of freckles. Martina was taken aback and might've been alarmed, if she'd had a moment to think.

"You're American, right?" the boy asked her, slightly out of breath. His accent came at her like a fly ball from Ebbets Field.

"How could you tell?" she asked sardonically, peering from behind her magazine, sprawled on a blanket labeled *Cape May, N.J.* in a nicely matched summer outfit her mother had bought for her at Woodward & Lothrop.

The boy smiled briefly to acknowledge the joke. "Act like we're talk-ing," he instructed her.

She straightened her back. This was different, she decided; something new, therefore good. Still, she wasn't sure what to make of the redheaded stranger. He was scrawny for his age, which she placed at about seventeen. All his bodily extensions—arms, legs, neck—were strikingly thin. His pale skin was pink where the sun had found it. His eyes were sparkly and green, like a favorite marble she'd lost years ago. His nose was large and some-how bent—could it have been broken and healed kind of sideways? All in all he looked like a character out of a comic strip: next-door neighbor to the Katzenjammer Kids. For some reason you felt like smiling at him, and so—practicing this new skill, moving with the flow of her emotions—she did.

"Yeah," he said loudly, poorly imitating casual chitchat, "I don't know what got into me. I should have known better, falling for a stunt like that!"

"You ought to keep your voice down," she suggested, "if you're trying not to attract attention. Just talk normally, nobody will notice."

The boy thought about this, longer than Ingo would've. "You're right, thanks." Then he went back to practically shouting. "I think later I'll hike into town and drink a few bierskis, ja?"

"For heaven's sake," she laughed, giving up on him. It was like dealing with a child. "What are you—hiding from somebody? Are you in trouble?"

"Shh!" With a furtive glance over his shoulder, the boy slid nearer on the blanket. He smelled sweaty, not dirty but healthy. "That's the guy over there. The butterfly collector."

Martina saw who he meant. A grown man, in his mid-thirties, she guessed, and thus one of the oldest people on the mountain. "Butterfly collector" was a weird description, but you could see what the kid was getting at. He wore khaki garments with an excess of pockets, and a wide-brimmed hat, and under one arm he clutched a leather-bound notebook.

"Is that man chasing you?" she asked, aiming for a tone of severity that wasn't easy to achieve with this kid.

He gave her a wry little smile, raised an eyebrow, twitched one corner of his mouth. "He's chasing *somebody*. He didn't get a good enough look to know it's me."

"Know it's you who what?"

She got only a shrug. Little wrinkles formed on either side of his mouth, as though he had too much skin for his bone structure. When he shrugged, his bony shoulders stuck up through his V-necked jersey. "Anyway, it doesn't matter. The guy's a jerk. Thinks he's some big Aryan bwana—know what I mean?"

Martina did not. But she suspected that whatever the man might be, he wasn't chasing this kid for nothing. She looked the boy in the eye, as she imagined you might look at a little brother: Tell me the truth, shrimp, or I'll kill you. "What did you do—steal something?"

Again, the shrug. It reminded Martina of her grandmother.

"*I* don't know," he said. "Maybe he dropped something. And I kind of, you know, maybe, accidentally picked it up." He gave her a wink.

She didn't know whether to smile back or tell him to get lost. Slowly, the man in khaki moved past, poking through the dozens of little campsites in the vicinity, all of them laid out more neatly than Ingo and Martina's. Now and then he paused to glance sharply in someone's face. A couple of tents away, a brawny German youth made a rude-sounding remark.

The redhead laughed. "Did you hear that? That guy called him a Schwuler." He looked at Martina a moment, thinking his own thoughts, then stuck out a goofy-looking hand, too big for the arm it came on. "My name's Isaac. Where you from? I didn't expect to meet any other Yanks here."

She shook the hand because she couldn't think of a reason not to, but didn't answer his question. To reveal herself as Martina Panich, junior at Catholic U., would've shredded whatever veil of mystery she might have possessed.

"Don't talk to strangers, right?" Isaac nodded, allowing her hand to drop. "Can't say I blame you. You didn't get all this way on your own, though, did you? Couple of other girls come along?" He cast a critical eye over the pup tent.

Martina followed his gaze, wondering what you could deduce from a kid-sized tent, sloppily pitched and sagging in the middle.

"Or maybe a boyfriend," Isaac mused. His forwardness knew no bounds. Catching her eye—God knows what expression he found there— he held his empty hands up, signaling benign intent. "Hey, I don't mean to pry. Just a little curious is all. You know—another Yank."

"Tell me about yourself, then," suggested Martina. "What are *you* doing here?"

The smile never quite left his lips, though now it took on a shade of bashfulness. "That's kind of a long story. I've got family in Poland—an aunt and uncle—and my folks decided maybe I ought to spend a little time with them. Get off the block awhile, you know?" His gaze drifted across the meadow. Not really looking, just moving his eyes.

She ventured, "So you're here for the summer."

"Well, I guess longer than that. Forever, if my dad has anything to say about it."

She reappraised him. A note of family tragedy here. "What about school? Are you going to school in Poland?"

This time the shrug came from someplace inside him; you felt more than saw it. "I'm done with school, it looks like. I was never any good at it, to tell you the truth."

"So you live in Poland but you don't go to school. What do you do?"

"Well. I don't actually—" His eyes were still out there on the meadow. They were pretty, Martina thought, the way they picked up colors. When Isaac turned back he looked as though he'd slipped on a different mask, this one also smiling but made of something harder. "Things are kind of boring in Poland, you know? My uncle lives on a little farm, and there's all these animals to take care of. So anyway, this one time, I met these you might say *artistic* types who've got this place in the country, sort of a commune. They make pottery and toys and stuff. There's a lady who paints, and some people who want to make movies if they can get the equipment together. So I stayed there awhile, and then a few people were coming out here, so I came along." He concluded by briefly spreading his hands wide: *Ta-da! And here I am.*

As stories go, Martina found this one threadbare. But it did place the boy in a certain context. A runaway, she thought with a degree of wonder. A runaway, living in some Wandervogel commune. Not an everyday sort of thing back home. Over here, who knows? "You can call me Marty," she said on impulse.

He rewarded her with a flash of those sparkly eyes. "Marty. That's a good name for a Yank. So listen, Marty." His glance cut back and forth, conspiratorially. "You must be getting kind of restless, sitting here all by yourself. Want to come meet these friends of mine? I mean, they're Germans, but they're okay, you can talk to them. They aren't bündisch or Nazi or anything."

She had no idea what he was talking about. But then she imagined he was just throwing jargon around to impress her. Old hand in the Movement—and look, he doesn't even shave yet! Had she not been cross with Ingo, she never would have gone off with this stranger, a kid who was at least peculiar and possibly criminal. But she was, and so she did.

He led her down the mountain and up again, onto a lower rise called the Hanstein, along paths she couldn't have found again. Trailing a few paces back, she observed with silent amusement the boy's jerky progress, his bony limbs jostling within a random assemblage of pawned-off, mismatched clothing. She puzzled equally at his silences and his episodic sorties into conversation, primarily elliptical commentary on the people brushing past them on the trail: that fellow is Weisse Ritter; don't get this one started on Paragraph 175. She supposed it didn't matter if he was making it up. He'd become part of this adventure she was having, and if he were a scamp or a scoundrel, so much the better.

Also, she was grateful to have something, a single person, to focus on, struggling as she was with cognitive saturation. She must have seen thousands of kids today, every one of them exotic in some fashion, gathered in bunches, or marching in files, or drifting in twos and threes, or dozing alone in leafy bowers among ferns as high as your waist. Here now, they passed under an oak limb where a shirtless boy perched spritelike, dangling his legs, trilling a tune on his recorder. A little further, rival teams of boys young enough for grade school stood on opposite sides of a campfire bellowing *Volkslieder* at one another. In a shadowed glade, amid dangling bones and other spooky paraphernalia, a girl whose dark complexion came straight from a jar of stage makeup read fortune cards for giggling, flaxen-haired Heidis. You will meet a handsome man . . . the circumstances will be tragic . . . this card speaks of a departure . . . but see here, a sum of money is involved. Martina was wearily charmed.

Isaac halted before a wide tent whose front panel had been furled open, its interior furnished with makeshift tables, wooden planks supported at either end by stands of cleverly lashed wood, and stools to match. The

tables were laden with pamphlets, broadsheets, academic journals, gramo-
phone recordings, cheaply bound books. A handful of earnest university
types sat here and there, engaged in evidently purposeful activity.
Stretched between a brace of saplings, a banner declaimed in red on white

NUR EINE INBRUNST LÄSST SICH TREU ERTRAGEN:
ZUR GANZEN WELT! —R. Dehmel

Turning pointedly from the quotation to Martina, Isaac rolled his eyes.
"Nobody does do-goodism like Berliners."

At the sound of his voice, one of the young Germans looked up. A
tanned, outdoorsy-looking *Fräulein*, straight blond hair tugged back and
pinioned with a barrette, she broke into a smile and came forward to greet
the two of them.

"Kamarad!" she exclaimed. "Wir haben noch Angst für dich gehabt!"
She turned to Martina, aggressively cordial, and said something that,
based on her expression alone, could only have meant "So you're a friend
of Isaac's, are you?"

"Easy on the Deutsch, Kat," said Isaac. "Denn Marty ist Yank."

The young woman's eyebrows went up. "Stimmt? Ah, good day then!
How do you do? I am Käthe. Welcome in our little headquarters."

Martina, at a loss, only nodded. They're Germans, but you can talk to
them. Even if Käthe looked only a couple of years older, Martina felt some
wider gap between them. "Headquarters?" she said, grasping at anything.

"We are the SAJ, the Sozialistische Arbeiterjugend."

"Socialist Worker Youth," Isaac translated. "Don't get them confused
with the Socialist Loafer Youth."

If his sarcasm crossed the language barrier, Käthe chose to brush it off,
continuing in careful English delivered with occasional pauses over word
order. "Most of the Youth Movement pretends that they are not political.
Also the groups which refuse women or Jews to admit. Would you believe
them, this is not politics! Our group is at least honest over this. We will tell
you what we believe."

"So"—Martina thumbed quickly through her spotty recollections of
Modern Civ—"Socialist Workers. Is that anything to do with Communism?"

Käthe's response suggested that Martina had slapped the English right
out of her. "Mit dem Kommunistische Jugendverband haben wir nie
zu tun. Nie! Nothing! These are . . . Unruhestifter." She turned to Isaac
for help.

"Kat says the Young Commies are troublemakers. The SAJ will have nothing to do with them."

The German girl nodded. "By the Jugendtag, the Communists are not allowed, nor the Hitlerjugend nor the Wehrverbände. None of these terrible people. We are all here hoping for a New Reich, to the brotherhood of nations and people dedicated, and with the past not forgotten, toward the future unblinkingly turning . . ."

Martina's thoughts drifted back toward Catholic U., where her political awakening was still at the groping-for-the-alarm-clock stage. She had no means of grappling with the complexities of faction versus faction, the New Reich versus whatever the alternative might be—an old Reich, or a new something else?—and felt therefore unreasonably grateful for Isaac's sympathetic smile.

"Don't bother trying to keep score," he said. "The lineup changes every week. All that matters is, who are the real Arschlöcher? It doesn't matter what they call themselves. As of now, the Arschlöcher are mainly on the right, though the Reds aren't much better. If we're lucky they'll claw each other's eyes out. If not, it's a question of who pushes Weimar off the cliff first. I'd take Hitler over Ulbricht, at even odds."

Big talk—she understood that much. A teenager playing man of the world. But it must mean something, perhaps something important. For all she could tell, the kid knew what he was talking about.

Käthe gave Martina a woman-to-woman look. "Our friend Isaac is sometimes vulgar in his speech. I hope you do not know all these words."

"I can guess." Martina gave a shake of the head that signified, in any language, men—drawing a laugh from Käthe. She felt the warm glow of international amity.

Isaac beamed at them, unrepentant. "Oh, and—" Waggling his eyes like a matinee villain, he pulled something out of his baggy shirt that looked, from Martina's brief glance, like a much-folded clump of paper. Käthe's hand closed quickly around it, leaving Martina to wonder if the two of them were playing at skullduggery or genuinely up to something. She couldn't decide.

The minor excitement attending Isaac's arrival soon ebbed and the Arbeiterjugend settled down to what Martina gathered was business as usual. Hewing wood, toting boxes, slicing up trugfuls of gathered food, stenciling banners, practicing woodcraft, laying a fire—there seemed no end to the tasks waiting to be done nor the ranks of Young Socialists willing to do them. Isaac, alone in his lack of industry, stood outside the tent chatting up a pair of girls even younger than himself, neatly attired in clothing of the sort Pocahontas might have worn to receive John Smith, had she enjoyed the services of a punctilious German seamstress. Käthe took up the chore of folding pamphlets into exact thirds—there seemed to be a trick to it— and stacking them on a table. She gave Martina a smile that fell between apology and invitation. Seeing nothing better to do, and curious about what these people were like beneath the hale-and-hearty exterior, she ducked under the canvas brow of the tent and before long had fallen with Käthe into an easy rhythm of lifting, creasing and arranging. Women's work.

Out of the blue, Käthe asked, "Have you long known Isaac then?" in a tone that seemed excessively casual.

Martina glanced toward where he'd been standing, but the two little squaws were alone now, one plaiting the other's hair.

"He just goes away," Käthe said, following her gaze. "This is Isaac. And then he returns. Always bringing something. A gift, a stranger, a problem." She bit her lip, seeming to realize in the same instant as Martina that at least one of these characterizations applied to present company. Yet she made no apology. Fact was fact.

Martina nodded. "No, not long—actually we just met."

"Oh, yes?" Käthe's slight frown seemed to pose the question of whether meeting Isaac was an entirely good idea. "We also have not known him so long." A pause, a fold. "But he has been generous in his help to us. He seems to have . . ."

"A knack?" guessed Martina.

Käthe didn't know the word. "One might say, the ability to learn things. A few months ago, so he says, he could speak no German." She hesitated, arranging her thoughts. "Isaac is a unique type, is he not? I mean, unique also for an American?"

"I barely know him. But yes. That's my impression."

"Has he then told you his story?"

Martina raised an arm to brush her problematic hair away, in the process noticing fingertips stained oily black by printer's ink. These pamphlets, she guessed, were hot off the press. "What *is* this stuff? Some Socialist thing?"

Käthe cast a worried eye toward the hillock of paper. "An important vote comes tomorrow. There will be a debate—should the Meissner-Formel be amended? This is the guiding text of the Movement, adopted in 1913 at the first summit. The Formel now states"—her brow furrowed with the effort of translation—"Free German Youth intend to shape their lives by their own choice, responsible only to themselves, following their own inner truth."

She paused, as though awaiting Martina's ratification. "For its time, you know, this was revolutionary. But that was many years ago, before even the World War. Now we believe the text must go further. Tomorrow, therefore, the SAJ will propose to exchange 'freideutsche Jugend' for 'Free Youth of the World.' It will then be clear that the freedom of self-rule, self-decision, belongs not to Germans only but to everyone, all the new generation, not separated by borders or citizenship."

To Martina it sounded sensible enough. What did borders count for in the Radio Age? "So, the vote on this—you think you'll win?"

Käthe gave her a wistful, worldly smile that Martina could only marvel at. "We cannot know what will happen. None of us here, I think, really understands so well the democratic process. All the campaigning, the arguing, the secret vote—this is for Germany something new. We have had only a decade to learn, and the results, one must be truthful, have not been so good. Perhaps yes, our motion will pass. Or it may fail, which is not so terrible. The worst is that something bad and unexpected might happen. We have heard the Right is drafting a counteramendment. No one has seen it, but of course it will be *bündisch*, do you have a word for this? Nationalistic, full of swagger and patriotism, talk of young German warriors, 'War is the highest expression of our destiny.' Also it will have perhaps angry words about progressives, and feminizing influences on our youth, and Bolsheviks—this means anyone more liberal than the Kaiser— and especially Jews. Only now they like to say 'rootless cosmopolitans.' That is, people not of our blood, not of our soil—everyone understands who they're talking about. And so. When the vote comes, the outcome could be bad indeed. It could be dangerous."

"Dangerous how?" said Martina. "To who?" What difference could it possibly make, she thought, if some words on a piece of paper are voted up or down by a bunch of kids on a mountain somewhere?

Käthe's eyes drifted across the tent, as if the answer might be lying around there. "Dangerous," she said finally, "to people like you and me. But even more, to our friend Isaac."

Just for an instant, for no reason Martina could name, she felt a chill. It was how you feel hearing a fairy tale, at the moment when the forest path takes a sudden turn and there, from behind a tree, steps a snarling wolf or an ugly, stooped crone. But there were no witches here, only healthy kids and brilliant sunlight and clean air filled with music. For heaven's sake, it was 1929. The Great War was past, the market was booming, the world was learning to swing.

Taking a step back from the whole subject, Martina said, "So what *is* Isaac's story, anyway?"

Käthe gave her a thoughtful look followed by a short, diplomatic nod. "You know, this story changes somewhat with every telling. But it seems that back in America, our friend got himself in quite bad trouble."

"A little young for that, isn't he?" said Martina.

"You know America, of course, better than I. But from all I learn, New York is for some people a difficult place. Bad things happen, though also good. Where Isaac lived, it was a neighborhood full of people from many countries. Italians were there, and Irish, and Greeks, also many Jews, especially from Poland."

"Could be the Lower East Side," said Martina—not that she knew the first thing about New York. She had been there exactly twice: once as a small girl, during a visit to her grandmother, who was not yet too old to fuss with schedules and stations and crowded streets, and once a week ago, when she and Ingo had boarded a ship of the Hamburg-Amerika Line and doubled back on the path of their ancestors.

"Isaac began spending his time with a rough group," Käthe went on. "These were older boys. His family could not control him. He stayed out at night very late, many days he would never go to school. Soon came trouble with the police. Isaac was made to stand before a judge, and the judge might have sent him to a special place for young criminals. This was no safe place, Isaac says, even worse than the streets. But his father rose to speak in the court. Back in Poland, he said, we were respectable people. Educated people like yourself, Honored Judge. To this day we have family there. My wife's brother is a veterinarian. My cousin is a respected merchant, he sells timber at an honest price to the largest German mills. Let our son Isaac go live with this family in the old land, he will not find trouble there. Let him become a man and learn a trade and live far away from these unhealthy influences."

"And the judge said yes?"

Käthe shrugged. "Isaac has told this in different ways. In one story the judge says, All right, you go to your Onkel Eli and Tante Rachel. In another Isaac is sent up the river, as he says, but after a time he escapes and travels to Poland with the help of bad friends. Another time, good relatives. Whatever is the truth, this new situation also does not last. Because when Isaac learns what is expected of a young man in a respected deutsch-judische family—the schools, the books, the private tutoring, the helping with Onkel's veterinary practice—very soon he runs away. He discovers the Wandervogel life and finds in this a new kind of home."

Martina pondered for a moment how you could derive "home" from such a formless thing as "the Wandervogel life," which she took to mean a vague ideology of personal liberation, wrapped up with reverence for the countryside, the fields, the forest, the mountains. The idea made no sense from an American standpoint—in those wide-open spaces you felt liberated, all right, but also very much alone—yet here in Europe, perhaps . . . This landscape did have a drawn-in quality; it surrounded and enfolded you; it bound you and your comrades as intimately as clansmen around a fire.

"You said his family is German Jewish?" she asked. "But they live in Poland?"

Käthe nodded. "This is ordinary. All the Jewish bourgeoisie think of themselves as German. They speak Hochdeutsch at the dinner table and send their children to German universities. They plan often to immigrate here, or to Vienna, for instance. Germany is the land of Kultur, you see, of Bach and Goethe and Hegel, and also of famous Jews like Heine and Mahler. Poland is what? A mere outland, some would say, a former German colony pretending to be a nation, always slipping back to the chaotic rule of heathens and Slavs. Many Polish towns keep their old German names from when the land was governed by the Holy Reich. That was centuries ago, but the Germans do not forget. Neither do the Jews. In fact the Jews, I think, remember more clearly, because they read history, they do not mythologize it. We Germans feel about the East—the Ostland, we say—how you Americans might feel about your West, had you won it and then lost it back to the Red Indians. A great destiny lies unfulfilled there, so many people think."

Martina tried to absorb it all. This was more confusing, she thought, but also more interesting, than the stuff they spooned out to you in Modern History.

Käthe sighed. "It is a dark and corrupting romance. But we have always loved such things."

For the longest time, Ingo slipped cleanly out of her mind. Afternoon drifted toward evening yet she no longer fretted over where he had gotten to or when they would hook up again. If she thought of him at all, it was only to tell herself that he was missing an eye-opening experience and had only himself to blame.

It was inevitable, she supposed, that the two of them should have taken separate paths; what was amazing was that they'd stuck together for so long. What, when all was said and done, did they have in common? Not a thing she could see, beyond the accident of having grown up on the same block in nearly identical red-brick houses on a boring, middle-class, suburban street. A matter of socioeconomic happenstance, nothing more, and it certainly didn't mean their fates were intertwined.

Just look at him: bookish and timid, sallow from living indoors, temperamentally conservative and, let's face it, something of a stuffed shirt. He sang in the *church choir,* for God's sake. Whereas Martina was . . . well, she wasn't so certain about that, only about what she was not. And that was the least bit Ingo-ish.

If anything, she was more like these Socialists. The longer she was around them, the more she felt at home, among friends. Comrades. She admired their confidence, their fellowship, their dedication to a cause. She envied their well-formed ideas about the world. She approved their practical clothing, simple uniforms of good, durable cloth that blurred differences of age and gender. She liked how they pooled the chores of running the camp. She even came to appreciate—after somebody handed her a multilingual edition—the poetry of Richard Dehmel, whose words flew in red and white on a banner over the campsite.

ONLY ONE PASSION CAN BE BORNE UNTIRINGLY: THAT FOR THE WORLD AT LARGE.

She was grateful to be spared Ingo's commentary on this, and on Dehmel's other stirring, plainspoken verses—"The Working Man," "The Martyr," "Harvest Song." Martina had never much cared for poetry, but this was a different thing, a nearly opposite thing, from the precious, lilac-scented, art-for-art's-sake confections that Ingo shlepped around in his rucksack. Dehmel's writings honored struggle and pain, the joy of children's playtime, the tears at the graveside, all the ordinary hopes and sorrows that were the real stuff of people's lives. None of that sighing, dreamy nonsense like *Death in Venice* or *Remembrance of Things Past,* those neverlands where Ingo tried to lose himself.

Martina felt her eyes had been opened. She knew this was a cliché—Ingo would have mocked her for saying it—yet it was true. She was looking at the world with a different, more honest and unclouded kind of vision. Opening Franz Werfel's "Friend of the World," she felt her heart quicken even at the preamble:

It is my sole desire, oh Men, to be related to you!
Whether you be a Negro, or a circus performer,
Or you still rest deep in your mother's arms,
Or your maiden-song rings through the courtyard . . .

How ironic, she thought, that you had to come to Germany to find someone who would write this way. In America, such thoughts were unutterable. You could go to Catholic University, right there in Washington, D.C., and learn all about Christ's New Covenant, wherein the old tribal admonitions are brushed aside and everything hangs on love for one's fellow man—yet nobody ever mentions that he might have dark skin. Here in Germany, the land of castles and knights and magical pipers, you were free to read, and to think, and to say whatever you liked, in your very loudest voice.

And the people here—these near-adults, a whole swelling tide of youth—weren't living in the Dark Ages anymore, but boldly in the present. Having cast off the moldy Thou Shalt Nots, they were plunging into the future, the new decade about to dawn, with no rules, no fears, no inhibitions. They might do anything! The Thirties would be a time such as the world had never seen—Martina was now sure of that, if not much else.

"Come now," Käthe called from the golden circle around the campfire. "Come, while there still is something to eat."

Martina had been sitting alone at the edge of camp, her thoughts adrift, while darkness rose up around her, like smoke from the land itself, out of the rocks and old trees and hard-worn earth, while the sky became a tapestry of shining lights, the million stars woven together by an unseen hand and spelling out endless prophecies, if only the mortals below knew how to read them.

Near the big iron stewpot she found a dozen or so Arbeiterjugend whose faces she had come to know, and an equal number of fresh arrivals who'd been out spreading the Socialist gospel across the mountainside. They accepted Martina matter-of-factly, another sister-in-arms. A dark-eyed boy handed her a bowl of leek-and-potato soup, steaming and fragrant with wild herbs and mushrooms gathered that afternoon; without tasting it she knew it would be delicious.

She looked around for Isaac but did not find him.

Through gaps in the trees, all over the Hanstein and up the higher slopes of the Meissner, she could see the orange-yellow pricks of campfires. All day people had been trying to guess the size of the crowd. Twenty thousand, she had heard. Then thirty. Then, unbelievably, fifty. You could imagine this if you looked at the fires and thought about all those campsites large and small tucked into every niche and fold and glade for miles. Fifty thousand young people: enough to fill Griffith Stadium back home, twice over.

One of the SAJ—a young man she'd noticed jotting entries in a ledger— turned to her and spoke in careful, almost too-polite English. "Käthe tells us that you are from Washington come?"

"You come from Washington," a second boy corrected him, the dark-eyed one who'd given her the soup.

Martina smiled and nodded, to assure them that either phrasing was fine.

"I think that it is a beautiful city," said the first boy. "Not like Berlin. Berlin is a great city but ugly. Like Chicago. Do you know Chicago?"

"No, I'm afraid not."

"Over Chicago Brecht has written," the boy said. "A real workers' city. Like Berlin, big and dirty, but so full of life! The people, warm and true."

"Do you know Berlin?" Dark Eyes said.

Martina shook her head. "I've never been anywhere in Germany. Only here. And the train from Hamburg."

There was quiet murmuring as this was translated and Martina felt somehow inadequate. These people were just so . . . good. So calm and sure and open to knowledge in all its forms.

"I think Germany's a beautiful place," she said hastily. "I'd love to see more of it. I wish I could just, you know, wander around, like you all do."

Hearing herself say it, she decided it was true. She wanted to cast off the constraints of college and home, a life scheduled down to the minute, and strike out along these enticing forest paths.

"If you wish that," said Käthe, from her place halfway around the fire, "why should it not be?"

"Does the SAJ," Martina said, awkwardly assembling her question, "just camp out anywhere? Do you have regular places, or . . ."

"We have a main home," Dark Eyes said. "It is not so far from here, a place called the Leuchtenburg, near Jena. And we have a project in the East, a model village. There is a little farm there, and an artisans' work-shop. We make everything for ourselves."

"But our chief work is in the cities," Käthe said. "Organizing among the working-class youth. Helping at soup kitchens, setting up libraries. This is our first duty, to serve and unite the ordinary people."

Her voice had an edge, and Martina wondered if she was annoyed that the boy had mentioned these other, less-serious-minded matters.

"But you must come to Leuchtenburg!" Dark Eyes persisted. "Always guests are welcome there. It is a lovely old place, with a wonderful legend. A knight of the Holy Reich took refuge there, pursued by pagan bandits—"

"Na ja," said Käthe, clearly annoyed now. "Just the sort of tale the Weisse Ritter like to tell. Armored aristocrats dashing about subduing the peasantry, crusaders sticking their lances through infidels."

The boy only smiled; this argument had a rote quality, its themes probably oft-repeated. "It is only a tale, you know," he confided to Martina. "Unlike the White Knights, and some other bündisch people we could name, we SAJ do not believe in old legends, though we may freely take pleasure in them. We do not believe either in new legends, as the Marxists do. We don't even believe in Wagner!"

There was laughter around the fire, and Martina dearly wished she got the joke, that she could be just another good, honest Socialist. When I get back to Washington, she promised herself, I'll take an interest in politics, figure out how the world works. And then I'll do something about it— mark my words.

Caught up in these thoughts, Martina was probably the last to notice the strange noises coming from the other side of the camp. Somewhere beyond the tent, off in the shadows, there was a scuffling, like a heavy object being dragged over rocks. Then a tumble, something falling or being thrown to the ground. Finally voices: two at least, male, cursing or laughing, possibly both. As the sounds got closer, a few Arbeiterjugend slipped away into the darkness like soldiers preparing to meet an unseen foe. Martina moved to follow them, but Dark Eyes held her back.

"Before, we have had trouble. People have been hurt."

At last the source of the commotion came lurching into the wavering circle of firelight: Isaac, his face begrimed and clothing torn, his hair askew, blood-slick gashes running down one bare arm. His eyes shone with fevered brightness as he stared back and forth, like a child waking from a dream and trying to recognize the faces swarming around him.

Then, to everyone's amazement, he began to laugh. His mouth opened wide and the laughter was that of a wild creature of the woods. He took a step forward, nearly lost his balance and had to be jerked upright by the young man beside him. This second boy didn't look crazed, though he too was a shambling mess, his clothing soiled, his hat knocked sideways. Martina's first thought was that he must be some German kind of Eagle Scout: he had the stiff, clenched-jawed look of someone working extra hard to win that merit badge. Her next thought was that the boy holding Isaac on his feet was Ingo.

Ingo it was, wearing a hat she'd never seen before, some silly loden thing with a feather poking out of it, and an unfamiliar peasant-style smock that was torn and stained. Ingo the timid bookworm from Brookland. Ingo the Dull and Predictable.

"Isaac!" someone shouted—Käthe, Martina dimly thought. "Bist okay? Bist du verletzt?"

"Verletzt?" Again the crazy laugh. "Injured? Nie—ich wäre tot. I thought I was a fuckin' goner."

Ingo led him forward, one stumbling footfall at a time. A German boy grabbed the opposite arm and together they carried him to the fire.

When Isaac saw Martina, his marble eyes sparkled. "I met another Yank!" His voice was unreasonably loud, the voice of someone who'd had a close shave and lived to tell about it. "This guy here, Ingo Miller, he's a fucking hero. I'm serious—this Arschficker saved my life."

NEAR STARY SAMBOR

War, thought Butler, is Tolstoyan: it obeys the formula laid down in *Anna Karenina*, the famous passage about families. Every successful military operation is more or less the same, but disaster comes in limitless variety.

Sometimes the problem unfolds gradually, over weeks or months, with ever more depressing clarity, like the Eskimo technique for killing a bear by feeding it sharpened bones in blubber, so that it bleeds slowly to death from inside. That's how the annihilation of Hitler's army in the East was proceeding, from the German point of view.

Other times, trouble leaps upon you so fast you have no time even to imagine what went wrong—rather as though munitions engineers had fed the bear an armor-piercing explosive. That's how the war felt to Butler this morning. That little click in the gut, just before the *boom*.

After five years as a front-line correspondent—six if you count the dress rehearsal in Spain, months devoted largely to screwing, reading Cavafy and smoking hashish—Butler had come to feel about the war as an experienced, intuitive mechanic might feel about a high-powered engine. He could clear his mind and gently touch the keys of his modified Remington, and the living pulse of the war would come throbbing into his fingertips. He could tell when the great, ravening machine was running smoothly. He could sense the changes in rhythm when it was roaring ahead or chugging wearily to a halt. He needed no inside source at Front HQ to tip him off to a new offensive: he could read it in the grinding teeth of motorized traffic, the whine of aircraft overhead, the tense, excited faces of young staff officers with secret orders behind their eyes.

Butler knew when a battle was going well from his bedroll, hearing the rolling thunder of artillery, the gentle shudder of the earth under advancing tank columns, the electric crackle of radios as messages came through. Just so, he could tell at once when the great engine faltered, when something got stuck, a connector snapped, an artery gushed blood. He felt it, somehow, in his own flesh: a sick churning in the belly, a tightening at the throat. A dry hacking of field guns. A silence when there ought to have been noise.

He was lying in bed this morning, an hour past dawn, wrapped in a bearskin blanket in his cozy bivouac near the railroad junction at Stary Sambor, a town that might have been in Poland or Galicia or the Ukraine, depending on when you drew the line. Today, in the autumn of 1944, this was Soviet territory. So why were the guns firing?

His head ached and his knee throbbed from having been twisted hard a couple days previously, as he crawled in or out—he was drunk at the time—of the political officer's tent. The *politruk* was angry because Butler, in connivance with his new pal Seryoshka, had snagged a private bunker: a neatly excavated little den with birch-log walls and a ceiling covered with turf to keep the rain out. The Wehrmacht built such things when it went over to the defensive, and once made they were damned hard to destroy. The *politruk,* not a popular guy—in point of fact an asshole—had been assigned a low round yurt. It was warm enough, double-layered in sheep's hide, but prone to blow over, especially when its stakes had been loosened by subversive elements among the lower ranks. By virtue of its roominess it had become a popular gathering spot for battalion staff officers, who liked to keep the *politruk* in their line of sight. Hence Butler's throbbing knee and a head that, pain withal, felt much too terribly clear.

"Good morning, comrade," Seryoshka said from across the musty little space. Dawn light streamed through crevices angled away from what, during the German tenancy, had been the front; since then the sides had changed and the light slits now faced the wrong direction, offering a glimpse of the Carpathians. Werewolf country. Nasty things crawled through the woods out there.

"What's happening?" Butler said groggily. "What is that shooting about?"

Seryoshka was bent over lacing his boots and probably had been awake for hours. Some nights he hardly slept, especially when a battle was in progress. Other times, he could hibernate for days. "A limited action, they say. Advance along a narrow front. Who knows? Maybe they're straightening the lines before the freeze. Or just keeping the Huns off balance. You know the sort of thing."

Butler knew. Small-scale movements, which seldom affected the reconnaissance battalion, had become standard Red Army procedure in this latter stage of the war. Now that the Germans were essentially non-mechanized, owing to lack of fuel and deteriorating equipment, Soviet commanders liked to keep things mobile along the sharp edge—obliging their foes continually to adjust their positions, burn a little more petrol, fire off a few more shells. Maintain the pressure, was the general idea; don't give the enemy time to catch his breath. *We can breathe during peacetime,* Zhukov's political officer, a man named Khrushchev, had famously said. *Today, we fight.*

"Where are you off to?" asked Butler.

"To Division. Pay a call on our friends over there. Catch up on the news."

Butler unwrapped himself from the bearskin. "Wait for me."

If Front Headquarters was a floating city, then Division HQ was one of its smaller industrial suburbs. There was nothing to it, really, except for the offices of core divisional staff, housing for support troops, radio and encryption facilities, a maintenance shed, a galley and the usual comic opera of Red Army logistics, a production with more of Groucho Marx than Karl about it. The division commander was a one-star general, recently assigned, and Butler had yet to take his measure. Seryoshka's "friends" were on the operations side, field men kicked up to headquarters, not often happy to be there. A sturdy lot.

The pair of them crossed the encampment and stepped quietly into the command post, sited in what was left of a schoolhouse. You would expect such a place—the brain of the fighting organism—to be a scene of purposeful frenzy, but effective brains are not frenzied, and a working CP often falls, at the pitch of fighting, eerily quiet.

So it was this morning. From the hall where Butler and Seryoshka stood, you could look into the operations center, which reminded Butler—such places always did—of newsrooms he'd known. It was dominated by a huge table on which maps and manuals and field reports and decrypted dispatches were arranged in an order apparent only to the men who needed them. Around this, ordinary slate boards smudged with chalk provided a continually updated accounting of unit strength and disposition. Except for the uniforms, the scene might have been taken for a wearisome gathering of the Math Department at a grubby provincial college.

The senior staff was present en masse. The division commander sat immersed in paper at the head of the table, chewing a cigar and swearing calmly under his breath. His ops deputy hunched beside him, grunting into a field telephone. The political officer sat opposite, doing nothing in particular; ostensibly an advisor, a helpful emissary of the Party, he provided by his mere presence a reminder of the stakes they were playing for. Heads were going to roll, if not Fascist then Red ones. The selection of heads on offer—the tank man, the infantry specialist, the logistics chief and so forth—sat in their designated spots, according to a seating arrangement standard throughout the Red Army. Sundry junior staff huddled near their bosses, while along the wall couriers stood at the ready to run dispatches or fetch more coffee. From an adjoining room you could hear a platoon of clerks aggressively engaged in the battle of the typewriter— one of the few theaters in which they were still outclassed by the enemy.

Cautiously, Seryoshka led them to a chart table just inside the door, where a trio of aides-de-camp quarreled *sotto voce* over a situation map. Preparing these entailed reconciling numerous, often conflicting status reports from subordinate commands engaged in battle, some of whom inevitably had gotten things wrong, while others, caught up in this and that, had not made contact for several hours. The present task was mostly finished; the only point in dispute being where to place a red block identifying a certain infantry formation. Either this side of the river or the other—it couldn't be both.

"Put the damn thing anywhere," growled the captain in charge. "Flip a fucking coin. The comrade general is waiting."

Looking smug, as though he personally were responsible for the collapse of German resistance, a peach-faced lieutenant affixed the unit in question to the farther bank. The captain nodded curtly and the map was rushed over to the big table, where the assembled officers pounced on it like so many night editors when a hot dispatch comes off the wire.

"Someone explain to me, please," General Krivon said loudly, with a thump on the table, "what the hell is going on out there. This makes no sense at all."

An anxious look crossed the captain's face, but his commander's dissatisfaction seemed to concern something larger than the map per se. The whole damned operation, for example.

"Something's gone wrong, hasn't it?" said Butler.

Seryoshka made a quick motion—*Keep quiet*—though nobody at the big table seemed to have heard. The captain, a pal of Seryoshka's from somewhere, whispered, "What makes you say that?"

Butler shrugged. "I've been hearing artillery all morning. Why hasn't it stopped by now? What are they shooting at?"

The captain took on a shrewd look, seeming to suspect Butler of being privy to closely guarded secrets. In a cautious voice he said, "The fire-control reports are inconclusive. It would appear the targets have been knocked out. But then—you know how it is. Until definite information is received . . ."

Butler considered this, trying to connect it with the vague unease that had troubled him all morning. Ideas swirled in his mind, barely out of reach, known facts and wild conjectures mingling chaotically. It was like the moment when, upon sitting down to write a story, you reach into a maelstrom of words and fish out the perfect lead. Suddenly, it's there.

"The reports are inconclusive, you said. You mean you've had no reports at all. Not for a while now. Your forward fire-control observers are out of contact. Is that it?"

The captain's lips tightened; he seemed to be resisting an urge to respond.

"Don't you see what this means?" said Butler.

He must have spoken too loudly, because in the subsequent silence he heard his own words ringing across the room. Abashed, he looked around to see the whole operations staff staring back at him. General Krivon— flicking cigar ash on the floor—said with teeth-grating courtesy, "What does this mean, comrade? I would dearly love to know."

Butler had spent time enough with the Red Army to understand that at moments like this you didn't try to be diplomatic. The old man got enough diplomacy from his underlings. He was asking you, ordering you, to answer in plain words.

"This means you're in deep shit, Comrade General."

Into the vacuum of shock, Butler moved a step toward the command table. He knew he was playing a role—Gogol's *yurodivy*, the village fool, speaking truths no one else dares even to think—and that having taken it up he must now play it wholeheartedly. In the same cocksure manner he went on, "This means the Germans have taken out your forward observers. They've blinded you. And there is only one way they could have done that."

Krivon glanced at his operations chief, who was glaring at Butler with a distinctly carnivorous avidity. "And how is this, pray tell us?" the general asked, his voice mocking. He played his own role quite well.

Butler took another step.

"The only way to take out forward observation posts—unless you make some incredibly lucky mortar shots—is to send assault teams through the line. They have to move fast, they can't get bogged down in the fighting, and they have to make their kills silently. Your observers have probably had their throats cut. Now your guns are shooting at nothing, at empty woods. The German forces have shifted position, but you can't tell where. And there's something else."

Now he had everyone's attention. They might not believe what he was saying—probably they hadn't decided—but they were damned well listening.

The general made a hand gesture, a sign of impatience: Very well, get on with it.

"You're not facing the SS, no matter what front intelligence tells you. That's a Wehrmacht man, over there. Classically trained. Old-school. Generalstab, more than likely. This sort of ruthless finesse, this bloody-minded coolness—you don't get that with the SS. You get the newer model tanks, and formations manned at nominal strength. You get tenacity in defense, fighting to the last bullet, dying in the foxhole. And you might, at worst, get a competent commander—as opposed to some Nazi brute chosen for political reliability. But you don't get military keenness. You don't have to worry about the enemy reading your mind. And that, Comrade General, is what you've got to worry about right now."

The division's intelligence man shook his head. "This cannot possibly be true." He addressed himself to Krivon. "We're not depending only on information received from the front. We've sent out our own patrols, we've snatched a few tongues. The prisoners come in wearing Waffen-SS patches. Some of them are Hungarian. We know the Wehrmacht has no use for Hungarians—only the SS. Himmler slaps a tag on them that says 'Ethnic German,' then into the line they go."

The general acknowledged this with a smirk. He kept his eyes on Butler. "What do you have to say to this?"

Butler thought quickly. He believed, as a guiding principle, you should always trust your intuition. But he guessed it didn't hurt to hedge your bets. With as much panache as he could scrape together, he said, "Comrade General, I think it is possible you are up against something very unusual. Something we may never have seen before."

A little smile came to the general's lips. The idea seemed to appeal to him. "And this is?"

"An SS field officer who has read Clausewitz."

It was too much, finally, for the operations chief. A stocky colonel with a breastful of battle decorations, he shook his head and said, "You've given us your grand theories, comrade. Clausewitz—splendid! But you've never got around to telling us what in hell any of it means to us ordinary fighting men."

"That's quite simple," said Butler. "Your forces are going over the wire. Soon you'll be swallowing territory like a thirsty man draining a canteen—only at some point, you'll feel a little scratch in your throat. And next thing you know you've got a viper in your belly."

"What percentage of that in there," Seryoshka asked him later, in the *politruk*'s yurt, "just as an approximation, would you say, was absolute horseshit?"

The other men present laughed. Even the *politruk,* a generally humorless sort, monkish in his gray tunic, broke into a grin.

Butler waited for them to have their fill. He toyed with the glass of vodka before him, rotating it carefully like a precision instrument. At last, professorially, he said, "I would not go above fifty. Sixty perhaps. Definitely no higher."

Seryoshka broke into fresh bellows of laughter, and the others joined in.

"I meant what I said about the SS, though," Butler added. Nobody cared by now; he was speaking mainly to himself.

"God, that was a good show," Seryoshka said, wiping his eye. "I wish you'd all been there."

The *politruk* nodded. At times you felt he wished to be human but his job prevented it. Most of the time you thought of him as a squid. "Comrade Sammy is an excellent speaker," he allowed. "He is highly persuasive. Perhaps he will try his hand sometime at writing for the official journals."

The remark was typical, Butler thought: neither positive nor negative, it could have been a pat on the back or a knife in the kidney.

After a while the other men in the room excused themselves, leaving only Butler, Seryoshka and the *politruk.* An ensuing silence was not uncomfortable—they were accustomed to one another's company by now—but nonetheless made Seryoshka restless. He stood up and paced a few steps, as far as the cramped interior of the tent allowed.

"I wish I was out there myself," he said, waving a hand roughly in the direction of the fighting, which had changed in the past hour to tank and infantry fire. "I hate sitting around, waiting. If they don't send orders down soon, I may think up something on my own. And you know that's all too likely to get us killed."

Now was the moment, perhaps, Butler thought, to rub the lamp and let the genie out. "I've got something for you," he told the *politruk.* "It came yesterday, in a package of stuff from Moscow. Here, let me show you."

He crossed the tent and picked up his Astrakhan coat. From one of its many interior pockets he withdrew what appeared to be a thick square of brown boxboard. Across the top, like a scrolling red ribbon, was printed the well-known symbol of the Moskva State Recording Studio. He held it before him, advancing toward the *politruk.*

"This is something for me?" The man didn't bother to mask the suspicion in his voice.

"I hope you like it," Butler said blandly.

Of course he would damn well like it. To feel otherwise would be tantamount to treason. Butler had just handed him a newly pressed recording of Shostakovich's Symphony no. 7, the *Leningrad.* It was a famous work, the artistic embodiment of the Great Patriotic War. Legend held—and in this case Butler believed the legend might be true—that the first three movements had been written as it were on location, during the siege of Peter's capital. Hitler himself had ordered that the city be reduced by starvation rather than direct assault: an unspeakable calamity that claimed a million lives. Shostakovich could have gotten out—his fame would've won him a seat on an aircraft fleeing the encirclement—but chose instead to stay and share the fate of his fellow citizens. He spent the early months of the siege as a volunteer firefighter, rushing from one bombed-out site to another, working on the symphonic score in his spare time. Finally in midwinter, enfeebled by hunger, he acceded to Stalin's order to pack up and go.

The magnificent work, completed in some godforsaken industrial town east of the Urals, was said to depict thematically the glorious defense of the "City on the Neva" against the Fascist hordes. It had special meaning for Butler, too; he'd gotten good American ink—the *Chicago Trib,* among others—for his review of the premiere performance at the Bolshoi in March of '42. The recording he'd just placed in the *politruk*'s hands was made only a couple of months ago, after the final lifting of the siege, by the Leningrad Philharmonic itself, the very orchestra Shostakovich had had in mind. As patriotic icons go, this was right up there with *Alexander Nevsky.*

The *politruk* raised his eyes to meet Butler's. He was a shrewd fellow— they usually were, in his line of work—and from his expression two things were apparent. One, he understood what Butler had given him. A career *apparatchik,* he knew the symbolic status of the *Leningrad* and could guess how tricky it must have been to obtain a copy. For this reason he would be wondering now what motives lay behind such a gift—surely something more than uncomplicated generosity.

Two—all doubts aside—he was touched, deeply and truly. What Russian would not have been? The man's expression softened, his gaze taking on something of that famous sentimentality. Turning away, he placed Butler's gift reverentially on an ammo crate, then reached underneath to pull out a bottle of fiery pepper vodka—the good stuff, such as the Chairman himself was said to enjoy. "Please join me, gentlemen," he said, filling their glasses. "Now we shall listen to this noble piece of music."

Butler eased back into his chair while a phonograph was wound and the needle carefully lowered. He let a few minutes pass while the symphony got off to its lyrical, unhurried start. Seryoshka was watching him—interested, waiting—but Butler declined to return the look. These days, paranoia came to him easily and naturally. War was Tolstoyan, yes—and this one was spiked with a strong dose of Kafka.

A second round was poured, a toast offered by the *politruk* to the citizens of Leningrad, and after that no one spoke for a while. The orchestra quieted down; a folkish little melody made the rounds of the upper winds. In his *Tribune* piece, Butler had noted the striking serenity of this opening movement—a marvel, when you thought about what was actually happening while Shostakovich toiled away. Shells were landing in the square outside the Winter Palace, a few blocks from the composer's apartment; miraculously, they failed to crack the domes or knock Peter off his horse. Fires were breaking out at all hours, fists pounding the door, people running around in terror. Then time began to slow, the food supply trickled down, winter crept over the city and the great hunger set in. The starving shuffled like zombies, going home to scrape off the wallpaper, using the paste for soup stock. Before long, people began lying down in the street to die—a civic-minded gesture, saving another hungry soul the bother of dragging your corpse down from the flat. Thinking about all that while listening to this wonderful, lilting, purely serene and unruffled melody . . . it made you wonder if artists of Shostakovich's caliber were altogether sane.

"This part here," Seryoshka said, "this part with the drums—that's the German panzers rumbling over the steppe. At first they're quiet, then they get louder till you can't hear the flutes anymore. I think the woodwinds are the peasants, working out in the wheat fields—good humble folk overwhelmed by the tides of war. Something like that."

The others nodded without replying. They'd heard it before, and other narratives as well—every trumpet call, each boom of a timpanum, was said to signify this cruel blow or that daring counterstroke. And by the third movement you had snow on the roof at the Kirov, the German guns fallen quiet, tanks frozen in place and babushkas dragging corpses on children's sleds up the wide, empty promenade beside the river.

You had to wonder, though. What would this music have sounded like in Peoria? It had been broadcast, Butler had heard, over the radio, Toscanini pinch-hitting for Samosud, the NBC Orchestra for the Bolshoi. And yet, though every note in the score might be the same, could such a performance have any meaning, any power, over there? Folks in Peoria had barely heard of Leningrad. They knew next to nothing about the German assault or the Russians' heroic stand before the city gates; all this had happened the summer before Pearl Harbor, while the Yankees were steaming toward another World Series win and the nation was enjoying its long isolationist nap. The *Leningrad,* in its majestic unfolding, could evoke for them no landscape of moon-white marble façades, nor the black waters of Lake Ladoga, nor the sky stretching unbroken to the Arctic.

Glancing surreptitiously, Butler found his comrades sunk into misty-eyed absorption. One of the pleasures of going to a concert in Russia was to watch how the audience responded. And they did respond, like no other people in the world, even the Germans. They would bow their heads and sob, or open their mouths in delight, or crane their necks in breathless anticipation, as if expecting the Firebird to come whooshing down from the chandeliers. The day Russian composers discover irony, Butler thought, will be the end of the world.

Movement four began. The weakest, in Butler's opinion. Shosti must have hated that tractor town in the east. "It was rye," he said quietly.

The other two men stared at him as though he had spoken in Japanese.

"It was rye in those fields, where the peasants were working. They don't grow wheat around Leningrad."

Seryoshka shook his head and grinned. "You know a bit of everything, don't you, my friend?"

"Only a bit." He knew one thing: now was the moment, if ever. "I have a proposition to make. To both of you."

Out of the phonograph, the string section galloped like the Tsar's cavalry. The *politruk* lowered his eyelids, but it was too late for cynicism now.

"I want to get into the action over there," said Butler. He nodded westward, where the sound of fighting could be heard behind the gathering finale. "To see the war like nobody else ever has—nobody on either side. But I need your help. It could be a good thing for all of us."

Seryoshka stared at him, a wary interest in his deep Georgian eyes. The *politruk* waited with his fingers knitted.

"We're not far from the Carpathian Mountains," said Butler. "That's wild country—the Huns have never properly conquered it. No one has. Those hills around the Moravian Pass have sheltered renegades and rebels and deserters for so long, you've got third-generation outlaws in there. And now you've got partisans, ours and everybody else's. You've got escapees from the prison camps. You've got soldiers from the Czech and Polish armies who wouldn't surrender in thirty-nine and have been fighting ever since. And of course you've got the damned Germans, shooting everyone not in feldgrau. Hell, by this time they may be shooting each other. I want to get in there. I want to hook up with the Underground— the Red formations, they're the dominant force now—and get *their* story."

He made a bracket with his hands, framing an imaginary scene, like Zanuck briefing a cinematographer.

"Here you've got this clandestine Red Army, supported by a secret proletarian society. By some stroke of providence, they've survived the Fascist occupation. They've taken terrible losses, unspeakable losses, but they haven't been knocked out. They've kept up the fight, they've attacked supply dumps and rail lines and raided armories and who knows what all else. They've struck the Nazis at every tender spot. They've surely targeted local collaborators—we've got to be honest about this—as well as the Germans. But in doing so they've forced the enemy to hold units back from the line, to police the whole rear area. That's weakened the front, which in turn has hastened the Soviet victory."

He slapped the table. "Think of it! Behind every partisan there's a story. Real human drama. A husband who's seen his family shot. A girl who fled from a slave-labor camp. A Red Army man, caught behind enemy lines, bravely carrying on the struggle. Somebody has got to go in there and meet those people and tell those stories. And whoever does it first is going to be"—barely nipping off the word *famous,* which one would leap for in a room full of Americans—"a hero. A genuine hero of the Revolution."

With sweat gathering on his brow, Butler wondered if he should spell out for them exactly what sort of hero he was talking about. He was thinking, and he wanted his listeners to think, the *politruk* especially, of those young propaganda officers who'd broken the news—manufactured it, some would argue—of the Stalingrad snipers. Or for that matter the imaginative soul who did the flack work for Shostakovich. Butler would've given short odds that the no. 7 wasn't called *Leningrad* before the Ministry of Culture got hold of it.

"Such a story," said the *politruk* at last, "might be inspirational. Were it not for certain obstacles. Chief among them, the German army. Which, if

I am not mistaken, unfortunately stands between ourselves and the partisans whose stories you wish to tell."

Seryoshka gave a grunt of amusement. He must have known Butler would have a ready answer.

Like a stage magician reaching into his hat, Butler dipped once more into the folds of his coat and pulled out an outdated situation map he'd nicked off the floor of the operations center. Moving the vodka glasses aside, he unfolded this on top of the ammo crate. It showed the territory between the Pripet Marshes and the Parczew Forest in Poland, as far south as Vinnitsa—most of which, according to the map, still lay in German hands.

"Last summer," Butler said, "when the Red Army hadn't yet reached the Dnieper, a lieutenant colonel named Kovpak led a small armed reconnaissance force over the line right here"—tapping at a town called Konotop—"then crossed the river, slipped right through the enemy rear, breached the Dniester eighty kilometers on, and made it all the way to *here.*" His finger came firmly to rest on Delatyn. "Which is a long fucking haul. En route, he destroyed several German targets and freed a number of your people being held by the Gestapo. Made it back home alive, and won a medal for his trouble. Two medals—Rokossovsky personally pinned them on his chest. I was there, I wrote a piece about it."

"I may have read that," said Seryoshka, fingering his mustache.

Butler didn't doubt it.

"Let me understand you, Comrade Sammy." The *politruk* stared down at the map, the better to conceal his thoughts. "You propose that an element of our forces should be dispatched on an exceedingly risky mission, the goal of which is to obtain a story for you?"

"Not just for me. And that's not the only point. We could carry in supplies and reinforcements for the partisans."

"That is already being done, by parachute."

"*And* we could bring some of the partisans out. Not many—not the key leadership. But interesting people, sympathetic people. Mothers, children. People who can give testimony of Fascist cruelty. Poles awaiting their Red Army liberators. Jews who—"

The *politruk* raised a hand, a quick and subtle gesture. "It is not the attitude of the leadership," he said primly, "to give special attention to any particular religious or cultural group. This goes against the spirit of Socialist unity."

"That's fine—but you can see what I'm talking about. The potential here. Not just for us, not just for today. For history."

The *politruk* turned thoughtfully to Seryoshka. There was no sign the two men despised each other. "What do you say about this?"

Seryoshka ran his finger through his thick black hair, making a show of deliberation that was, Butler felt sure, entirely feigned. "I think," he began finally—but then the flap of the tent rustled open.

A young lieutenant stood there, flushed and panting. "There is a general alert, comrades. Excuse me, but the general has ordered everyone to prepare for combat. Our battalion is going into the line as soon as we can mobilize. I was sent to inform you." Belatedly, he came to attention and offered a salute.

Seryoshka snapped off a quick return. "What is the situation? To what mission are we being assigned?"

The lieutenant stammered. "I—I am sorry, Comrade Major. I was not informed of these things. There has been an enemy counterattack, this is all I know. Our advancing forces were trapped at the river bend. Heavy casualties, they are saying."

Seryoshka did a most surprising thing then. He laughed, loud and heartily. "You were right, my friend!" Slapping Butler on the shoulder, hard enough to cause pain. "Not for the first time. And I'll wager not for the last." To the lieutenant he said, "All right, go get yourself ready. We'll be right behind you."

When the young officer had gone, the *politruk* laid a hand on Seryoshka's forearm. "So you are getting your wish, comrade. To be out there in the fighting."

Seryoshka grinned. He was indeed.

The *politruk* nodded. "Listen to me now. Don't take foolish chances. Go out and kill Fascists, if you like. But I need you back here as soon as it's over. Back in one piece. Is that understood?"

Seryoshka looked at Butler, then both of them stared at the *politruk*. The man's narrow eyes had a peculiar light in them. "If we are going to attempt this thing," he said, "this big scoop of Comrade Sammy's, we all have work to do."

SECRET GERMANY

One thing that must be said—one thing irrefutable, though everything else may be in doubt—is that Ingo Miller was a methodical young man. And careful, and patient, and deliberative. Yes: Ingo Miller, belying his youth, was all these things to a fault—and he was perfectly well aware of it. For he observed his own actions, his own thoughts and feelings, in the same quiet, attentive, unhurried manner that he observed the world around him. He watched himself move from place to place, passing from one day to the next, climbing out of one stage of life into another, and had been doing so—silently watching—for a long time now. He had gotten rather good at it.

This habit of self-observation he'd taken up at the age of twelve. That had been a signal year for Ingo, during which he'd embarked on something—a quest, a private exile, a purifying ordeal—that now had brought him, in a surprising turn, to the Höhe Meissner. At twelve he began, all on his own, to choose what books to read. He volunteered to sing in the church choir, having conceived an interest in religion generally, and started earlier than most to prepare for his First Communion. In school he signed up for German, a language spoken at home that he'd never systematically investigated. He joined, at his father's urging, the newly founded Boy Scouts of America. He suffered acutely the early symptoms of adolescence. And one summer's day, in a patch of woodland near Olney, Maryland, he experienced what he could only call, borrowing a term from the Christian mystics, an epiphany.

Since then, Ingo had been laying his plans, preparing himself through readings in the classics and the most *avant-garde* Continental authors, through listening to evocative music, through secret experiments, but mostly through deep and lonely contemplation. By the age of twenty, his preparations were complete; he was ready to take the next step. Only he had no clear idea what that step should be, and—let's be honest—for all his virtues, he was not much of a step-taker.

At which moment, as if on cue, enter Marty Panich. Who blithely had strolled up one afternoon and started babbling about the German Youth Movement. About which, needless to say, she knew almost nothing. Oh, she'd picked up a few stray facts in Anthropology class; but chiefly she was guided by a general feeling, emanating from her fashion bone, that here was a New Thing, as epochal as bobbed hair, possibly more so.

Also needless to say, Ingo knew everything: Wyneken and Wickersdorf and *Jugendkultur,* Blüher's writings and the furor they aroused, the schism between the Wandervogel and the Free German Youth, the fragile truce of 1913 and the unmitigated horror of the Great War, in which one in four Movement members had perished—and from which Martina's professor, an Austrian coward, had absented himself. He knew, too, what was happening now, in the fractious Weimar era—the scandals, the public shaming of Wyneken and Tusk, the tendentious cult of Stefan George and the rise of dangerous, adult-led factions on both right and left.

But beyond all that, in a more personal way, he knew about the Gemeindshaft der Eigenen (the Society of the Exceptional) and its illustrated journal, *Der Eigene,* which billed itself, ingenuously, *"ein Blatt für Männliche Kultur."* Deep in the university library he unearthed the *Jahrbuch für Sexuelle Zwischenstufen*—though, to his disappointment, it shed little light on these "sexual in-between stages," which was perhaps all one could expect from euphemisers. He even managed by transatlantic parcel post to obtain rare issues of *Schönheit* (Beauty), *Der Insel* (The Island), *Lieblingsminne* (Courtly Love), and the scarcely believable, nor translatable, *Blätter für Nacktkultur.*

A whole world was there. Ingo had discovered it. And while he knew it belonged not exclusively to the young or to the Germans—Marcel Proust was French, and dead—it struck him that only since the rise of the Jugendbewegung, and only in places the Movement had touched, could this new world be mapped, explored, experienced. And he yearned, he ached, he needed desperately to experience it for himself.

Martina knew none of this. If she had, Ingo doubted she'd have understood it. To Marty, this was just the latest craze she didn't want to miss out on because, hey, it was swinging! Whereas for him, it went far deeper than that. Therein lay the difference between them.

Well, one difference. There was another, equally crucial. Ingo, knowing all he knew, and having made all his preparations, had still, by the ripe age of twenty, done nothing about it. He stood motionless, becalmed, the per-petual observer of himself and the great world around him. Whereas Marty—who understood nothing, or precious little—was ready to hop on the next boat, regardless of when the boat sailed or where it was headed. She had no idea how to get from there to wherever this mountain was. She had no plans for eating, sleeping, bathing or attending to bodily needs whilst in Germany. Presumably she took it for granted Ingo would take care of all that. And of course, she was right.

Shaking himself free wasn't difficult. In fact he got the impression Martina wanted to get rid of him, the better to sprawl shamelessly on that ludi-crous beach blanket, waiting for some strapping young Teuton to stumble over her.

So he slipped away and ambled for a while along the paths on the moun-tainside, taking in the scenery, noting the goings-on both banal and aston-ishing, meanwhile planning his next move. The first thing, he decided, was to change out of these clothes that his mother had felt were suitable for traveling. No doubt they were, but he had arrived now. At least he was very close. He didn't want to look like an *Auslander.*

At a glance, there seemed no particular order to how things were arranged at the *Jugendtag.* People pitched their tents and formed their music circles and sprawled in the sun, in some cases mostly naked, just like in the magazines, wherever the fancy seized them. But with Germans there is no such thing as "no particular order," and after a while Ingo began to detect an overarching logic by which certain areas had been reserved for special purposes. The open ground near the summit was kept clear for large public gatherings, like tonight's oath-taking ceremony, which involved a huge bonfire. Other spaces had been claimed by certain factions—the Pathfinders, it seemed, had taken a whole face of the moun-tain to themselves. And a stretch of paths and fields on the lower ap-proach, down by the Meissner Haus, had been made over into a midway like that at a county fairground. Here you saw booths and exhibits where, within a few steps, you could purchase handmade wooden cups or the writings of Karl Marx or a purportedly authentic reproduction of the sword wielded by Charlemagne, the original having been entombed with him at Aachen. A dozy girl offered brochures said to reveal an infallible method of discovering your past lives, cheek-by-jowl with a boy in a yel-low shirt loudly hawking a fat tome called *Mein Kampf,* apparently the memoirs of a new, self-anointed Messiah.

It did not take Ingo long to find what he was looking for. From photographs, he'd acquired a conception of what the well-turned-out Wandervogel ought to wear. He'd even formed definite likes and dislikes: neither the androgynous look nor the pseudo-military costume affected by the *bündisch* crowd held any appeal for him. He approved, conditionally, of the *Minnesinger* style, meant to evoke the wandering minstrels and scholars of the Middle Ages, a period vivid in the collective German memory—but for his money, skintight leggings and hats with bells on them were taking the thing too far.

He chose, in the end, to keep his trousers—plain khaki twills that wouldn't, as his mom pointed out, show dirt—and to swap his shirt for a straw-colored, loosely woven jersey, its hems threaded decoratively in cobalt blue. You could tighten the V neck with a lace, also blue, and you wore the tails hanging right down over your belt. Ingo had never owned anything like this before and he liked the way it felt, the breeze flowing up around his body. His *body:* something he hadn't thought much about, not since age twelve or so, when along with everything else it had become strange to him. Wearing his new shirt, it felt strange all over again.

As a cheerful afterthought—a whim really, something Ingo rarely indulged in—he bought himself a hat. A jaunty sort of hat, pointed on top and widening toward the brim, made of undyed wool with a wide ribbon for a band. The young woman who had made it, eyeing him up and down, chose a long feather from a vase and stuck this on with expert nonchalance. She stood back to smile at the effect, then pointed him toward a mirror at the back of her stall.

Ingo gawked at himself. His neck and the top of his chest looked pale and very bare. But the blue of the shirt's piping brought out the color of his eyes, and the way the fabric hung about his shoulders made his upper body look broad and muscled, his belly trim. The hat, meanwhile, gave him a bold, mirthful, devil-take-the-hindmost air that was so different, so very different, from how it had ever felt to be Ingo Miller.

He thanked the young woman, and she astonished him by reaching out and giving him a quick embrace. "Viel Spaß!" she said. Lots of fun.

He responded with a low, humorous bow.

By the time he left the midway he had bought a rucksack—the old Boy Scout number would never do—into which he jammed his traveling clothes, a cheap wooden recorder, and the all-but-official Movement songbook, the *Zupfgeigenhansl*. Only one stop remained: long awaited, much delayed and, now that it was imminent, nerve-shattering.

A booth near the first turn of the trail bore a banner that read *Geheimes*

Deutschland—Secret Germany. There was nothing secretive about the booth, sitting there with its side flaps rolled up and its wares on display. In every visible particular it was no different from other booths, no bigger or smaller, no cleaner or *schmutlicher,* and the two young men who staffed it looked no smarter or duller, no more furtive or swarthy or strange, oily of palm, shifty of eye, jaded or jaundiced or sick of heart, than anyone else on the Höhe Meissner that morning. They looked like ordinary German youths, and when one of them greeted Ingo, his manner suggested that Ingo looked like an ordinary German youth, too.

"Are you a member?" the fellow asked pleasantly.

Ingo didn't understand. It wasn't a problem with vocabulary: his conversational skills were quite good, really, but he had come by them in a roundabout fashion, the watered-down immigrant's Deutsch of the family breakfast table having merged with a bookish, German Lit–major dialect, neither of which was quite the same as the language spoken on the Höhe Meissner. He had no way of knowing whether some everyday word— "member," *Mitglied*—might have a special, coded or vernacular connotation. Was he a *member* . . . of what?

"Here is a leaflet about our organization," the young man said, having read nothing into Ingo's confusion beyond a simple no. "We are called Geheimes Deutschland. Please, you are welcome to take this. It contains a membership form, should you be interested. The cost of dues includes a subscription to our monthly journal. Here, please take a sample issue. We lugged a ton of them up here, we do not wish to lug them down again."

His partner laughed, rubbing an aching shoulder.

Ingo smiled. The easygoing sales pitch had allayed some of his nervousness. When you boiled it down, this was essentially a bookstore, and bookstores were nothing new to him. And yet . . .

Here it was, before his eyes, laid out for the world to see. The proof— solid and irrefutable—that it was all real, that such a place as Secret Germany existed. These young men were real, too, and unremarkable; they were not freaks or sicklings or Satan's newest conscripts. They were just people, like Ingo.

While he stood there, flipping absently through a German translation of *Leaves of Grass*—pleased to have his suspicions about this confirmed—a pair of newcomers arrived: two boys somewhat younger than himself, he thought, though all these German kids looked so fresh and bright-eyed, it was hard to be sure. In their cautious, hesitant manner, Ingo recognized himself, as of five minutes ago. His own uncertainty, his trepidation and excitement. Finally, with a burst of relief, his sense of having arrived at last. Safe in the homeland, the *Heimat,* he had long been hoping to find. Ever since that afternoon seven years ago, the epiphany in the Olney woods.

They are people like me, Ingo thought, watching the two boys while the young man behind the table offered them a free issue of the monthly *Blatt.* People like me . . . yet Ingo didn't even have a word for the kind of person he was. Did it matter? He couldn't decide.

He leafed through some current novels—*The Puppet-Boy, The Battle of Tertia*—and an intriguing collection of essays by someone called Sagitta, *Books of the Nameless Love.* He glanced at a collection of poems by August von Platen but soon put it down because Platen's anguished verses, though beautiful, belonged in a place like Catholic U., where the *namenlose Liebe* could not be spoken of, let alone committed to paper; you had to grit your teeth and content yourself with cryptic references to Grecian statuary. Instead, Ingo scooped up a year's worth of *Der Eigene,* which always made lively reading, and the pictures were nice, though its occasional plunge into Weimar politics left him feeling punch-drunk.

While paying for these in devalued marks, he noticed a change, subtle but definite, in the young man behind the table.

"There is a gathering today," the fellow said quietly. "Not just our group—others as well. A discussion and, who knows?" There was in his smile something mildly conspiratorial.

Geheimes Deutschland, thought Ingo. I've bought some magazines and suddenly I'm a citizen—a Secret German.

"At Frau-Holle-Quell," the young man said, "do you know this spot? You will find it easily on the map in the program book. The trail is not so hard—a pleasant hike and, who knows?"

Ingo stuffed the *Blätter* into his new pack, which now was pretty full, then stepped out into the midday sun and pulled his hat off, letting the cool breeze dry the nervous sweat on his brow. He felt the kind of shakiness that comes from hunger, but it was not from hunger.

He studied the fold-out *Karte,* then tucked the program book away and set out down the trail to Frau-Holle-Quell. He was entering an unfamiliar homeland—a journey that he wanted to take, and needed to take, but that nonetheless frightened him more with every step.

The Quell was a small lake shaped like a rounded eye, most of its surface glossy black where it reflected the walls of dark spruce rising steeply on either side. But at its far end, perhaps a kilometer off, the water gleamed opalescent, a pale confusion of colors resembling mother-of-pearl where it reflected the northern sky. Just beyond the Quell lay a wide meadow, hazy green in the afternoon sun, dusted with drifts of goldenrod and pricked out with tiny moving figures, perhaps a hundred in all.

Ingo stood for a minute or two staring from the ridge. The trail tumbled before him, bumping down the spine of a draw and then skirting the edge of the pond until it vanished into a lush and shadowed land, full of mysteries. The landscape read like a fairy tale. Frau Holle's well was a motif from the Brothers Grimm: a bottomless shaft leading straight to the Otherworld. The virtuous daughter falls through and returns covered with blessings. The feckless stepsister follows and winds up suffering an awful curse. Watch your step, Secret German.

Suddenly he felt an odd sensation, like a hand laid softly on his neck, and he realized he was not alone. Turning, he saw a boy, a pale boy about his own age, who had stopped a little farther back along the trail. He didn't seem to have noticed Ingo yet, for he stood there peering outward unselfconsciously, across the forest and the lake toward the distant meadow.

The newcomer did not seem the usual Wandervogel sort. His clothes were wrong—they looked like something Ingo's mom might have picked out, sensible clothes to ride a train in. His hair fell thick and brown over a high white collar. His eyes, fixed on the horizon, were dark and somehow older than the rest of him. A satchel hung from one shoulder, its strap bone-tight. Suddenly a breeze whipped down from the summit, tugged at the loose sleeves of his shirt and the folds of his baggy trousers; the cloth flapped around slender limbs and the boy looked like he was about to blow over. Moving to steady himself, he caught sight of Ingo. Immediately he seemed to draw back into himself, though the movements were so slight that you could barely register them individually. What you perceived was the change in affect. Now the boy looked away and stood there motionless, wary.

It was a weird moment. The two of them were alone in a great empty place, too close, really, to ignore each other's presence. Normally—that is to say, in America—Ingo would have just said hi and given him a nod; that would've taken care of it. Now was different—*here* was different—and he couldn't think of how to greet the boy or what to do otherwise. Did you just walk away? Or stroll over and address this stranger on some pretext, ask for the time, *Können Sie mir sagen, wie spät ist es?*

Nicht zu spät. Not too late.

Suddenly the boy turned to look at him and opened his mouth but said nothing—apparently surprised by whatever expression he'd met on Ingo's face—and the scene veered into comedy.

Ingo laughed, his throat tight, releasing tension.

The boy's mouth formed a tentative smile—confused, perhaps, though that must have felt more comfortable than what had come before.

"Hallo," said Ingo, his equilibrium somewhat restored.

"Grüss Gott," said the boy, using a Bavarian form of speech. But his accent sounded more eastern than southern, and nearly as foreign as Ingo's own. "Ich bin Anton."

"Bin Ingo."

They had been too close and now were too far apart. Their voices strained to cover the distance.

Anton stepped awkwardly down the path. The footing was irregular and his gait uncertain, coltish, as if his legs were too long. Ingo moved closer but had no sense of his body doing so. The wind came in quick, hurried gusts.

Anton halted a couple paces off and brushed the hair out of his eyes. The gesture was artless, long fingers raking an alabaster forehead. Ingo's feet stopped moving; he felt in that instant something pop open inside him, something in his chest. The mountain air seemed too thin, starved of oxygen. The effort of breathing made him dizzy.

Anton didn't notice, or perhaps he was noticing other things. He appeared to be studying Ingo's shoes. "I come from Poland," he said then, raising his eyes. "From Galizien. But now I am studying in Germany, at the university in Jena. Where, you know, the earliest of student movements began, in Hölderlin's own time. A dueling society, the Burschenschaft—quite forbidden, of course, and so doubly appealing."

His expression was earnest, his eyes as dark and bottomless as Frau Holle's well. A few freckles dusted the skin around his nose.

Ingo relaxed somewhat. "I come from America. Washington, D.C." He couldn't think what to add. Until recently, nothing about him had seemed to require clarification. Now every single thing was ambivalent.

Anton only nodded; Ingo's origins must not have struck him as remarkable. "It is important to have come here, I think. To have returned to the homeland. This is a crucial time for all Germans, but especially the youth. We have a sacred duty to the future. We must become, as George tells us, the flag-bearers of a new order."

Mentally, Ingo took a step back. The college kids he knew back home didn't talk like this. Did they talk like this here? He felt a tickle of excitement, a growing certainty that he was in a new world, a world so fresh it was still in the act of self-creation. None of the old constraints need apply here—you could talk differently, behave differently, become a wholly different person.

"In America," Anton said, "do you know Stefan George?" Without waiting for an answer he went on, "George is very important for our Movement. He is a prophet, I think."

Ingo smiled. He had read George, especially the love poems. *You slim and pure as a flame, you blossoming sprig on a proud stem—I breathe you in every breeze, I sip you with every drink.* But he knew Thomas Mann as well, and had read his story "At the Prophet's," a very funny send-up of the George cult.

"There is a discussion today, about the master and his writing," Anton said. He turned to gaze down toward the bright blurry meadow. "Quite where, I am not certain. I was only now going to look. Would you like to come along?"

He had switched to the familiar "you." *Willst Du mitkommen?* And while Ingo couldn't sort out the deeper implications of this, or what had provoked it, he wanted to come along very much.

Their path led through spruce woods so dark you could not have guessed the hour was not far past noon. The trail was narrow and winding but well laid, its carpet of amber needles tamped flat by many passing feet. After a time the spruce thinned out into a sparser woodland of ash and elm, whose open canopy admitted streaming cataracts of sunlight. The two boys walked in silence, Ingo tending to lag a couple of paces back. It felt odd, rubbing shoulders with a virtual stranger. At the same time, irrationally perhaps, he already thought of Anton as something more than that. Not a friend exactly, more a comrade, a brother-in-arms. A native of the same mysterious homeland.

All at once Anton stopped in his tracks, stooping down to look at something beside the trail, and Ingo nearly tumbled over him. Between two slender fingers, the boy held a cluster of tiny white flowers borne upright on a narrow stalk.

"*Siebensternen,*" he said. "Do you have this in America?"

Ingo was hardly the one to ask. He had never noticed flowers particularly, and always skimmed ahead when Proust went on and on about them. "Seven stars," he said thoughtfully in English, but the plant's name meant nothing more to him in translation.

"The folk-name refers to the Pleiades, I think," said Anton. "Formally it

is called *Trientalis europaea.*" He straightened, leaving the flower unmo-
lested and facing Ingo with that same open and guileless expression.
"Goethe tells us, we perceive only what we are able to appreciate. The
coarse-minded do not see beauty, the unlettered do not hear poetry."

Ingo didn't know Goethe so well. Too cerebral, he thought, too daunt-
ing, like Beethoven. Himself, he was a Schubert man. "Do you study literature in Jena?"

Anton shook his head, fluttering his long hair. "I am reading in Botany. I
hope that if someday I see the famous blue flower, I should be able to recognize it."

Ingo laughed before he had time to wonder whether this was meant to
be funny. To his relief, Anton responded with a smile—the first Ingo had
seen—and it revealed a whole new facet of his sensibility; for on that face,
lit by the glow of those clear eyes, the smile had a hint of irony about it,
and you glimpsed a deeper awareness of the world than the boy's ingenu-
ous manner would lead you to expect.

"None of my comrades in Botany find that so witty," Anton said. "They
are quick to explain that the blue flower must be a type of *Gentiana.*"

Ingo had no idea what a *Gentiana* might be, but he was pretty sure the
genuine *blaue Blume*—an emblem of impossible yearning, invented by a con-
sumptive poet—had no Latin designation. The whole scientific enterprise,
this hubris-laden project of reducing the world to minute descriptions and
quantifications—killing and drying the specimen, pinning it to a mat in a
display case—was anathema to the old Romantics and their twentieth-
century heirs. "There probably aren't too many botanists who read
Novalis," Ingo said, meaning this as a compliment, among other things.

"Science need not be sterile," said Anton, who sounded more grown-up
now, more sure of himself. "Love is an observable fact of Nature, as are
friendship, eros, loyalty. There is no need to talk about such fine things in
terms of anatomy or the 'evolution of species.'"

Having spoken his mind, he turned and headed down the trail. Ingo
caught up and they walked for a while in silence, shoulder to shoulder
now. At intervals, Anton would point out this or that bit of local flora—a
creeper known as wood louse plant, *Pediculans silvatica;* pink-blossomed
fever clover, *Menyanthes trifoliata;* and tall, reedlike flute grass, *Molinia
caerulea,* bearing its seeds on golden stems as high as your shoulders. Ingo
thought Anton himself was a bit like these botanical specimens: you came
to appreciate him more and more as your faculties attained the proper
atunement. It was like dialing in a radio signal, faint and wavery at first,
then clear and strong. He scarcely paused to wonder what kind of signal

he himself might be sending out. In his mind, he was just a quietly humming, reasonably faithful receiver.

At last they reached the meadow. It was larger than he'd expected and its
features were more complex—a rippling expanse of knolls and dales with
tufts of hedge between them, sloping gently to the dark clear lake,
hemmed protectively by the muscular shoulders of the mountain. You felt
pleasantly isolated here—safe in your own little world—and with that feeling came a delicious sense of liberation.

Then of course there were the people. Young men, every one of them,
from what Ingo could see. He didn't try to look at them all at once, in fact
was rather afraid to. He felt like a kid who's tiptoed downstairs on Christmas morning to find not just what he hoped for under the tree but more of
it, in larger boxes, more extravagantly wrapped, glistening more brilliantly,
filling every corner of the room. Some kids would have rushed forward
with open arms, but it had always been Ingo's way to advance cautiously,
eyes lowered, and start with the smallest presents—trying hard, for as long
as his childish powers allowed, to ignore that gleaming red bicycle by the
fireplace.

Instinctively he drew closer to Anton, the only familiar object in sight.
Never mind that the other boy was a stranger an hour ago. Anton might
have felt the same, for the pair of them entered the clearing in hesitant
lockstep, like cowboys in a Karl May adventure, cagily advancing through
a lawless Western town, hands on their holsters, each watching the other
fellow's back.

They passed the little hollow, a natural amphitheater where high-
school-aged kids in Hellenic garb awkwardly declaimed a Greek drama
entitled, according to the placard tacked to a tree, *Alkibiades*. They passed a
hill where a group called FKK-Jungen were holding an archery match. The
competitors wore sandals and leather wrist guards and quivers that hung
from their shoulders—nothing else. Ingo declined, with a proper if pan-
icky *Vielen Dank*, an informative pamphlet presented by one of the archers.

They came to a stretch of curving lakeshore crowded with cattails
where the open water was clean as the sky, pale as a pearl. A narrow
wooden pier had been fashioned of spruce beams—freshly scarred where
limbs had been axed off—and this had been claimed as a diving platform
by a gang of perhaps two dozen swimmers, ages assorted. They took turns
in orderly German fashion heaving themselves out of the water, queuing
up at the pier, joking among themselves and shivering while the cool

mountain air brushed over their naked bodies, then leaping back in again, with varying degrees of athleticism and grace, to the hoots and applause of those already in the water. Ingo could have lingered there a while longer, but Anton seemed restless. And so they moved on.

They had not spoken now for some time, perhaps a quarter of an hour. Ingo was uncertain how much of his own emotional state—unsettled, topsy-turvy, unprecedented—it was safe to assume that Anton shared. But he looked discomfited, and that made Ingo feel for him. Without thinking, he reached across the short distance, less than an arm's length, and touched his shoulder. You could feel the bone in its thin wrapping of cotton and flesh. You could feel the warmth of his body.

Anton started, just perceptibly, blinked a couple of times, then glanced back at Ingo and bashfully smiled. The smile was slightly ironic, as before. He took in a quick deep breath and let it out forcefully, giving a funny sort of shrug. All this seemed to Ingo like a private form of communication, comprehensible only to the two of them. A language for secret sharers.

"Look there," Anton said with adolescent nervousness—nodding toward a thin hedge of alder that ran ahead of them.

Ingo followed his eyes. He sensed he was about to glimpse the red bicycle, ready or not. What he saw, though, was nothing remarkable—the most ordinary thing, perhaps, he'd witnessed since waking up that morning. A wide path, rutted by carriage wheels, led through a gap in the alders to an overgrown pasture, its grasses tall and interspersed with late-summer wildflowers. There someone had built a small stage on which a musical performance was under way: a singer in a white smock accompanied by guitars, recorders, powwow drums and a small accordion—more or less the staple Youth Movement instrumentation. The audience was small, forty or fifty at most, scattered sparsely around the field. Most sat not facing the stage but chatting among themselves, sharing sandwiches, passing a flask around. It looked like a good place to rest one's feverish, overloaded brain.

The two of them ambled over without need of consultation, wading through grasses topped with nut-brown heads that shattered on contact, the seeds clinging to skin and hair and clothes. They found a place to sit where the ground was relatively clear and the footing soft, with a clear view of the stage. Ingo recognized the song-in-progress, a ballad about a bird that warbles happily for an afternoon but at sunset dies in sorrow. The singer's voice was high and clear, a countertenor. Ingo breathed slowly in and out, in and out, feeling the nervousness and anxiety ease out of him. Then belatedly, like a joke sprung with masterly timing, the truth struck home. The red bicycle. Undeniable. In plain view. And suddenly, the only thing you could look at.

A short distance away, close enough to toss a paper ball at, two other boys sat listening to the music. One was a little bigger and stockier than the other, but they were dressed alike in green tunics and both wore their hair closely cropped. The first had his arm draped around the smaller boy's shoulders. It might have been a brotherly sort of embrace, but just about the time you started to think so, the second boy turned to gaze up into his friend's face, staring intently into his eyes, and there was no mistaking what kind of look that was. Then they kissed: lightly, delicately, lip-to-lip, holding it for the longest second Ingo had ever lived. After that, they went back to listening to the music. The song was the same; the bird had not yet tumbled from its branch. Only the Earth was different.

It was Anton, after that, who spoke—the older-seeming Anton, the botanical authority, an expert on native life-forms. "This is common in the Movement," he said. "I found it strange at first, coming from Galizien. But here . . ."

He gave Ingo a particular kind of look, and Ingo responded with a look of his own. They were deep in the secret language now, somewhere past ordinary consciousness but short of Dionysian rapture. An in-between stage, *Zwischenstufe,* no euphemism after all.

They turned to follow the performance, or at least to look in that direction. The music played on. The world rotated around them. It was a glorious afternoon, deep in the countryside at the center of Germany, toward the end of summer in the year 1929. There never had been a day like this, never in human history, and Ingo was certain it would go on forever. The sun would never sink. He would never get tired or hungry. Nothing would change that really mattered. The future would unfold, his destiny would dawn, when Ingo was good and ready, not before. He knew these things with sublime certainty. And he was not, repeat not, going insane.

The discussion of Stefan George and his work began at three o'clock and drew a sizable crowd. He and Anton found themselves pressed between two packs whose contrasting uniforms represented, Ingo feared, antagonistic *Bünde.* Onstage, half a dozen guys representing various factions of the Youth Movement, all about Ingo's age or a bit older, sat in deck chairs arranged in a semicircle, shuffling notes and eyeing one another with what, even at this distance, seemed a notable lack of comradely warmth.

The whole affair was highly organized and well-thought-out until the moment when, right on schedule, the first speaker opened his mouth. Within seconds, Frau Holle awoke from her hundred-year nap and the whole mountain gave a shudder. Whatever Ingo had expected from a poetry discussion, if anything at all, it certainly was not this.

The speaker was a tall fellow dressed like an assistant professor in a jacket with flaring lapels and many buttons. Armed with a monograph, a severely knotted tie and a pair of half-glasses that made him look ten years older, he declared in crisp, Lutheran German: "There can be no doubt that the Master, Stefan George, is a hero of the Homosexual Emancipation Movement."

Immediately a second young man, this one dressed in Wandervogel style, rose from his chair and shouted: "I protest! I object to the intrusion of this kind of language, which is all too typical of the Hirschfeld cabal, into this forum. Such a manner of speaking degrades noble Eros by reducing it to the status of a medical diagnosis. Moreover, this is anathema to genuine Friend-love, which is healthful and beneficial for any youth of finer temper, and which has *nothing* to do—nothing whatever!—with the gross cravings of degenerates and effeminates and male prostitutes, or those denizens of noisy basements whom we may call Berlin's Third Sex."

Fighting words, evidently. The ensuing furor erupted even before the man had finished uttering them. The scheduled speaker tried to go on with his prepared remarks, but whatever he was saying in that academic voice got drowned in the clamor. Ingo caught a few isolated phrases, slogans perhaps, but could make no sense of the arguments tossed out from the stage and hurled back from the meadow. Off to the left a boy stood shaking his fist, declaring that one of the speakers (Ingo was not sure which) ought to go back to France, where he belonged. Anton shrank from the ruckus, pressing himself closer to Ingo's side.

Finally a tall and solemn-looking man rose from a chair at the center of the stage. There was nothing remarkable about his appearance— university-age, conservative clothing—yet there was an air of authority about him, a strength in his silence. The others must have felt it, because one by one they took their seats. A sudden calm spread like a wave through the crowd until the whole field was, if not silent, at least down to a murmur.

"Who's that?" Ingo whispered.

"One of the Counts von Stauffenberg," Anton said quietly. "The younger one, I think. They are very close to George, part of the inner circle. The Master himself has chosen not to attend—they say he never goes anywhere these days—but he sometimes sends one of his Elect."

All this with no tinge of cynicism. The Master. His Elect.

Every eye was on the young count. He spoke finally in a voice just loud enough to carry across the meadow. "Wer je die flamme umschritt," he intoned, "bleibe der flamme trabant!"

"He's reciting George!" breathed Anton excitedly.

Ingo knew. It was a famous poem, a kind of anthem. *Whoever has circled the flame will forever remain its vassal.*

> *Wie er auch wandert und kreist:*
> *Wo noch ihr schein ihn erreicht*
> *Irrt er zu weit nie vom ziel.*

By the end, the crowd had taken it up like a liturgical chant, a rote invocation. *However he may wander and roam, the radiance will still reach him, and he will never stray from his goal.* Ingo felt the hairs rising on his neck. Beside him he sensed Anton's body stiffen with the electric thrill of the moment: hundreds of young Germans speaking as one, uttering the words of the Prophet. So much for irony.

"Now, we have all come here," said the young aristocrat, "to talk among ourselves as friends, and to honor the man whom we all admire, whose words have touched us so deeply. We may not agree always on what those words mean. But we all are brothers in the Movement and I *hope*"—pause—"that we may disagree without mistaking the other man for an enemy."

"But there are enemies here!" someone called back from the crowd.

"There are no enemies here," Stauffenberg said calmly.

"There are Jews!" A different voice this time. "There are Bolsheviks! Parasites that feast on the blood of the German people."

The handsome count held his ground. "We have come to talk about Stefan George."

"Indeed we have," said another man onstage, a muscular-looking fellow whose snow-white tunic gave him the look of a medieval squire. "And has not George himself foretold the coming of a 'leader with his völkisch banner'—"

"George does not use this term in a crude racialist sense."

"—and warned us to seek the company only of the superior breed of men? And does not your own sect, mein Graf, open its meetings with the words 'Leave the temple of foreign gods'? Surely these commandments are identical: to eschew what is alien to the German folk-soul, and instead to join with others of our own kind to forge a 'new nobility'—saving your feelings, sir, I'm simply quoting George here—'whose warrant no longer derives from crown or escutcheon.'"

The young count gave a slight, mocking bow. "I'm sure we're all impressed by your aspirations to nobility, Herr Gruppenführer. And I certainly shall not embarrass you by correcting your quaint misimpression of the dj.1.11, which, after all, it is not your business to comprehend. But I assure you, no one would be more surprised than George himself to hear that in all these passages, he was really talking about—what was it again?—*the German folk-soul.*"

Laughter ensued, but the other man kept his composure. "What, then, mein Graf, do you make of the Master's call to heed 'germ and breeding in every waking movement of your tribe'?"

"It is more to our point here," the Wandervogel broke in, "to heed George's deeper message: 'The new salvation will come only through a new kind of love.' Here is the clue, gentlemen, to what superior breed of men the poet was thinking of. It is a question not of blood, but of beauty. Beauty of spirit as well as body. This is stated explicitly in *The Seventh Ring,* when the Master tells us, the greatest service one can render the Volk is to bring forth one's own deepest loveliness. Only then may one understand what it means to 'bind oneself in a circle closed by love.'"

Ingo glanced at Anton, who was sitting raptly, nodding now and then in agreement.

"George speaks here," the man went on, "of the love of friends and of male youth—the love extolled by Socrates and Hölderlin, by Shakespeare in his sonnets, and not least by the Master himself, in his many poems to young Maximin. This love that is higher than mere reproductive lust, and infinitely more spiritual, indeed more sacred, than the crude libidinousness which is of such fascination to certain psychoanalytic types—I say this with all respect to our friend from Berlin."

The assistant professor glowered. Count von Stauffenberg sat down. A smatter of applause came from the group of boys on Ingo's right, but this was not enough to silence the burly fellow in the white shirt.

"Very good, gentlemen. If you wish to speak of Friend-love, let's do so in plain German. It hardly does the poet honor to make him out to be weak or naïve, in either political or sexual matters. The Master knows perfectly well what is entailed when we set out to create a New Reich. In the first place, the Old Reich must be got rid of. Yes, I'm speaking of the sickness that is Weimar—but more than that, the gross distortions of our Kultur that have transpired since the year 1849. You know what I am talking about, my good gentlemen, and so naturally does Stefan George. I say this as an admirer of the poet! As one of you, in blood and spirit! George has instructed us to look back to the noble Athenians—but what does that mean, exactly? It means harking back to a time when our community was ruled rightly, by a peerage of strong men, a brotherly elite. Not this en-feebled, modern, bastardized, cosmopolitan 'society' wherein women enslave us by the tyranny of the womb and Jews wrap us in chains of usury and priests heap upon us an intolerable burden of guilt!"

There was a stirring in the meadow, but Ingo couldn't figure out what prompted it—agreement, repulsion, surprise? Maybe a bit of everything.

The burly man strode back and forth, flexing his arms powerfully, as if to clinch the argument by sheer physical force. "George challenges us to find the strength within ourselves, not merely to cast off such un-German accretions, but to destroy them, utterly and forever! We are to ascend from the plain of Sodom and Gomorrah to the 'aeries of dread birds.' We are to become as gods. Not the weak and forgiving god of the desert people—no, the fierce and avenging gods of the North! We are bound in a circle of love, yes—for our comrades, our brothers within the circle. Toward those outside, it is correct, in fact it is necessary, to feel otherwise. We must feel—here I am sure the Count will understand me—the cold, steel-hard sureness of our own superiority.

"Friend-love is noble: on that we can agree. But it is noble precisely because it strengthens and purifies us. By withholding our seed, we deprive women of their power to weaken and distract us. By preserving German blood in its full vigor and potency, we avoid the racial morbidity that has weakened other nations of the West. And by consorting only with other young men of a good type—except insofar, of course, when in due time we must choose a proper candidate to bear and raise our healthy progeny—we avoid the danger of odious corruption by all that is foreign or unwholesome, all that is unworthy of our tribe. That is the message of Stefan George. And I can say quite firmly, gentlemen, that any full and honest reading of the text will bear me out."

That was not the last word. One thing Ingo was learning about this move-ment was that no word, however loud or cutting or resolutely spoken, could ever be the last. There were too many viewpoints, each more eccen-tric or alarming than the last. After a while you felt dazed by it all; you longed for a bit of straight, Yankee-style talk. Sit down and shut up. That's nuts. Pass the mustard.

It was funny, in a way. Ingo had waited so long to find this place. Yet now that he'd arrived, he was ready to move on. He was tempted to slip away and join the boys swimming around the pier. They were still at it—you could hear splashing and laughter from that direction—though the sun had drifted lower and the chill of a mountain evening crept in on the lengthening shadows.

What held him back, of course, was Anton, sitting there upright and alert, attending to each little speech and every question and retort, not all of them polite, from the audience. His brown hair, pulled back behind his ears, gave him an elfin look, and his skin had taken on olive tones in the yellowing light. There was something quirky about his face, something not quite perfectly arranged or matched-up. Whatever it was, it suited him, like some stray adornment—a scarf, say, or a hat—that shouldn't have looked right with the rest of his outfit, only it did.

Anton must have felt himself being stared at. He turned to look Ingo straight in the eyes. His own eyes were round and dark, almost childlike in their unguardedness. Most of his attention was still directed toward the stage, though he freed up enough of it to give Ingo a warm, happy smile. Then back to the stage again, the smile still on his lips.

You could have read any number of things into that smile, as you apparently could read practically anything into Stefan George, if you wanted to. But Ingo was enough of a Catholic to believe that only one reading could be correct. And he hoped, fervently, his own reading was true.

The program finally broke into smaller disputations that floated off in many directions, fading like sparks in the sky after a fireworks display. Ingo and Anton joined the general drift back through the meadow. The sun had dropped behind the mountain now and people were starting fires, singing songs, laughing together, enjoying their citizenship in this strange, makeshift republic.

What happens next? Ingo wondered if there was some kind of script that just came to you, without effort, the way your lines pop into your head at the last moment in a school play, even when you think you've forgotten them. Or do you have to ad-lib your way through? Does Anton know?

Anton, at least, was talking—chattering away, excited by the debate, playing parts of it back, commenting on this or that speaker, agreeing or disagreeing with points Ingo could hardly remember having been made. Ingo offered scant response but Anton did not seem to mind. It was pleasant to listen to his voice, which was still boyish and seemed to come largely from the upper part of his throat, the long slender neck. Sometimes he gestured with hands that, like the neck, were long and smooth and faintly tinged with olive. Ingo could not recall ever, at any point in his life, having actually noticed someone's hands. Well . . . perhaps when Timmy Nye, his scouting mentor, showed him how to tie a clove hitch.

"Oh, look"—Anton's fingers pressed lightly on his forearm—"there's that horrible man again."

He was looking at a little knot of people some dozen paces off, marching through the field behind the burly man in the white tunic, the racial hygiene fellow: half a dozen kids all dressed in the same medieval-style clothing, all jabbering breathlessly. All but one. Close by the leader, occupying a place of honor at his side, was the most flawless boy who had ever walked the Earth.

He was perhaps sixteen, an archetype stamped in flesh: the Teutonic boy-god, fair-skinned Baldur, eyes bluer than cobalt, hair paler than spun gold, limbs more cleanly sculpted than Donatello's David—quite a bit less beefy than Michelangelo's—and each feature the epitome of its type and in perfect harmony with every other. Even his movements were those of a being who knows himself to be finer than merely human. He walked beside the Gruppenführer yet set his own course, changed directions when it suited him. The others didn't care, they were being festive, they must have thought they'd won the George debate. Only the snow-blond boy seemed to have a destination, and whatever it was he kept it to himself. From his companions, he remained as distant as any star.

Ingo could not wrench his eyes away. He found the boy terrifying. Ice-cold in his beauty. Cruel in his aloofness. Repulsive in his knowledge of his own perfection.

For an instant those cerulean eyes brushed over him. They paused just perceptibly, as though by their limitless power they were lifting Ingo for inspection, then tossing him back to the dreary realm of mortals. The eyes clicked a notch sideways and repeated the procedure with Anton. Then they were gone.

The group altered course, heading off on a side trail into the forest. Within moments they were lost from sight.

Only then could Ingo regain his equilibrium, blinking like someone just emerged from a hypnotic trance. The whole incident, if you could call it that, had lasted, what—fifteen or twenty seconds? Anton had seen nothing. He was still talking, something about the Jungdeutscher Orden. Still warm, still real, still fully human.

Ingo felt a surge of emotion he could not have named—or rather, that the obvious name would have done nothing to clarify—and in that moment, before thought could interfere, he placed a hand on Anton's back. The hand moved slightly, as if of its own accord, along the bumpy ridge of the spine. Anton did not react except for a pause between words— "very right-wing, very . . . threatening, I think"—but after that, somehow, he was walking closer, near enough for Ingo to get a physical sense, just short of actual touch, of his body inside the floppy clothes.

What happens now?

Whatever it might be, Ingo felt it pushing outward from his breast, a pressure demanding release.

Then Anton decided the matter, absolutely. He stopped walking and turned to face Ingo, an odd sort of firmness in his expression. "It is time for me to go back," he said. "Past time, actually. I am staying at the hostel in Vockerode, a few kilometers' hiking from here. If I tarry longer, there will be no dinner. So I must say 'until later.' "

Ingo felt as though the air had been sucked clean out of him. But he could think of no grounds on which to object. He could hardly invite Anton up to the campsite for dinner. For starters he wasn't sure he could even find the campsite, not with evening coming on. And what would they eat? Martina was no more cook than Ingo; thus far they'd scraped along on food scavenged from the *Gasthaus* in Kassel, mostly hard bread wrapped in one of Ingo's undershirts. Hardly a meal to offer a guest.

But still. The disappointment was so sharp, so sudden and painful, Ingo feared for one dangerous, wobbly instant that tears were about to form in his eyes.

Anton must have seen it. His expression did not change, but he stepped closer and took both of Ingo's hands in his own. "I hope we can meet again tomorrow." His breath smelled of sunshine on fresh-mown hay. "I'm afraid today I have done too much talking. I have hardly given you a chance to tell me about yourself, about your life in America. But tomorrow . . . perhaps, if you are willing, we could meet again on the trail there? Where we met before?"

Ingo said something, he did not know what, he would never remember. Evidently it was enough.

Anton took half a step back, then a full step forward, and kissed him lightly on the cheek. "We shall be friends, then," he said, backing away again.

Sure, friends, okay, thought Ingo, foundering, well beyond his depth. Whatever the hell "friends" means. He guessed he would find out tomorrow.

In the meantime he watched Anton striding confidently down his separate trail, the long legs bending rhythmically and the narrow haunches twitching under the weight of that thin, slightly awkward, miraculous body. Ingo realized he was hungry—Christ, he was starving—but that was nothing. On the whole, he felt like a million bucks.

He must have ambled for some time with no thought of where he was headed, eyes down among wild thyme, tufted grasses, soft German soil. When he raised his head, the day had passed into twilight, *Dämmerung*, that in-between stage where your vision plays tricks on you.

He had been following a path through sparse woodland, mostly birches that gleamed white like pillars in a crumbling temple. Since Charlemagne—Karl the Great, as he was known around here—the Germans had identified themselves with ancient Rome, or more exactly with a misty, romanticized vision of empire, *Reichtum*, and all its glories. Even their countryside seemed to reflect this, both the landscape and the lens of art and legend through which it was apprehended. These smooth-worn hills, haunted forests, weathered rocks, waters that housed fallen goddesses, mountains beneath which bearded emperors slept—everything spoke of some lost grandeur, a hidden but still palpable subterrain of the German soul. The Holy Reich was dormant but not dead. Frederick Red-Beard might wake and gallop down at the head of his wild legions, more wolf than man now, sweeping all modernity aside. At the *Dämmerung*, on the magic mountain, you could believe such things. You could think you glimpsed those risen knights, bloody crusaders who sang love songs and observed the niceties of *Lieblingsminne* when not slashing infidel heads off.

There, just now, in the clearing ahead. What were those white figures flickering through the shadows?

A chill ran the length of Ingo's spine. Not for the first time today, he felt in danger of losing his mental competence. He wanted to turn and flee, but that would have granted the hallucination a claim upon reality. So he pressed ahead, facing the ghosts of the past as every stouthearted German must do.

As he entered the clearing he saw that the spirits were only human—of course, who could have doubted it?—and were in fact none other than the young men in white tunics, the Gruppenführer and his pack, their number grown to a dozen or so. They were gathered into a huddle or a circle, as if enacting some esoteric rite, and why shouldn't they? It was a natural part of the Middle Ages fantasy—Grail quests and hidden castles, blood-oaths sworn at sunset.

Only by degrees did Ingo realize that it was some kind of fight or struggle—an asymmetric affair, like the aftermath of a hunt, the stag in its death throes, lashing out dangerously, the hunters circling, vying for the honor of dealing the coup de grâce. Ingo tried to pick out the boy-god among the others but the darkness was too heavy now. They were just pale figures, more or less human, with something else in their midst, darker, nearly indiscernible on the ground. Moving, though. Rolling or crawling, fighting wretchedly to live.

One of the boys struck a match and held the flame to a stack of small branches, forest debris that appeared to have been hastily thrown into a pile. The newborn fire leapt up and the light spread itself around the clearing, though at first this only made it more difficult to see, for outside the flickering circle all was thrown into blackness.

At last, coming very near the flames, the hunters dragged their prey, which was writhing and bucking in a final burst of strength. Ingo glimpsed filthy, blood-streaked limbs and—what, surely not a baseball jersey?

The victim was no beast of the woods. It was a scrawny kid. A kid whose clothing was torn and hair tangled with leaves. He was smaller than the boys who held him, yet fought them with crazed ferocity.

"Bring him into the light here," the Gruppenführer commanded.

Half-seen hands thrust the prisoner forward. He landed face-first, rolled a bit, started to rise, but his captors were on him immediately, pulling his arms back, someone grabbing him around the neck. After a few moments the victim gave up his struggle; it was all he could do now to breathe. His face was red and his eyes seemed to bulge; still you could see a glint of defiance there. The kid had guts, even if all his strength was gone.

A new figure stepped forward, and to Ingo's surprise this was no boy but a full-grown man, thirty at the very least. He wore not a white tunic but a khaki suit with many pockets and a wide-brimmed hat, as though just back from safari.

"Yes, that is he," the man said, after a quick glance at the prisoner, his voice high-pitched and pompous. "That is the little Jew who took my papers. Be sure to turn out his pockets when you're done with him. Though I suspect by now he has passed the documents to his confederates. They work in groups, you know—the actual term is *cells*. We are dealing here with a hive-culture, such as one finds among insects." He gave a short nod, then turned away and stepped quickly into the shadows.

To Ingo, who could barely take in what was happening here—*here*, at the very center of modern Germany—the man appeared simply to vanish.

"Filthy pest!" the Gruppenführer spat in the boy's face. "Give back what you stole or I will kill you this minute, I swear I will."

"No," said another voice. "Please. Allow me."

Ingo knew immediately who had spoken. The perfect diction, a chorister's clear and ringing contralto. The beautiful boy stepped so close to the fire that, had he truly been carved out of ice, he would've started to melt. The flames brought a red flush to his cheeks, a dangerous gleam to his eye. You could see exactly why Zeus had hurled himself down from Olympus to pluck up Ganymede—or why Loki had plotted the murder of young Baldur, whose beauty transfixed the other gods. There was something dire, a whiff of the afterworld, the *Nachwelt,* in these rare creatures.

None of this was real—Ingo was sure of that. These figures were archetypes, the forest clearing an open theater, the scene drawn from one of the bloodier myths, of which there were plenty to choose. The whole thing was a queer sort of play, an acting-out or living-out of certain resonant cultural themes—that was the only explanation.

The object of the ritual sacrifice seemed to know his lines well enough. "You stupid arschgefickten Hitlerjungen," he drawled in a voice that was weak and clotted yet strangely self-possessed.

There was something American about that voice, Ingo thought, but also something uprooted, untraceable. A voice to go with the motley, ruined clothes.

"You love this, don't you?" the victim said, plainly now addressing the boy-god himself, speaking in a curious argot that was neither English nor German. "This is how you get your little Würstchen up, I bet."

Unaffected by this outburst, the blond boy came a step closer, holding what appeared to be a riding crop. He gazed at the prisoner with a far-off, superior air, twitching the crop like a schoolmaster's rod.

"Go on," said the Gruppenführer. "Let's get it done."

The boy-god would not be hurried. He paced slowly like an actor onstage, commanding not just your attention but your admiration as well. The kid on the ground thrashed with a free leg and almost managed to trip his tormentor. The blond boy stepped hastily out of range, quickly recovering his stride.

"I expected something better than this," he said. "Aren't you supposed to be dangerous?"

He used the plural form of *you,* leaving Ingo to wonder whom he meant—Americans? Jews? Rival bundists?

"Don't worry, you'll get more," said the prisoner.

The German's expression grew . . . not angry, quite. Vexed, out of patience, annoyed—the face of someone accustomed to having his way. "This can be over quickly," he said, "or it can be prolonged and very unpleasant. Tell us what you did with the papers you stole. Tell us right away. And then, perhaps, things will not be so bad for you."

The kid on the ground seemed to have caught his breath. An expression almost like a smile appeared on his face. When he spoke—his voice notably clearer than before—it was to pronounce a startling colloquialism Ingo had never encountered, even in Brecht, though he recognized the body parts involved.

That seemed to do it. The blond's brittle composure cracked. He raised the crop high like a *Magier* charging his wand for some shattering invocation, and the magic took immediate effect: the texture of time thickened and events took on the slowed-down, rather balletic quality of something happening underwater.

The firelit scene spread itself out, as a movie screen does when you walk down toward the front of the theater, the projected images becoming larger and more distinct. Several heads turned—something had interrupted the bloody ritual, violated the sacred circle. Lastly the face of the boy-god, more beautiful than ever in close-up, swiveled toward the camera, its otherworldly pallor blanching everything around it. But the deathly blue eyes never quite came into focus. The riding crop—a fine piece done in willow and braided leather—leapt out of his hand and floated through the air in a perfect arc that ended at the heart of the circle. From offscreen came a maelstrom of voices—languages running together, the voices of no particular age, it might as well have been the forest itself crying out or the spirits that drift in the twilight.

Suddenly another face, looming close, swelled to fill the screen. The Gruppenführer's mouth opened, and somewhere behind it, shadowed and out of focus, one of those powerful hands clenched into a fist.

Ingo slugged the guy so hard he was afraid he might have broken a knuckle or two. The man, a puzzled look on his face, did not look hurt so much as taken by surprise. His thoughts ran slowly, like time itself, whereas for Ingo everything was clicking along at ordinary speed. He hit the burly fellow again, this time lower, down in the gut. It felt even better than before.

"Try it like this," said the scrawny kid, who in the confusion—half dead or not—had managed to wrench himself free and climb to his feet. While his captors stood dumbly, as if waiting for their leader to rally them, he squared off before him and delivered a kick straight to the groin that crumpled him like a paper bag. From the heavy fallen body came a long, plaintive moan. The rest of the pack stood frozen in a jumble of alarm, disbelief and open fear. The older man was nowhere to be seen.

"As for you, bottom boy," the kid said, turning on the blond god, his voice a polyglot sneer, "you better keep out of my way, or my pal here will *really* get sore next time. Come on"—this to Ingo—"let's get out of here."

He limped for a step or two, then threw a hand around Ingo's shoulder, pulling himself upright. For all his bravado, the boy was hurt so badly he could barely walk on his own. Yet he managed to set a brisk pace for the two of them, tugging Ingo along even while half dangling off him. They hobbled along for some distance without speaking, the boy dripping blood over Ingo's new shirt, until neither of them could go any farther without a rest.

Dark now, the moon nowhere in sight. The boy's face was indistinct, but Ingo could hear his labored breathing and smell the animal scent that rose off his body and clothes.

"You're American," Ingo said finally, in English.

At first the boy did not respond. Then Ingo felt a hand taking hold of his upper arm, and the boy's face pulled in close. A pair of half-demented eyes screwed into his own, the oddly shaped nose pointing from one feature to the next like a specialized instrument being used to examine him.

Suddenly the kid laughed. "Another fucking Yank!" he loudly exclaimed, as if to an audience out there in the darkness—hamming it up for the peanut gallery. "An honest-to-God Yankee Schwuler. Wouldn't you know it?" He settled back with an honest sigh. "Well, pal, I owe you. I'll remember this one for a long time, you can believe that. I thought for a minute there the fucking Huns were going to kill me."

Ingo wanted to downplay the incident, but in truth that's how it had looked to him as well. "You know, I haven't the faintest idea where we are." He spoke in German—having done so all day, it seemed natural to continue.

The boy understood well enough. "Not to worry, pal. I'll get you right where you need to go. I've got kind of an instinct." He braced himself on Ingo's shoulder and heaved himself back to his feet. "Let's get going. I could use some grub. Even that scheisslich vegetable stuff."

Ingo was loath to move. The events of the day—an almost insupportable load of new experience—weighed more heavily on him than this insubstantial kid with the nasal voice whom he somehow, despite an intimation that he ought not to, found himself growing to like. "Those things the guy back there was saying," he began hesitantly. "That you stole something from him. Is it true? What was all that about?"

He felt he had earned the right to some explanation. But the kid didn't seem inclined to provide one.

"You'll like these friends of mine," he said. "They're Krauts, but they're okay."

Friends, thought Ingo: that problematic word again. With a feeling of resignation—he was lost in darkness, steering by unfamiliar stars—he allowed the strange boy to direct him onward. After a while the boy stopped abruptly and said, "Hey, you saved my butt back there, and I don't even know your name."

"Ich bin Ingo."

"Is that so? Well, ich bin Isaac. Glad to meet you, pal. Really and truly I am."

He slapped a hand into Ingo's. It felt big for the size of him, the grip strong, the skin damp and hot. Something odd moved through Ingo at the moment of contact, a raw kind of energy. He dropped the hand but the feeling, the energy, stayed with him for a while. In a way it never left him.

He could not have known at the time, but it came to him later, with the startling clarity of a dream, that maybe what he had felt in that instant was nothing less than the pure stab of his long-awaited destiny.

ILLYRIA

Thank you, Lord, for Timo. Really, I mean it. I'll make this up to you. Trust me.

Martina couldn't remember how or when or at whose suggestion the ex–D.C. cabdriver had signed on for the long haul. Maybe somebody managed to find Serbia on a map. Maybe it was just another fuck-up. In any case, by the time SS *Paloma Roja*, a round-bottomed steamer of Portuguese registry, had cleared Gibraltar and Martina was able once again to keep down solid food, she had come to depend on Timo for everything from weather updates and policing the cargo hold to apprising her of morale and gossip among her shipmates.

The problem with the Varian Fry Brigade, she felt—now that it was too late to change anything—was that it had grown into a multiheaded beast. Head no. 1 belonged to Aristotle, the veteran guerrilla chosen to command the volunteers upon their landing in Yugoslavia—which should happen, so she'd heard, in a matter of hours. Head no. 2 bore the raptorlike features of Rabbi Harvey Grabsteen of Agudas Israel Worldwide, whose Hollywood donors were footing the bill, his overseas contacts handling the logistics. If Grabsteen wanted to tag along on this little voyage, who was going to tell him no? The same nobody that was going to tell him to shut up, go back to his stateroom and stop getting on people's nerves. Which was to say: Not me, thanks.

And Head no. 3—like it or lump it, boys—demurely adorned the shoulders of Miss Martina Panich, duly appointed Girl Wonder of the U.S. War Refugee Board and hence, *ex officio*, the brigade's sole link with any recognized governmental entity, if not, indeed, with reality as it is commonly understood. Never mind that for the record Martina had taken a leave of absence from her duties in Washington. Or that the Secretary, if pressed, would deny all knowledge of her activities. The fact remained that Martina's presence aboard *Paloma Roja*—even as a chronically seasick bystander—constituted the only practical response of the Roosevelt administration to the annihilation of the Jews of Europe.

Martina knew it. Aristotle knew it. Even Grabsteen, who knew everything, just ask him, knew it.

She was not at all certain what this singular historic position required of her. Not much, she hoped. With any luck, the boys could handle the tricky part: get in, find Isaac, grab the paper and scoot. Under such happy circumstances her role would entail what was known in *Realpolitik* circles as "maintaining a constructive presence." Things might, of course, take a less happy turn. Martina might find herself obliged to deal with Nazi assassins the way she dealt on a workaday basis with shit-heeled Dixiecrats—a bloody business best not dwelt upon. In either case: the thing to bear in mind was, she damned well did *not* intend to be nudged aside while the boys made all the decisions.

Hence, Timo. Her closest ally. Her strong-arm man, father confessor, messenger and spy. And perhaps, now that she was feeling better, her something else as well. We'll have to think about that. There are those yellow teeth to consider.

Timo—the man, not the prospective lover nor the multifaceted wish-fulfiller—smiled at her from across the cabin, where he sat on the bunk assigned to a spunky gal named Sara Weiss, the only other dame on board. Martina suspected she'd made the cut so there would be two of them—*Let's give Marty somebody to talk to*—though what she had to say to a twenty-year-old typist was beyond her. Nice nails, sugar. As things fell out, Sara spent no more time than necessary in the stuffy little cabin, which suited everyone.

Martina sat cross-legged on her own bunk shoveling down a late breakfast of Spam and reconstituted eggs that tasted heavenly. "What did the message say?" she asked, prompting Timo to resume the daily briefing, an ordeal she equally dreaded and could not wait for.

"Unfortunately, the rabbi would not show me the text." He flicked invisible lint off the lapel of his olive gabardine. "So I had to wait till late at night, then had a chat with the radio operator. This"—withdrawing a slip of flimsy paper from a pocket—"cost one bottle of bourbon. We are running out."

"Yeah, well, we've made it across, though." Martina squinted at the paper by the dim light oozing through the porthole.

"We have not yet made it so far as the dock. This is the beginning of our problems. I hope you brought plenty of money."

Martina shrugged. She had some money, Department money, of assorted denominations. There wasn't much, and she wasn't at liberty to talk about it. Skimming through a gabble of international radio signals, she reached the content of last night's signal from Grabsteen to Agudas headquarters in Palestine. Halfway through it, her jaw was bouncing off the wafer-thin mattress. "He told them *what*? My God, I can't believe this. I'll kill him. I swear it, Timo, I will murder that man."

Timo grinned. The malicious twinkle, the problem teeth. "Let me do it."

Martina tossed the paper at no particular target. "Why doesn't he cable Himmler and tell him where to meet us? That's the only thing he left out."

The cable in question, its text on onionskin drifting to the cabin floor, took the form of a press release (dateline: Somewhere in the Mediterranean) announcing that as of today, heroic Jewish freedom fighters were poised to strike a blow *into the very belly of the Nazi beast. No longer*, crowed the dispatch, *will the Jewish nation depend upon empty assurances from the Western powers. Henceforth we shall take up arms in our own behalf. Let the Fascist killers tremble in their lairs!*

"I assume," Martina said dourly, "that if this message is intercepted— *when* it's intercepted—the Germans will be able to figure out where it came from."

Timo retrieved the paper and ran a finger down the chain of alphanumeric designators. "It's probably all right," he said. "There's not really much here to go on."

"Still, that man is an idiot."

"Indeed." Timo shrugged. "On the other hand, it makes no difference."

"How do you mean?"

"This dispatch? Nothing but empty bluster. The Germans will laugh. They understand, at this stage, they have nothing to fear from a tiny, ridiculous band of Jews."

"Thanks, Timo," Martina said, feeling the eggs deconstituting in her stomach. "That's really a comfort."

She stood on deck, wearing rumpled fatigues and clutching the rail just aft of the boat davits, when the first line hit the wharf at 2:45 that afternoon. Grabsteen had managed to insert himself into the rank of ship's officers lining the bridge wing two decks above. Aristotle was up in the bow in conference with his three Moes.

Before them lay the ancient, drab and battered city of Sibinik, a lesser port of entry into the Yugoslavian province of Dalmatia, cleared of German forces only weeks ago. Behind them lay the Adriatic Sea and most of the food Martina had consumed for the past week and a half. While the *Paloma*'s winches hauled wearily at hemp lines as thick as her leg, Martina scanned the deck and eventually located Ingo, slouched against the railing between his two best buddies of late: Stu the dentist, whose inclusion was based solely on his medical credentials, and the prelaw kid from Charlottesville, Eddie, whom Ingo seemed to have taken under his wing. Martina, performing an old and dependable trick, held her eyes on Ingo until he looked back at her, at which point she gave him a sly, knowing wink. He affected not to see her.

The vessel shuddered beneath them as it was winched against the current to the wharf. Martina gazed past the waterfront to the surrounding hillsides, where the city lay swabbed in orange with smoky afternoon sun. Buildings clumped up around the old seaport, whose wharves and piers welcomed everything from oceangoing rigs like the *Paloma* through rusted-out coastal steamers to humble fishing boats propelled by oar and Gypsy-rigged sailcloth, manned by crews consisting of a father and one or two of his shirtless, umber-skinned sons. Sibinik must have seen street fighting not long ago, for the appalling consequences of modern warfare were everywhere on display. There were buildings with walls and roofs blown in, burned-out vehicles no one had bothered to drag off the streets, the charred carcasses of locust trees jutting from a hillside north and east of the harbor. The pavement was cratered from shelling. Rubble lay everywhere, some of it gathered into neat little hillocks, scampered over by half-clothed, feral-looking children. There were few other people in sight. Tito's partisans were setting up a new government, yet the streets still had the look of a no-man's-land.

"We've got to be careful here," she said quietly to Timo.

"I am careful everywhere. But especially in the Balkans."

A stench of live coals, wetted down but still smoldering, arrived at intervals on a puffy eastern breeze that also carried smells of peppery cooking, rotting fish and broken sewer mains. It reminded Martina of the sluggish breeze off the Anacostia River, fetching odors of undrained swampland and the municipal water treatment plant.

Amidships, a ratcheting sound. The ship's gangway was being lowered. The first lieutenant took his post on the quarterdeck, fidgeting as he watched a party of uniformed men stroll unhurriedly along the wharf. Port authorities, she guessed, the sort of men who might need special encouragement to overlook the crates of ammunition and weaponry stashed belowdecks. Captain Aristotle approached wearily from the stern, accompanied by One Moe, the most impressive of his noncoms. When Martina moved to join them, Timo raised an arm to block her.

"It might be unhelpful," he said, "for these people to think a woman is in charge. A woman like you, most particularly. I will go. Just to make sure there are no . . . errors in translation."

She nodded, though it galled her—*A woman like you?* What did that mean?—but she forced a smile, making a good show of it. From inside, the smile had an Eleanorish feel. Make no mistake: the First Lady was a great woman, Martina's personal heroine, a living saint. Yet you couldn't help noticing the strain, the wistfulness, in that smile of hers. Which made you wonder what really went on in the Lincoln Bedroom.

Ashore, negotiations ensued in plain sight at the end of the gangway and seemed to require, on the Yugoslav side, much raising of arms and shaking of heads and gesturing with automatic rifles. The American side had recourse chiefly to stoic glares and official-looking documents. This went on for half an hour. Finally Aristotle lumped off toward the harbormaster's office, a seedy wooden shed resting on piers at the foot of a jetty, in company with two of the natives. A second pair of Yugoslavs stayed behind and One Moe stuck with them, passing out cigarettes. Timo started up the gangway with a noncommittal expression. Grabsteen, always hungry for news, hurried down from the bridge to intercept him.

Martina gritted her teeth. "What is it this time?"—venting her annoyance at Timo.

"They will allow us to land, in consideration of certain . . . factors that have been mutually agreed upon. But there are no trucks."

"What do you mean, no trucks?" said Grabsteen. The pitch of his voice reminded Martina of the gulls that circled the wharf, searching for choice bits of garbage. "There were supposed to be trucks!"

"There are no trucks." Though Timo's expression didn't change, you got the feeling he was enjoying this.

"There have to be trucks! How else are we supposed to get to—"

"Shh," Martina hissed. "Not so loud, for God's sake."

"Ah." Grabsteen got a shifty look. "You're right. Loose lips and all that." Dropping to a whisper: "What happened to the trucks?"

Timo shrugged. "You don't sign contracts with a revolution."

The other two watched him, curious as to what you did do.

"Arrangements must be made on an ad hoc basis. Forget yesterday, and leave tomorrow to fend for itself. Aristotle will sort things out, don't

worry. Only it may take a while. And there may be other factors to consider."

"What do you mean, a while?" Grabsteen's voice edged up the stave.
"How long is a while?"

Martina's mind snagged on something else. Had Grabsteen just said
"we"? *How are we supposed to*—as in, not just the competent members of
the Brigade, but also the rabbi personally? Did he now fancy himself a
gun-toting avenger, dropping over the line with the rest of them? This
terrible thought was leavened only somewhat by the near-certainty that
the Germans would make quick work of him.

For no reason, she glanced up to find Ingo looking at her from his perch
on the foredeck. His expression was out of place, almost cheerful. There
was no figuring him. Maybe he, too, was a gun-toting avenger, a fact only
now coming to light. Maybe all these guys, Timo included, were like a
gang of little boys who love nothing more than hiding in the bushes and
shooting off their cap guns. Leaving Martina to tote up the losses, and Sara
Weiss to type the letters home.

"You know what the problem is," she said.

Grabsteen gave her a surprised look, as if he'd forgotten she was there,
and Timo's eyes flashed a question mark.

"I've got cabin fever," she declared. "I need to get off this damn boat.
I'm going ashore, right this minute."

And so she did. Who was going to stop her?

The waterfront at Sibinik, crimped around a U-shaped harbor, fell roughly
into two halves. The right held the usual things you find in any port
town—warehouses, saloons, cheap pensions, a shuffle of shady characters
with time on their hands. The left was more original, with small boats of
varying description, none of which looked remotely seaworthy, lined up
gunwale to gunwale along a broad wharf. The masters of these boats had
laid down blankets on the shore or erected little stalls. Fires snapped and
coughed smoke from pits banked with rubble, over which hung skewers
of unidentifiable food. An open-air market, evidently. Martina wondered
what was for sale.

She headed over that way, ignoring the efforts of one of the harbor
cops—a very young man who shouted in some incomprehensible language,
then switched to Italian and, in extremis, German—to impede her. Over
her shoulder she sensed, and also ignored, Timo hustling to overtake her.

"May I ask what you are doing?" His eyes scanned the street.

"Shopping." She waited to see what kind of reaction that provoked, then added, "I'm kidding."

"You must not speak to them," he told her, seriously. "Nor to anyone. Yes, I know"—raising a hand, forestalling her—"you are a freethinking person who refuses to be told what not to do. But think. The appearance of an . . . English-speaking foreigner—"

"An American woman, you mean."

"—would be . . . *interesting* to these people. And interesting things lead people to talk."

He was right. She didn't care to admit it. "Where do those boats come from?"

"From the islands." He gestured toward the open Adriatic. You could see low, gray-green mounds a few kilometers offshore. "People have fled there over the years, whenever there is trouble. And always there is trouble. But the islands are very poor, it is almost impossible to live there. This"—sweeping a hand over the wharf—"is how the people support themselves. They sell whatever they can find, or catch, or grow. Some of them are said to be pirates."

From the look of them, Martina doubted it. But what did appearances count for? "Have Jews fled there, too?"

Timo looked at her, puzzled by the question. He shook his head. "When I say over the years, I don't mean the Nazi time. I mean the last four centuries. There may be Jews out there, I don't know. They may not know themselves, not by now. They are all just islanders."

Martina looked at Timo and then, mournfully, at the market for a while longer.

Back in the cabin, she surprised Sara Weiss in the act of snipping off fistfuls of her Bergman-blond hair.

"I decided," Sara announced without looking around, "I don't want to be called Sara anymore. I want to have a partisan name, like Aristotle."

Martina wasn't sure what to say. She thought Sara sounded nicer than Marty. "Have you picked one?"

Her cabinmate turned with a puckish smile, her hair as short as a boy's. "I think I want to be called Tamara."

Nobody left the ship again that day or the day after, except for the crew on regular shore leave and a small delegation led by Aristotle that got no farther than a café on the built-up side of the harbor. By the second evening there was still no word on trucks, and Aristotle spoke of a new arrangement involving mule-drawn wagons. Harvey Grabsteen chose this moment to say, "I don't understand what the holdup is. The pilots are probably waiting out there in the hills, wondering what's become of us. It wouldn't surprise me if they've flown right back to Palestine."

Aristotle's response to this intrigued Martina. The three of them were up on the bridge, which was otherwise deserted, and spread before them on the navigator's bench were maps and aeronautical charts showing the terrain from here through Bosnia and Hungary all the way into Czechoslovakia. The last light of day came at double strength from sky and water through windows on three sides. Aristotle's eyes were a complementary gray and for a moment, as he raised them to study Grabsteen, looked equally ancient.

"Has your organization, Rabbi," he said slowly, turning the thought over in his mind, "also taken upon itself the task of arranging air transport?"

"Naturally," said Grabsteen. "We have resources worldwide. We're in daily contact with the Haganah."

"And the Haganah are under daily surveillance by the world's intelligence services. Not the British alone. Is that where your weapons came from?"

Grabsteen shrugged. "I'm not a detail man. We needed certain things, and we got them—that's what counts."

"Indeed. A full platoon's worth of Mausers and Machinepistole, all in new condition. And the proper bullets to go with them. And not just hand grenades, but *German* hand grenades."

"So what?" Martina demanded. "What are you driving at?"

"Nothing really. Only that it gives one pause for thought. This confusion with the trucks, that is perfectly ordinary. It is the most natural thing, in a time of war and chaos. Matériel is desperately short, Tito is scrambling to secure his hold on power, and of course still there are Germans about, being uncooperative. So—a few trucks are misdirected, or perhaps there never were any trucks. Such things happen. But now and then something different happens. A much needed item is immediately available. A ship of neutral registry passes through a war zone without attracting undue notice."

"I don't get it. Are you saying there's something fishy going on?"

"I say nothing of the sort."

It seemed Aristotle was going to leave it at that. Then he turned to

Grabsteen and said, "But I am curious now, whether these airplanes of yours will be waiting when we arrive. Fueled and ready, with expert pilots, and plenty of parachutes to go around."

"Sure they will," said Grabsteen. Not getting it, or perhaps feigning obtuseness.

Martina said, "What is it you're worried about?"

Aristotle sighed. "I have been at this too long to worry about anything. Rather, to worry about any *one* thing. But a special problem in the Underground, which only increases as we come to the endgame, is that one never really knows who anybody is. What strange bedfellows have they acquired? What is their deeper purpose?" He turned back to Grabsteen. "I agreed to join this expedition because I am a Jew and a patriotic Czech. But I am not a puppet. I will resign—believe me—if I conclude that I am being played. It makes no difference, Rabbi, which side is playing me."

In the end, it was mules. Mules and wagons, like something from another century.

Martina guessed it could be worse. It beat sitting on the *Paloma* twiddling their thumbs. At least she didn't actually have to ride one of the animals. Though that might have lent the ordeal a nice biblical flavor.

As it was, everything fell out neatly. There were six mules, three wagons, thirty humans: the Brigade's twenty-odd dogfaces, the Three Guys Named Moe, Grabsteen, Aristotle and the hoary Bosnian who owned the mules. They loaded supplies and munitions first, starting an hour past sunset. Sentries were posted along the wharf to discourage onlookers. The moon had not yet cleared the hills behind Sibinik. Loading went smoothly, with only a modest amount of stumbling in the dark, smashed knuckles and crates that landed with a crack on the pavement. On the whole, you might have been watching an organized military operation.

Martina figured it wouldn't last.

The hitch arose toward the end, when the time came to decide who was going to ride on which wagon. On paper, the brigade was organized by squads. But during the ocean passage an unofficial realignment had occurred. Now there were people who did not care to be crammed into close proximity with certain other people. And there were spontaneous groupings, such as Eddie, Ingo and Stu, that did not accord with the official roster.

"This ain't gonna wash," grumbled Eat Moe, the smallest of the noncoms. He strutted up and down the wharf like a bantam rooster, clucking out orders that the volunteers mostly ignored.

"What's the point?" Martina asked, of nobody in particular. "Why not let people sit where they want? It's just a damn wagon ride."

"It is not just a damn wagon ride," said Middle Moe. "It's a question of discipline. Of order."

"Order is for Aryans," Stu's voice quipped from somewhere in the dark.

Oddly, that appeared to settle it. People boarded higgledy-piggledy. The military contingent—Aristotle, the Moes and a handful of toadies—commandeered the first wagon. Martina was slow in collecting herself and heaving her kit bag to her shoulder, and in consequence was left with no choice but to hop on the last wagon as it began creaking off into the night. Hands reached down to yank her up, and she landed in a graceless heap amid a thicket of kneecaps and GI boots. She strained her eyes to make out who she was riding with.

It was the wise-guy caucus. The old D-for-Dog Squad, plus or minus. Ingo and his pals, Sara—no, make that Tamara—and a bunch of people Martina had barely gotten to know. She had been, as she now realized, pretty isolated of late, what with *mal de mer* and the general fretting over what lay ahead. Now that whatever it might be, doom or glory, lay practically on top of them—only a few hours' bumping along by wagon, then a quick hop by airplane into the jaws of hell—she felt strangely lighthearted. Or perhaps the pervasive mood of terror, her own and everyone else's, had disguised itself as something different, an irrational gaiety.

"Hiya, guys," she said.

There were return greetings, and Ingo gave her a hand up from the floor planks, clearing a little spot for her between himself and a pile of ammo crates.

"Mm, cozy," she said, squeezing into it.

"Haven't seen you around much."

"I know, I've been . . ." She shrugged, peering into the hollows where his eyes must be. But he said nothing more, and she listened instead to the sparrowlike chatter of Tamara and a cluster of young men farther back.

The wagon groaned up from the harbor to higher ground on an old pitted road stretching along the spine of a hill. Suddenly the moon was hanging there, huge and round, casting an eerie dimensionless light over the landscape, which closely matched Martina's notion of the surface of Mars. Everything was reddish, dry, strewn with rocks the size of automobiles, lifeless for millennia.

"What is this, some kind of desert?" she asked, hoping to rouse Ingo to conversation. It bothered her, now that she thought about it, that the two of them hadn't talked for so long.

"It's no desert," he said. "It's a ruin. A wasteland. This once was Illyria."

Just like Ingo, she thought. Ever the Romantic, seeing moonlit ruins where everyone else, every normal person, saw nothing but . . . nothing. For the good reason that there was nothing to see.

"I'll bite. What's Illyria?"

"It was a paradise when the Romans discovered it. They came here and built temples in the cypress groves. Then they started cutting the trees down for their fleets and their fortresses. Then the Goths came in. Then the Mongols, then the Venetians, finally the Austrians. The Venetians were the worst. This is what's left. There's no soil anymore for trees to grow in, and if there were, the peasants would chop them down for firewood."

You could hear the melancholy in his voice, but Martina suspected it had little to do with the lost forests of Illyria.

"Are you worried about things back home?" she asked him. "The Ring, all that?" He shrugged. His face looked thinner, she thought, more drawn. "Vernon can handle it. I've put it in writing that the place is his if I don't come back. Only, no more goddamn chickenwurst once rationing's over."

A little joke, she guessed, though she found it a sad one. Poor Ingo. His world had become so small—the proverbial grain of sand. Eternity in a lunch hour.

"So, how are things with Timo?" he asked, a casual slap on the cheek.

"What do you mean?"

"I mean, how's Timo? The two of you seem to be hitting it off."

That was Ingo, too. To turn a companionable moment into a sparring match.

"What's that to you?"

"Nothing. I envy you, truthfully. It's a convenience, I think. Falling in love with whomever you happen to be with."

She could have socked him—almost did, in fact—except she realized in time that it might not be her he was thinking about.

They rode on in silence, not a peaceable silence but restive, seething. The clomp of the mules and the clank of the wagon wheels seemed loud in the empty wastes.

"I wonder if we'll find him," Martina said after a long time.

"Find who?"

But she didn't answer and he didn't ask again. When they reached the landing strip shortly after midnight, two Heinkel aircraft were waiting. Squarish, too-small-looking planes, their corrugated skins painted white, still bearing the squared-off crosses of the Luftwaffe, they stood tail-down, side by side, gleaming like metal ghosts in the moonlight.

ON THE TRAIL

The White Russian princess was bored by the time they reached Hannover-am-Münden, which was okay with Butler because he'd begun to find her boring as well. They did little these days but snap at each other between bouts of French champagne and Berlinish lovemaking. In truth he felt sorry for the poor gal, with her clutch purse of family jewels, her cold-water flat in the Kreuzburg and her threadbare memories of having danced as a young girl in the Winter Palace.

Maybe it was a there-but-for-the-grace deal. If their situations had been reversed, the lost estates and the shabby exile's life his and not hers, perhaps Samuel Butler Randolph III would have been every bit as petulant as Sissi. But as things stood, she was the down-and-out aristocrat, praying for an end to Bolshevism, while he was the commissar-in-waiting, biding his time until Capitalism breathed its last and he could write an epic novel, a *War and Peace* for this half-spent century. Tolstoy meets Marshal Chuikov meets Cecil B. DeMille.

The jaunt down to this place near Kassel had been Sissi's idea: a different sort of weekend outing, a change of scenery, a frolic. Buy some sandals and do the Wandervogel bit. Butler couldn't see it. On the other hand, he divined possibilities in there for, say, a *Collier's* piece. German youth sunbathing bare-assed, singing folk tunes and living the natural life. Toss in a few hints about free love; titillate the innocents at home.

Butler was twenty-two and had a few years left, he figured, before taking up the serious business of literature. In the meantime it couldn't hurt to keep his name in print, bridge the gap between *The Crimson*, whose editor he should have been had not university politics gotten in the way, and the *Times Book Review*. He could have done postgrad work anywhere, but he had chosen Leipzig, whose university was already venerable long before the first brick was laid in Harvard Square. It was important to be in Germany now. While the Weimar Republic might be a transient phase in the history of Europe—an epiphenomenon, in Hegel's lexicon—it was the fulcrum, the turning point, where the imperial past tilted against the proletarian future. In Leipzig, which lay east of the Elbe, facing out over the steppes toward Asia, the musty halls echoed with the footsteps of Schumann and Schiller even as the curtains flew back before bracing winds of revolution.

He had fallen in with Sissi at Bayreuth. What on earth had she been doing there? She loathed German opera, Wagner worst of all. But so did Butler, in the box adjacent to hers, subsequently in the same suite at the spa. Then it was off to Berlin, rising at noon to browse the *International Trib* at a café in Unter den Linden; afternoons hazy with humidity and brown coal whiled away on a blanket in the Grünewald, or adrift in a hired boat on the Wannsee; nights that never went dark in the sweaty radiance of their private midnight sun. And now this romp in the Kaufunger Forest, a hike up some mountain, *Licht und Luft* and all the rest of it.

How quickly one thing turns into another, Butler reflected. A snatch of detested Wagner came to his mind. *You see, my son, here Time becomes Space.* He hadn't a clue what it meant. Probably nothing, just sounded impressive, like Wagner in general. A hash of badly told stories, misunderstood myths, all blown up with the sideshow gimcrackery of *Gesamtkunstwerk*—clashing cymbals and blaring trumpets, singers bleeding to death while they bellow at one another across the stage.

Screw Wagner, and the white horse he rode in on. Screw German opera and the whole bloated, pestilent body of High Art: that's how Butler felt, and he wasn't alone. Everybody was quoting Spengler this year, commenting blandly over coffee on the West's imminent *Untergang*, which means "sinking," damn it, not "decline." Few people had given any thought to what came next, after the last bubbles rose from the deep. Most seemed to feel it didn't personally concern them.

"Are we almost there?" the Princess mumbled from a champagne drowse.

"No, we are not," said Butler. He stared out the window as the train appeared to leap across a river gorge. The gloomy, spirit-infested waters below looked like a proper sort of place to drown in—ease oneself down, clutching a wept-over copy of *Jungen Werther,* one's lifeblood oozing slowly from the hole just at the heart, pierced by the blue flower's unsuspected thorn.

Such an end was not for Butler: never. His great destiny lay ahead of him. He sat comfortably in the first-class carriage feeling the journey unroll beneath him, staring through clean German glass, studying his reflection there.

There was no room at the Meissner Haus. Apparently not all Free German Youth were inclined to rough it. Butler was for turning back; they could hop a local train to Kassel or—here's a thought—Göttingen. But the Princess surprised him, declaring with an exile's hard-won adaptability that she intended to go right up the mountain and sort things out when she got there.

"We can buy a tent," she said, brightening at the thought. "A tent and some food, that's all we need."

"You'll want something to drink, surely. I don't know if we can carry more than a magnum or two, if we have to hoof it."

"Don't be a bore, darling. The Wandervögel don't touch alcohol, you know that. We must live cleanly from here on! Now komm mit, before it gets dark."

The trail wasn't hard, thank God. So many young German feet had trodden it down the past couple of days you could've found your way by the dark of the moon, just from the feel of the ground. The landscape was predictably picturesque, scattered *Dörfer* and smallholdings that petered out into more thickly wooded terrain, Hölderlin oaks of requisite antiquity, Nietzschean crags and gorges. Butler was no naturalist. The most he would give the scenery was an acknowledgment that it was, as the locals would say, *charakteristisch.*

You smelled the campfires before you could see where the smoke was coming from. You heard sounds as well—nothing as clear as speech or as evocative as voices raised in song, more a kind of buzzing or murmuring such as often rises from a meadow at the height of May, the combined life-sounds of bugs and bees and scurrying rodents and chittering birds and screeching crickets—except this had a human timbre, hard to define yet unmistakable. Finally you rounded a turn and before you lay the whole amazing spectacle: a mountainside bright with banners, prickling with bodies like so many moving cilia, specked with the orange of open fires and the black of those tents known as *Kohten,* shaped like lathed-down cones and said to derive from a Lappish original. Again, wholly *charakteristisch.* Nevertheless impressive, if you were impressionable. Butler was not. Sissi surprised him with a girlish capacity for awe.

"Oh, Sammy, look!"

"Why do you call me that?" he said, knowing even so that it was not the nickname that annoyed him.

She gave him a twinkling Russian smile, innocently mocking. "Because it suits you better than the other one. Butler is a foolish name, don't you agree? A butler is the chief servant of an English household. And you are nobody's servant, dushka moy. Maybe you long to be, maybe that is the secret of your name. But let us go now and find an icy mountain stream so that I can splash my face. That's all I need, then I will be ready for the party."

"Party? What makes you think there'll be a party?"

She gave him a look he knew well and detested: the one that implied he was, after all, only a naïve American.

"Here we are, Liebe, in the middle of . . . did you see the *Tagesspiegel* gives the attendance at thirty thousand? Thirty thousand young people, not all of them children, either. There certainly will be a party."

One thing turned into another. The quest for a tent led them to a booth on the arcade run by the summit's organizers, from whom you could acquire such needful things as a program book, a box of matches, and a cloth patch to sew on your rucksack, "Freideutscher Jugendtag August 1929" scripted around an emblem carried over from 1913: a bird in flight over a trio of squiggly lines that might have suggested water, or a musical staff, or the strings of a guitar. The booth was manned by a harried-looking fellow in his mid-twenties, clearly a Meissner vet. His name was Karlheinz but he had chosen, in the fashion of the Movement, to be known as Kai.

This much Sissi got out of him in a matter of seconds, along with the fact that he lived in Chemnitz and had published a smattering of poetry. Since poets tend to be aware of other poets, if only to disapprove of them, Sissi quizzed him until they turned up a mutual acquaintance, a gloomy expatriate named Vlad. From Kai's expression you would guess he had little good to say about Vlad, but that was of no account. Sissi shrieked in delight and fell upon Kai like an old friend, grasping his arm and murmuring into his ear—tales of amusing mishaps on the journey from the capital, a joke at her own expense concerning inappropriate footwear, all in a torrent of *Berlinersprach* Butler could barely comprehend, with its blurred consonants and catlike vowels, and probably neither could Kai. That was of no account either.

In twenty minutes, a perky young woman arrived to take a turn in the booth, and Kai was striding arm-in-arm with Sissi, Butler some paces back, on a path through the woods to a smaller mountain that was not, he promised, too far off.

"The dj.1.11 are up there," Kai told them. "Do you know of them, the deutsche Jungenschaft von 1. November? Quite a distinct group."

"Those are the ones who write everything in lowercase," said Butler.

Kai nodded, overlooking the possibility that Butler's comment might be sarcastic. "They are quite selective in their membership, and seem always to get the best of everything. Now they have the best campsite. The view at dawn! You can scarcely imagine."

Butler thought that, for Sissi, to imagine the view at dawn from anyplace—even her own bathroom—would be a stretch.

"If there is no extra tent," said Kai, "then you can use mine. I should not mind sleeping under the heavens. As long as I can sleep. This has been a most wearying day."

By the time they reached the top—Butler soaked in sweat, Sissi fresh and irreverent as a mockingbird—they found everything just as Kai had described. The spot was magnificent, a stark promontory of silver-gray rock rolling like petrified waves to a thrilling drop-off in the southeast. They had climbed above the haze that clung to the lower slopes, and the view seemed to stretch out forever, right to the Iron Mountains on the Czech frontier. The Höhe Meissner itself stood an uncertain distance to the north—two kilometers? five?—and between the two peaks you could look almost straight down into the lake called Frau-Holle-Quell, whose dark oval face was aswirl in clouds, like Snow White's magic mirror.

The vegetation at this height consisted of stunted conifers and a furze of waxy-leaved bushes with tiny berries the color of eggplant. As for tents, a quite large one was set back from the cliff—surrounded by boys in dark blue open-necked shirts who Butler supposed were the dj.1.11—and several smaller ones scattered like satellites, some of them pitched at odd angles, others barely hanging on against the pull of the wind. Butler had no idea what held any of them upright; there seemed too little soil up here to drive a stake into.

At the center of the open space, half a dozen blueshirts were building a wooden pyramid out of roughly sawn logs. It must've taken them all afternoon to haul the wood up here. A deal of trouble just for a bonfire; but that was German Youth for you. He pulled out his notebook. He would jot down some impressions.

"Sammy, darling!" Sissi sprang from a rock with a tall, stiff-backed youth in tow. "Look who I found over there, with all those nice boys—it's Count Berti! Alex is here too, he says. Can you believe it?"

Of course he could. The upper classes of Europe lived in a very small village that happened to be spread over the entire continent: a salon here, a hunting lodge there, an overfurnished flat somewhere else. They all knew one another and they shared a faculty, like a blood scent, for stumbling upon their peers in unlikely circumstances. If a Prussian baron were shot down while bombing France, his parachute would touch down on the lawn of a marquis who happened to be his third cousin, and there enjoy a luncheon of freshly bagged quail before being sent off to genteel internment.

Count Berti, who looked no older than twenty, extended a hand and gave Butler a clever, ironic little smile, perhaps a wordless confidence regarding their mutual friend Sissi, while saying in an unimpeachable tone, "Von Stauffenberg. Please call me Berthold, I am often confused with my brothers Alexander and Claus. Alexander is around here someplace. Claus has just finished his officer training and cannot be bothered with the affairs of youth. Sissi tells me, Herr Randolph, you come from Virginia?" Without waiting for an answer he switched to flawless Oxbridge English. "It is a beautiful state, I am told. Regrettably I've never had a chance to visit America, though I hope someday to do so. Germans and Americans are of a type, I believe."

Butler disagreed but it didn't seem worth mentioning. The Count was just being gracious. *Noblesse oblige.*

Now Kai legged it over toting a great stoneware jug that was evidently full. "Berthold!" he exclaimed, seeing Stauffenberg. "That's perfect, I was certain you'd like to meet our new friend from America. Berthold," he explained to Butler, "has always been interested in foreigners. That is refreshing, isn't it, in these days of hurrah-patriotism."

Butler nodded absently; he must remember this term, *Hurra-patriotismus.* That sort of detail would do nicely for *Collier's.*

"Berthold also is a poet," Kai purred on. "A protégé of the famous Stefan George. Are you an admirer of George, Sammy?"

Butler sensed this was some kind of test. Rather than admit he wouldn't know a George poem if it were carved by the hand of God in the rock before him, he said, "Most people call me Butler. Only Sissi here—"

"Ach, Sissi!" Berthold laughed. "She has her own names for everyone. Ist das nicht wahr, Fürsterin?"

"For myself, I do not care for George," Kai announced. "I find him elitist, revanchist, overly nationalistic, and a terrible snob. They would drum me out of the dj.1.11, I'm afraid—they're all George 'fans,' as you Yanks would say. Fine fellows nonetheless. Look here what I've got from them! Some of their famous tchaj!"

He hefted the jug, and from the Mephistophelean nature of his smile, and the knowing look that passed over Stauffenberg's face, Butler guessed Sissi was right. There would be a party. A jolly little party by firelight.

"The Left made a tactical error," the young Count declared, tossing a pebble toward the edge of the cliff, where it vanished in the darkness. "They should never have moved to amend the Meissner-Formel. Once that door was opened, the Right came charging through, and now see the mess we've got."

He spoke in quiet, measured tones as though they were gathered around a table in a candlelit *séparé,* and not at a bonfire on a mountaintop, their conversation drowned at times by raucous singing from the dj.1.11 side. A chilling wind came from the east but occasionally changed directions, whipping smoke around in Butler's eyes.

"But the Left was correct in its arguments," said Kai, louder than necessary. His passions were inflamed. "The amendment is needed precisely *because* the Right has become so radicalized. So angered."

"I am not speaking of the merits of the proposal," Stauffenberg said stiffly. "I am speaking of cause and effect. Now the newspapers are going to have—what do Americans say, Butler? A field day, yes?"

"We ought to be talking about tradition." This was Petra, the young woman who had taken Kai's place in the organizers' booth. She was *ostelbisch,* perhaps Silesian, with straw-blond hair brushed back from a wide Slavic face and light brown, almond-shaped eyes. Her features looked especially striking in the light from the fire, which by this late hour had burned down to an orange heap that reminded Butler of a smashed Halloween pumpkin. "We ought to remain true to our own history. It was Wyneken himself who told us in 1913—you were here, Kai, you must remember—'The Youth Movement does not end at the borders of nation or language or race.' What the Left wanted to achieve was to make the language of the Formel embody this principle, on which all of us agree."

"We don't all agree," said a yellow-haired student from the Sudetenland, his face pink from several mugs of tchaj. "If we did, the motion would have passed. Instead we've got people stealing from one another, having fistfights, hurling racial insults . . . it is a kind of sacrilege."

"The original Formel was a compromise, Ulrich," Stauffenberg said calmly, his face half in shadow. "That was the only way to get anything accomplished in 1913, with so many factions at the table, and it remains so today. Indeed more so, as the Movement has become more fragmented. Our problem is not that we disagree. It is that we have lost our willingness to compromise, to find some meeting ground. Unmistakably, the Right came hoping for a quarrel—something they could turn into an open struggle, a street brawl, over who should control the Movement."

"No one should control the Movement!" Kai practically shouted.

"And the Left," persisted Stauffenberg, "has been happy to oblige them. Now I fear there may be no way to save the situation. It is Jena 1919 all over again. Perhaps even worse this time. Think how terrible this must look to outsiders! Though I suppose you could say this too is in keeping with our tradition." He smiled at Petra, who beamed back at him, seemingly thrilled by his attention. Then he sighed. "And all this over a couple of words on a piece of paper."

Butler waited a few moments, to be sure no one had more to say. The dj.1.11 lads were rocking back and forth in an imaginary storm, roaring a comical sea chantey: We're off to Scandinavia, crossing the cold North Sea, leaving this land where we're *mehr bekannt und mehr verbannt* (notorious and widely banned). Then he asked, "Fistfight? Stealing? When did all this happen?"

Count Berthold rose from his place at the fire, stretched a bit, then strolled off into the shadows, the topic of fistfights apparently not to his liking. The pink-faced student leaned closer. "They say Americans were involved. Jews, they say. Some of the Jungdo boys claim the Americans attacked them."

"Jungdo?" said Butler. He did not want to be so indiscreet as to pull out his notebook. On the other hand, he needed to get the facts straight.

"Jungdeutsche Orden," explained the pink-faced Sudetenlander.

Order of Young Germans: a name, thought Butler, some might find redundant.

Kai made a rude noise. "Yes, I'm sure a gang of American Jews came all the way to Hessen to pick on the innocent Jungdo. That's the lot that got thrown out of Stuttgart last summer for disrupting a performance of Mahler. *Song of the Earth*, I think."

"What's wrong, don't they like the Earth?" bubbled Sissi, half drunk. She swooned with laughter at her own joke, leaning on Kai's arm for support. He didn't seem to mind.

"No, the Second Symphony," said Petra. "A beautiful work. So sad, though."

"Mahler was ein rassischer Jude," explained Kai. "Racially Jewish, though nonreligious and culturally assimilated. That's too much for the Jungdo to bear. *Jewish music must not be played on German soil!* No, this tale of marauding Americans is too preposterous. It cannot be true."

Butler agreed. But then, truth was not what chiefly concerned him. He wanted to hear more. This might be the angle he was looking for.

The Sudeten boy did not need much encouragement. As he heard it, someone connected with the Jungdo—a grown-up, perhaps a group sponsor—claimed that some of his private papers had been stolen, as well as a sum of money. He identified the culprit, who turned out to be an American Jew working in collusion with SAJ—the Sozialistische Arbeiter-jugend, who everyone knew to be traitors to the Fatherland. Only no sooner had this criminal been arrested, and an investigation begun in keeping with the honorable tradition of German justice, than a gang of the Jew's confederates swooped in, beat the innocent Jungdo senseless and ran off into the night. Now their whereabouts were unknown, but the Order meant to track them down and right the scales.

"This is great stuff," said Butler. "Now if we can only figure out who they are. We need to get the other side of the story."

Kai was aghast. "You can't possibly believe—"

"Oh, I know it's hogwash. But that's exactly why there must be some truth in it. Nobody would make up anything so ridiculous. A Jew, yes—but why an *American* Jew? Why Socialists, not Communists? And why admit you captured this guy, then let him get away? People don't invent stories that make themselves look bad."

Kai looked downcast, as though dismayed by Butler's credulity. He poured himself more tchaj, a curious beverage, meant to be served warm, that tasted strongly of herbs but seemed to consist mainly of red wine spiked with brandy and quantities of sugar, and fatally effective. "What will you do with this 'story'?" he asked, choosing the English word over its German equivalent, which carried a connotation of factual historicity. "Will you recast it as a heroic romance? The mysterious Yankee as Robin Hood, stealing from anti-Semites and giving to the common people?"

Butler swirled his mug, studying the dregs down there. "That might be exactly how to play it," he said thoughtfully. "The folks in Iowa might get that. Thanks, pal."

Something was wrong with Butler's pillow next morning. Of the two heads lying on it, neither ought to have been there.

The one attached to Butler's neck was a bloated, throbbing thing, rendered hateful by a day of champagne followed by a night of that stonework jug. The second head, which ought to have been Sissi's, was not. The hair was too thick, the bare shoulder and rounded breast—from which the blanket had slipped—too fleshly, and the skin lacked her blue-blooded pallor.

It came to Butler in fragments. Petra, the girl with Slavic cheekbones. Bellowed camp songs that grew increasingly bawdy and off-key. The ebbing fire, the enveloping darkness, the longing for body warmth, Sissi asleep on Kai's shoulder, Butler awake and amorous. Then the ease with which everything followed—the steady escalation from glances to furtive touches to a full-on embrace, starting by the fire but ending here amid tangled bedclothes in a tent that now, by daylight, was too bright and too hot and sagged ludicrously as its pegs worked loose.

Butler hoisted himself on his elbows and regretted it. Yet there was no going back; the day was advancing with or without him, and somewhere out there—this came to him now—a story waited to be told. A tale of American avengers, two-fisted innocents abroad, with "Butler Randolph" all over it.

He dragged himself out of the tent without waking Petra. Sunlight covered the world like a buttery glaze. Around him, the mountain stirred. Young Germany had arisen, the dj.1.11 had already marched off. The air was dank with heavy sweetness like that of a million overspent roses. You sensed renewal yet suspected an inner decay—lotus rising from the cesspool, that kind of thing. Jot these impressions down, old boy, before you lose them.

Sluggishly he retraced his path from the day before, coming at last to a quick-running brook where he dunked first his hands, then his entire head. Time to make a plan. Start with the Jungdo. Lock them into a version of the story, then go after the Yanks. Wrap it up by mid-afternoon and we may yet tuck in to a civilized dinner in Kassel.

There was no stopping Butler once he set his mind to something.

At first it seemed the pieces would fall readily into place. The Jung-deutsche Orden was conspicuously installed on the Meissner proper, in a campsite that bore a passing resemblance to a medieval tournament ground: colorful pennants flapping from high shaved poles around the periphery, watchtowers made of lashed timbers, an inner courtyard squared off with tents. Butler wondered how long such a fad for things troubadourish would last in America. About eighteen months, he guessed.

In Germany, it was well into its second century with no sign of anyone getting bored. They even had a name for it, *Teutschtümelei,* as untranslatable as the thing itself.

The gate to the camp, a swinging log that pivoted around an elm, was manned by a sentry who looked all of eleven. The lad's shrill command to halt and identify himself pierced Butler's aural nerve like a surgical instrument. Wincing, he brushed past the boy and knocked the gate open.

"Alarm!" the sentry cried. "An intruder has stormed the courtyard!"

The modest commotion that ensued was opportune, insofar as it brought a dozen older members of the Order out of their tents and away from their breakfast fires into the open, where he could size them up. They didn't look like a gang of bullyboys, such as one saw on the streets of German cities nowadays—more like members of a sporting club at a competitive *Gymnasium* in some staunchly bourgeois suburb like Berlin-Steglitz. Most were in their teens, though a couple looked old enough to be recent university grads. All were in uniform, a white jersey over baggy tan britches, and a few wore hats on which insignia of rank or degree had been sewn. Butler picked out the one with the most silver crosses, reckoning him to be the leader.

"I'm a journalist," he said, uncapping his pen. "I'm looking into an incident that happened yesterday, when—if my information is correct—a member of your group reported that certain items were missing, and that the person or persons responsible had been apprehended. What can you tell me about that?"

The fellow worked his jaw muscles but did not reply. He studied Butler with narrow eyes. He was a solidly built character who could have held his own in a street fight, and in fact might have done so quite recently; a pair of tiny bandages made a neat white cross on the bridge of his nose. Butler judged him to be just young enough to have missed the last war, and determined not to miss the next one.

"I should tell you, I intend to write up this incident whether or not you're willing to provide information. But I'm sure you'd like to see your own side of the story fairly presented."

"As opposed to what?" said a voice from the side.

Butler turned to see an older man, thirty-five-ish, wearing a wide-brimmed expedition hat, a crisply tailored waistcoat and a pair of tall riding boots. The only thing missing was the horse crop. He stood arms akimbo some paces off, fixing Butler with a look that aspired to withering condescension.

In a haughty academician's voice he went on: "As opposed to the usual sort of bias and distortion one expects from the Jew-run press?"

The stout, bandaged fellow gave a quiet chuckle, then cocked a thumb toward Butler. "Herr Professor, this person has entered the camp without permission. I was about to help him leave."

The older man shook his head. "Not quite yet, I think. Let us learn first who he is, and on whose behalf he has come."

It irritated Butler to be spoken of as if he were incapable of understanding. "I came on my own behalf. And as to who I am, I'm a representative of the press—that's all you need to know. Listen, Professor, if you don't want to talk, that's fine. Just let me make a note of this for the record."

He scrawled *break the fucker's nose again* into his notebook and then glanced around the circle of Jungdo boys. They were much of a type, not in physical appearance but in their arrogant demeanor and pseudo-military bearing. They seemed to have taken the concept of *Orden* very much to heart.

"You may put your pen down," the Professor said. "No one has refused to speak to you. We ask only that you reveal the true nature of your investigation. Also, if one may inquire, mein Herr—your accent. Are you of foreign nationality?"

Butler believed a reporter's job was to ask questions, not answer them. But the man's supercilious manner was getting under his skin. "My name is Randolph. I'm an American writer, studying at Leipzig. All right? Now, what can you tell me about yesterday?"

The older man's smile was hard to read; something about Butler seemed to amuse him. "If we are to have a talk, it would be well to sit down. Come, we shall go to my tent."

He led Butler across the open space to a square pavilion of white canvas, the stout young man following with the rest of the Jungdo. At the door the younger boys paused; the Professor motioned them all inside. The interior was furnished like a movable study, complete with a folding wooden desk on which books and papers were stacked. An ornate tapestry—the slaying of a huge stag by a knight on horseback—hung from the rear panel, an imposing backdrop. There were only a couple of chairs, but the floorcloth was well supplied with pillows. The Professor took the largest seat and the younger boys arranged themselves in a semi-circle at his feet. The burly one perched on a stool, looking edgy, ever ready to leap up again. This left a rickety-looking chair for Butler.

"To begin," the older man said, "my name is Professor Doktor Konrad

Freiherr von Cheruski. I am honored to serve as chief scholar of the Jungdeutsche Orden—my title is Oberbachant. This is Gunter, our Gruppenführer. At his side there is one of our Stamm leaders and an aspiring Bachant."

The youth in question, a boy about sixteen, was notable chiefly for his bland Teutonic features: limp blond hair and empty eyes, with a complexion that was almost white except for a faint blush of pink through the clear skin, like a healthy vampire. He stared blankly at Butler, who could detect no trace of a soul through those unclouded irises.

"Now," said Cheruski, "I must proceed by correcting certain of your 'facts.' The incident to which you refer was, indeed, *reported* yesterday. However, it took place on the previous evening—that is, the second day of the Jugendtag. Several of these lads were present."

Butler made a little business of writing in his notebook. Yesterday, the day before . . . it made no difference to him. He cared more about getting this scene right: the glowing, worshipful eyes of the boys, the leatherbound edition of Tacitus weighting down a corner of the *Schreibtisch*. He hoped also to convey the self-satisfied pomposity of the Herr Professor, whom Butler judged to be a second-rate scholar, unimpressive to his colleagues, who had found in the Youth Movement a ready market for otherwise unsalable theories. Probably there had always been such people, in every nation, but Weimar Germany seemed awash in them.

"All right—day before yesterday. Now, could you just tell me exactly what happened? In your own words, please. I don't want to rely on hearsay."

Cheruski was not ready to drop his supercilious attitude; nonetheless he complied, more or less. His story was much the same as the one Butler had heard the night before, with minor variations. In this telling, the number of thuggish assailants was not specified, and certain other details were left purposely vague. The Deutsch subjunctive mode, thought Butler, is a fine vehicle for using many words to say nothing definite. It didn't matter. He had what he needed: a look at the supposed victims, a strong dose of local color. Still he supposed he ought to play the hard-nosed Yankee reporter.

"What makes you think"—returning to what seemed to him a weak spot in Cheruski's account—"the young man you've called, let's see, 'an American Jewish type,' was, quote, 'in league with Bolshevik elements'?"

"I made that quite clear. I have no wish to repeat myself."

"You say, 'He had been seen often in company with known agitators on the Left.'"

"This I saw with my own eyes."

"So the young man was not a stranger to you?"

"Of course he was a stranger," Cheruski insisted, toying with the German term *Fremder*, whose meaning could be slippery. "An individual of that type would be a stranger even should he reside in the house next door. He is a stranger to all honest men and to all wholesome places, by his very nature."

"By his race," explained the blank-eyed youth, the budding *Stamm* leader.

Cheruski tightened his lips, as though nothing more need be added.

"Thanks," said Butler, shutting his notebook. "Now I need to track down these other people—the ones who, you say, physically assaulted you."

"That is a waste of time. They will deny everything."

"Oh?" Butler feigned puzzlement. "I should think you'd want them found, if everything happened like you say it did."

Cheruski said tersely, "I will bid you good day then."

Butler rose to depart, then paused. "One more thing. What's your field, Professor?"

"I am a philologist," said Cheruski, enunciating slowly, as though he did not expect the foreigner to understand. "I study archaic manuscripts. I investigate the deeper levels of truth encoded in the text. You may say that in studying a given document—let us say, a heroic saga—I seek to understand what it really means, as opposed to what it merely says."

"I'll send you a copy of my story," Butler promised.

In the August sun—strong for Germany, more like the sun of his boyhood in the West End of Richmond—Butler's headache made an impressive comeback. He slumped in the shade of an oak tree. Another two hours' sleep would have been wasted on him. Nearby, in a sloping field whose yellow, rasping grasses made his throat feel dry, a javelin-throwing contest was under way. *That's correct,* Butler told an imaginary editor, raking over the text of his unwritten article, *a fucking javelin-throwing contest. And in the background, you could hear some kind of singing competition. One side was armed only with folk tunes, the other fired back with depressing ballads about fallen comrades. It wasn't even close.*

Jesus Christ, laughed the imaginary editor—an acerbic Maxwell Perkins sort. *What was that song by Uhland? The real hankie-wringer.*

"Ich hatt' ein guter Kamarad"—*yeah, they sang that one, too. Only Jesus had nothing to do with it. Try Wotan.*

Not Thor? I thought he was the warrior.

Thor is mighty and stupid. He's the god of the Fritzes in the trench. Wotan is the sneaky son-of-a-bitch back at headquarters. He's also the dispenser of the mead of poetry, which makes him the patron deity of propagandists.

Sounds like you've been over there too long, old man. You ought to come back to this side of the pond for a spell.

Maybe. Someday. But the future is over here. I want to stick around to see it. I want to write it all down.

And the future is what—singing contests? Hurling javelins?

The future, Butler would say, *is barbarism. The death of reason. Raging delusions of vengeance and heroism and destiny. It starts with toy weapons and 'The Hunter Is to Green Woods Gone,' but it doesn't stop there. You watch. You'll see.*

Only in Germany, Perkins would laugh.

No, said Butler. *It doesn't stop there, either. It's the millennial complex, the dream of a thousand-year empire. Bring light to the dark corners of the Earth, break the shackles of history. Germany is next up in the queue. But sooner or later . . .*

Perhaps he had begun muttering aloud. Butler looked up suddenly to find himself being stared at. The staring face was blurred by the glare of backlighting—he had to shade his eyes to make it out. He was surprised to recognize the Jungdo boy, the blank-faced blond, hovering before him. That vampire complexion, those empty Aryan eyes.

"They have gone away," the boy said. No greeting, no ceremony. His voice was uncolored, a pure tone, like a radio test signal. "The Jew and his friend, the ones you are looking for. They left early, just at dawn. The friend was German, I think. And a third also, a woman."

Butler shook his head, trying to clear it enough to think. Had the boy followed him here? Was he acting on his own or at the behest of the Professor? If the latter, why had the story suddenly changed—the tally of bad guys dropping to two? And this new character, the lady friend—where did she fit in? Butler felt like laughing at such an unlikely spin of the wheel. His reporter's intuition, such as it was, told him he'd tapped into something here, a seam of glittering metal. Whether it would prove to be more than fool's gold required further analysis.

"You're sure about this?" He didn't bother opening the notebook. "You're saying only two people were involved in the attack? One of them a Jew and the other, what, a German?"

"The second one spoke in English. But he seemed German to me."

"He *seemed* German. And they left this morning?"

"With a Fräulein. I believe, a Jewess."

Butler peered at the boy but it was like staring into a stream. You saw patterns, but no meaning. Facts without truth. "Why are you telling me these things?"

"I know where they have gone," the boy said.

For the first time, a faint expression came over his features: a look you might see in a courtroom when an attorney—careful to make no overt display of triumph—calmly adduces what he knows to be the decisive piece of evidence.

Butler didn't ask Where?—he figured that the kid, having come this far, would get around to that. Instead he said, "What's your name, Wölfling?"

"Wolf cub" was a term of rank, denoting the very youngest of the Pathfinders, Germany's Boy Scouts. Butler figured it would needle the Jungdo boy.

"If you want to find these people," the kid said, "you will have to follow me. But we must set out immediately, the path is long. I hope you are not afraid of hiking."

Butler shrugged. He could hike when he had to.

The boy stood there a moment longer, his demeanor once again opaque. "I am Hagen von Ewigholz," he announced in a formal voice. "I come from Saxony. I hope someday I shall become also a writer. But not a journalist. A writer of history. I am especially interested in the history of war. Have you read Clausewitz?"

Butler blinked. He recognized the boy's expression now, and it was not that of an attorney. No—the boy wore the mask of a hunter. An old-fashioned *Jäger* of the greenwood, not lacking in courage or stamina, but blessed above all with patience, with instinctual caution, with a gift for moving through the forest methodically—first the stalking, then the sighting-in, and at its appointed moment, neither a breath too soon nor a moment late, the ecstasy of blood.

SLOVAK PARADISE

R ight up until the explosion, Ingo pretended to believe everything was fine: the mission was well planned, the volunteers adequately trained, the leadership competent, the logistics in order, the objective attainable. Even afterward, he did not abandon this pretense at once. It was like any other sort of belief—in Catholicism, for example, or the Washington Redskins—that after a time becomes habitual.

Also, the moment itself was not dramatic. *Explosion,* the word, poorly represents the subtlety of what he experienced: a brief shaking of the Heinkel aircraft, as if a large hand had momentarily gripped it and then let it go, followed an instant later by a rather soft, low-pitched thump. There was no way to know what had happened. The transport bay of the craft, designed to hold twelve paratroopers, was windowless and overfull. The only light came from a red bulb over the hatch leading forward to the cockpit. The noise of the twin engines was very loud, the vibrations were ceaseless.

In the seconds after the thump, Ingo glanced at the faces around him. It was not hard to read the thoughts there. Was this kind of thing to be expected in air travel? What did it mean? Was there any danger? Nobody seemed to know.

This suspended state lasted until someone—it must've been Stu—said, "What the hell was that?" Then it became clear that something was wrong, because the engines rose in pitch and the plane rolled into a sudden leftward bank. Ingo realized he was afraid, yet felt strangely untouched by his fear. The phrase *evasive maneuvers* came to his mind—something from a war movie, he guessed.

The big Moe, the guy they called M-1, decided he'd had enough. He struggled out of his cramped position and lurched forward, bent over, toward the cabin door. In the red light his expression was a dreadful thing, a mask of anger stretched over a face of confusion. He yanked the door open and shouted some incoherent question at the pilot, a young man from the Haganah, who shouted back a long and complicated reply.

"My God," the big man said. He took a step back into the transport bay as though something had hit him in the stomach. The Haganah man slammed the door. "Something has happened to the other plane. A fire in the tail section. We don't know what went wrong—we have to maintain radio silence. They're able to fly but there's trouble with the steering, they seem to have lost control of the rudder." He paused, still hunched over beside the door. He seemed to have forgotten to sit down. "We're pulling farther away, in case it blows up."

All Ingo could think was that there was something distorted about this announcement. The rationality in the big man's voice made a lie of what he was saying. Half the Brigade was on that other plane. Aristotle. The two other noncoms. Fifteen comrades in all. Also, half their supplies, including the maps. An irrecoverable loss.

But it was not lost yet. How much farther to the drop-off point? Already they'd been in the air more than three hours; they must be over Slovakia by now. Ingo wished he'd paid better attention at the briefing. The plan, as he remembered it, had been to keep well clear of Budapest, where the Germans were making a stand, and head northeast into a region called Slovensky Raj. About which Ingo knew nothing except that its name meant Slovak Paradise. A wild backcountry, Aristotle had said, far from any strategic points, empty of major combatant forces, nothing there worth dying over. Only of course the dying never stopped.

The landing zone lay somewhere in the foothills of the Tatry Mountains, "the Alps of Slovakia," said to be controlled by partisans. Ingo could picture the place as it had looked on the map, peaks and valleys crowded along the frontier, the border jigging its way through. Kraców to the north, the Moravian Gap to the west. In between, old German towns, Ostrau, Teschen, Auschwitz, lining the trade routes of a lost empire. Nearby, a great lake, its dark waters spreading like blood between two stricken nations. The land around the drop-off zone was keyed green, the color of forest, with splotches of white where the higher peaks remained snow-locked. On the map it looked empty except for the tiny dots of villages, mostly unnamed. Nothing to fear but the elements, and whatever spirits haunted the high passes.

If Ingo's experience held true, everything would look different on the ground. He clutched at this thought, *on the ground*—it implied they would land in one piece, he would live to walk the Earth again. After endless days on a ship, then a mule cart and now an airplane, he longed for something firm and unmoving under his feet. Even the killing grounds of Mitteleuropa.

Marty sat across the aircraft bay, squeezed between Timo and Harvey Grabsteen. She glanced up and gave him an anxious little smile. Ingo could not imagine what he gave her back. His mind was a shifting screen of images, white on gray, like fading photographs. There were people in some of them, but the faces were hard to recognize. Everyone was young, while the world around them was very, very old.

The aircraft lurched. Cables groaned as the wing flaps shifted to a new position; knocks and clunks issued from various moving parts. The Heinkel had belonged to the Luftwaffe, not long ago the terror of the skies. Tonight, suspended in blackness, the plane itself seemed terrified, quaking with cold and dread. The round heads of structural bolts looked ready to pop from the strain. Moisture from the passengers' breath had condensed on metal bulkheads. Back toward the tail, a wide hatch stood ready for the brave *Fallschirmjäger* to drop like Valkyries on their foes.

Ingo's old affection for the German language was still alive; this lovely compound, "falling-shield-hunters," seemed infinitely better than the ugly English *paratroopers*. Even now, it was hard for him to grasp that the language of Hölderlin, that subtle and sensuous code in which the deepest secrets of humankind had been confided, was today the language of tyrants, torturers, child-slayers, beings so crude as to seem barely human. It was hard to believe Luther's High German was capable of admitting such a term as *Vernichtungslager*—meaning a camp, *Lager*, in which people became nothing, *nichts*. The English approximation, *extermination camp*, sounded clinical by comparison. You lost the sense of profound annihilation, the veiled thought that an evil deity, an anti-Creator, was at work.

The plane seemed to be easing itself to a lower altitude. The roar of the engines dropped to a growl. More groaning of cables, more knocking of flaps. The cabin door popped open and the Haganah pilot shouted something Ingo couldn't understand.

"Hold on tight!" the big Moe translated. A needless command: everybody was grasping whatever lay in reach, including one another. Eddie, the prelaw student, braced himself against Ingo's shoulder; his canteen had gotten wedged between their hips. This would have been damned uncomfortable except that any bodily sensation, right now, was proof you were still alive.

There came a loud clump, first from one side of the plane and then the other. Grabsteen gave a yelp.

"For God's sake," hissed Tamara, erstwhile typist, "it's only the landing gear."

You could see the sheen of sweat on her forehead.

The plane swung from side to side, like something dangling from a sling. David's rock, about to be slung at Goliath's forehead. A familiar story, though you never hear what happened to the rock. Ingo sensed a struggle in progress, the unseen pilot wielding whatever it is that makes a plane fly straight and level, while his opponent—a wind off the Ukrainian steppes, raging over the rough landforms of Slovensky Raj—fought back hard.

Suddenly the floor of the plane thrust up at them, as if the ground was breaking through. Then everything reversed itself and the craft seemed to bounce, giving you for an instant that weightless feeling as when an elevator starts down. Then the wheels hit the landing strip and the plane began to buck and brake like an automobile that has run off the road into a cow pasture. It bounced crazily for a while and finally lurched to a halt.

There was an immediate, palpable release of tension, a shared relief verging on joy. But then, the next moment, everyone seemed to remember the other plane. *A fire in the tail section.*

M-1 pushed down the center of the bay and spun the hand-bolts on the parachute hatch. He was the first out and the others crowded after him, creating a jam. By the time Ingo made it to the ground, the landing field seemed crowded and he felt an unreasoned surge of panic. His hand moved to his Schmeisser.

Fires were burning. He saw two and then three of them: piles of flaming brush that marked the landing strip, a long arrowhead pointing into the wind. The strip itself was a narrow clearing, like a channel between two stretches of black woods. It was amazing, he thought, that the pilot had been able to find it, a glowing needle in the haystack of Europe. But Ingo had read about the exploits of the Maquis in France—commandos dropped off at night by two-seater RAF Mosquitos with the reliability of His Majesty's Post. Such things were possible, if you had help on the ground.

He wondered who had lit the fires.

As his senses adjusted, the scene began to make a degree of sense. The plane had rumbled to the end of the cleared space, leaving the field open for the other plane to follow. People were gathered off to one side, staring up the strip in the direction they'd come from. Waiting.

Ingo counted heads. Five people extra. No, four, he had forgotten the Haganah man. Four strangers among the Americans. He tried to pick them out but the firelight was shifty and nothing was clear. There, next to Grabsteen, that short fellow with a stubble of beard . . . no, that was Bobby Zilman, a band teacher from somewhere out West. The strangers, the men on the ground, must be keeping themselves back from the light.

Carefully Ingo unstrapped the machine pistol from his pack. He winced at the *clack* when the ammunition cartridge snapped into place. A couple of heads turned his way. One belonged to Bloom, the big Moe, who stood a distance to the side with his hand on the Walther at his belt, looking fidgety. Good, thought Ingo. It's not just me.

A minute passed slowly, then another. The moon had sunk low near the jagged ridge of the forest. The wind was light but steady and cold. Clothes that were warm on the shore of the Adriatic felt pitifully thin in Slovakia, which lay at the latitude of southern Canada. Winter here came early. *Es ist schon spät, es ist schon kalt.* Already it is late, already it is cold. That was Eichendorff, a poem about a witch, and the ending was not a happy one.

The noise reached them first. A buzzing, like a drill, that grew louder as a queer sort of meteor appeared low in the heavens: a dull orange streak that plunged straight toward the landing strip. The second plane came down fast and hard, bumping to a stop some eighty meters from where everyone was waiting. Even at that distance you could see what a wreck it was. The fuselage that had gleamed white was now charred gray. The tail smoldered dully like a dying cigar.

There was a general move in that direction, but Bloom barked out: "Hold on! I'll go see what's what. Miller, come with me. The rest of you stay put."

They stepped onto the landing strip in tandem, Bloom moving with a rapid, stealthy gait, surprising in a man of his size. Ingo felt like a little boy playing soldier. His gun felt too big, his head too light. The ground underfoot seemed to vanish as they stepped away from the fires. When they were halfway to the second plane, the cockpit hatch popped open and a body forced itself out, like something emerging from a charred chrysalis. This figure—the pilot, Ingo supposed—dropped to the ground, lay still for a moment, then struggled to rise. Bloom broke into a trot. Ingo heard another set of footsteps and spun with his Schmeisser at the ready, but it was only the young Haganah man. *Ein guter Kamarad* who'd grabbed a fire extinguisher from the undamaged plane and was loping along with it under his arm like a leaden football.

The fallen pilot had clambered to his feet by the time they reached him.

"Help," he said, dazed, motioning toward the rear of the plane. "The others . . ."

The smell didn't hit Ingo until they stood before the parachute hatch while the uninjured pilot hosed down the fuselage with a stream of white, foaming liquid—a smell at once alien and obscenely familiar. The eastern wind whipped it away with the smoke, but not fast enough. They struggled with the hatch, which seemed to have fused shut from the fire. Finally Bloom, in a paroxysm of frustration, threw his body against the metal surface and the panel crunched inward. The pilot gave the handle a vicious yank, and the door broke free.

Bloom moved up into the opening. With a strangled cry, the pilot stumbled back, right into Ingo, who caught him when his body went slack. The stench was overpowering. Ingo fought the urge to vomit as he eased the pilot to the ground, then stepped over to join Bloom. The Haganah man had turned away; he appeared to be staring at the moon.

"They're all dead," Bloom said. In these words, simple but uttered with deliberate weight, you could hear the memory of the Great War, and you could see in his weary stance a man who'd known his share of fallen comrades. The dozen-plus souls in the scorched plane took their place in a column that already stretched long.

Ingo made himself look; he wasn't sure why. Observing, bearing witness, seemed to be what he was meant to do. His eyes moved from one corpse to the next, and he thought how strange it was that each had stiffened in a distinct posture, as though each man had met his death in a unique, personal way. The bodies near the tail were partly burned and hard to recognize. But those farther forward seemed merely to have asphyxiated, suggesting that the plane had become, for a time, a high-altitude gas chamber. Aristotle sat upright, his head tilted forward, as though he were taking a long-needed nap.

Bloom laid a hand on Ingo's shoulder. "Come on," he said, his voice calm, eerily serene. "We'll need help taking care of them."

The first argument came at once. Bloom insisted the dead be decently buried. The local partisans saw no sense in it and were all for blowing up the plane and getting out of there. Their leader was called Shuvek. He was slightly built and had the quick-eyed, feral look of a lesser member of the weasel clan; a stoat, maybe. Of his few English phrases, he relied chiefly on "You come now."

Bloom wouldn't give the man the courtesy of an answer, which Ingo feared might be a mistake. The big noncom led his burial detail out to the landing field armed with handheld entrenching tools—standard GI gear designed for grubbing foxholes. Eddie started after them but Ingo grabbed his sleeve and held him back. Any last shred of innocence, he felt, was a precious thing, a thing to cherish and protect. No doubt the cause was doomed. But after two decades of reading German poetry, Ingo had come to embrace doomed causes as his own, even to find spiritual consolation in them, the more hopelessly doomed the better.

While the diggers went about their grim task, Ingo tried to bridge the language divide. He reasoned that for better or worse they were dependent on the locals, especially now with Aristotle gone. "Verstehen Sie Deutsch?" he asked Shuvek, with a bartender's unassuming geniality— inviting the customer to chat, but not pressing it.

The question didn't strike him as unreasonable. People in this part of the world often did understand German, the traditional language of the educated class. But Shuvek behaved as if Ingo had cast doubt on his paternity, spewing a lengthy torrent of Slovenian and then turning away to glower.

Eddie murmured, "I think he said, he will not speak the tongue of pig-fuckers."

"You understand him?" Ingo gave the boy a hard look, wondering how long he'd planned to keep this amazing ability under his hat.

"Not really. I mean, a little bit, maybe. My grandma, see . . ."

"Your grandma."

"She lives in Poland. Or I mean, she was living in Poland, the last we . . . Anyhow, you know, these Slavic languages. They're all kind of similar, right?"

Ingo had no idea. "Look, can you ask him where we need to go from here? How far we've got to travel before daylight?"

Eddie gave him a helpless shrug. "I don't even speak Polish, not really. My grandma, she talked mostly in Yiddish with a little English thrown in, when we were around. She only used Polish to curse in."

In the days when things were funny, this might have earned a chuckle. But people were dead and the cold wind showed no sign of slacking up, and it was hard to imagine anything ever being funny again.

Kommst nimmermehr aus diesem Wald—Nevermore, quoth Eichendorff, will you come out of this wood. But that was only a poem. And what was poetry worth, in the end? Not a whit compared to young, doomed Eddie. Ingo addressed himself to Shuvek, whose back was still turned. "Do we have far to travel tonight?" he asked in German.

A second partisan muttered something from the shadows. Ingo blinked: the new voice was a woman's. You couldn't have guessed from her rough clothing, the cap pulled down across her forehead, the way she stood with her feet spread and her Russian PPD submachine gun, with its round ammo canister, dangling from her neck like a grotesque medallion.

Shuvek answered her in annoyance, and Ingo looked hopefully at Eddie.

"I'm not sure, I think she asked what's eating him. He told her to shut up. Look, I could be getting this wrong."

Ingo thought it sounded close enough. At this point Harvey Grabsteen wandered over, having given the grave detail a pass. He jabbed a hand toward Shuvek and introduced himself like they were mingling at a cocktail party. Shuvek gave him a hard stare. He repeated, "Grab-stein?"

"Steen," said the gangly man with enthusiasm. "Steen, as in . . . Grab-steen."

Shuvek shook his head and muttered to the woman partisan.

Eddie translated: " 'There, see?' What do you suppose that's about?"

"Grabstein means gravestone," said Ingo. "Sounds like the locals think your name's a bad omen, pal."

"That's absurd," said Grabsteen. "Listen. It's obvious this man understands German. Tell him I am in charge of this expedition, now that we've lost Captain Aristotle. Tell him I represent the organization with which his group has been in contact. Remind him of our agreement. And let him know I expect the full support and cooperation of the forces on the ground. We have an urgent mission to complete, and we've no time to waste on this sort of pantomime."

Mentally, Ingo took a step back and gave Grabsteen the professional once-over. He tried to picture him at a table in the Rusty Ring, speaking in a tone like this to Bernie Fildermann during an especially hectic lunchtime shift. Bernie was the soul of forbearance and would never have responded in kind; no, he would've gone calmly about taking the customer's order and then, carrying the food to the table, lost his footing and dumped the tray in the fellow's lap.

"It might be better," Ingo suggested, "if you waited till Marty and Bloom get back."

"That's not your call, is it?"

"No, but"—regretfully smiling—"if you want a translator . . ."

Shuvek followed this exchange with a gleam in his weasel eyes. Ingo wondered in passing what sort of character traits would help a man stay alive through the Nazi occupation. Warmheartedness, he guessed, was not among them. Perhaps an instinct for sizing other men up, a knack for making timely alliances—coupled with a readiness to break them, should circumstances change. One would do well, Ingo thought, to deal cautiously with this man.

Beware of strangers you meet in the forest: the oldest lesson in the fairy-tale book.

It was five in the morning, local time, before the burial was completed. All the Americans wore a dispirited look. It was hard to imagine they still had a march ahead of them. But the surviving members of the Varian Fry Brigade formed up behind Bloom and headed out on a trail chosen by Shuvek—a tight passage between short, bristly pines better suited to wild boar—with minimal chatter and no complaints, and with Grabsteen's blustering speech still untranslated. Ingo watched for signs of a power struggle between the rabbi and the big, intimidating noncom. He saw none. The challenge came instead from Martina, who scooted up behind Bloom and positioned herself dead-center in the trail, elbowing Grabsteen back into third place. Ingo might have found such fractiousness entertaining had he not known Shuvek was seeing it, too.

They walked until the sky grew light and the stars began to fade. All this time there had been little change in the land around them. The pines pressed in monotonously and the terrain neither rose nor fell. But as dawn arrived and the first yellow beams touched the boughs in this stunted woodland—the oldest trees no taller than Ingo could have hurled his weapon—it became clear that they were moving parallel to a gorge whose edges were so sharp it looked like something hacked out by a giant's sword. The landscape was starkly drawn with a narrow palette of colors: dark green of pines and leathery ferns, umber-red where rock faces showed through a thin coverlet of soil, and the unearthly blue of an empty, comfortless sky.

You could believe the world was vast. You could believe there was within it the possibility of escape, independence, sanctuary. Ingo knew better. He knew, from his own life's journey, that the world was finite and confining. What you thought was wilderness was only a walled garden. Every vista was artfully contrived. Each noble tree, each blade of grass and tuft of moss had been placed there in accord with some grand, unknowable design. You trod a path that wound back upon itself, repeating the same actions, meeting the same people and suffering the same disappointments over and over again. Even your mistakes were repetitious; you never did more than retrace the calamitous footsteps of your forebears.

This war was a new thing only in the sense that with practice and growing expertise, the process of destruction had become more efficient, the
mechanisms of death more dependable. Apart from that, the mortal agonies of the Third Reich were only the fall of the House of Burgundy all
over again. Heroes and villains would be, at the end, not only united in
death but nearly indistinguishable, like the bodies in the airplane. Those
limbs tangled together there, did they represent some final struggle or a
farewell embrace? Was it hatred that drove men to murder or was it an
excess of intimacy, the despair of men trapped behind the same wall? Did
the Aryan strike down the Jew because he found him strange, a despised
and alien thing? Or because he knew him only too well, from having
roamed the garden together, having trod the same path side by side—
knew him as intimately as one knows a brother or a lover?

The hike ended finally an hour past daybreak. They had reached a spot
where the tree cover thickened, pines mixing with taller spruce.

"Here we wait for dark," declared Shuvek in English. "You rest now."

The local partisans did not, however, seem inclined to rest themselves,
at least not yet. A pair of them moved into positions up and down the trail
while a third—the woman—hovered near the Americans, close enough to
eavesdrop on their conversations. Ingo guessed it was prudent to assume
she understood English. Shuvek headed off through the trees and after a
quarter-hour was still gone. It was a relief not to feel those weasel eyes
boring into you, yet Ingo felt equally troubled by the man's unexplained
absence.

The Yanks settled in to their makeshift camp. Stu and Eddie collected
fallen branches and kindled a small fire. Over this they set about boiling
water for coffee and heating up tins of processed meat. The woman partisan glared at them and looked nervously at the sky, but Ingo couldn't tell
whether this represented a genuine fear of overflying aircraft or a condi-
tioned response brought on by years of running and hiding from every
shadow.

"Ain't this grand?" said Stu, leaning back with a hunk of Spam speared
on his bayonet. "Clean air, tasty food, good company—and no dishes to
wash."

Ingo sidled over to where Martina, Bloom and Grabsteen were huddled
around the charred remnants of a map. It looked like the one Ingo had
seen before, with its green and white terrain markings, the jagged scar of
the Polish border.

"There's no way to tell how far anything is," Grabsteen complained.

"It's not far," said Bloom. "Your little finger is about twenty kilometers long. That's an easy day's hike, even in this country. Most days you could make thirty. If you really pushed it, you could be in Auschwitz by next week."

Grabsteen looked affronted, as though this were an actual suggestion. Ingo heard a smirk beside him and turned to see Timo standing there. The Serb appeared very relaxed, in his natural element. But then he'd looked the same manning a taxi on the Anacostia riverfront and shuttling supplies to a Maryland chicken farm. The man was at home everywhere. Which made him nearly the inverse of Ingo, who was at home nowhere at all. Or at any rate, nowhere you could get to in 1944.

If you wanted proof of how small and tangled the world was, Ingo thought, look no further than Timo. Who had somehow, courtesy of Earnest's Hackney Service, made his way from the Balkans to a side street off Dupont Circle, thence to the cold, empty heart of Europe. What sort of pattern could you find in this? Yet there must be some pattern, as there was in all Creation. Even if, at the bottom of it all, lay God's own flaming madness, *Flammenwahnsinn,* just as Heine suspected.

As the morning grew warmer and the Americans finished eating and smoking, a kind of moral stupor set in. The awful events of the night seemed to fade in the sunlight. People unrolled sleeping bags or stretched out wherever they happened to be. Before long most of them were dozing. Ingo sat for a while looking down at Eddie, whose dark hair had fallen across one eye, whose arms were crossed and body folded into a childlike bundle, oblivious. He envied the kid not so much his youth as his ability to just *be* there, to fit in, to float with the current instead of kicking and sputtering against it. Finally he sighed and turned away.

He was exhausted, but could not relax. Perhaps the morning light disturbed him. It seemed unusually harsh, even filtered by a canopy of evergreens. It was like the unsparing light of a public locker room, a merciless illumination in which everything was revealed and nothing looked good.

Restless, he stood and stretched his limbs. The woman partisan threw a catlike glance in his direction. He resented her, standing there like a snoop. So he stepped out of her field of vision, losing himself among the trees— walking with no destination in mind, just needing time to himself. Time and space. A return, however fleeting, to his accustomed state of solitude and secrecy, the nearest thing he had now to a homeland.

Alone in the woods. It felt oddly familiar, as if he'd been here before. His muscles relaxed. He was immensely weary yet also alert, his senses sharpened, his breathing quiet and slow. After a minute or two he stopped walking and only stood there, inhaling the autumn morning, the smell of fallen needles on damp earth, the sharp upland air. He closed his eyes and listened to the birds quarreling in the treetops, red squirrels chasing each other from branch to branch, a rumor of larger game far off. After an uncertain time he heard a different, stealthier sound. Human feet. Boots mashing the undergrowth, moving quickly in his direction. Ingo touched his Schmeisser but he felt no sense of threat. He was on home ground; he need only hold his position.

Out of the trees stepped Shuvek. The partisan saw Ingo and stopped. His eyes moved down to the gun and back up again. He raised his hands slowly, palms open. For a few moments the two men stood there appraising each other.

"You're the one, aren't you?" Shuvek finally said, in clear though thickly regional German. "The one the Fox asked for."

Ingo's mouth opened in surprise, but before he could speak the surprise evaporated. A tumbler fell; a puzzle piece dropped into place.

Shuvek smiled. Not a pleasant smile nor a friendly one; still there was something disarming about it, a texture of sincerity. "They said we should expect someone who looked like a German pretending to be a Yank. *That* was some riddle, I thought. Then you showed up."

He reached around for something on his back. He stopped when Ingo leveled the gun at him.

"No trouble, Kamarad," he said, with the same smile. "I'm only following instructions. Here, I've got something for you. I'll go as slowly as you like. You can see I am not armed."

He took off a little rucksack and tossed it lightly in Ingo's direction. It landed softly, like a moccasin. Ingo kept his eye on Shuvek while he bent to pick it up. In the sack was a set of clothing. Ingo shook it out, letting the pieces fall to the ground.

"That's good," said Shuvek. "Dirty it up a bit. It'll look more natural."

It was a German army uniform, greenish gray, bearing a sergeant's sleeve insignia and, at the collar, the chevron of the Waffen-SS. "What the hell is this?" said Ingo.

"It's for you to put on. Not now. Later. Soon."

Ingo glared at the man. He wanted an explanation and didn't want to dig for it.

Shuvek gave a shrug. "Like I said, I only follow instructions. You've come to see the Fox, but that's not so easy to arrange. Not at this stage. The front is collapsing, you know. The Germans are falling back. For them, that means less territory to patrol. Where you're going, it's thick with blackshirts—I'm talking about regular SS, not the lousy *Hilfi*. It's a question of how to hide an elephant. You know how to hide an elephant, don't you?"

"In case you hadn't noticed," said Ingo, "I haven't come alone. Do you have uniforms for all of us? You think you can hide a herd of elephants?"

Shuvek shook his head. "Your companions can't be trusted. Not all of them. Something is wrong there, I am not sure what. The safest thing is to get you away. I was planning to wait a couple of days, watch how things played out. But now . . . well, you've wandered off on your own. It's an opportunity. We ought to take it."

"No." Ingo tightened his grip on the gun. "I'm not going anywhere without the others. Anyway, this whole business smells fishy."

"Yes, I'm sure it does," said Shuvek. "Look in the breast pocket there, you'll find something to convince you."

Doubtful but intrigued, Ingo plucked up the jacket, which looked about the right size for him, and examined it awkwardly by touch while keeping his eye on Shuvek. After a bit of fumbling his fingertips brushed a lump of paper.

He risked letting go of the Schmeisser for a moment, extracting the paper, unfolding it. Shuvek kept still; only his eyes skittled this way and that, making sure the two of them were alone.

The paper was thick, like parchment, and roughly as wide as two hands laid together. It seemed to have been torn out of a book. On it was an artful pen-and-ink sketch of a flower: bloom, leaf, stem and seed head, all rendered in precise, botanically exact detail. The drawing was labeled *Gentiana poetica* and signed *Anton Krolow*, 13. Sept. 1929.

After several seconds, Ingo remembered to let out his breath.

Shuvek watched him dispassionately. "They said it would mean something to you." He waited a couple of seconds and said, "Are you ready to come now? It's best if we leave while the others are asleep. Don't worry— I've ordered Petra not to harm anyone. She won't disobey, though to be honest, she doesn't care much for Jews. She blames them for all this trouble." He gave a bitter laugh, perhaps at the idea that this trouble, this all-devouring catastrophe, could be blamed on anyone in particular. It had simply come in the manner of all misfortune, storms and invasions, malign government, mortal illness, faithless women.

Ingo paid him no attention. He folded the paper as lightly as possible, this blue flower whose petals would shatter at the merest touch.

★   ★   ★

They reached the guerrilla encampment by nightfall, just as the first pale stars were coming out. It was like a tiny village, a dozen rough but sturdily made structures crammed between boulders and tree trunks beside a racing, icy-looking stream. A wooden pen held chickens and a shed housed a blacksmith-cum-armorer. There was such a fantastical air about the place that Ingo felt like a character in an adventure novel, a tale of wilderness survival.

The guerrillas turned out en masse at their arrival. There were fifty at least, and for the most part they fit their surroundings like the wood-gnomes of German folklore, furtive creatures who dart among the ferns and toadstools of the forest floor, unglimpsed by all but the keenest eye. Only a few stood out: children so tiny they might have been born here in the forest, and one old woman so bent and shriveled she looked like a *Hexe* who survived by purely magical means, dispensing strange herbal reme-dies along with the occasional curse. Most of the adults, men and women alike, carried weapons as naturally as farmers go about with the imple-ments of their livelihood. They dressed like Gypsies in all manner of cloth-ing, layer upon layer, nothing matching anything else. As Shuvek and Ingo came among them they pressed in close, and Ingo felt hands running over his fatigues, fingers touching the smooth American fabric. It was as though the partisans needed to assure themselves he was a real human being and not some trick of the forest, a dangerous Black Elf in disguise.

Shuvek steered him toward one of the crude huts and under its low doorway into a squarish chamber, lit by a fire in a small stone hearth and by the chilly gray light of dusk that drifted through a window facing the stream. Here, on a stool by the fire, a man sat calmly, as if he were await-ing them. He was gaunt and his face was lined, but his hair was still yellow. Ingo guessed he was no older than himself.

In German, Shuvek said, "This is the one. His name is Müller."

Ingo did not suppose the error was great enough to need correcting. His name was indeed Müller, or anyway it would have been had not his grandfather, fresh off the boat, chosen to Americanize it.

"Müller," the man on the stool repeated. "Well, that's easy enough." Shuvek nodded.

Ingo was mystified; this man spoke *Hochdeutsch* with only a trace of Eastern inflection. He had the air of a Sudeten aristocrat, an ethnic Ger-man in a land of Slavs, who instead of heeding "the call of the blood" had chosen to go native.

"And the uniform?" the man said.

"Haven't tried it," said Shuvek. "I'd say it's about right, though."

They looked Ingo up and down like a tailor's dummy.

"He hasn't slept," Shuvek said.

The man nodded. He rose from the stool and came closer, staring Ingo in the eye. "God help you," he said after a couple of moments. He spoke simply, as though he meant this and nothing more. In the same straightforward tone he added, "I'll have someone bring hot water. A good bath will help you rest tonight. Tomorrow . . ."

He gave a little nod, as if he were alluding to a well-known truism—*Tomorrow is another day* or something of that kind. Then he left the hut and Ingo heard him speaking outside in the local tongue, presumably giving instructions about water.

When he dragged himself an hour later, groggy with fatigue, out of the old-fashioned washtub, his muscles felt like they'd dissolved. He must have dozed off because the water had turned tepid. The day's long walk had drained more than just his energy. By the dancing firelight, shadowy figures flitted at the borders of his vision.

He dried off as best he could on a ragged towel no bigger than a washcloth. Then he discovered his clothing was gone. In its place, neatly folded on a stool, was the German uniform. *Feldgrau,* field-gray, with a tinge of green, its color was roughly that of the underside of a white-oak leaf.

"Try it on." Shuvek addressed him from a dark corner of the room.

"What happened to my fatigues? There were things in those pockets, personal things."

"You'll find it all right there." He pointed to where Ingo's belongings had been arranged beside a stack of threadbare blankets with his bedroll on top. Shuvek's small eyes glistened out of the shadows. "If that uniform needs altering, we'll have it taken care of tonight. So you will be all ready in the morning. Ein ganz guter Soldat."

Ingo, remembering how the people in the encampment had run their hands over his clothing, imagined pieces of it distributed among favored members of the group. Irritated, he said, "What happens tomorrow? What is it I have to be ready for?"

"Tomorrow?" said Shuvek, as if the word was strange to him. He sat forward, bringing his face into the firelight. "Forget tomorrow. There is no tomorrow. There is no today. Today is nothing but a dream. The only thing real is yesterday, last evening, just before we all fell asleep. Try to remember that—the chair you were sitting in, the book you were reading. Perhaps you'll wake again, and there you'll be, right where you left off. Your family around you. Everyone laughing. And from there, your story goes on."

BETWEEN TWO WORLDS

Martina sat on a big rock at the edge of a river gorge and cast an eye glumly over what was left of the Varian Fry Brigade. She tried to imagine how Ingo would see them, what Ingo would think. Pigheaded and cynical and politically troglodytic he may be, but he was also disconcertingly observant, and he had a habit, in down-to-earth matters, of turning out to be right.

For starters, he'd make some crack about Grabsteen. How foppish the man looked in his custom-tailored khakis, which must have been the product of some Burbank costume shop, tapered at the waist and fitted out with Edwardian epaulets. And how he strutted like a martinet, lecturing the stone-faced partisan gal on the *comprehensive agreement that exists between our respective parent organizations.* As if such jargon had any meaning at all in the Tatry Mountains.

And surely he'd be in full-blown I-told-you-so mode over the collapse of the Brigade's best-laid plans. Back on the Eastern Shore—no, before that, a September evening in Martina's apartment in Cleveland Park, red neon spelling U-P-T-O-W-N one letter at a time outside the window—he had ticked off a laundry list of reasons why the plan was botched from the start. His analysis, typically thorough, began with the implausibility of the whole *casus belli*—the existence of a document, a piece of paper, for God's sake, so historically precious it was worth staking dozens of lives on—and proceeded from there.

What exactly, Ingo had wanted to know, is this Agudas Israel Worldwide? Are they mixed up with those terrorists in Palestine, setting off bombs at the King David Hotel and attacking British administrators in the streets? Are they frustrated actors, looking for a war movie to star in? Or worst of all, are they exactly what they appear to be: a fuzzy-headed but well-funded rabble of Roosevelt Jews, all worked up about something they read last week in the back pages of the *Times* and determined to, quote, do something—never mind what, we'll figure that out as we go along—about these awful Nazis who are even less pleasant, we now suspect, than Republicans?

He hadn't stopped there. Who exactly will this team of guerrillas consist of? Great War retreads? Or do you intend to recruit a bunch of 4-Fs and COs and *vin-de-pays*-sipping Hemingway fans, bundle them in jumpsuits and drop them behind German lines, armed with a compass and a box of matches and a secret decoder ring?

By the time he shut up, even Martina was hopeless. Martina for whom hope was a substitute for religion—hope in the warm, tolerant future envisioned by Eleanor in her happier moods, hope as sung between the lines by melancholy Ella, hope as dispensed by those plucky USO gals high-stepping for boys at the front whose numbers might be up tomorrow. Without hope, how could you carry on?

Which brought her now, in circular fashion, to the deepest mystery of the whole affair. If Ingo was so damned sure the Varian Fry Brigade was destined to go the way of the *Hindenburg,* why in God's name had he hopped on board?

To ask such a question was to answer it.

Martina closed her eyes. For an instant, Slovensky Raj was swept away. Nineteen forty-four dissolved, and in its place was a different time, another place—a world so different it seemed to have no relation to this one, not a single point of contact, no path from one to the other.

What was that novel, so popular back then, that Ingo had gone on about? *The Man Who Walked Between Two Worlds?* Something like that. Martina never read it. She wasn't reading much at the time, not even Spengler, not even Freud. Now she regretted it, but regret was the least of what she felt when she thought about those times, the very least. The chief thing was wonder—disbelief, actually—that such a time and a place had ever been. And such a Marty. Such an Ingo.

Were they really better people in those days? She believed they were. Marty herself had been so . . . so open, so unafraid, so hungry for new experiences. She hadn't learned to substitute political engagement for genuine human passion. And Ingo hadn't yet forgotten how to feel; the mask he wore was still loose enough that his true face could now and again be glimpsed behind it. Even Butler, as calculating and cold-blooded as he was, still had a core of genuine belief—if not in world Communism, at least in himself, his sacred vocation as an artist.

And the German boy, Hagen—he'd been fired by a sort of idealism that was transparently heartfelt. It seemed reprehensible now, but only because you knew what it had led to. At the time, in that context, it seemed genuine enough. Like the rest of us, Hagen thought he had found a new world, a new kind of person to be.

As to Isaac . . . well. Who really knew what Isaac had ever been, then or now?

So of course, she perfectly understood—there was not the slightest doubt—why Ingo had come here, and why he was willing to throw his life away, if that's what it came to.

"Are you *listening?*" shouted Harvey Grabsteen. Not to Marty, as it turned out. But his high-pitched voice jolted her back to the present, the notably less-real-seeming world of 1944.

"Shuvek will come soon," was all the woman partisan would say. It might have been the only English she knew.

Martina shook her head. Slovensky Raj reassembled itself before her, along with its unlikely inhabitants: A dejected crew of would-be guerrillas lolling at the edge of an ancient, shadowed and dangerous forest. A blank-faced woman with Slavic cheekbones and a Russian PPD. A Serbian man with brown eyes to die for and terrible teeth. A skinny kid from Charlottesville. A wiseguy from St. Louis. A hulking Great War vet with his jaw clamped and his eyes staring at nothing, waiting for the next battle.

"I said, *Are you listening?*" Grabsteen snapped, turning in exasperation to the wider audience. "I am trying to get this woman here to tell us where they've taken Miller. Also whether she intends to lead us where *we* need to go. Because otherwise, I'm determined to press on, with or without local support. We'll make new arrangements as we go. I've got plenty of Swiss francs. I'm sure we'll have no lack of possibilities."

"Where do you think you are?" said the big noncom, Bloom. "Strolling around some studio back lot? Trying to clinch a production deal?"

Grabsteen wheeled on him. "No. I believe I am—I believe we all are— performing a *mitzvah,* a holy task that's been given us to fulfill. You can take me for a fool or a bully or a soulless Hollywood shill, whatever you like. But I'm willing to use whatever means are at my disposal to get this job done. Surely all of you would agree that our first duty is to history, to a full and just accounting of the crime that has been perpetrated against our people. If any step we take brings us nearer to that, then it's not only justified, it's morally necessary. More than this, I don't think we should say in front of an outsider."

Bloom bristled. "You can pickle the sermon, Rabbi. I don't need anyone to tell me what I'm doing here."

Martina let them argue. Grabsteen's *mitzvah,* not so long ago the driving obsession of her life, seemed a fool's errand now, a snipe hunt. Where *has* Ingo gone? she wondered for the hundredth time. Walking between two worlds, she supposed. The warm and the cold. The first in color, like the paintings on the wall at the Rusty Ring; the second black-and-white, like wartime newsreels. The first true. The second preposterous, nightmarish, untenable.

It was clear enough why Ingo had come here. Because somewhere in the dark heart of Europe, hidden deep in the forest, was a secret crack in the wall of time, a passage from one world to the other. Martina hoped he would find it. And she yearned to follow him. She wished they could be together again, all of them, if only for a little while—an afternoon, an hour—in that warm green place.

*   *   *

AUGUST 1929

Say what you will about fairy-tale castles. For Martina's money they were drafty and dark and every little noise echoed like crazy and just try finding a bathroom in the middle of the night.

None of which was to say she was immune to the charms of the Leuchtenburg. No: there was a beauty to this old pile of rocks, even a kind of romance, for those of susceptible disposition. She glanced pointedly at Ingo, who stood leafing through the guestbook on the other side of what once had been some margrave's private chapel. The room doubled now as a miniature museum, where a selection of the castle's surviving artworks was displayed, and as an office for the youth hostel that had sprung up in one of the less ruined wings. Ingo was smiling to himself.

"What are you smirking about?"

He looked up, as though surprised to find her there. "Nothing, really. Some of these entries, they're just so . . ."

"So?"

"So *German.* Listen to this one, it's a poem by 'Two Mädlein from Leipzig,' from back in May:

> *We are young, the world is open,*
> *Oh you beautiful wide world!*

All our longing and desire
Lies in yonder wood and field.

"And here's one from a couple of weeks ago, must've been some guy on his way to the Jugendtag. He writes in this really dark Gothic. 'Your best weapon will always be the word: *Ich will.*' "

"That's two words," said Martina.

"Exactly."

She looked him over. He had become strange to her, these last few days. Ever since the Höhe Meissner. Being in Germany seemed to bring out some hidden aspect of his temperament. But that was ridiculous; the whole point of Ingo, the safe and boring kid next door, was that he *had* no hidden aspects. That is what Martina's parents had counted on, and what, she now realized, she'd been counting on as well. So much for the eternal verities.

Ingo fished out his pocket watch—an affectation acquired, she believed, from a photograph of Thomas Mann—and said, "I guess I better be going."

"Going where?"

He paused a moment, as if deciding whether to divulge a great secret. "Orchid hunting."

"*What?*"

To be surprised by Ingo was doubly surprising, because he'd always been so predictable. What had changed? It wasn't just the clothes. Though come to think of it, where *had* these new hiking shorts come from, and this troubadour's tunic? No, his skin had taken on a healthy sort of glow, and his face looked thinner, like he'd finally shed some of that baby fat. His eyes shone with an unfamiliar light, and he carried himself with a new sort of assurance.

Martina crossed the room; she gave him a companionable jab on the arm. "Since when did you become such an avid naturalist?"

He turned his head away, feigning a sudden interest in a statue of Saint Sebastian, commissioned four hundred years ago on account of his reputation as a defender against the plague. The martyr was scantily clothed and naturalistically rendered. "There's nothing wrong," Ingo said lightly, "with taking an interest in one's surroundings. Is there?"

"I didn't say—"

"For example." Staring through her, eyes alight. "Did you know, thirty-eight species of wild orchids have been identified in the countryside around Jena? At least fifteen can be found near the Leuchtenburg. And not only orchids. The Saale Valley marks the northernmost spot in Europe where a number of plant species naturally occur. It's because of the climatic influence of the south-facing sandstone outcrops. Crocuses bloom here in February."

Martina was at a loss. She personally didn't know a crocus from a croquet hoop, and Ingo's sudden interest in such things left her modestly flabbergasted. Also, admit it, left out. "Did it occur to you that *I* might like to go orchid hunting?"

His expression plainly said that it had not. "Do you really want to go crawling around in the woods looking for tiny flowers that probably aren't even in bloom?"

"No, of course not. But I would like to do *something*." Her voice sounded sniffly, even to herself.

"Why not just go out and get some fresh air?"

"I've had nothing but fresh air. I'd like to breathe some exhaust fumes, just to remember what century I'm in."

"You could see what Isaac's up to."

"Isaac? That's a laugh. What, is it afternoon already?"

"Or go help out in the woodshop. Or the kitchen. There's always plenty to do."

"Yeah? How come I don't see *you* volunteering to scrub pots and sweep sawdust? What have you been doing with yourself? You take off in the morning and I don't see you till dinnertime."

Under questioning, his manner became twitchy. But all he said was: "Orchid hunting."

"Yeah, right. It wouldn't surprise me if you had a Mädlein out there somewhere."

His ears reddened. She supposed it was unfair to tease him. Poor Ingo.

That afternoon it rained. You could see the storm approaching, purplish clouds unrolling from the northeast. A change came into the air, a queer sort of inverse pressure, forceful emptiness. The light grew otherworldly, streaming sideways as though from a parallel dimension, casting trees into bright relief against the dark sky. Martina, who'd never noticed such things before, wondered if this was an early symptom of Romanticism.

Isaac appeared as usual around two p.m., padding into the third-floor chamber where Martina sat before a tall window watching the weather change. Somebody else's clothing drooped from his bony frame like laundry hung out to dry. He approached sleepily, toting an oversized mug.

Martina smiled at him like he was a little brother. Not her own, somebody else's, an object of entertainment and frequent annoyance.

"What's going on?" he asked, his voice a teenage croak.

"It's about to rain. Look."

He cocked an eye toward the window. "It rains all the time in Germany."

"It rains everywhere."

"Nah, it's different here."

"How?"

He shrugged. "It feels different. You get soaked and you don't dry out. Everything turns gray. People get cranky."

Outside, in the castle close, there was an orderly sort of commotion. Frau Möhring, the tirelessly cheerful hostel *Mutter*, directed her gang of kitchen helpers in a rapid harvest of vegetables from the courtyard garden. Most of the couple dozen kids currently bunking here were *Arbeiterjugend*, and they took the "worker" part seriously. Martina felt tired just looking at them. Their little baskets filled rapidly with produce.

God, she thought—cabbage soup again. All these pure-bodied young Germans. No meat, no drink, no polluted air, no unwholesome jazz music. She knew there was a point to it, but what this might be continued to elude her.

A long rumble of thunder shuddered through the castle and came bouncing off a nearby cliff—a place called the Dohlenstein, where the young Germans liked to take their clothes off and lie in what passed for a summer sun. Martina gave an involuntary shudder.

"Here," said Isaac, offering his mug. "Want some of this? It's elderberry, I think."

"No"—almost snapping at him.

"See what I'm talking about?" He gave her a drowsy smile.

"I'm sorry. I'm getting a little stir-crazy. You feel like doing something?"

"Like what?"

"I don't know. Go out, get rained on. Hike to Seitenroda. I'm starting to feel like Rapunzel in here."

Isaac gave an appreciative smirk. "I'm supposed to be laying low, remember? Käthe's orders."

Martina remembered. It was why they'd come here, after his run-in with the Jungdo. Ingo had sprung for train fare to Jena—Isaac being clearly in no shape to walk halfway across Germany—and Käthe had drawn a map from there to the Leuchtenburg. *Go to ground for a while,* she told Isaac. *Lie low, but keep your nose to the wind. Like a clever little fox.*

When the first drops arrived—and not until then—there was a bustle through the arch-covered gateway as the hostel guests ran indoors. Martina watched for Ingo but he didn't appear. The afternoon darkened to a false twilight and the castle roof began to leak in too many places to count. For all its size, the place felt crowded. Every room in the habitable wing had its little cluster of young people plucking lutes or arguing over Nietzsche's unknown god or rehearsing for a performance later of Hofmannsthal's *Death and the Fool*. These German kids seemed to like being crammed together—maybe it was in the nature of Social Democracy— and Isaac settled in among them with his characteristic lack of self-consciousness. An advantage, perhaps, of being essentially homeless. They accepted him as they might an interesting animal, say a pup, suitable for making a mascot of. As for Martina, she was ever more aware of her status as an outsider: the meat-eating, crow-haired, brashly spoken and politically innocent foreigner.

Vaguely unsettled, as though niggled by foreboding, she paced from one paneled and tapestry-hung chamber to the next, blinking at the occasional flare of lightning. Eventually she found herself in a stairwell leading up through a circular turret called, for historical reasons unknown to her, the Veil Tower. Half a dozen boys too young for *Gymnasium* raced one another up and down winding steps so tall as to guarantee knee strain, all the while shrieking with the excitement of imaginary battle. Martina climbed until they were well below her. Their voices, high-pitched and ecstatic, floated upward blurred by masonry into a diffuse trill, like a boys choir misbehaving in a cathedral. From the uppermost story, perhaps sixty feet above the ground, narrow paneless slots through the enormously thick walls gave fragmented views of the countryside.

The heart of the storm had already passed to the west; the sky above the Saale was starting to brighten. A thin blanket of fog lay across the valley like cotton, the green of summer soaking through. The view from each cannon-slot was different, but all were lovely and each as implausible as the next—surely no landscape had looked this way for at least a hundred years. These Germans, so gullible, to believe any of it was real.

Out of the mist, two riders materialized, guiding their mounts up the old dirt lane beside the river. Martina watched them in suspended disbelief. As they came nearer, she made them out to be male, one older and larger of frame than the other. The latter was very pale beneath a wet, drooping hat, but he rode with assurance, like someone born to the saddle. The other was bareheaded and dark-haired and sat stiffly on his

horse as though trying to impress someone—a pompous knight cantering
onto the tournament field, accompanied by his squire. Only of course, in a
proper legend, it is the golden-haired boy who bears the mark of destiny.

Now would be the moment. If Martina had long golden tresses, this
was her cue to send them cascading from the turret. Improvising in haste,
she pawed through her pockets and discovered Käthe's crumpled map. She
folded this sloppily into a paper airplane, which on its maiden flight tumbled into a fatal nosedive. Martina watched with dismay as it spiraled
down the face of the tower toward a fringe of hawthorn at the base of the
wall.

Just before it vanished, the pale boy turned and pointed. You could see
his mouth move. His companion turned to look, but by that time the airplane was gone. Slowly the dark-haired stranger raised his head, his eyes
moving up the tower until they reached Martina's window. She felt like an
idiot. It was too late: he'd seen her, and now raised a hand to give her a
little wave. Even from this distance you could not mistake the irony in the
gesture. Then he wrestled his horse sideways and made for the castle gate.

His name was Samuel Butler Randolph—the Third, if you please. An
American expatriate, a writer, and a Communist. Martina had never met
any of these things before. Nor had she met anybody quite so . . . well, she
couldn't make up her mind whether he was supremely self-confident or
insufferably stuck-up. A bit of both, she thought. And terribly handsome,
so handsome it seemed almost dangerous.

She worried that her Romantic symptoms were growing rapidly more
acute. If she wasn't careful, she'd end up throwing off her clothes and sipping herbal infusions and crooning *"Mein Vater war ein Wandermann"* like
all the rest of them. Well, who knew? Maybe she'd enjoy it. She was enjoying this little game of Fair Damsel and Handsome Prince.

It did not take long for the dark-haired man to find her. She waited there
in the tower while he charmed his way past Frau Möhring and then
slashed brazenly through the castle's indolent defenders. As he surmounted the last steps, the blond boy close on his heels, he greeted her, to
her considerable surprise, in English.

"I know you're not a Kraut," he said, his voice pitched low and so
inflected as to suggest that the whole thing was some urbane joke. "If you
were, you'd know how to build a proper airplane. What are you, a
Spaniard? A tempestuous Italian? Surely not a Yank?"

Even in her slightly addled state she guessed that he knew the answer.

Otherwise, why was he talking in English? She allowed her attention to wander from his broad shoulders to his squared-off jaw, coming to rest upon a pair of eyes that seemed both world-weary and alert, even somehow jumpy, though they didn't stray long from her own. "I loved the entrance," she told him. Going for a flip, flapperish routine: a gin-sipping native of East Egg fetched up in a castle in Thuringia.

He acknowledged this with the briefest of bows. The horses, he explained, were a matter of simple expediency. "I would have rented an automobile, but there didn't seem to be any to spare in Kassel. Maybe I should've just bought one, it would've been a lot faster."

"What's the hurry, Sam?" Talking to this man—how old would you say he was, twenty-four? twenty-five?—she felt like an actress in some *avant-garde* play whose every line was improvised, and whose plot might therefore take any number of dizzying turns.

"Please, call me Butler." His voice was soft and deep, like a lion's purr. "There isn't any hurry. I simply prefer to waste as little time as possible *en passant.*"

"*En passant* to where?"

"Oh, you know . . . just hunting around."

Martina chose this moment to glance aside at the ghost-pale boy who had sauntered over to a window, through which he stared motionless as a sentry. His eyes were ice-blue, his features unexpressive. What is *this* one, now, she wondered, and why is he traveling with Samuel Butler Randolph III? What nefarious doings are afoot here? Something frightfully scandalous, she hoped. "Hunting?" she prompted.

"For a story," Butler said amiably. He stretched back against the tower wall, flattening his spine on the aged limestone. It made him look even taller. The rain had stopped outside but continued to drip from his hair and clothing.

She ought to have pressed him a little harder. But the mystery surrounding this handsome stranger was not without its appeal. There was, too, the relief of having an American to banter with. And so before long Martina found herself answering Butler's questions, at length and unguardedly, instead of asking her own. His attention flattered her. Not until much later did she pause to reflect that he seemed especially happy to be told about her companions, Ingo and Isaac. He was curious as well about the Socialist Worker Youth, and how the whole bunch of them had gotten acquainted, and what, by the by, brings you out here in the sticks to—what do they call this place, the Leuchtenburg? All this as though he were jotting down notes for future reference. Martina made nothing of it, assuming that Butler found her comments informative, her opinions sharp and well formed, her delivery amusing. Hardy-har-har.

"So this friend of yours," he said, "this Ingo. Odd name, isn't it? German-American, I suppose. Is he a *rough* sort of fellow, then? Likes to throw down some beers and bash around a bit?"

"*Ingo?*" She couldn't suppress a titter. She felt Butler's stare grow heavier. "No, he's not really the bash-around type."

"How would you describe him? Physically strong but slow to anger? Formidable when roused?"

"Not exactly."

"You smile. Is there something I'm missing?"

He was smiling, too. But there was something private about that smile, like you were seeing it through a window, a face fleetingly glimpsed in the first-class car of a passing train.

From the cannon-slot, the German boy uttered a soft syllable. "Da." His whole frame had become taut. He stared down into the close of the castle, where people were once more venturing out. "Da ist er," he said. "Das Jüdling."

To Martina, this didn't sound good. She stuck her head out the next window over and craned her neck to survey the open space, hemmed by the wings of the building and partly occluded by an old tree. At the center was a giant chessboard formed by alternate patches of green and silver creeping thyme clipped mercilessly into squares, its pieces artfully carved from heavy logs. A crowd had gathered to watch a match that had started before the storm and now resumed. Black's position looked hopeless, though the onlookers were free with suggestions. Among the kibitzers, half hidden by a waist-high bishop, was Isaac.

"You're sure that's him?" said Butler. No more lion's purr, the voice was all business.

"Yes, this is the same little Jew," said the German boy in stiff but well-spoken classroom English. "You can see, he shows bruises still."

"Okay," said Butler, "I'm going down there."

Now, the notebook. Martina blanched. Who was he? What had she told him? His face had taken on a hawkish look. She felt vulnerable, almost violated, yet even this—as she would later reflect—was far from unpleasurable.

Should she call out to Isaac? Call out what, though? Butler Randolph might not be what he seemed, but he surely was no right-wing bullyboy looking for heads to smash. And the little German: no worry there. Yet even as these thoughts ran through her head, she glanced down to see Isaac staring up at the Veil Tower, his eyes locked uncannily on the window where the blond boy stood. The pair of them stood that way for several moments, bracketed, motionless, as though caught together in a private time-stream. Butler meanwhile bounded to the stairwell and *pfft,* he was gone.

Martina turned to the German kid. His face was cleansed of expression by the cool gray light, like a stone carving worn smooth by centuries of rainfall. "Who are you?" she said. "What do you want with him?"

The boy turned to look at her. He was terribly young, younger than Isaac, yet his calm, controlled manner and his eerie self-possession made him appear grown-up.

"I am not come here," he said, "to make any harm."

"Oh, yeah? What are you doing here then?"

"I am come to warn your friend."

"To warn? Don't you mean threaten?"

The boy retained his composure. "Your friend is in danger. The other one, too, who was there with him. Both are . . . marked out. It is a question of honor. There is a need for . . . I don't know your word, Vergeltung. For my comrades, this is very important. Especially while a foreigner is involved. Even more so, a Jew."

Martina stared at this ghost-pale youth. He seemed sincere, perhaps only because it took some effort to express himself in English. She nodded toward the empty space where Butler had been. "Where does *he* fit in?"

The boy answered readily: "He paid for the horses. He is a Bolshevik, but I believe a man of honor."

Martina doubted it. She preferred her Black Knight fantasy.

When she glanced out the window again, she saw Butler down there in the close, striding heedlessly through the chessboard, ignoring the players' objections, his head scanning the faces. But Isaac was nowhere to be seen. The little fox had given them the slip.

Ingo turned up not long afterward, as Martina was making her way to the dining room. He came bouncing across the wide and gloomy ancestral hallway with its faded portraits and coats-of-arms. The storm had drenched him to the bone, yet he seemed cheerful about it, his face in a healthy flush from the day's outing, the ends of his hair, already drying, bleached straw-yellow by the sun and dangling over his eyes.

Martina started to tell him about the latest arrivals when he gestured with a tan arm and said, "I'd like to introduce a friend. Marty, this is Anton Krolow."

She was surprised, but not overly so. It stood to reason that Ingo would make friends, given his fluency in German and his new habit of rambling around the countryside. This Anton was a pleasant-looking youth, an inch taller than Ingo, lanky and long-haired. Shaking hands with him, she said, "Are you an orchid-hunter, also?"

Anton gave her a perplexed smile.

"His English isn't so good," Ingo explained, then quickly murmured a translation.

Anton responded with an easy laugh. "Ja," he said, "ich bin auch orchid-hunter."

"Anton is really the expert," Ingo said.

Martina felt a curious pang as she watched the two of them. The way they managed to communicate in glances and a few soft phrases, you would have thought they were not new acquaintances but old and intimate friends. Was it jealousy she felt? Was it envy? She thought of dangerous, dark-haired Butler Randolph, imagined him speaking softly in her ear as Anton was murmuring in Ingo's. But that was a different thing, of course. More dangerous and thrilling than simple friendship—more 1929.

"What's for dinner?" said Ingo. "We're both famished."

"Oh, you know, the usual. Frau Möhring's cabbage surprise."

"Herrlich!"

She watched the two boys tramp off into the dining hall, arm-in-arm, like good German comrades. It wasn't fair.

That night they had a bonfire. Young Germany loved its bonfires and this was a noisy one, logs still damp from the rain hissing and popping and bursting into clouds of sparks like tiny fireworks. The whole gang from the castle came out onto the sloping field where it was lit, but as time passed many drifted off into the knee-high grasses and wildflowers. The sky had mostly cleared and the remaining clouds moved with dramatic speed across the face of a waxing moon. Martina moved in slow, widening circles looking for Isaac, someone she knew, anyone to talk to. Near the fire she had been sweating, though now the night air felt chilly and there were goose bumps on her bare arms.

"Gansfleisch," said a voice behind her, deep and filled with latent power.

She turned with a jumble of feelings shaken together like a cocktail at a gin joint.

"German term," said Butler. "Means the same as the English. Here, take this, it'll warm you."

He handed her something dark and heavy, a leather jacket, rich with manly scents with which she yearned to become familiar. His eyes were as dark as the trees. He stood with his back to the fire, whose orange glow limned the fringes of his hair.

"I owe you an explanation," he said.

"An apology, how about. You tricked me. On purpose. I thought you were being friendly. But you were *interviewing* me. All those questions— who was I with, what were we doing, how long we'd been here. I didn't suspect a thing. I *still* don't get what you're up to." She could make out the sparkle of perfect teeth—damn him, he was smiling.

"Who are you angry with?" he asked her. "Me, for making conversation? Or yourself, for being so naïve?"

She raised a hand to slap him but he caught it easily. She was glad he did. He lowered it slowly to her side and, after a couple of moments, relaxed his grip. What did those moments mean?

"I told you," he said in that relaxed, gentlemanly drawl, the oral equivalent of a slouch. "I'm hunting for a story. Think I've found a good one, too. Young Americans abroad, carefree summer vacation, seeing the sights, doing the Jugendtag—then all unawares, they get tangled in German politics. Chance meeting of strangers becomes a collision of worldviews. Ancient hatred erupts. There's treachery, there's violence. But wait, what's this? A new twist: young Deutscher pops up, offers his hand in friendship, only to find himself spurned like an unwanted suitor. Young America is tired of playing by Old World rules—can't tell who the players are, even *with* a scorecard. But 'leave us alone, please' doesn't play in Thuringia. Like a small town really, always bumping against one another, feelings easily bruised. And so we come to what you might call the moment of catharsis—only what does this consist of? A reconciliation among enemies? Does the German break bread with the Jew? Or is this a story of prejudice and betrayal, violence begetting revenge? Either way, it's ripping good, don't you think? Excellent magazine piece, if not more."

Martina was already shaking her head. "Or maybe it's not a story at all. Maybe it's real people's lives that you have no business messing around in."

He accepted this with a nod. "Fair enough. I'd still like to talk to your friends, though, if you can arrange it. Both of them—but the German-American especially intrigues me. A sort of bridging character. One foot in either camp. Next time you see him, I wonder if you'd just let him know—"

"Tell him yourself. He's standing right over there. See, by the fire, next to that tall skinny kid?"

Butler followed her gaze. Martina enjoyed the thought of what Ingo—

the new, self-confident Ingo—would say to this arrogant so-and-so. He'd give Butler hell, she hoped. Somebody ought to.

"*That's* your friend? That's our good pal Ingo?"

Something was wrong here, Martina thought. Butler's tone was sarcastic. He peered at her closely enough that she could make out the unsavory gleam in his eyes.

"You're telling me, that fellow over there is the terror of Frau-Holle-Quell? On whom the Jungdo have sworn bloody vengeance?"

"I guess I am. Sure. Why not?"

Butler laughed. "I noticed him at dinner tonight. Him and his pretty friend. Well—there must be some confusion here. At the very least an exaggeration of facts." In the consequent silence, she formed the impression of someone scratching his earlobe or chewing a pencil, one of those manifestations of inner thought. "But you know, it might play even better this way—not for the *Saturday Evening Post,* of course. Perhaps *The New Yorker.*"

"What are you going on about?"

"My dear," said Butler, taking one of her hands, pulling her toward him until they stood eye-to-eye, moonlight and firelight merging in their faces, "I strongly doubt your friend Ingo could have done what people claim he did. Mauled a bunch of strapping Germans, hauled the sacrificial lamb out of the fire? Great God, woman—he's a raging queer."

A *what?* Martina's mouth was open, ready to argue. But the words never formed in her throat. She felt as though a missing piece had dropped into place—but more than that, a piece whose absence she hadn't even noticed. Suddenly, things made sense that she'd never thought *didn't* make sense. An aspect of Ingo she had assumed was merely dormant or underdeveloped turned out to be alive and kicking after all. Only secret, hidden. Inside-out. Paradoxically, she felt almost no surprise.

Butler chuckled. "Here," tugging gently on her hand, drawing her toward him, "you look rather blanched. Why don't we find a dry place to sit? It's a beautiful summer evening, and I don't expect we'll have too many more of those."

She could not have known that this was to be her last night in the fairy-tale castle. Even afterward she would not remember it that way, but rather as the night of the bonfire or the evening after the rain, when the grass was damp and the moon was huge and yellow and the first kiss of autumn was in the air. She wondered sometimes how Ingo remembered that night, and

Isaac. Because for each of them it was the end of something; and the morning that must come all too soon would be the beginning of something different. It was unusual, she supposed, to be able to date with such precision one of life's great turning-points. But now and again it must happen, and perhaps not infrequently to a group of people at once. Friends, fellow travelers, even strangers thrown together by chance. Rarely, an entire generation.

The morning would be sunny, the treetops east of the castle gleaming like emerald cobblestones, the tile-roofed houses of Seitenroda neatly arranged as toys in a well-run nursery, the River Saale rushing as swift and full as the night's last dream.

The German boy, Hagen von Ewigholz, delivered his warning to Isaac in person over the midday meal, which was Isaac's usual breakfast. *They must know you have come here,* he said, or words to that effect. *I myself could guess where you had gone, and I am only young, so they must know as well, for they are older and more clever than I.* That was how the kid talked, in careful, schoolboy's English. Under other circumstances, it would have had appreciable charm.

Afterward, naturally, there was more talk, too much of it, breaking out finally into open argument. Plans were proposed and rejected and finally settled upon, decisions taken and instantly regretted. There were partings, vows, prophecies, promises, irreverent asides. Embraces and tears and drollery. Butler striding about, giving someone instructions about the horses, counting out mark notes. Anton jotting an entry in the guest book. Isaac giving Frau Möhring the finger. Ingo staring hard at Saint Sebastian, until Martina walked over and touched him on the arm. The look in his eyes then. Hagen in the background, half noticed, spectral, until his abrupt declaration—*I will go with you, I know this area quite well, there are paths I can show you*—taking everyone by surprise. Isaac apologizing and Frau Möhring bestowing forgiveness, as people always would. Käthe arriving from the *Bahnhof* barely in time to bid them farewell. And Martina . . .

But she had no image of herself from that day. No clear memory of what she'd done or said, how she'd felt, what position she'd taken in the long debate over what to do. Already, perhaps, she was torn between the onrushing future and the fast-receding past. When all was said and done, she probably could have stayed forever in that falling-down castle. Leaky roof, cold floors, frightful plumbing and all.

*　　*　　*

Grabsteen's face was red from shouting. The woman partisan, Petra, tried to maintain her air of stoic indifference, but he wasn't making it easy for her. Her fingers slowly tightened around the tommy gun that dangled from her shoulder.

"You must take us to your headquarters," Grabsteen yelled at her. "I demand to see your commander. You must take us *immediately*. And I'm not talking about some little field camp. I'm talking about the place where orders are given. Are you hearing me? If you don't understand English, go fetch the other one. That Shuvek person."

Eddie tried to calm him. "If she doesn't understand English—"

"She *does* understand! Can't you see it? Look at her eyes."

By this time the commotion had attracted the other two partisans, posted as sentries up and down the trail. These men in their ragtag clothing, coats sagging with ammunition and grenades, stood hesitantly at the edge of the encampment. Evidently the task of dealing with the Americans had been assigned to the woman alone.

"Shuvek will come soon" is all she would say.

"That's not good enough," said Grabsteen. "I'm sorry, but we can't afford to wait any longer. Our people are being murdered while we stand here. It's vital that we proceed with our mission, with or without your Shuvek." He glanced at Martina, then away. "And with or without our Miller. Now, I'm going to head up that trail, and I'm going to make for the Polish border. On the way, I intend to find a radio and make contact with . . . some people who can help us."

"That's just crazy," said Bloom.

"Is it? Just a Hollywood stunt, huh? Something only a crazy Jew would think of? Try to take action—to *move*, to *strike*—instead of just, be sensible, don't get excited, just sit there, we'll take care of everything, can't you see the President is a busy man?"

"Save it for your contributors, Rabbi. That crap doesn't flush with me."

"Without Ingo," Martina pointed out, "there is no mission. He's the whole point of it. The only one the Fox will trust—remember? We've been over and over this."

"Indeed." Grabsteen turned his anger on her. "And the more we go over it, the less willing I am to swallow it. This operative, this so-called Fox— nobody's even certain who he is. *You* say he's your friend, but the odds are pretty strong he's not even American. The analysts I've spoken to believe that in all probability he's a Silesian Jew who went underground in 1939, and has been fighting the Nazis ever since. Naturally such a man would take great pains to obscure his real identity—in order, among other reasons, to protect any surviving relatives from reprisals. He operates independently of the ZOB, which is smart—look what's happened to the rest of them. It's thought he receives minor support from the Jewish Brigade in the Ukraine, but of course you can't trust the Russians to tell the truth about something like that. From all we've been able to learn—"

"*We* meaning who?"

"We meaning Agudas and certain well-placed overseas contacts. You'll understand why I can't be more specific. This Fox has managed, nobody knows how, to live off the land, right through the occupation, in one of the most venomously anti-Semitic places on Earth."

"All that aside—"

"Wait, I'm not finished. What I'm telling you is that nowhere, in any intelligence I've been privy to, is there a *hint* that the Fox has maintained ties, even distant or indirect ties, with any person or organization in the United States. Not with you, not with anti-Nazi groups, not with distant aunts or cousins, and *damn* sure not with some goy bartender at a second-rate uptown saloon."

Martina glared at him a few moments, then made a game attempt to shrug it off. "You don't know everything, Harv. Neither do your well-placed overseas contacts. No matter what you guys think."

"I'm afraid I have to agree," said Stu, who'd been uncharacteristically quiet through all this. "It doesn't make sense. Let's think: how did this whole business get started? It started with a personal message from the Fox, delivered to Miller and Martina via an old pal of theirs, some left-wing journalist. Miller was singled out by name. 'The only one I trust,' or some such thing."

"Well, of course he was—and quite an artful gambit, wouldn't you say? Because this deflected our attention from the true target of the communication."

Stu shook his head. "*What* true target? Who, and why?"

Grabsteen pointed a finger in Martina's face. "The target was *her*. A publicly recognized official of the United States War Refugee Board. Hence, a point of access to the Roosevelt administration. The purpose of this entire scheme is to involve the American government, to bring a Washington insider here, into occupied territory, to witness firsthand the crimes of the Nazis—thus to make it impossible for Roosevelt to claim ignorance or to remain personally uninvolved. It's an immensely clever plan, and the only shame is, it was hatched a couple years too late."

A few moments passed during which everyone considered this. Eddie was the first to speak.

"It still doesn't add up, I don't think. Even if what you say is true—the Fox was aiming at Martina, so as to bring the government in—well, that proves that the guy *must* be her old friend, right? Because who else could possibly know about their mutual connection with a private citizen named Ingo Miller? Unless you think, what—somebody's gotten hold of their high school yearbook?"

"Oh, I don't know." Grabsteen's mouth curled into a mean smirk. "Let's imagine that somebody—it could've been anyone—happened to stumble across the April 1930 issue of *Harper's Bazaar*? Eh, Miss Panich?"

She rolled her eyes. It wasn't enough, she thought, that Butler's damned article, when it finally appeared, had made her the object of scandal and notoriety—and, she supposed now, secret envy—among her college set. There she was, portrayed to all the world as a dizzy, big-mouthed brunette whose chief function, story-wise, was that of a typical Hemingway gal: a convenient and adoring sexual accessory for the hard-drinking, two-fisted hero. Even Ingo had come across as a more compelling figure. And so, of course, had Isaac.

"Did your well-placed overseas contacts dig that up for you?" she asked Grabsteen. "Or did you manage to find it all by yourself?"

"What's the difference? The point is, anyone reading that article and making the connection between *that* Martina Panich and *this* one—it's hardly a common name—would know everything they needed in order to push the right buttons. Names, relationships, personalities. Every little quirk and foible."

"Not every one. Not even Butler knew—" She caught herself; though really, it was a bit late to acquire the habit of discretion. "You know what, Harv? Sometimes a cigar really *is* a cigar. Maybe not in the circles *you* move in, but sometimes, if a person says he'd like to see so-and-so, it's because so-and-so is who he wants to see. End of story."

"That is utter crap, and you know it. Why would a man like this Fox— no matter who he is—want to see a man like Ingo Miller?"

"I guess you'd have to ask them about that, wouldn't you?" she said, scoring a small point. Then the afterthought struck her: *If we ever see either of them again.*

Bloom pushed forward. "None of this makes—excuse me, Marty—a fucking bit of difference, does it? The only thing that matters is, we're stuck here till Shuvek gets back. I'd suggest we all sit down—"

"No!" shouted Grabsteen. "I am *not* sitting down. I am moving onward *right now.* With or without," he added, turning to gesture at the woman partisan, "this fool's cooperation."

"Without it you won't get very far," Stu said mildly.

"No? Then *you* try communicating with her, why don't you? I've done everything I can think of. It's like talking to a rock."

Martina had forgotten about Timo. He'd become all but invisible since the plane landed, as though some Serbian instinct for furtiveness had reawakened in him. She didn't notice him now, really, except as a shadow moving at the edge of her vision. Perhaps she felt the slightest flicker of curiosity—what's *he* up to?—but certainly not alarm. Nothing like that, not until Timo raised his gun and blew the first man's head apart.

By the time she turned her head, the second partisan's eyes were wide in terror. Almost instantly they vanished in a burst of scarlet as his face split open like a water balloon.

Timo spun, aiming his rifle at Petra. She was gripping her PPD, but Timo's left eye was already squeezed shut and his right peering down the barrel, which was perfectly steady and pointed straight at the woman's heart. "Ask her again," he said. "I think you will find she understands much better."

Martina thought she might vomit. Or else shriek like a madwoman and strangle Timo with her bare hands. She waited for someone—Bloom, Grabsteen, sensible Eddie—to react in some coherent way. But everyone stood there, as stunned as she was. Everyone except Petra, whose face merely showed a passing sadness, or perhaps disappointment. *Why wasn't I able to stop this?*

In the end, Martina watched dumbly, her knees wobbling beneath her, as Grabsteen said something quietly, his head inclined toward Petra's ear. Martina didn't catch what it was, her own grasp of English seemed to have left her, but she saw the woman nod. There was no discernible expression on her face—only a profound weariness so deeply ingrained in her features that it was part of her being. Petra turned up the path and began walking.

"Should we take her gun?" said Grabsteen. It was not clear whom he was asking, and at first no one responded.

"I shouldn't bother," said Timo, reslinging his rifle. "There won't be any more trouble. Not from that one." Then he bent quickly and began stripping the dead bodies of weapons and grenades, dropping everything into a rucksack.

Wordlessly, they moved up the trail. The woman leading them never looked back. Maybe that's the secret, thought Martina.

LUBLINLAND

The place was not what Butler had expected. It was not, after all, a fetid and smoldering city of the dead.

For months now, since the Red Army slugged its way onto Polish soil, Butler had been horribly titillated by reports of a so-called Nazi death camp near Lublin, an old university town whose chief distinction heretofore had been its exceptional concentration of Catholic churches, said to be the greatest in Central Europe. That changed at the end of July when Konstantin Simonov, sometime novelist, landed a sensational story in *Pravda* about a facility known as KZ-Majdanek, where—so he claimed—upward of one million Jews had been "exterminated": poisoned by gas, then burned in industrial-scale crematoria. Similar reports came thick and fast from all the Soviet papers. *Red Star* ran a shot of two captured SS guards taken shortly before their execution, standing in a vegetable garden among enormous heads of lettuce, grown, the caption explained, in a mixture of manure and the ashes of murdered Jews.

It was a pornography of evil. The public was mesmerized. Butler as well. Yet the Western press made next to nothing of the whole affair, deeming it, apparently, something cooked up by Soviet propagandists. Red meat for the masses. Well, who knew? Butler, however—who knew something about propaganda and its reigning *auteurs*—believed the stories to be true, more or less. True enough.

In mid-August, Marshal Rokossovsky—indignant that the word of his officers should be doubted—had invited a select pool of Western correspondents to tour the site. They were chosen for "credibility," which is to say the likelihood their stories would run in leading periodicals, especially in America. Butler's widely known pro-Red leanings ruled him out. But a few weeks later, on a rare visit to Moscow, he bumped into Alexander

Werth, the *Sunday Times* man, at the bar of the Hotel Lux, that grubby mecca of expatriates on Gorki Street.

Werth, an Oxbridge Fabian sort, was still miffed that the BBC had refused to run his Majdanek piece. "And it was good stuff," he grumbled, "exclusive stuff. Spent several days there. Spoke to the local Poles. Not just Party types. They all knew what the camp was for. Hell, it was barely two kilometers outside town. When the wind was in the east, the whole place stank of it. One little boy showed me the shoes he was wearing—good as new, he was quite proud of them—that he'd nicked, you see, from a big clothing dump the Germans ran on, wait for this, Chopin Street, don't you love that? Shoes off the feet of some poor Zhid, undoubtedly. Must have been from one of the last batches to be liquidated, otherwise they would've been sized and boxed up and shipped off to the Reich. But the Poles, they're quick to grab that sort of stuff, soon as the Germans clear out, and who can blame them? They've had a bad war."

Werth had been drinking for a while; Butler let him talk. During a pause he said, "So it's true, then? The gassing rooms, the ashes, all of it?"

Werth turned in his chair, looked Butler straight in the eye. His stare had a certain bluntness, as though he were about to say something rude. "You've been here awhile, haven't you? In the war, I mean." He nodded, answering on Butler's behalf. "So you've seen things by now, places liberated from the Nazis. You've interviewed survivors. You've seen what's left of the liberated zones. How can you doubt for a moment it's true?"

"But the stories," Butler persisted. "The details. The cabbages. A million dead."

Werth's eyes rolled. "One million, ten million—that's numbers. You know how Russians are with numbers. How many people can grasp what a million means? You say a million, what you mean is, an inconceivably large number. What the stories say is, an inconceivably large number of human beings were murdered at Majdanek, under circumstances more ghastly than you can comprehend. Yes, the bloody stories are true."

So when Butler at last came to Lublin—by special invitation of Osoby Otdel, Special Department, Bureau 1965—he expected to find some nightmare conjured out of the blackest depths of the German imagination, like those medieval woodcuts creatively depicting the torments of the damned. Only worse, many times worse, as Stalingrad is worse than Agincourt, because the capacity for bestiality is so much greater today than at any time in the past. What he did not expect was a placid, medium-sized

Old European city, laid out on a generally flat and sparsely wooded landscape, its buildings in decent shape, its streets filled with people who looked neither downtrodden nor half starved, its markets reasonably well stocked, and those famously plentiful steeples pointing hopefully toward a blue and cloudless sky. But that is what he found, and it gave his visit, on this sunny and windless day, its quality of surrealism.

You reached KZ-Majdanek by a narrow lane running east out of the city through copses of elder and pine. At first glimpse the place had a clean, well-ordered look. It was, above all, nonthreatening. You might have guessed, standing outside the perimeter fence, that it was workers' housing for some big war-related industrial concern, a Farben or a Krupps. True, there was a double rank of barbed wire fencing, but this was wartime, after all; barbed wire could be seen around many a stately home in the British countryside and many a cornfield in the American South. You grew habituated to its presence, and also to the message it contained: the world today is full of places where you are not meant to go.

Butler hopped out of the Yankee jeep and thanked the Red Army man who'd given him a lift. The main gate stood wide open, manned by a cluster of soldiers from one of the Central Asian republics. As he drew near, he tried to suppress the natural jauntiness of his stride, to turn his thoughts to the many souls who had passed this way on a journey with no return. It was difficult. A recent dusting of snow lay gently on the landscape, like a clean white sheet pulled discreetly over a corpse. Just inside the barbed wire ran a cheering row of young beeches, from whose twigs fluttered yellow leaves as bright as daffodils. One of the soldiers scrutinized Butler's papers, noticed the NKVD seal and handed them quickly back.

He paused to take the lay of the land. Beyond the gatehouse, the main camp road ran straight as a Roman highway for a kilometer or so. Bootprints by the hundred, imprinted before the freeze, were preserved in its cinder surface. On either side stood wooden buildings painted institutional green. The Hammer and Sickle hung limp from a flagpole in a courtyard surrounded by shrubbery; it might as well have been the Stars and Stripes. The creepiest thing about this place, Butler thought, was its humdrum normality.

A couple hundred meters off, a line of soldiers filed out of one of the larger buildings and formed up in columns on the roadway. He could hear an NCO barking orders.

"What's going on there?" he asked the closest guard.

"New arrivals, getting the grand tour. Marshal's orders."

Butler pulled out a pack of cigarettes, the white-papered kind issued only to officers. He soon had the whole bunch—Uzbeks, as it turned out—gathered around him, chattering in a Russian even worse than his own.

"The Marshal wants all the fresh troops brought through here on their way to the front," one of the men said.

"So they'll know what kind of enemy we're up against," explained another.

"What about the veterans?" said Butler.

The first man spat into the snow. "We've seen enough already, haven't we?"

"I don't know," his comrade said. "This place is a little different."

"What's the tour like?"

"Oh, it's pretty thorough. You go into the big room where they all got undressed, and then down the hall into the gas chambers. You stand in there, and they shut the door, and the only light is from this little skylight, high up over your head. And your guide says *Look up there, look at the tiny blue Zyklon crystals coming down, aren't they pretty? Just like snow.* It gives you a chill, that does."

"This lot's finished now," a soldier said, pointing. "Now it's off to the ovens—they've cleaned up a bit over there. Had some German prisoners in a couple of weeks ago. Before that, there were bits of skeletons lying around, the pieces that hadn't got burned all the way."

"One of them looked like the top half of a little girl."

"You don't know it was a girl. Could've been a boy."

"It looked like a girl to me."

"Hurry now," a man told Butler, "before the next lot comes in, you can get a tour all by yourself."

He took a few steps forward. He stared up the camp road, past the *Bad & Disinfektion* building with its twin rows of skylights. The company of fresh conscripts marched away from him, toward a half-ruined structure that seemed to have collapsed around its single red smokestack. He recognized the place from Simonov's vivid description in *Pravda*. As with the camp as a whole, it looked much less horrible than he'd imagined.

Once again he tried to make himself feel something. He wanted to empathize properly with the countless human beings whose earthly existence had ended a few steps up the road there. Most of them had been Jews from a place called "Lublinland," a make-believe province that existed only on the wall-charts at the SS Race and Settlement Office. Into this arbitrary corner of the Generalgouvernement, the Nazis had herded racial undesirables from the newly acquired territories of the Reich during those early, dizzying months after the fall of Poland. The plan had been to hand

their homes and farms and businesses over to *Volksdeutsch* settlers, who
were themselves being coerced into "coming home" from all the old German enclaves of Eastern Europe—all part of a grand scheme to redraw
the ethnic isobars of the continent. Butler wondered how things had
turned out at the other end, the places from which the Lublinlanders had
been "evacuated." Had they become model German hamlets, as envisioned by the planners at the *Siedlungsamt*? Or just burned-out, depopu-
lated zones like so much of the Nazi empire?

A wave of revulsion swept over him. He had wanted to feel something
and now he did, though it was more nausea than compassion. Turning
away from the crematorium, he began walking in the opposite direction,
aimless, passing one block of identical buildings after another. Prisoners'
barracks, he supposed, but they might have been warehouses, horse stalls,
repair sheds. Beyond them, he came to a fence that divided the camp into
unequal sections, its gateway open and unguarded. On the other side, the
buildings were sturdier, more permanent-looking. Perhaps this had been
the administrative area: offices where records were kept, a dining hall
where SS men shared wholesome meals, a recreation hall to pass one's off-
duty hours. Butler moved from one to another, imagining the function of
each, composing little mental narratives. *Over there is the sauna, and here is
where we watch the latest films from Ufa. And along here—watch your step!—
Hauptmann Schuler likes to walk his Doberman bitch, he calls her Freya, isn't
that the goddess who likes to fuck?* He came to a little building with a high-
pitched roof that in any other place might have been taken for a chapel.
But there were no chapels for Himmler's SS. Curious, he tried the door. It
yielded easily, the heavy, cross-braced wood swinging back on well-oiled
hinges.

"You're a bit early," said Puak.

The little man sat on a large, wide bed that occupied a place of honor
against the far wall, draped on either side with opulent folds of crimson
velvet.

Butler was too startled to reply. His mind crackled with a static of detail:
stag's antlers mounted over the bed, Puak's gray silk jacket smartly
adorned with a white carnation, a log fire blazing in the wide stone hearth.

"I thought you might want to inspect the facilities." Puak spoke in his
perfect, slightly effeminate English, his tone neutral and his smile, as usual,
open to interpretation.

"No thanks."

"No? Then I suppose it is down to business."

"What the hell *is* this place?" Butler was past the surprise now and on to the customary struggle of composing himself in the presence of the Spider, whose gleaming black eyes seemed capable of melting things down to their essence.

"Precisely what it appears to be"—switching now to collegial Russian. "Here, sit down, see how that chair feels, I believe it is bison's leather."

Butler stepped closer to the outlandish chunk of wood whose upholstery sat like an expensive saddle on a torture device.

"This is a shrine," Puak continued, now in *Hochdeutsch,* "to the heroic act of procreation. You stand in a sanctum for the breeding of German heroes!" Then English again: "From what the villagers tell us, the SS officers were always on the lookout among the political prisoners—that is to say, the non-Jews—for females of the ideal Nordic type. Blond, long legs, good breasts, proper small noses. When they found one, they would bring her back here and a few of the lads would have a go at her. They fed the girls well and kept them around for a few weeks. At the end, they offered the girls a deal: their freedom, in exchange for their promise that should a child result, it would be given over to the SS Lebensborn—a sort of baby-farming operation."

"What happened? Did both sides keep their end of the bargain?"

Puak's smile did not change. "The prisoners were released, but their fate beyond that point is hard to determine. To the best of our knowledge, few progeny of these matings survived to full term. The Poles did not fancy a new breed of monsters being spawned among them. They killed many of the girls as a precautionary measure. It is a case of denying the enemy much needed resources—the resource in this case being a fresh supply of wombs."

"War is biology by other means," Butler said; cleverly, he thought.

Puak pursed his lips. "Clausewitz has nothing to say about this. We are not fighting here a Clausewitzian war. We are back in the days of Nevsky, the peasantry rising up to repel the Teutonic Knights by any means necessary. And remember, it was not *we,* nor was it the Poles, who chose to fight such a war. The Germans have allowed themselves to become drunk on their own mythology—which would not be so bad if they stayed home and listened to Wagner and stabbed each other in the back, like Siegfried and Hagen. But no. They must impose this irrational construct upon the rest of the world, and that cannot be permitted. History itself will not allow it."

"You speak of History as though it were . . . an angry pagan god. Isn't *that* a kind of mythologizing?"

Puak shot him an annoyed glare, which Butler took to mean he had scored a point. "I shouldn't be so smug. You Americans also tend to mistake your own myths for objective truth. Look at your national archetype, the Lone Gunslinger—a strong and independent man, unconcerned with culture or manners, set on doing what he pleases, irrespective of the consequences. Especially if the consequences affect only such lesser breeds as Indians. That sort of legend makes for a good Saturday matinee but hardly a sound foreign policy. Then there is your homegrown version of Christianity, which is every bit as crude and apocalyptic as the Germans' Götterdämmerung, with the disadvantage of being also self-righteous. We had a taste of that in your recent Prohibition. One suspects things will only get worse as your society spins further into decline. Someday, my friend, these strands are going to intertwine, and your great nation will become as daemonically possessed by this mythic, Bible-toting cowboy as the Germans by their white knight singing the *Nibelungenlied*."

Butler was surprised to find that he resented this; it had been many years since he'd thought of himself as American. A Yank, yes, as long as the word was preceded by "expatriate," which spared him from lugging all that heritage around. "I suppose you Russkis are above all that," he said, trying not to sound too flippant. "No myths of any kind. No ghosts. No tendency toward hysteria. Bulgakov got the whole thing wrong."

"The triumph of the Soviet Union," said Puak, speaking primly as a schoolmaster, with pauses to facilitate the taking of notes, "is to have transcended national consciousness—to have dissolved the artificial boundaries between Russian and Georgian and Azerbaijani—and to have opened, to people everywhere, the greater wisdom that resides in the collective consciousness of the proletariat. The clear Communist mind is not haunted by archetypal daemons, nor ruled by outmoded conceptions of manhood and vengeance and honor. It shines forth with the light of science and understanding. And it offers this same understanding, this liberation from mythic bondage, to all humankind." He smiled benevolently, a Marxist boddhisatva.

Butler slid tentatively back into the bison-leather upholstery. The chair was built for the Teutonically postured, hence a bad fit for the average Western spine, which yearned to slouch. "All right, what's this about?" he said. If he were to be regarded as a damn American, he might as well behave like one. "Why this little tête-à-tête in a death camp?"

"Because it is not the only such place." Puak leaned forward from his perch on the bed. "Nor the largest. Nor the most horrific. I wanted you to see it by way of preparation."

"Preparation. For what?"

"For your assignment. The difficult business ahead."

"I thought my assignment was to grab a piece of paper."

"Just so. But not an ordinary sort of paper—no, this is rather like the parchment on which Tacitus scrawled his *Germania*. A seed, you might say, from which a new and dangerous mythology could emerge."

Butler stared at him. You did grow tired, at times, of the little man's parables. "I thought we were getting down to business."

Puak gave a gentle laugh. "And so we are. You are a man who likes stories, Comrade Sammy, isn't that so? You like to hear them, but especially you like to tell them. Let us think then for a moment how you would tell the story of what happened here at Majdanek. You would make it out to be a tragedy, I expect. Not in Aristotle's meaning of the term, but in the commonplace sense: a stage strewn with corpses. There is even a *deus ex machina*—the T-34 crashing with Olympian power through the gate, its hatch popping open to reveal a strange being with almond eyes."

Butler only shrugged. "Okay, a tragedy. Maybe. Why not? Love the almond eyes, that's a nice touch."

"Very well. Now, at the center of this story there is a man, the prime mover of events, by whose command such places as Majdanek came into being. This man might be thought of as the villain, but the role does not fit him. For one thing, he never appears onstage. For another, he is no mere foil for the protagonist—and who is *that*, by the way? No, this man is more than a villain. He has assumed the godly prerogative of life and death; he has dared to reshape the world to his own design. He is guilty, that is to say, of the classic sin of *hubris*, which we know to be the downfall of tragic heroes. He must be the hero, then—the dark and terrible protagonist of the story that will be told of this place, and of the war at large."

Butler did not need to give this a lot of thought. "That's ridiculous. Pure sophistry. Hitler's no hero. You said yourself, this isn't a tragedy as the Greeks understood it. It's something unique to the twentieth century. Call it an epic horror picture. Hitler's the producer, the DeMille. Which is why you never see him on-screen."

Puak knitted his fingers. "Perhaps that is saying much the same thing. In any case, it shares the same problem. Everything revolves around a single man. The masses who fought and died are relegated to the chorus. Moreover, in this version, the story has no historic meaning. It becomes merely a case study in exceptionalism, like one of your Horatio Alger fables: a man can accomplish anything if he sets his mind to it. But is this the kind of story good Communists want to tell their grandchildren?"

"Tell me a different one."

Puak rose from the bed. He stood near the hearth, making a strange figure there: the little Slav in his silk jacket, dwarfed by massive German stonework. "Of course, I lack your narrative gift. Yet it occurs to me, this tale might be spun as a piece of popular history, an exciting yet very distant-seeming object lesson that shows, among other things, how far we have come as a people, how much different and better is the world we live in today. Consider the story of the Crusades, a fantastic account of knights in shining armor marching off to glory—or to death, if that be their fate—under the banner of Christianity. Better perhaps, think of the Black Plague, a horror raging unchecked across the land, its symptoms hideous, its causes unknown—it was commonly felt to be a sign of God's displeasure—wiping out families, entire villages, erasing centuries of progress. Such stories fire the imagination. And in the hands of a politically astute narrator, they also have practical uses. They impart useful lessons about the folly of religion, the life-saving power of science."

"The Nazis liked the one about the Crusades, too," Butler said. "But they read something different into it."

Puak rounded on him. "The point is that in such tales, the motive power is no longer an individual man. It is a broader thing, a widely distributed force—the people as a whole, an entire epoch. Surely our present story, of death camps and Blitzkriegs and deportations, the whole Nazi saga, can be better understood in such a telling. Not as tragedy, with a single protagonist, but as a horrifying, yet safely distant, saga from an age long past. Because then, you see, it will have a lesson to impart."

"That the noble Soviet peasant always triumphs over Fascist Crusaders?"

Puak gave Butler an indulgent smile. "I would put it differently. Capitalism, with its stratified society and its Darwinian ethic of competition, must always lead to conflict. And the victims of that conflict must always be those most distant from the rulers, in terms of race or class or geography. Whatever its cultural achievements, and its pretense of morality, Capitalist society is at its core barbaric. Strip away its pleasant material trappings, as was done to Germany after the last war, and the inner beast emerges. No institution in Western society has the power to tame it, indeed none finds it advantageous to do so. They all, as you say, are in on the deal."

"Maybe so. But it's academic, isn't it? You can't dictate how people who aren't even born yet are going to think."

"No? Perhaps not. But I believe we may exert some influence, at least.

We may, for a start, manage to dethrone the tragic hero. We cannot write him out of the story, any more than you can rid the Crusades of Richard Lion-Heart. But we can deny him the leading role."

"And how, dare I ask, are we going to do that?"

Puak turned from the fire, casting his expression into shadow. "If indeed there exists a document proving that all this"—flicking a hand toward the death camp outside the walls—"is the responsibility of one man, a single deranged mind whose force of will once held an entire continent in thrall . . ." He looked at Butler, his dark eyes glinting in the orange fire-light, his lips forming a spider's smile. "If such proof exists, then your task is to find it and destroy it. A tale so great and terrible must have only one meaning.

"The correct one."

WEREWOLF COUNTRY

D olina Zimnej Wody—Cold Water Valley—possessed a naked beauty Ingo found unnerving. Every feature was exaggerated. The river-beds were gouged from sheer rock like battle scars. The water coursing through them ran so icy and blue you feared to drink it, lest the chill go right to your bones. On all sides the Tatry Mountains climbed at a pitch that seemed geologically implausible, shooting upward to peaks that might have been honed by a storm-god's ax. Life clung precariously to the land here: sand-colored wisps where grasses had waved in summer; dark holds of spruce whose ragged tips imitated the mountaintops; more rarely, stripped-down blackened stalks of some native flower jutting from gaps between pale gray rocks, their pods rattling faintly with the tiny seeds inside.

This land was shaped with no regard for soft-skinned creatures. And so history had flowed around it, crossing and recrossing the Polish plain to the north, creeping east onto the Ukrainian steppe, welling like a tide from the old imperial cities in the south. The war, too, had mostly bypassed the Tatrys, as it had the rest of Carpathia. But now the Reich was collapsing like an empty bag and the bloodied remnants of the Wehrmacht were retreating, mostly on foot, into territory they had skirted in the heady days of the Blitzkrieg. It was partisan-held territory, according to one school of thought. According to another—the thinking to which Ingo's guides subscribed—it was held by no one and never had been. Inherently, and like no other place in Europe, on account of its roughness and isolation, the land belonged only to itself.

Ingo had set out two days ago with the partisan Shuvek and the yellow-haired man who spoke like a Sudeten German and whom Ingo believed to be the chief of the guerrilla encampment. He was called Uli—short for

Ulrich?—but of course his given name could be anything. No one talked much, which was a relief; Ingo needed every ounce of energy for coping with the journey. And he wanted his thoughts to himself.

What these thoughts were was not easy to say. To an extent that surprised him, his mind was simply open, like a window, admitting views. These shifted from time to time, but certain things came around repeatedly, shifting *Leitmotive* that included another journey he had taken a long time ago. *Journey* made too much of it; all it had been was a drive into the country. Ingo was about to turn twelve. It was his first Boy Scout camping trip. He was frantic with anxiety; he had never spent a night away from home or needed to relieve himself in a place without indoor conveniences. He sat tensely in the backseat of somebody's rattling Ford with his friend Timmy Nye. Timmy was slender and confident, someone to whom the business of boyhood came naturally. As such he was of great interest to Ingo, who made a continuing study of his characteristics: how he wore his clothes, how he walked, how he behaved toward other boys. Riding in an automobile was itself an unusual experience—Ingo felt slightly carsick—and riding in an automobile to a place in the woods near Olney, Maryland, where he must survive without home or family for an entire weekend was without precedent.

But what he remembered most clearly now, from this distant perspective, was that during that car trip, in spite of his queasiness and dread, he had felt paradoxically happy, even strangely at peace. He had treasured every moment, each glimpse of the unfamiliar landscape, every breath of country air through the car's open windows. Because he knew that very soon now, before he was ready, the journey would be over.

They made frequent stops, at times and places chosen by Uli. Ingo supposed this was on his own account. He didn't mind. His leg muscles were all but spent, and the coarse fabric of the German uniform, which was the proper size but somehow wrongly proportioned, chafed the skin raw at his neck and his knees. In early afternoon they halted in a sunny hollow that narrowed to the northwest, its slopes littered with rocks the color of old newspaper. Ingo had nearly dozed off when he heard the sound of an airplane. It was impossible to guess which direction it was coming from until suddenly the plane appeared in a gap between the mountains: a two-engine craft, painted gray, buzzing along at low altitude.

"Russian," Shuvek said, indifferently.

Uli was prying at a rock with a length of sun-bleached wood.

"What are the Russians doing way out here?" said Ingo.

Shuvek shrugged. "No one knows what the Russians are doing any-where. Except smashing the Germans to a bloody pulp."

"It's too low to be a reconnaissance flight," said Uli, more deliberatively. "They might be dropping supplies to their partisans."

"Are *their* partisans different from your partisans?"

Uli gave him a wistful half-smile. "We have an enemy in common. For the moment, that's what matters. To the Russians as well."

"Yet here we sit," Shuvek noted sourly, "the three of us, speaking the enemy's language."

Ingo decided to voice the question that had been tugging at him. "Where do you come from, Uli? You don't sound much like a Czech."

Uli looked thoughtful for a moment. "As to where I come from, that's easy—a place called either Bratislava or Pressburg, depending on where a certain line falls on your map. As to what I am, whether I am a Czech, or speak as a Czech ought to speak, these are questions I cannot answer, and indeed questions I might never have troubled myself over, had it not been for Uncle Adolf." He stared at Ingo, his eyes rimmed in pink from long weariness. "You cannot understand this, I think. To be American is simple, a matter of having a piece of paper stating your citizenship. There is no question of blood, or ancestral homelands, or borders that move from one place to another."

Ingo wasn't so sure America was as simple as that. But Shuvek went on: "Do you think so? This one here, he doesn't seem like a Yank to me."

"Have you known many Americans?" Uli asked gently.

Shuvek shook his head. "No need to. I know what Americans are like. Just the way I knew what Germans were like, before they ever came and started shooting people. Some things you don't need to see up close to understand."

Uli frowned. "Perhaps you're right."

"Have you ever met the Fox?" said Ingo.

Shuvek gave him a sharp look. Uli said slowly, "I have met him. And he does seem very much an American to me. An American of a certain type. If that is what you're asking."

It was. And Uli's reply reassured him somewhat, but also gave him a strange, shaky feeling. He was almost there now. Only one person away.

The method of the partisans was to travel around the clock: move a while, rest a while, move again. They stayed in the hollow until the sun dipped below the neighboring ridge, then headed off toward a pass that would take them through a turn-of-the-century spa village and ultimately to the Polish frontier. Timing was important; Uli wanted to reach the village just after nightfall. The problem was that near the border they must travel by roadway; the High Tatrys were too difficult to cross otherwise, even for seasoned climbers. But the road was narrow and in places ran along the edge of deep mountain lakes, with no place to flee or to hide short of diving into the icy water. If they were caught by a German patrol there was no way out, they would have to stand and fight. And there were only three of them. And one of them was Ingo.

He made a quick inventory. He still carried his stubby little Schmeisser, which by now felt almost comfortable, snug in its leather sling at his elbow. His uniform came with a supply belt of the standard German type, holding a bread bag, bayonet, ammo pouch and water canteen. His backpack contained a frayed wool blanket, a few stick-type hand grenades and a volume of poetry. All these things—the poems as well—came from the German soldier whose body, now rotting somewhere, this uniform had fit.

Ingo doubted that it was the same man, Corporal Josef Müller, whose identity papers he carried in a breast pocket. Yet it was hard, all the same, not to imagine so—not to feel that he had slipped into the empty space left by the other man's passing. A characteristic folktale of the Carpathians. One night, deep in the forest, beneath a full Hunter's Moon, Ingo Miller transforms mysteriously into Josef Müller. The soft-bellied American barkeep becomes a hardened *Sturmmann* of the Waffen-SS. His beer mug turns into a machine pistol, his bar rag a *Brotbeutel*. In place of a warpainted Redskin, his cap sports a leering Death's Head.

And yet—here is the authentic fairy-tale touch—on his back, tucked in a blanket, he still carries the same volume of poetry. *Beliebte Gedichte der deutschen Romantik:* Hölderlin, Heine, George, Hofmannsthal, magical verses that have always brought him such comfort and such sorrow. The little book, bound in red, is a kind of talisman, though its exact function is not revealed. Maybe it holds the power to reverse this terrible enchantment—or maybe it's the very thing that sparked his transformation in the first place.

"Now listen," said Uli, when they reached the edge of the village. The three of them crouched behind a fence; soft amber light spilled from cottages a hundred meters away. Uli was looking hard at Ingo. "Here is something you must remember. There are worse things a man can do than die. I do not say this as the SS do—die a glorious hero's death and go straight to Valhalla. I mean that if something goes wrong, if you still have the power to choose, it is better not to be taken alive by the Nazis. Because they will kill you regardless, but they will not do it right away. Do you understand?"

Ingo nodded.

"No, you do not. Be thankful you do not. But perhaps, let us hope, you understand enough." His face softened and he placed a hand on Shuvek's shoulder. "Despite what my friend says, some things you must see yourself—see up close—to truly know."

Shuvek gave a nasty sort of smile. He spoke briefly in Slovenian.

Uli shook his head, then translated: "He says not to worry. If it becomes necessary, he will shoot you himself. And he hopes you will do likewise."

"Keine Sorge," Ingo told him—no worries. "It would be my pleasure."

The village slipped past like a dream. Smoke curled from its two dozen chimneys. Shingled roofs were pitched at the same angle as the mountainsides. The lane twisted past outlying farmhouses where no dogs barked, whose barns stood empty of livestock. All domestic animals had long been eaten by the Germans or the partisans, or else their owners had hidden them in high secret glades. At the far end of the village, tucked at the foot of a craggy *Berg* whose summit shone with early snow in the moonlight, stood an old rambling spa, built in the Swiss style with massive timbers and an overhanging roof. From one of its hundred diamond-paned windows, faint lantern light flickered. A caretaker, Ingo supposed. He looked around at the shadowed landscape and imagined Party bigwigs hiking and shooting in this rugged forest, swimming in dark blue waters that never became warm.

The village fell behind them, and they were climbing out of the valley on a tortuous, pebble-surfaced lane. The moon hung bright over the peaks, the sky was clear, the stars more luminous than Ingo could remember. Frozen night air moved in and out of his lungs, charging his brain with unusual energy, and he felt like one of those tiny figures in a painting by Caspar David Friedrich, standing with his back to the artist, hand on a hiking staff, rendered insignificant by a breathtaking landscape, alone at what looks very much like the outermost edge of the world.

But this was not the edge of the world—it was the heart of an old and populous continent, the eye of a thousand-year *Sturm*. On every side lay ruined lands, burning cities, unmarked graves. And he was hardly alone, for besides his two companions the Carpathians teemed with hidden life, creatures familiar and uncanny, ghosts who sang in long-dead tongues of a time that had never been, devils in tall black boots, avenging angels toting automatic rifles, the golden eagle shrieking high above clutching its *Hak-enkreuz* while Wotan's twin ravens, Thought and Memory, feast upon the souls of the walking dead and the soon-to-die.

This is what comes, Ingo thought, of reading those well-loved German verses over and over again. After a decade or two, they get stamped so deeply in your mind that you no longer know the sense of them, only the feeling. Then you are right at home here in Werewolf Country.

The road took them down then higher up. The moon crawled west across the sky. They hiked and rested, nibbled some bread, rubbed their sore feet, hiked again. The temperature continued to drop until the cold seemed a part of Ingo's body, something you carried everywhere without thinking much about it, like age. After that, it no longer bothered him.

Only in such an isolated spot, with a view of a perfectly clear sky, do you notice the subtle gradations of daybreak. "Darkest before the dawn" is a gross misstatement, at least here. Long before dawn you could detect a graying-out along a wide arc of horizon, so slight it seemed at first nothing more than your imagination. You noticed it chiefly by a dimming of the eastern stars. Next came a penumbral half-light that waxed, by immeasurable degrees, into the predawn state known as first light, the favored time for launching infantry assaults. By now they were close to the border.

"I say we stop here," said Shuvek. "Keep out of sight in those woods there. Rest till mid-morning. Warm up a bit."

Uli gave this some thought, or waited long enough to make it appear he had done so. "We'll be easier to spot then," he pointed out. "And the Huns will have finished their porridge and sent their patrols out. No, if we're going to stop, I'd rather do it on the Polish side."

Ingo, too exhausted to venture an opinion of his own, accepted Uli's decision as stoically as did Shuvek. The three men resumed their plodding, mulelike progress through the mountain pass.

Not long afterward—fifteen minutes, or another kilometer of desolate roadway—Ingo became aware of a sound that did not belong here. It was faint and seemed to come from many directions at once, bouncing off the hard surfaces all around them. By the time he stopped to listen, he saw that Uli and Shuvek had stopped as well. Their faces were blank. The noise grew more distinct.

"It's not a motorbike," Shuvek said.

"No," Uli agreed.

A few moments later: "I don't think it's a truck."

"No? That's good."

Until then, Ingo couldn't have guessed that it was a motor vehicle—as opposed to an airplane or, who knew, a Tiger tank.

"It's a car," Shuvek declared at last. "A big car."

They looked around. Their position, though not as bad as it might have been, was bad enough: midway along a gradual curve where the road skirted a steep, smooth outcrop. On the downslope, inches past the edge, the terrain plunged steeply into a gorge. Still, there were places you could think of hiding. Only you had to think right now; the noise of the car was getting louder fast, coming up the road behind them from the Slovak side.

"Down here." Uli pointed to a narrow cleft in the rock face that seemed to offer hand- and footholds. Below it, the chasm was so deep and shadowed you couldn't see its bottom. Shuvek scrambled down first. In his haste, one of his feet slipped loose. He hung there for a horrifying moment, struggling for balance, clinging to the rock face with one hand while the other groped blindly for something, anything, to grab hold of. Uli dropped to the ground, stuck both arms over the edge and seized Shuvek's free hand. After that Shuvek was able to regain his balance and edge a bit lower, making room for the others.

They had lost precious seconds. The sound of the engine was clear enough that you could guess the number of cylinders. Ingo fought an urge to stare up the road, waiting dumbly for fate to roar down on him.

"Now you," Uli said. "Hurry."

"No."

The surprise in Uli's face mirrored his own. Ingo hadn't planned on saying this. Nonetheless he blundered on. "I'm wearing the uniform—they'll just think I'm—"

Uli clapped him on the shoulder. It might have been agreement, or thanks, or simply goodbye. Relief, perhaps, at getting rid of this troublesome charge. There was no time to talk or even to acknowledge what Ingo was doing. Uli's head had scarcely dropped below road level when a big Mercedes touring car appeared around the bend. It was moving fast, its tires kicking up dust. The round, protruding headlights burned cold and bright, like the approaching sunrise.

Ingo began walking straight toward it. Every stride carried him farther from where Uli and Shuvek were hidden. He'd taken no more than a dozen before the car began to slow, its brakes engaging with a suppressed groan, its great engine falling to an idle.

He could not see who was inside. The windshield only mirrored the silver-blue sky. At last, as the sleek machine ground to a halt barely an arm's length away, Ingo saw himself reflected in the glass: a small and

insignificant figure, like that poor schmuck captured by Friedrich, alone
at the bitter end of everything.

His right hand was on his Schmeisser. He expected the car doors to fly
open, jackbooted stormtroopers to leap out. *There are worse things a man
can do than die.* Instead, the rear window on his side of the car slid
smoothly down. Ingo stepped hesitantly nearer until he could look inside.
A thin man with a mustache, wearing a dark leather coat over some kind
of uniform, peered out at him. The Mercedes's passenger compartment
was so high above road level that the two of them were almost eye-to-eye.
Ingo figured the man was about ten years younger than himself.

He spoke without thinking, in the roughest German he could muster:
"I'd be careful driving this way, meine Herren. The mountains are full of
partisans. You'll never see them until it's too late." He took a step back,
pretending to admire the automobile. "Those Ungeziefer would love to
knock out a beauty like this."

Despite the cold he was sweating. He tried to adopt a pose of uncon-
cern. The thin young man looked about to say something, but only ran his
lips together. Nervous, Ingo thought. Which put him several grades above
Ingo on the scale that runs from dead calm to shitting yourself. But everything was unfolding so fast that Ingo, near exhaustion, could hardly grasp
that any of it was real. He felt like a drunk, oblivious of the conventions,
with no recourse left but bluster.

From the shadowy interior of the car a second voice spoke—quiet, pars-
ing the words carefully, like an orator rehearsing his lines.

The man with the mustache looked briefly away, muttered something,
then turned back to Ingo. "The Brigadeführer would like to know what
you are doing out here alone. And why you are not with your unit. I suggested that you are perhaps a deserter."

This was the moment, Ingo supposed. Two men in the backseat. Up
front just one, presumably a chauffeur. All probably armed. He might get
the drop on them—maybe one chance in ten. And after they shot him,
they'd go looking for his confederates, or radio for an anti-partisan squad.
No, it would be best to contain the disaster; let their thoughts run the way
they were going.

"It's like I told you—there are partisans all over this area. There was a
fight. I got separated from my comrades. We had just made camp for the
night. I found myself lost in the woods. It was dark. This happened night
before last. Since then I've been trying—"

The thin man cut him off. "What is your unit, Sturmmann?" he said in a clipped, angry voice, like a Hollywood Nazi. "What is the name of your commanding officer?"

Ingo started to raise his hands—*All right, you got me, boys*—when the other man in the backseat leaned over to the open window. This one was older, in his mid-fifties, perhaps, and though he wore the same black uniform, he didn't strike Ingo as a fighting man.

"Excuse me, please," he said, examining Ingo through small rimless glasses. "Your accent, I have been trying to place it. How you roll the R. And something about the intonation—it drifts lower on the final syllables. As a boy, did you by chance live in . . . could it be South Africa? Or perhaps—Canada?"

Ingo was afraid to respond. He'd always been proud of his German, which he'd kept in fine polish through countless hours of half-drunken banter with staffers from the German embassy. But now his confidence deserted him; he feared that by any small lapse, the shadow of a Washington drawl upon a vowel, he might betray himself. Was this a trap? he wondered. Was it some kind of test? He stared at the face behind the little spectacles but saw no guile there. Perhaps the old fellow was just dotty and fancied himself an amateur linguist.

"Repeat something for me," the man said, his eyes brightening with inspiration. "Wer der Schönheit angeschaut mit Augen, ewig währt für ihn der Schmerz der Liebe."

Ingo hesitated, wondering what exactly was expected of him. "Wer der Schönheit," he began at last, "angeschaut mit Augen—" And at this point something turned inside him, and he corrected the ending of the verse: "Ist dem Tode schon anheimgegeben." Then he said it all again, his voice falling into the meter like water finding a channel in the rock. *He whose eyes have gazed upon true Beauty is already given over to Death.*

The one with the mustache rolled his eyes, a supercilious little bastard.

Mainly to annoy him, Ingo went on: "*Death in Venice* in twenty syllables—that's what one of my professors used to say."

The older man laughed—a dry sort of laugh, but it sounded genuine enough. He stared at Ingo for a few moments, dispassionately. He might have been a naturalist in the wild, evaluating some new specimen, deciding whether it was worth carrying home and putting under glass.

"I am surprised," he said at last, "that anyone is still teaching Platen. But then, you're not so young, are you? You were educated before all this." He sighed. "If I didn't know better, I would say you come from the United States. That is improbable, I realize—the days of the Bund are long past.

But I have heard there are still a few such people around, from the early days. People who heeded the Call of the Homeland and, as it were, missed the last boat leaving Hamburg. But I don't suppose . . ."

There was something almost plaintive in his expression. An aging Romantic, Ingo thought: the most pitiful thing on Earth. So perhaps it was out of sympathy—or worse, a twisted sense of comradeship—that he said without forethought, like a student trying to please his teacher, "I am American. Originally, that is."

Hearing the words, he was horrified to have said them. The old man's eyes opened wider.

Ingo blurted, "But I came here . . . I mean, came to Germany, many years ago. Back in 1929."

The younger man in the automobile, turning his back on Ingo, murmured something in a rapid undertone. The old man shook his head.

"I tell you, he is no deserter"—sounding exasperated now. "Where would he be deserting to? This road does not lead to California, I can assure you of that." He leaned forward to rap on the driver's seat. "Albert, would you unlock the door, please?" He turned back to Ingo. "If you please, Sturmmann, take a seat there in the front. Don't worry, I'll see that you get back to your unit in due course. We can always blame your absence on the eccentric old Brigadeführer. They will understand that, won't they, Jaekl?"

The thin man offered a lackluster imitation of a smile.

The passenger door opened heavily, as though armor-plated. A prewar model, Ingo guessed, from the years before steel became a strategic commodity. He heaved himself into the stiff, leather-covered seat. The driver, a teenager wearing the field-gray of a Waffen-SS *Soldat,* gave him a brief cold glance and shifted into first before Ingo could close the door.

As the big car gained speed, the Brigadeführer tapped Ingo on the shoulder. "I hope we shall have time to talk," he said. "Not now—the damn motor. But later. I have spoken only once before to an American. Language is a special passion of mine. My life's work really. The written language, primarily, though the spoken is not to be scorned. One can discern many things from a voice. And of course, the great epics were meant to be *declaimed*—writing them down was an afterthought. Hence, so much is lost to us. But listen to me!" That dry laugh again. "Here I am, babbling away, and I haven't even asked your name."

"Müller," said Ingo. At last, back to the script. "Josef Müller. Sergeant, SS."

"Very well, Müller. And I am Professor Konrad Freiherr von Cheruski—

I prefer to be called Professor, though you see they have given me a military commission, it is the only way of trumping the bureaucrats. Lately of the University of Prague, also the Department of Race Ancestry. Presently engaged in special research at the direction of the Reichsführer-SS. But at heart—and I say this to you as a man who knows his 'Tristan'—at heart simply, an old man who has spent a great many years with his nose in a book."

At what point they crossed into the Generalgouvernement of Poland, and at what later point they crossed again into the province of Lower Silesia, incorporated since 1939 into the Greater German Reich, Ingo could not have said. They traveled at imprudent speed along back roads through the Carpathian foothills. Around mid-morning they reached a flat, open space where they stopped for a while at an official checkpoint. Was this the border? It had not been, the last time Ingo was in the neighborhood.

There was a train station nearby and all four of them got out and walked over there. The platform was crowded with refugees, mostly German families trying to escape to the west, surrounded by heaps of their belongings. Most of them looked as though they'd been waiting for days. Girls in white uniforms were serving ersatz coffee out of a big metal urn, and one of them offered to pour some in Ingo's canteen. Cups were in short supply, she explained; it was important to save them for the boys on the troop trains, bound for the front. Ingo nodded to the girl, who spoke with a strong Polish accent. He supposed that with her washed-out skin and blue eyes she had been deemed suitable for "Aryanizing." The black liquid was very hot, with no identifiable flavor.

Back in the car they drove with the sun on their left rear quarter. Soon they were in foothills again, though the landscape was less drama-filled than in Slovakia. Trees grew taller and fuller-bodied, and there was an abundance of little ponds. For the most part the farms and houses looked untouched by the war, except that many of them, especially in the villages, seemed empty. Overall the countryside wore a sleepy look, as if it were lying there in the sunlight waiting for something.

They passed a sign reading "Reich Nature Protection Territory," which Ingo made out to signify some type of game preserve. There wasn't much to it, mostly old woods and rolling meadows, all in drab winter colors. For many kilometers they drove without passing a single building, though it seemed to Ingo that in some of these fields—over there, beside those wind-bent apple trees—cottages once must have stood. He glimpsed a squared-off enclosure that he guessed might have been the foundation of a barn. The land felt not so much empty as emptied.

They pulled in to a long straight drive bordered with elms. Years ago these trees had been pruned into boxlike shapes but lately the practice had been abandoned, the boxes left to burst open, spilling branches that dangled in their path. The drive ended in a circle around a statuary fountain of remarkable monstrosity: Poseidon lustily chasing sea-nymphs, or maybe they were Rhine maidens. A flight of crumbling concrete steps led in tiers up a hillock whose elaborate formal plantings had gone to thistle and bramble. At the top squatted a small mansion made of black timbers and skin-white stucco, with windows whose tops were rounded into Palladian arches. Here and there a pane was gone. The thatched roof needed re-thatching. But as Ingo lifted his eyes he noticed a column of smoke rising from one of the half-dozen chimneys. And as they climbed out of the car, smells of burning wood and molding autumn leaves filled his nostrils, and he was stirred by the strange, slowly decaying beauty of the place. What once had been somebody's dream house, with its spacious grounds and formerly well-tended garden, now belonged, so it seemed, to this black-uniformed professor, lately of the University of Prague. An SS brigadier who knew his "Tristan."

"We call it the Hunting Lodge," said the thin man, Jaekl. He passed in rapid little strides across a very large square room whose ceiling was two stories above, divided into vaults by enormous, crisscrossing beams. Two hearths, each big enough to hold a bridge foursome, gaped at each other from opposite walls, but only one had a fire going and that was scarcely enough to drive the chill from the cavernous space. A mounted knight impaled a stag on a wall tapestry, both prey and hunter dwarfed by natural-istically rendered oak trees on either flank. A row of antlers, sawn off the heads of mythically huge beasts, circled the room at rafter level. Had there been a unicorn's head with its phallic horn, the scene would hardly have seemed more fantastic.

"The place was built by a Jewish merchant," Jaekl went on, using a term, *Käufer*, that carried a taint of venality, corruption. "It dates back to Bismarck's day. That was Bismarck's one weakness, you know, his soft spot for Jews. Let them finance your wars, that's fine—but don't bring them home to dinner afterward."

Ingo supposed the man was talking to fill up the emptiness of the room, whose few furnishings were marshaled into a little group in one corner, the frail chairs looking as though they were trying to edge closer to the fire. But Jaekl stared at him like he was expecting an answer. Maybe this, too, was a test.

"Every hero has a weakness," Ingo said amiably, barkeep-style. "Look at Siegfried."

The thin man gave him a thin smile. "I don't know how long you'll be staying, so I've asked Magda to make up the coachman's room for you. Properly speaking that should be Albert's, but Albert"—lips tightening in distaste—"is sleeping elsewhere."

Ingo nodded. His eyes drifted to the fire. He felt as though he had stepped into one of those country-house mysteries, without benefit of a murder to solve. Or perhaps there were thousands of murders and an endless list of suspects.

"You know," Jaekl blurted unexpectedly, "it was that comment about Mann that did it."

Ingo looked around in surprise to find the thin man watching him with eyes that had gone hot and bright.

"That coy little reference to *Death in Venice*. The Brigadeführer has a horrible fascination with Mann. Dangerous as well, considering what that traitor has been saying over the Voice of America. And here you come along, *Vox Americanus* in the flesh, quoting your sexually tormented poets and reminding him of his days at the university. Which is the *last* thing he needs to think about right now, with the Reichsführer himself waiting—"
He looked away.

Ingo guessed he had said a little too much. Reichsführer was a title reserved for Heinrich Himmler. "I thought," he said, deciding the provocation was worth the risk, "your boss prefers to be called Professor."

Jaekl shot him a glare. "I address the Brigadeführer at all times with the respect that is owed to a man of his position. And I expect others to do likewise. At present, we are called to arms in defense of the Fatherland. Whatever we may have been before the war, and whatever we shall be after, we are for now German soldiers joined in a Struggle of Destiny, fighting for the very survival of our race."

He took a couple of steps in one direction, then spun on his heel and paced back in the other. His movements took on a martial quality to match his words. The effect was something of the tin soldier.

"Before all this, I was one of the Brigadeführer's students. First at Göttingen, then, from 1938, in Prague, where I became his teaching assistant. What a wonderful time that was! But it is over now. There is no telling what will come. For the present, I am honored to serve as his personal adjutant. I hold the rank of Untersturmführer, second lieutenant, but this is a formality, I would be of no use at the front. My place is here."

He stared at Ingo and his meaning was clear enough: This is *my* place, and there is no room in it for you.

Which suited Ingo fine. He had every intention of making a speedy exit. The problem was, he needed a plan. And this plan must take into account the unsettling fact that beyond the elm-lined drive lay the embattled Thousand Year Reich. His own Fatherland, in a hand-me-down sort of way. But not the most hospitable place in the world right now for anyone remotely like Ingo Miller. Who was pretty much the same person, war or no war, as he had ever been.

The woman Magda led him to the coachman's room. She looked Gypsy or Magyar and embodied the phrase "hardy peasant stock"—sturdy, uncomplaining, capable of yoking an ox or pummeling dough or delivering a baby with equal efficiency. She was, on top of that, adept with the meaningful sigh, as she demonstrated when she pulled back the faded green drapes from the high window, letting light spill into the mildew-smelling but homey enough little chamber.

"Things aren't how they used to be," she said, gazing at something outside on the grounds, perhaps something only she could see. "There used to be six of us on staff here. I only had the downstairs to do then. That and helping out in the garden, during the high season."

Her German was a mix of formal and colloquial phrases, like patches added randomly to a fraying garment until the original could barely be recognized.

"And there were parties, too. Real events, they were. People would drive out from Kraków, sometimes from Dresden and Leipzig. The house would be full for the whole weekend. They kept us running then."

"How long ago was that, Magda?"

"Oh," she waved dismissively, "ages. It was when the family still owned the place."

"You mean the Jews?"

She looked at him in surprise. "Yes, that's right. Their name was Grünberg. Funny, the names Jews have. 'Green mountain'—where do you suppose it comes from, a name like that? Someplace they remember? Or maybe a place they dream about."

Ingo watched her bemusedly. She kept her back to him, folding down the blanket on an old-fashioned cupboard bed, the sort with a curtain to block out the chill of night.

"I suppose you'll be wanted at dinner," she said. "That's at seven-thirty—pünktlich." And then she was gone.

He unclipped his uniform belt, laid it on a dressing table and slowly undid the buttons of the jacket. As the layers of Josef Müller came away, Ingo Miller, trapped inside, was able to breathe again. He perched on the edge of the bed to loosen his boots. They had let him keep his American boots, the risk being deemed acceptable in consideration of the long walk ahead. He tried to remember the last time he'd lain on a real bed. Not a stack of blankets in a forest hut. Not a narrow bunk in a rolling ship. And not a bag in a tent on a Maryland chicken farm.

It must have been his last night at Dupont Circle, his farewell to the Rusty Ring. He'd stayed up after closing time with Vernon and Bernie, sharing National Boh from the tap and then a bottle of malt whiskey, worth its weight in ration coupons, upstairs in his sitting room. It was a Monday, and getting late, but there was noise outside; the noise had never stopped since the war got going. There must have been a ruckus at the Officers Service Club, a private establishment around the corner, because a police car came flashing up the road and hooked left onto R Street. WRC was featuring lady singers that night. They listened to Helen O'Connell and Margaret Whiting and Fran Warren and a Negro vocalist named Ivie Anderson whose voice was like brushed velvet. All these things Ingo could remember, though it seemed like they'd happened a hundred years ago. But he could not remember what he and Vernon and Bernie had talked about. Not one word.

It was dark when he opened his eyes with a jolt of panic, fearing he'd slept through dinner. But he realized there had been a loud thump at the door—someone, probably Magda, had come by to rouse him.

He dressed in darkness and groped his way out to the corridor, which was barely lit by a lantern hanging at the far end. Groggily he retraced his steps from several hours ago to find Jaekl and Albert waiting in the great square hall. Evidently the Professor had not yet shown himself. An out-landish Schwarzwald clock read 7:22. Jaekl said, "Do you take brandy?"

Well, since he was offering. The liquid glowed like it had a fire inside, and it felt much the same in Ingo's throat. He looked around the room, mostly in shadow except for a half-circle in front of the big hearth. It was odd that Germans, of all people, this race of sun-worshippers, had been reduced to living in semi-darkness for want of lamp oil. He looked at his companions, but neither returned his gaze. The clock clunked out the minutes.

Precisely at *halb acht* Cheruski appeared in the doorway. Wordlessly they followed him into a long dining room with a row of windows running down one wall. Here, at least, candles had been lit to supplement the hearth fire; their burning tips were reflected in the windows against the black of night like dull, flickering stars. Cheruski took a seat at the head of the table and Ingo settled into the only chair left unclaimed, directly across from Albert.

If he had expected a comradely meal—breaking bread among fellow soldiers, all ranks sharing Magda's excellent rabbit stew like social equals— that notion was laid quickly to rest. The dinner conversation took the form of a monologue by Cheruski, punctuated at intervals by obsequious questions posed by Jaekl and the occasional mutter from Albert, who wanted Ingo to pass the rolls. The Professor's topics ranged over history and literature to the lamentable state of popular cinema—"In their eagerness to *divert*, these people at Ufa forget that their duty, first and foremost, is to *entertain*"—and it would have been easy, half listening as Ingo was, to believe Cheruski was not aware that a war was in progress. Now and then the old man would drop some revealing phrase or lapse into a sort of reverie, his eyes seemingly fixed on a scene conjured out of the candlelight.

"I had rooms in Göttingen," he said in a dreamy tone, "which Hölderlin himself was said to have used. There was an old desk and people said, You know that was Hölderlin's desk. That's why they hung on to it, for it was nothing but a piece of junk. Had it been Heine's desk, it would long since have become firewood."

He paused, smiling at the image: the Jew *Dicter*'s desk being fed piecemeal into the flames, spreading a cheery warmth through the room. Jaekl stared at his master as if sharing the same happy thought. Ingo got an inkling now of the sort of professor Cheruski must have been: encircled by his acolytes, a following bound by love of their master and vying jealously among themselves for his favor. It was easy to imagine Jaekl among that crowd. Albert was another matter.

Ingo had time now for a closer look at the young driver, whose own attention was concentrated on nothing more complicated than his dinner plate. If Magda struck him as good peasant stock, Albert seemed a different but related sort: the farm boy given to indolence, too lazy to rise at cock's crow, too eager to nap in the hay, always with an eye out for the road to an easier life. He was well mannered enough, and pleasant-looking with his clear eyes and sturdy shoulders and cropped, straw-colored hair. Over the years he would grow heavy, like Ingo. But that was over the years—meanwhile, he had landed a safe and comfortable posting, while his peers were being sacrificed *en masse* to the Red Army so that the Reich might endure a few more months.

Dinner ended when the Professor set down his fork. The four of them moved back to the great hall, where Magda had heaved fresh logs on the fire. Over the past couple of hours the wind had risen. On its hilltop perch the old house caught gusts that had sailed for miles unobstructed over treetops; now they whispered at the windows and sometimes came puffing down the chimney, forcing a gout of smoke back into the room, where it drifted slowly toward the ceiling. Everyone sat in the frail-looking chairs a safe distance back.

"Those are nice boots," Albert said unexpectedly. His tone was petulant. He stared at Ingo's feet. "When I went for training they didn't have boots to fit me. I kept getting blisters. Finally they got a new shipment from somewhere and they said, Here, try these. So I got this pair that fits, only the leather's too thin. My feet are cold all the time. I bet they came off some schmutziger Jude who sat indoors all day, counting his money. I wish a had a pair like yours."

There followed an uneasy silence during which everyone seemed to be looking at Ingo's boots. Were they waiting for him to offer some explanation?

After several moments the Professor said, "Jaekl, why don't you pour us some brandy."

The thin man stirred himself, crossing the room to a sideboard.

"Why can't we have beer?" said Albert. "It's been an age since I've had a beer."

Cheruski studied him for a moment—an expert, a specialist, making a cool and detached observation—and Albert stared back. At last Cheruski said, "I believe there is beer in the cellar. Go ask Magda to fetch you some. And drink it upstairs, why don't you?"

Albert stood, pleased with himself, failing to understand, or not caring, that he'd been dismissed. Jaekl served brandy to the others and Cheruski began speaking before Albert had left the room, as though the boy had ceased to exist.

"And so"—raising his glass—"I should like to say how pleased I am by the appearance of our guest from America. This seems to me more than simple coincidence. Does it not, Jaekl? I feel there must be some deeper meaning here—that Müller's appearance must be taken as a kind of omen. Or, if you will, an affirmation. For those inclined to doubt the fundamental premise of my research."

Ingo couldn't help noticing—nor did Jaekl make a particular effort to hide—how Cheruski's words caused him to fidget in his seat. As lightly as possible, Ingo said, "You mentioned you were doing some kind of special research? Something for the Reichsführer?"

Cheruski's eyes twinkled. Clearly this was something he longed to talk about. His eyes flicked over toward Jaekl, who sat glowering. "I work, of course, at the Reichsführer's direction. But I may say, with no false modesty, that the project I am now engaged in derives purely from my own research, conducted over many years now. When I put it to the Reichsführer at Posen last spring, he was most enthusiastic. It tallied quite nicely, so he told me, with a certain urgent undertaking of his own."

Jaekl could not contain himself. "Do you really feel, sir, we should be speaking of such matters in front of this stranger?"

"What do you imagine?" He spoke sharply, as in a household quarrel. "Do you suppose this man is an American spy? Tramping about like a Wandervogel on the chance that some high-ranking person might give him a lift? Snooping into rear areas our own General Staff does not see fit to defend? God in heaven, Jaekl, the man is SS, like ourselves. He comes from America, which means that he has *chosen* to join us in our time of national struggle. Unlike the traitors of 20 July, who were, every one of them, native-born." He tightened his lips.

Jaekl fell into a surly, resentful silence.

"It can be no secret," Cheruski resumed, pointedly now speaking only to Ingo, "there are those in our government, including persons I shall not name, quite close to the center of power, who would like to make a separate peace with the Anglo-Americans. For some, this is purely a tactical matter. Concentrate our defenses on a single front. But for many of us—I speak here of persons at the *very* highest level—this war with the Anglo-Americans is a regrettable lapse, on everyone's part. I do not exempt Germany itself from this error! For do we not, on both sides, share the same Northern heritage? Does not the same Aryan blood flow through our veins? Are we not equally opposed to the evil of Bolshevism that has arisen among the yellow-skinned people of the East?" He paused, but only for effect: the classroom rhetorician. "The hour has arrived when we must end this awful bloodshed. Our great nations ought rightly to see themselves as cousins. Any quarrel among us must be resolved in a manner that spares the blood of our youth, while preserving the national honor."

Ingo tried to keep his expression blank and attentive. Cheruski drained his brandy in a long swallow.

"Unfortunately," said Jaekl, leaning in to pour another, "there is the *slight* problem of unconditional surrender, upon which the Allies now insist."

Cheruski snatched his glass away. "Anyone with the least understanding of diplomacy—let alone the shades of meaning in even the simplest phrase—should understand this is a question of semantics, of a political utterance that need not be taken literally. Naturally there must be some pretense of an Allied victory, to satisfy the public over there. But I tell you—and I have seen the reports on this myself—the British people have no wish to drag this war out. They are sick of it, of having their cities bombed, cowering behind blackout curtains. And it goes without saying they are terrified of our new V-weapons. I assure you, they are eager to make peace. Still, it is a delicate matter. It is the same as any other proposition—an offer of marriage, for example. Both parties are ready to agree. Yet the question must be put forward very carefully. One false word, a misjudgment in timing, and everything falls apart."

Jaekl gave his master a sullen look and rose stiffly from his seat. "Unless you have further need of me, sir, I shall retire now. It has been a most wearying day."

"Yes, yes." A wave of assent. "Good night, then."

Ingo said, "Sleep well, Herr Untersturmführer."

With a cold nod Jaekl slunk off into the shadows. Cheruski swallowed more brandy. He was drinking now, not sipping.

"So, this project of yours." Like warming a pitcher up, Ingo thought; just keep tossing the ball back. "It has to do with the British?"

Cheruski gave a conspiratorial glance around the room. The stag's blood on the tapestry had turned black in the firelight. "I went to Posen last spring," his voice pitched low, "to hear an address by the Reichsführer to his higher SS and police leaders. It was quite a distinction, to have been summoned there. In those weeks, we were expecting at any time the Allies to launch their invasion. Meanwhile there were problems in Hungary, the Red Army was preparing its summer offensive. Everyone was anxious to hear what the Reichsführer would say."

"What did he say?"

"Oh, any number of things. The need to stiffen our resolve. The heroism of the ordinary German people, our duty to protect them from the Asiatic hordes. He assured us that this time around, there will be no stab in the back, as there was in 1918. Because this time the backstabbers have already been gotten rid of. He meant, you see, there are no more Jews to betray us. So the Reich is safe from the enemy within, all that remains is to deal with the enemy at the gate. At last he alluded to peace, the sort of peace he hopes to attain."

"A separate peace in the west."

"He did not say this directly! No—he only alluded. It was not until afterward, when I spoke with him in private . . ."

He paused for another swallow. The brandy was making him expansive, but before long it would make him groggy. Ingo could read the signs.

"I spoke with him after the address," Cheruski went on. "The Reichsführer was of course familiar with my work. He took me aside, just the two of us, and he said to me, 'Herr Professor, I wish to ask you a question.'" He paused, savoring this prized memory. A cozy chat with Heinrich Himmler. "'Herr Professor,' he asked me, 'what is the key to understanding a people—to knowing how they think, why they choose to act or not to act in a given situation?' I replied without hesitation: It is their literature, Herr Reichsführer. The stories they tell of themselves. Above all, the very oldest ones, the stories that have no author. The tales that seem to have sprung from the depths of their folk-soul.

"Upon hearing this, the Reichsführer grew very thoughtful. 'Now I ask you this, Herr Professor. If one were to examine closely the literature of, shall we say, the English—if, that is, an expert were to do so, a man such as yourself—might one discover perhaps some formula, a sort of code, an equation, something scientific, that would make it possible to communicate with these people in absolute sympathy? So that, should one make them a proposal, an honorable proposal, presented in good faith, they could not fail to agree?'

"Well, by this time, putting one thing with another, I understood what the Reichsführer was asking of me. He was saying, 'Can you find a way to make the British accept my peace offer?'"

Ingo waited out the melodramatic pause.

"'Yes,' I told him. 'Yes, my Reichsführer, in principle, one can do this. One can discover such a formula, such an equation.' What I did not tell him was 'If one has time enough to look.' Because you know, people in such positions are accustomed to giving an order and, *knick*, the task is done. But I assured him that every tool of modern philologic science would be placed forthwith at his disposal. After that, we had no more time to talk. Such a man naturally has many demands upon his schedule."

Ingo did not care to hear about the busy life of Heinrich Himmler. "So you went back to Prague"—nudging harder, the old man's eyes were starting to glaze—"and got down to work."

"I was already *down to work*." The voice became briefly mocking. "Our task in the Race History Department—this may not be generally appreciated—is to correct the many errors that have accumulated over the centuries concerning the role of the Germanic people in shaping Western culture. How many great accomplishments, how many works of art and literature, how many scientific advances, have wrongly been attributed to other peoples? To the Romans, for instance, or the French—even the Italians. Scholars like myself have worked for years to set the record straight. My own contributions have been, I say with modesty, solid but unspectacular—my specialty is ancient texts, and this is felt to be rather an out-of-the-way line of inquiry. Now suddenly, I found myself thrust into a timely, indeed historic, situation. My Leader had called upon me for a vital mission. I had been asked, if I may put it so, to provide him with a new weapon, a Wunderwaffe of the mind. I assure you, my friend, I got *down to work*."

He looked at Ingo but his thoughts were swirling within. It was easy to imagine him teetering with an expression like this before a roomful of undergraduates. Dotty old Cheruski, they must have thought.

"Now straight off, in this sort of inquiry, one faces a problem. It's easy enough to say—I have just said it—that we Germans and you Anglo-Americans are, in essence, the same people. That is true, it is a biological fact. We belong to what Professor Steiner calls the same root-race. Yet we speak different languages, we govern ourselves in different ways, and now a terrible war lies between us. Clearly then, from our common racial root has grown, in a manner of speaking, a widely branching ancestral tree. *So*"—crisply now, with a slap on the knee—"what one first must do is to locate precisely the point of division, the historical moment at which our respective national limbs began to diverge."

"And you've done that?"

"I have. Were there a slate board, I could draw you a diagram. But I can tell you, with a high degree of specificity, on the strength of detailed inquiry, that the break occurred around the year 1203, along a fault line that corresponds approximately with the rivers Rhein and Donau."

For an instant, Ingo wobbled at the edge of laughter. But having heard wilder theories at the bar of the Rusty Ring, he managed an encouraging nod.

"Do not imagine," Cheruski warned him, leaning forward, "that I am blind to your reaction. Listen to this old crack-brain, you think."

His eyes took on the sage look that comes to some men when they are about two-thirds drunk. The trajectory from that point is predictable. Were there a slate board, Ingo could have drawn a chart of his own.

Cheruski eased back in his chair. "I cannot, of course, lead you through the entire chain of reasoning—this is a technical matter, it would take up a full university course. But you have read Platen, you speak rather intelligently, I'm sure you can follow the basic thrust. My research has come to focus upon two things: the Matter of Britain and what I choose to call, by analogy, the Matter of Germany.

"With the first, you are no doubt familiar. It comprises a body of material known popularly as the Arthurian romances—though that term is inadequate, there's more to it than the frivolous business of the Round Table. The tales themselves, in their earliest versions, seem to be quite older even than the historical Arturius, who was a general, not a king, and whose task was to defend the island in the wake of the sixth-century Roman withdrawal. It appears that this Arturius or Arthur became a convenient national figurehead upon whom to drape a body of legend that had existed long before him, whose origins are now obscure. By the time the source material got cobbled into something like canonical form—that is, the form in which it comes down to us—it encompassed matters as diverse as courtship rituals among the ruling classes of feudal Europe, the life and teachings of a Druidical figure called Myrddin or Merlin, exciting battle stories, reports of jousting tournaments, an allegory about the slaying of the Green Knight, another about an incestuous union and a mystical, messianic birth, and—most puzzling of all—the distinctly eerie and symbolic quest for the Holy Grail. This mishmash is called the Matter of Britain because . . . well, what else could one possibly call it?"

Ingo wasted a moment pretending to think it over. "And the Matter of Germany, that would be what—Siegfried, the Ring, all that?"

Cheruski raised his nose, like a snob on the sidewalk. "Please, put every thought of Wagner out of your mind. Every note, every syllable of that outlandish opus, whatever their musical merits might be—of that I can offer no informed opinion—is the grossest imaginable corruption of an ancient, untainted and astoundingly well-preserved body of national mythology. Unlike the British material, whose origins are lost in prehistory, our Germanic legends have been passed down in something very like their original form, in such rich sources as the Nordic lays, Snorri's *Edda*, the early heroic poems and ballads, and above all, the *Song of the Nibelungs*—a medieval masterwork that, as my colleague Professor Burdach in Stuttgart points out, succeeds so wonderfully at invoking the spirit of its subject matter that it promptly dispatched all other contenders. It alone has come down to us." He rapped on the table, as if to make sure he had Ingo's full attention. "It is *here* that we come to the break point. This is precisely where we part company with our oceanfaring cousins."

The Professor poured himself another cognac. Ingo did likewise: why not? It was getting late; they were sitting in a drafty old mansion, rambling on about literature; they had passed, some while back, the last road marker of objective reality. The scene took him back to his last year at Catholic U., after coming home from Germany, when he discovered the tonic and mind-cleansing properties of alcohol. Sure, one more, a nightcap. Then off to our lonely bed.

"It is a remarkable fact," Cheruski said, twirling his glass in the firelight, "one of those coincidences that occur not infrequently in the history of ideas, that this masterwork was written at precisely the same time as the greatest, most elegant and comprehensive account of the Matter of Britain—and written moreover in very nearly the same place. Certainly the same *kind* of place. I refer of course to Wolfram's *Parzival,* which was begun around the year 1200 and finished no later than 1205. Its most crucial passages, recounting the Grail story, were composed in the winter of 1203–04 at the castle Wartburg in Thuringia, in honor of Wolfram's patron, the Landgrave Herman."

Thuringia, Ingo thought dreamily. A castle in Thuringia.

"Simultaneously, the *Nibelungenlied* was being composed by another court poet a short distance to the south, near Passau. In this case, we do not know the poet's name—and that is a cardinal point, because the anonymity was deliberate. By this time, you see, it was commonplace for a court poet, even an ordinary minstrel, to be identified with a particular work. We know about Chrétien, about Otto of Freisling, about Walther and Lucidarius. We know about Wolfram. But the man from Passau chose to hide himself, as it were, behind the work. And by so doing, he makes clear his connection with an older and more purely Germanic tradition, that of the tribal bard, the imbiber of Wotan's mead of poetry, who, in singing the great stories of his Volk, becomes, in effect, the voice and the memory of his people. That is the first point of divergence.

"The second is more blatant. Even at a casual reading, the two works could not be more distinct. You begin with roughly the same raw subject matter—kings and queens, oaths and champions, sacred objects, castles besieged, realms ravaged and restored—yet in each poet's hands, the material is fashioned into radically distinct form. In simplest terms, *Parzival* has a moral. The *Nibelungenlied* does not.

"All the Arthurian material, *Parzival* included, reflects the great change that had come over the European mind during the preceding three centuries: in becoming Christianized, it trained itself to think in dichotomies, good and wicked, sin and salvation, now and Hereafter. This binary thinking is present, often in quite explicit form, but always there at bottom, in even the most simple of the British legends, the pure diversions. Dragon meets slayer. Black Knight versus White Knight. The stories are quite varied but the moral is approximately the same, and it is the fundamental teaching of Christianity: If you do something good in the here-and-now, then you will be rewarded at some time in the future.

"Not so with our German legends. This is not to say they negate or deny such a meaning. It is simply that the question of lesson-teaching, or moral-drawing, or indeed any line of thought pointing to a reality outside the story itself, does not arise. The legend of the Nibelungs simply *is*. This is who they were, this is what they did, this is how it ended. *Finis*. At no time during all those adventures and surprises and betrayals and bloody disputations does any participant pause to give thought to any larger issue— neither the morality of his actions, nor the effect of those actions upon his own eventual fate, still less the fate of others. Above all, there is no thought whatever to the possibility of an afterlife, heavenly or otherwise.

"Günter desires to marry Brunhild. Is he worthy of her hand? We do not know; the question has no meaning. He arranges, by deceitful means, with Siegfried's help, to satisfy his desire. Siegfried lets Kriemhild in on the plot. Later, in a moment of pique, she comes out with it. Brunhild is shamed. She has quite a temper and vows to get even. The poet's sympathies appear to be with her, but that is no matter. She enlists Hagen to exact revenge. It is quite straightforward: they must murder Siegfried. Not so easy, but the deed is done. And now, of course, further revenge is required, and that brings the House of Burgundy crashing down—that's how things go, history proves it again and again. In the end, all the principals are dead, and the only thing one can say is, Well, now *that's* over. Who were the heroes? Who the villains? What are the lessons here? There are none. There can be none. It is only a story, a great story—a German story.

"Which of course is the astonishing thing. A full two centuries after the last bulwarks of heathendom were smashed in Europe—which campaign, incidentally, was directed by German emperors, Otto and his successors— we find this profoundly non-Christian epic being penned in the very heart of the Holy Roman Reich, commissioned by a duly christened noble, even as Wolfram, two days' riding north, was penning his *Parzival*. That is the second, really quite striking point of divergence.

"There is one other. And you may think it odd, but I have come to think this may be the most telling of all. *Parzival* was written to be spoken aloud—memorized and then recited. The *Nibelungenlied,* in contrast, was composed to be chanted or sung, to the accompaniment most probably of a lyre. Thus the former is an early work of modern literature, whose author we know, whose artistic intent is fairly clear. The latter is neither modern nor literary. Though beautifully worded and filled with compelling scenes, arresting images, even the sort of nuance we would now call psychological, it is not, in the end, a work of the mind. It is a pure matter of the heart, the blood, the enraptured consciousness. The author is nameless because the story springs from deep in our folk-soul. It is the Matter of Germany in the purest possible sense.

"So there"—setting his glass down, folding his hands, a monkish gesture, as though laying aside the quill—"in brief, is the problem I have undertaken to solve. How does one speak, how can one put forward a proposition of the utmost delicacy, to a nation of people who think in categories, who look for morals and believe in consequences, on behalf of a nation that does not?"

A fair question, Ingo thought. "So," he said, "how does one?"

Cheruski stared, eyes bleary now. He weakly waved an arm. "I have thought . . . well, you know, they were both *Germans,* it's hard to get around that. Maybe something about the Grail, the deepest mystery, the hidden truth . . . strip away the Christian stuff, it's pagan at the core—the sacred goblet, only a youth can approach it, an innocent, 'slender and pure as a flame'—"

"That's George, not Wolfram." Ingo sighed. Cheruski had seemed to be making sense there for a while. Now he was babbling, a tired and deluded old man.

"But I know," the Professor said, fixing Ingo with a darkly impassioned stare, "what you're wondering is, do I have anything for the Reichsführer? Have I found *an equation, something scientific?* No, I have not. It is such a pity. For if only the Anglo-Americans could be made to understand us, then we might put an end to this needless war. Our generals could turn to the true enemy in the East. And people like you and me, Herr Müller, could take off these uniforms and get back to our books."

Ingo slept fitfully, twisting beneath heavy blankets and coming partly awake again and again, unable to separate the strands of reality and dream, each as strange, as haunted, as the other. Footsteps echoing down cold hallways. A boy lifts a heavy cup to tender lips. A hunter rears on his steed, armor black and shiny as an automobile. Cries of terror, dragon's fire, a castle standing empty, a countryside left barren. Ingo is lost in an edgeless forest. His legs move but carry him nowhere, only deeper among the trees. There are furtive noises all around, invisible scurrying. Then a hush: the air is shot through by a hunter's horn, blazing clear and hard-edged as the sunlight.

He opened his eyes. The curtain of the cupboard bed was closed but the window drape must have been open because the coachman's room was flooded with light. He lay there blinking with the dream still in his mind, coloring his awareness. The echo of the *Jägerhorn* seemed to linger between these heavy plaster walls. Then he heard the snorting of a horse, and he could not have been dreaming that.

He thrust the curtain aside and struggled free of the blankets. The room was winter-cold. Outside the high window lay a hillside of naked trees whose branches, etched in white, shivered against a sky that was deep and achingly blue. The frost on fallen leaves was so heavy it looked like snow. Ingo pressed his forehead to the pane; his eyes probed the woods as if trying to locate the center of a maze. He thought of the Friedrich print hanging on the wall of the Rusty Ring, *Landscape with Oaks and Hunter.* The painting was a visual riddle, as this was, the question being: Where is the hunter? Because the oaks are plain enough, great craggy things with limbs broken by storms, and you can see a passing companionship of birds, the sky turbulent with cloud, a far meadow stretching pale green to glimpses of water . . . but in that expanse of *charakteristisch* Germania, can you spot the hunter? Long-standing patrons of the Ring had won rounds of drinks this way.

"Of course he's there, look at the title. All you have to do is find him. Tell you what, I'll give you an extra minute, starting—*now.*"

And suddenly, there he was. Fifty meters from Ingo's window, a gray-clad figure on horseback, motionless amid a confusion of boulders that lay like the bones of a fallen cathedral with a stream twisting between them. The horse, a large silvery animal, had lowered its head to drink from the half-frozen water. The rider's face was shadowed by a peaked officer's cap. When the horse had drunk its fill he moved just perceptibly in the saddle and the animal turned, clomping unhurriedly up the hill toward the house.

Then there was another, and another. One by one the hunting party came out of the forest. There were five of them mounted and another bunch, too far away yet to count, crossing a low clearing on foot.

Ingo felt a surge of panic—*they were coming for him*—that he tried to dismiss as irrational. Mainly, though, he felt wonderment. It was like a scene out of a different time, a more idealized version of this same countryside.

They called it the Hunting Lodge. Who would have thought they meant it literally?

He tugged on his uniform and found his way to the kitchen, a wide sunny room with hectares of counter space and copper pans dangling from hooks in mixed shades of oxidation. A cookfire blazed in an old woodstove where Magda was fussing over a pot you could have boiled a boar alive in, above which hovered a cloud of steam.

"Magda. There are people coming out of the woods. Men on horses."

She gave him a hurried smile. Agitating the contents of the pot with a huge ladle, she said over her shoulder, "You'll find coffee in the jug there. It's mostly roasted dandelion but there's some of the real stuff mixed in. And milk if you like, but go gently. That's meant to last us awhile."

"But Magda—do you know who these people are? They'll be here any minute. Should we . . . do something? Wake the Professor?"

She turned to him, ladle dribbling a grayish, gooey liquid, her temples pearled with sweat. "Do something?"—as though the idea were novel, or amusing. "A bit late for that, isn't it, dear?"

A clatter came from elsewhere in the house—a door flung open, boots stomping up a corridor. Voices raised, rambunctious, irrepressible, like revelers out on Connecticut Avenue, soldiers on leave, rousing Ingo in the wee hours, beyond caring—Whatta ya gonna do? Put me in the army and teach me to salute?

In the kitchen door a bulky figure appeared, a fairy-tale giant filling the space from sill to header. He wore a week's beard, a Russian-style fur cap, unmatched pieces of a Waffen-SS uniform and a long-barreled bolt-action Mauser. "By God, you old witch," he roared, "there you are, stirring your cauldron. What is it then, a sleeping draught? God, I could use one, I'll tell you that."

His sharp accent and reddened, fruit-shaped nose came from somewhere east of the Alps. Either of his hands could have crushed a coconut. He noticed Ingo and offered a grunt by way of hello.

"It's good porridge," Magda scolded him, "but you're not having any till you clean up. Now step away, you're blocking the door."

He complied indifferently, moving his bulk to the nearest sink and opening the tap, which gave forth a thin stream of water. Behind him came a second man, then a third, as unlike to one another as they were to the giant, except for their ragtag uniforms and their attitude of casual brutal-ity. Before long there were seven of them, filling the large kitchen with raucous laughter, curses in at least three languages and a faint but disgust-ing smell like that of putrefying meat. They paid Ingo no more attention than they would have given a household cat, but this was scant comfort. They looked the sort of men to kick a cat aside the moment it crossed them.

"The chief is back from the east," the giant told Magda when she handed him a steaming bowl. "Did you hear?"

She shook her head. The news didn't seem to interest her.

"He's been promoted," the giant went on, oblivious. "I can't even pro-nounce what he is now."

"Obersturmbannführer," said a man across the room.

"Right. Same as a light colonel. Gave him a medal, too. Something he did at the front. Counterattack against the Russkis, gave 'em a taste I'd say."

"*And* nabbed some horses," said a man with a long, thin face whom Ingo fancifully likened to a defrocked priest. "Ugly old draft horses that belonged to the artillery. Figured, if they can tug an 88 through that Ukrainian mud, they could even carry Janocz."

They all laughed except for the giant, evidently Janocz, who nodded grudgingly. "The both of them together might do it. Myself, I'd rather walk. Never got the hang of shooting from a saddle."

Magda stood with an empty bowl, eyeing the lot of them with uncon-cealed distaste. "Where is he now, then, this great hero? Will he be coming to breakfast or not?"

"Upstairs with the old man," said the priest.

This answer did not appear to satisfy Magda, who stared at the empty bowl as though it posed an intractable dilemma.

"Give it to that one," said Janocz, pointing to Ingo. "All good SS boys should eat their porridge. That's what Heini says, eh?"

Magda shrugged. She scooped out a portion of what looked like gelati-nous, overboiled oatmeal, placed it on the counter and left the kitchen without ceremony.

Now for lack of other entertainment, the rough-looking men turned their attention to Ingo. None of them spoke, but he figured it was only a matter of time.

"How was the hunting?" he said, taking the initiative, aiming for an easy, bartender's bonhomie.

For the longest while no one made a sound, only stared at him, and Ingo feared he had given himself away.

Then the defrocked priest shook his head. "Not so good this time. We had a tip about some Czechs who'd been hitting railroad lines from a base somewhere on Tatra Polskich. We spent five days up there and saw nothing but rocks. Finally went into a little mountain village and interrogated the peasants. Nobody would talk, so we shot a few. Still no talking, so we shot some more. Soon only women and kids were left, and they started babbling, but who could believe them? So we cleared the place out and had a fire and a nice dinner, then we came back down."

The other men nodded and muttered; a couple added details that Ingo tried not to hear. He dug into his oatmeal, which had taken on the look of liquefied brain matter.

"Know what I heard, though?" said a dark little man whose hair was cropped shorter than his dramatic, coal-black eyebrows. "I heard tomorrow we're headed out again, to the other side of the Gap. Hunting's always better there. And you know what else—"

"Not tomorrow!" groaned Janocz. "I need some rest. I haven't slept the night through in a week."

"You need a fucking bath, is what," another man said.

"What I heard was," Eyebrows persisted, "there's a bunch of Jews out there, somewhere. Out in the east, toward Zakopanje."

"They've *all* gone east," the priest said archly. "Haven't you heard?"

"I'm talking about *living* Jews. Fighters, in the mountains somewhere. That's who we're going after. So I hear."

Someone scoffed: "Jewish fighters."

"I haven't shot a Jew since 1943," mused Janocz, rubbing his chin.

"There *were* some Jewish fighters," Eyebrows said. "Back when you were still loading manure down in Croatia. The ZOB—that was a tough bunch, let me tell you."

"It was during Harvest Festival," Janocz said. "Remember that?"

"Who doesn't?" said the priest.

"I've heard there's Jews left in Lithuania. A whole brigade of them, men and women both. Breeding in the swamps like maggots."

"They were short of hands at the big camp up by the railroad, and they had a quota. You know, a certain number they needed to kill. Birthday present for Heydrich or some such thing."

"Heydrich was dead by then," said Eyebrows, apparently the historian. "It was more, a commemoration."

Janocz scowled. "This was before the snow started, anyhow—tail end of the transport season. Harvest Festival, get it? Extra pay and lots of booze, to help you get on with the job. Plus, if you went through their pockets, who knows what you might find? Take a look at this." He opened a flap of his filthy coat and dug something out of a pocket.

It was swaddled in red cloth, and at first Ingo thought it was a piece of jewelry. But as the giant let it dangle he saw that it was an exceedingly ornate military decoration; around the basic shape of a Prussian cross in blue enamel played an intricate filigree of silver and gold, topped by a silver lion and a pairing of delicate, green-enameled laurels. "What is it?" he couldn't help asking.

"Ah," said the giant. "Well, I wondered about that myself. Finally I asked the Professor and he looked it up in a book someplace. Turns out it's the Commander's Cross with Swords, First Class, issued by the Duchy of Brunswick at the end of the First War. Quite a rare sort of thing, only a few dozen awarded. Well this old Jew, he was wearing it that day, under his shirt. Must've bought it at a pawnshop, I reckon. Anyhow, it's mine now."

"Worth anything, you think?" Eyebrows said.

The giant shrugged. "Beats me. I keep it for good luck."

"Didn't bring the last fellow much luck," the priest pointed out.

Janocz frowned. He seemed not to have thought of that.

Then came footsteps, as regular as marching. Ingo didn't know whether to be relieved or more frightened. Could things get worse? Probably so. The giant cleared his throat, making a sound like a motorcycle kicking over. Around the room there was a general clamming-up; some of the men straightened their backs while others patted their uniforms into a poor semblance of order.

Through the kitchen door, at a crisp gait, stepped Cheruski followed closely by another officer in a field-gray cape. Jaekl came last, looking out of temper and seeming to shrink from the coarse, vile-smelling men; Ingo could hardly blame him. For an instant, the two of them exchanged an almost brotherly glance.

"The Brigadeführer tells me," said the officer beside Cheruski, "we have a newcomer. Another Volksdeutscher, gentlemen! We are becoming quite international, aren't we, in these days?"

Ingo longed to disappear. But he forced himself to meet the man's gaze straight on. The Obersturmbannführer was not large; he stood slightly shorter than Ingo and was as trim as Jaekl at the waist, though somewhat fuller in the shoulders. His most distinguishing trait was an exceptional pallor that extended from his surprisingly delicate hands—they could have belonged to a painter or a pianist—to his unemotive face, cold blue eyes, and thinning hair as fine and glossy as spun gold. His paleness became all the more striking when, in the steamy heat of the kitchen, the man whipped off his cape to reveal the all-black uniform of the Allgemeine-SS, the elite inner corps of the service, the Black Knighthood itself. He took a couple strides into the room, getting a better look at the name patch above Ingo's breast pocket.

"Miller," he said.

No, he said *Müller*, he must have. Ingo felt a shiver pass through him—invisibly, he hoped—and struggled to remain impassive, to return the man's stare as coolly as Josef Müller, battle-hardened *Sturmmann,* would have done. He distracted himself with irrelevant details: the creases beside the fellow's mouth, the exhaustion in his eyes.

"We head out tomorrow," the officer said. It was in effect an order. He spoke loudly, so that he appeared to be addressing the entire room, but his eyes were still on Ingo. "You come with us, Müller. I think you may find it interesting. Perhaps you will discover that you have an aptitude. The hunter's instinct." Then turned away and gave Cheruski a brisk little nod.

"Jaekl," the older man said, "go find Magda, would you? Tell her I shall be taking breakfast in my study, with Obersturmbannführer von Ewigholz."

Ingo's mind clicked on those ice-blue eyes. *My God,* he thought. The Black Knight was Hagen.

OFF THE MAP

Ingo in love.

It sounded—and perhaps was—absurd, buffoonish.

And yet: as he lay on a thin youth-hostel mattress with the early light of Thuringia in his eyes, listening to a distant clatter from the courtyard, Frau Möhring giving her poor kitchen staff no respite, breakfast will be served *pünktlich* at seven, he felt as though he were hearing a tinkle of golden chimes and breathing ambrosia-scented air. He could scarcely restrain himself form leaping up and running across the dew-soaked grass. And he would have done so, if there were any hope of meeting Anton earlier than 10:30.

His friend—*my lover*—would be hiking down from Jena and Ingo would hike partway up; they would meet in a woodland east of Jägersdorf, on a hill called the Sommerberg. It was good orchid country, though before long, said Anton, the game-hunters would be out, there would be danger—*es ist eine Schande,* for the autumn anemones bloom into October here, and the asters by the roadside, you should see them! There is one nearly pure blue, very pale, like the sky after a rain.

So Ingo hung around the Leuchtenburg feeling restless, jangly, half bored, half insane with happiness. He stared for a while at the painted statue of an almost naked Saint Sebastian. He inspected the castle's collection of medieval armaments. Finally, in a hopeless failure of inspiration, he flipped through the hostel guest book, and it was during this time that Martina tracked him down. He could feel her presence in the room—she radiated that sort of intensity—even before she spoke. He pictured her standing there, wanting attention, steam rising from her ears. He smiled.

"What are you smirking about?" she demanded.

He looked up, feigning surprise. "Nothing, really. Some of these entries, they're just so . . ."

"So?"

"*German.*"

As if he was anything but German himself.

In the forest, a different order prevailed. To come here among the ancient trees was to confront a stirring, unsimplified, complexly evocative environment. Your mind opened to a richer frame of reference. Your body reawakened to its primordial genius, its beauty-in-usefulness. To trade the bonds of floor and walls and ceiling for the unbounded freedom of the woods was like putting aside a comic book and opening *Faust*. You might find it alarming, morally chaotic, incomprehensible. But you must also—unless it was already too late, your soul already narcotized by modernity—find it thrilling, pulsing, raw, authentic, writhing with life, infinitely to be preferred to what you had left behind. Here, your senses grew sharper. Your pleasures and agonies grew more acute. If you were happy, you became ecstatic. If sad, you became like young Werther, lost, without solace, foredoomed. And if you were in love, there were no rules to follow, no limits or precedents to contain you. Anything was possible, everything was permitted, but there was no way to anticipate where you were heading. The forest was a land without maps.

Anton's shoulders were so thin you could see how the bones were joined together, how his parts moved. His skin, where the sun had not changed it, had a subtle tawny undertone, in contrast to Ingo's pink. It was like the wood underneath the bark of certain trees—only smoother, warmer, softer, sweeter, a miracle of texture and scent stretched gently over his sternum, his ribs, his hips. His hair had a slight curl and would not stay for long out of his eyes. One of his upper bicuspids, slightly uneven, lent a funny asymmetry to his grin. His mouth was wide, full, exaggerated. His eyes were chocolate-brown. There was a tiny dark mole on his left cheek, another just off-center near his heart, one three-and-a-half centimeters below his navel and another, slightly larger, midway down the left thigh. When he closed his eyes, his lashes cast a lovely shadow. When he stared hard at something close, something small, like a flower's trembling pistil, his chin tensed into a knot and fleeting frown-lines ran from his nostrils to the corners of his mouth, and his long, seemingly awkward fingers became as steady and exact as precision instruments. When Ingo kissed him those fingers raked his back.

They found several interesting specimens that day. The grass pink orchid, *Calopogon tuberosus,* rare in Europe but an errant cousin of a genus still numerous in North America. A gentian, sadly past its blooming period, which Anton was able to identify by the structure of its withered reproductive parts as *G. forsteriana* or forester's gentian—"which makes," as he put it, "a blue impression, but is yet not true blue." And a striking plant with deep green leaves, as glossy as if they'd been spit-shined, that looked half vine and half shrub; it had hoisted itself up by clinging to the trunk of an oak tree and then—at a height of slightly less than two meters, just above where a grown deer could nibble its foliage—had spread widely, flowered, and now was covered in small black berries like those of privet.

Anton laughed when Ingo expressed an interest in this plant. "That's ivy," he said. "Common ivy, *Hedera helix,* in its mature form. The seed probably flew here in some bird's gut. Maybe the parent lives in Jena, climbing the walls of my dormitory—who knows?"

The rain caught them under the ivy. They huddled there while lightning flashed and thunder echoed off the Sommerberg. For a while the glossy leaves held the water off. But after half an hour of steady downpour everything became saturated and the leaves drooped, spilling an accumulation of heavy drops that landed with a splatter. The water was not cold and at first it was welcome, washing the sweat off, making their bodies feel sinuous. The chill set in by the time it was over. They laughed through chattering teeth as they pulled their clothes on—the clothes they'd hoped to keep dry by tucking them in compact bundles at the base of the oak, failing to appreciate how water would channel down indentations in the bark like tiny vertical rivers, soaking the material and matting it with forest debris. Anton's skin was slick, his nipples contracted; he smelled like a warm loaf out of the oven, like grass, like sea-salt. Ingo needed him one more time. And then it was hopeless, they would die of chill, his heart would explode in bliss. They set off for the Leuchtenburg together.

"You," said the blond boy, "broke a fellow's nose"—pointing at Ingo—"and you"—at Isaac—"something far worse. You took his honor. To have been bested by a Jew! An American Jew! And all this"—swinging his head around to stare at Käthe—"over a scheme you Socialists cooked up. A political intrigue. A piece of paper."

It was impossible to know how the boy felt about what he was saying. His tone was lacking in rancor: give him that. Lacking in everything, from what Ingo could tell. But then, something had impelled him to journey here from the Höhe Meissner, dragging along some left-wing journalist whom Ingo detested on sight. Where was *he* this morning? And where the hell was Marty?

Anton at least was accounted for: outdoors, inspecting the castle grounds on the theory that there might be plants left over from some forgotten garden—native herbs, uncommon today, once cultivated for medicinal or dye-making purposes. It would keep him busy all morning.

"Should you ask my advice," the boy said, with precocious *gravitas,* "I would urge you to leave this place at once and go far away, out of Germany, even."

"Is that so?" said Isaac, in New York English that was more or less self-translating. "Well, nobody asked you."

So: an impasse. The four of them were in the woodworking shop on the second floor of the castle, surrounded by half-finished toys. Old lathes, operated by foot pumps, were mounted on work benches, and an assortment of hand tools lay amid piles of sawdust where the Young Socialist Workers had left them. It was Sunday. A row of jointed wooden clowns hung from strings in the window while their paint dried. Body parts of a dozen hobbyhorses were piled in stacks, awaiting assembly. Isaac lounged on the floor with his back propped against a pile of wooden torsos, Ingo sat sensibly on a bench, Käthe paced and—slipping out of character— puffed inexpertly at one of Isaac's cigarettes. The German boy, Hagen, stood at ease with one hand resting on a large open vise.

"You will just wait here, then," he said, "until they come looking for you."

Nobody answered him but he didn't seem to care. Ingo couldn't figure this kid out. It was hard even to decide whether to look at him or not. There was something a little frightening, even repellent, about his aloofness and his perfect, icy beauty. And yet there was that beauty: a breathing artistry. Hagen was like a statue that you could speak to and it would speak back. It would turn and move so you could examine it from varying angles. You could touch it. That might be interesting. It might also be dangerous.

"They will find you, of course." The boy was looking down at Isaac. "Many of the Jungdo live in Saxony, they know this part of the country well. They know the habits of their political enemies. For them this is not a single incident, a thing that happened once, they shrug and forget about it. No, they are fighting a war, and this is a battle. There have been other battles, there will be many more to come. Some they will lose—it does not matter. They are prepared to accept casualties, so long as in the end they are victorious. But this, this is a battle they can win. So they will choose to win it. This is how simple the matter is."

He turned to Käthe; he seemed to be calculating. "Perhaps I should add one thing more. To win this particular battle, they will need to get blood on their hands. That one"—gesturing toward Isaac—"almost certainly they will kill. The other one, perhaps not. He fought like a man, there is no shame in having faced such an opponent. But that one, the Jew . . ."

"His name is Isaac," Käthe said. Her voice matched his in coldness. "Around here we don't go calling people the Jew, the Catholic, the Saxon. Here we are all human beings."

"Perhaps. But not all Germans. And certainly not all patriots, not in the eyes of the Jungdo."

"Not all Germans? *Not all patriots?*" Käthe's eyes were on a tableful of sharpened tools and Ingo wondered if she was selecting one.

"Don't shoot the messenger," Ingo advised her. "Or stab him either. What *I* wonder is, why has he gone to all this trouble? Why come here in the first place? Why betray his friends?"

Obviously the questions were for Hagen, but Ingo was still having trouble turning his eyes that way.

The boy understood; he looked at Käthe while replying. "I cannot explain, except to say that it is a question of . . ." Ingo expected *honor,* that singular German obsession, but Hagen concluded, "of fair play." Now he looked at Ingo, gesturing with a hand. "It is as a hunt. There are ways of choosing the prey, ways of making the kill. It is necessary that there should be a balance. One does not bomb a stag from an airplane. One does not set out with a party of twelve to corner a rabbit. This is the rule: One must grant the beast one hunts its own nobility. Each animal has a kind of nobility, so does each person. Even a Jew possesses nobility of a kind."

"Did you just say"—Käthe's voice seemed to teeter between outrage and hilarity—"that *even a Jew possesses nobility of a kind?*"

"Yes." Hagen looked at her blankly. "That is just what I said. This is what I believe."

"What a champ," said Isaac from the floor. "I love this putz, don't you?"

The two boys, roughly the same age, different in every other way, sized each other up. Isaac pulled a comical face. He was dexterous in this regard—somehow he managed to stretch out his features as if they'd been shoved against a pane of glass. At the German's mouth, for the very first time, Ingo discerned the tentative sketching-in of a smile.

"You know actually," said Käthe, lighting another cigarette—she alone displaying an intensity of feeling appropriate to the circumstances—"there is a place, in the East. Which would be safe, I think. It is . . . we call it the Model Hamlet. A kind of experimental community. In the German-speaking part of Poland, the old province of Silesia—Isaac knows it already, his aunt and uncle live there. Near a rail stop called Auschwitz, just short of Kraków."

He caught Martina sneaking down from one of the castle towers, nominally off-limits on account of safety concerns. Safety concerns, that was a laugh. Trailing a few steps behind her new pal Butler, she looked—in Ingo's newly expert opinion—like she'd been fucking all night.

He felt two distinct categories of disbelief. One, that she had done such a thing. Two, that he hadn't seen it coming. It was so obvious, now that he thought about it. The pair of them acting last night like they were sharing God knew what manner of secrets. The strange looks she'd thrown Ingo's way at the bonfire. Now it all made sense. Anyway, what was it to him?

"Hiya, Marty," he said with what he imagined to be a sly and knowing smile.

"Hi, Ingo"—same smile, right back at him.

Butler himself they managed for the moment to ignore.

"Sleep well?" Ingo said solicitously. "I hear they have bats up there."

"Really? I didn't notice any. How about you? I hope you found somewhere to put Anton, there's hardly an extra bed in the house."

He couldn't penetrate her expression. Their stares crossed like swords. They'd come an incredible distance from their shady street in Brookland.

She laughed. He was *not* expecting that. She stepped over quickly and gave him a hug—a thing she'd never done before, not that he could remember.

"Oh, Ingo," she said, "I'm so happy. Really, I am."

She let him go, scampered after Butler. She never explained, then or later, what she was so damned happy about.

The most wretched day of his life began with a glorious sunrise. The light had a stabbing quality, as he imagined it might if he'd woken up with a hangover. (Ingo had never known a night of excessive drinking, though he began to suspect one might be coming.) Are there paeans in Deutsch, he wondered, to the breaking of day? None that he could think of. Your German poet is nocturnal, first stirring at the *Dämmerung;* if ever he sees the sun come up he must have been awake all night, weathering the usual torments. German literary sunrises are alarming developments, pregnant with ill omen. *Flecks of cloud flutter, weakly struggling, as red flames steal among them*—one of countless disheartening moments in Schubert's *Winterreise.* George of course is more Gothic.

> *Through storm and grisly portents of dawn*
> *He harries his flock to the day's work*
> *And plants the New Reich.*

Anton had said: It's only a question of timing.

Now Ingo stood before a slit window in the Gunpowder Tower, known during certain centuries as the Martyr Tower—he had not learned why. But he knew the story, everyone did, about the discovery during a nineteenth-century renovation of a tiny skeleton underneath one of the cornerstones: a *Bauopfer* or "builder's sacrifice," once apparently common all over Europe. In one version, the skeleton belonged to a cat. In the much preferred telling, however, it was the remains of a human infant. Dead babies would not have been hard to come by in those times, but in order to be effective, the Masonic rite required an actual killing. Everyone loved this story, it was one of the first things you heard when you signed in—right up there with the Black Death of 1506, during which people throughout the Saale Valley had sought refuge in the castle, bringing, need it be said, the plague along with them. Hence, half-naked Sebastian, protector against pestilence. And you were shown the ash tree, of course, from which some scant eighty years ago a peasant woman had been hanged, after having murdered her five, or was it six, innocent children. (Always *innocent*—as though surviving past childhood implicated you in some unnamed sin.)

Ingo supposed that old castles naturally inspired such legends. How many schoolboy nightmares had been spawned by Meyer's ballad about those *two feet writhing in the fire*? He wondered, on this particular morning, whether something about these places encouraged terrible things to happen. An architecture of calamity. Designed with a view toward violence, built at excruciating cost in labor and gold, attacked and defended with bloody-minded tenacity for hundreds of years—how could these stones *not* have absorbed some part of the anguish and battle ardor that had raged here? And now, to turn the place into a youth hostel! It was insane. But so was the world nowadays. Insane, needlessly cruel, remorseless.

Ingo felt like bellowing in his misery. His feelings had nothing to do with sinister Masonic rituals or the bacterium *Yersinia pestis*, borne by fleas—he understood that much. He was heartbroken, not stupid.

It's only a question of timing.

One decision having been taken—to leave here, to hike across the Iron Mountains into the Sudetenland, thence to the Polish border around Ostrava, and into Silesia—other decisions became necessary. The least of these, to rebook a liner passage with Hamburg-Amerika. Next, to notify Catholic U. of an unavoidable delay in their return for the autumn semester. Health problems could be cited, Butler suggested. An outbreak of Carpathian flu. More like a vampire attack, Ingo thought, eyeing Hagen with a surge of distaste.

Come on, Ingo—Martina never would take "no"—*it'll be worth it, you know it will. A real adventure!* He did not disagree. He imagined with hallucinogenic clarity just what kind of adventure it would be.

Only then, Anton. Forced to a decision of his own. Classes would start in a week, he noted with odd dispassion. The journey out and back must take at least twice that, even if the return were made by train. Those first lectures would be crucial: Anatomical Structure, with the well-known Professor Doktor Sippewitz—to miss the beginning is to lose the foundation for everything that follows. And the Theory of Eugenics, a recent offering, scandalous and popular, there was a danger of losing one's place on the class roster. No, it could not be avoided, emotions have no place in this matter, it's only a question of timing.

Hagen had said: This is how simple the matter is. And so it was, and there was no use in arguing. Nor in trying to sleep. Better to stand guard in the tower against the coming of dawn.

Nach irren nächten sind die morgen schlimm. George's deathly pentameter, precise as a scalpel. *After nights of madness, mornings are grim.*

One feature of being Ingo—*ein Eigene,* a singular being, for lack of a more helpful term—was that you were denied many of the ordinary opportunities for emotional display. Unless you happened to find yourself in an enchanted spot like Frau-Holle-Quell, where rules were magically suspended, you were advised to keep your feelings pretty damned close to your chest. Of course he was quite good at this, having spent half his lifetime honing a talent that already came naturally; but that was not the same as finding it easy to do. He remembered reading of a famous actor, a lion of the theater, who became violently ill from stage fright before every performance. Ingo felt sick now—not Carpathian flu, this was far worse—as the little band of hikers, making ready to depart, sorted itself out from those who were staying behind.

There were hugs for each of them from the good Frau Möhring—for Ingo, Martina, Butler, Isaac, even for Hagen, who failed to respond. More hugs from Käthe, along with a detailed map drawn on the back of an outdated flyer, pressed into Martina's hand. (Hagen: "We do not need this map. I can find any place you might name.") Effusive farewells and good wishes from some of the Young Socialists, Käthe's friends, the kitchen crew. At the end there were Ingo and Anton, standing eye-to-eye, with too much to say or nothing at all. How can you find a compromise, what sort of chummy goodbye would not be a vulgar apostasy?

Anton had given the matter some thought, it seemed. He opened his sketchbook, the one he used for field observations, and spoke with his eyes safely away from Ingo's, carefully removing a page. "I have heard of a certain flower," he said, "a blue flower—as I understand, it is not to be found in any of the scientific literature. Perhaps it is only a legend, yet there are those, my friend has told me, who claim to have seen it. I may have glimpsed this flower myself, only yesterday. Here, this is a drawing, perhaps you could help me make a positive identification."

Ingo took the paper but did not look at it; save that for later. "Do you know Hofmannsthal?" he said.

"Alas, no. He is modern, I think?"

"He died just this year. There's a poem called 'Infinite Time'—'Unendliche Zeit.' They'd probably have it in your library at the university."

"Thank you, I shall find it."

Scene—A wood near Wolfersdorf. Later that afternoon.

MARTINA: What was that business about a poem? Some
    kind of secret message?
INGO [*glowers*]: It's just a poem.
MARTINA: Sure. What about the picture. Can I see that?
INGO: It's just a flower.
MARTINA: I'm sorry, Ingo. Really, I am.
INGO (to himself): *About what?*

It's not like they didn't warn you. It's not as though the entire corpus of German literature from the *Nibelungenlied* onward was not one long, breathless chronicle of heartache and loss. Frequent spurting of blood and other body fluids. Then more loss, more betrayal, more loneliness. Ingo knew it, he had always known it; it was the worst-kept secret in all of Secret Germany. Yet look at him now—like a boar who manages to be surprised by the sudden tearing at his chest, even though he has been hearing *Jägerhörner* and baying hounds all morning.

It's only a question of timing.

Hagen, scorning Käthe's map, took unto himself the role of pathfinder. He marched ahead with Butler following and Martina alternately trying to keep up and not, ultimately falling back with Ingo. He found a silent comfort in her company. Then she would blow it by opening her mouth.

Isaac was not predictable. Something in him resisted being assigned a place, or staying in one. There were times when he lagged, others when he skipped ahead, probably to annoy Hagen, whose pace was brisk but precisely measured. More than once he vanished from the trail altogether—only to reappear half an hour later, lounging in tall yellow grass or squatting puckishly on an overhang, moving his mouth in amusement as if chewing imaginary gum.

"Was für einen Pfadfinder denn?" he said once, sarcastically, looking down on Hagen's head. What kind of trailblazer is this? Hagen pretended to ignore him but it seemed to Ingo, from his vantage point in the rear guard, that the German boy was tracking Isaac's movements attentively. There was an odd sort of game between them—fox and hound, or maybe, in the local tradition, hare and hedgehog. The rules were unclear and so were the players' motives. You assumed they were on opposing sides, though in the folktale the two hedgehogs, unbeknownst to the hare, are acting in sneaky connivance. Now and then Ingo wondered if these two were pulling something over on everyone. Pulling it over even on themselves.

During a longish stop for rest—which everyone pretended not to need, yet which no one was eager to see an end of—Hagen lectured them on the theory of hunting. Lesson one: Game Is Where You Find It.

"It is not best to be in deep forest. Nor again, the open Weide. These extremes are for the most part empty. No, what is needed is the edge, the in-between area. On this side the trees, on that side the meadow. At the edge the animals find cover. They find also leaves and berries and smaller creatures to eat. They find long lines of sight, so they may notice the coming of their enemies. In every respect, the edge is best for them—it is here the hunter should seek his prey."

Isaac heard only part of this. Hunting didn't interest him, apparently. He got up and wandered off somewhere—not far, Ingo suspected. Probably just out there in the undergrowth, eavesdropping on them from some hidey-hole. A native of the fringes, our Isaac. And in this, at least, a clansman of Ingo himself.

Camp that first night was on a hill south of Plauen. There was a youth hostel in town and another a few kilometers farther, in Greiz. They decided to pass on these because they had reached the western edge of Saxony, a stronghold of right-wing bands like the Jungdeutsche Orden. The arrival at a hostel of such an odd-looking group might, they feared, spark gossip. So under the stars it shall be tonight, perhaps tomorrow. Then we'll be in Czechoslovakia, a quiet country, the Sudetenland, Germans and Slavs living together peacefully—we'll have no trouble from that point.

Meanwhile, the question of dinner. The good Frau Möhring had packed some provisions for them, but hadn't they ought to save that for the long road ahead? Over the mountains and through the woods to a model Socialist hamlet.

"I will get food," Hagen announced.

"Yeah, how?" said Isaac in his most annoying tone. You could imagine him as a little kid, pushing through a crowd on the sidewalk to get his two bits in. And look, there's his mother, watching through the window, fretting. Someday, she knows, one of those larger boys is going to push back.

Wish you were here, Ma.

"I will set snares," Hagen explained. "It is a skill they taught us. I have everything I need. You may start the fire within the next hour."

Isaac rolled his eyes. "This I gotta see."

They set off into the underbrush together—one stepping boldly ahead, the other slipping after him like a thief, though after a few steps you couldn't tell which was which. Among the others, responsibility divided itself in a manner that was more or less spontaneous, or at least went undiscussed. Ingo scavenged fallen branches for firewood. Martina opened bags and arranged their equipment and brought a homey order to the campsite. Butler concerned himself with Ingo's pup tent, which couldn't hold all of them, and perhaps that was Butler's point: Might as well let him and Marty have it, what say? Thanks, old boy, you're a sport. Ingo didn't really care. He was in no mood for enclosure.

Hagen returned a good while later, not before the fire was well burned-down, looking disconsolate. He'd caught only a squirrel, thankfully plumped for the coming winter, and a scrawny fowl that had chosen the wrong patch of ground to go pecking in.

"That's great!" Martina exclaimed doubtfully. "We'll just throw in some, ah, green stuff. And it won't hurt to eat a *little* of the bread."

"Where's Isaac?" Ingo felt obliged to ask.

Hagen didn't give much of a reply; apparently the two had parted company. While Martina considered what to do with the meager catch, Hagen pulled from his knapsack a pretty wooden recorder, settled himself at a somewhat awkward remove and performed, flawlessly but with little feeling, a series of Youth Movement favorites. Martina tried to sing along—the gal's got heart, even Ingo conceded that—but she didn't know many of the lyrics. Her English-language rendering of "When I Go A-Wandering" was something he believed he would never forget. Afterward, Butler told off-color jokes as the light began to fail. Ingo contributed nothing whatever, beyond his brooding presence. Even this, he felt, was below par. This was the worst day of his life, and he was not about to let anything spoil it.

Now rub the lamp.

Poof!—a flurry of stage magic—and here before us stands Isaac. Isaac the Ever-Surprising. Isaac—can you believe it?—the Provider. In one hand a freshly slaughtered hen, well fleshed, sans head. In the other a piece of cloth, color deep azure, function unclear.

"There you go," he said, to no one especially. He laid the hen before the fire. It was too good, too plump and perfect, to be credible. At the very least, it begged an explanation that was not, however, forthcoming. Not then, not ever. The blue cloth he sent lofting through the evening air. It unfurled in flight, revealing itself to be an ordinary, Scout-style bandanna. "I guess you must've dropped that," he told Hagen. The German boy looked much less thankful than humiliated. Then, striving to top his tormentor in magical prowess, he fluffed the old make-the-hankie-disappear trick.

What do you know? thought Ingo. Nothing much, really. There were mysteries here and he supposed they would only deepen, as the better sort of mystery did.

After dinner (which was delicious, hunger being the finest sauce) he rolled out his blanket, turned his back to the others and carefully withdrew

Anton's drawing from a jacket pocket, just over his heart. It was a pen-and-ink sketch of a flower that—though technically nonexistent—was nonetheless rendered in botanically exact detail. Stem, leaf, petal, stamen, seed pod, each part labeled in a graceful, meticulous hand. The plant was identified as *Gentiana poetica*. The drawing itself was a poem, he thought, in its inspiration, its density, its rigorous composition. In the tears it brought to one's eyes.

What was that business about a poem?

> *In the shadow we stood trembling.*
> *It hadn't been an hour since the rain—*
> *Yet it felt like an infinite time.*
> *I had taken within me all your twenty-year-old being*
> *While the tree (so I believed)*
> > *Still clung to every raindrop.*

THE LINE

"The key to making this work," said Seryoshka, "is a narrow concentration of force leading to a rapid breakthrough. One quick thrust"—jabbing a finger at the map—"and we're over the line, into the enemy's rear. After that we're just dealing with partisan-hunters, not frontoviks. It isn't the same as being unopposed. But we should make rapid progress, especially if we keep to the backcountry."

He looked at the others, half a dozen men gathered in the political officer's yurt. Besides Butler and the *politruk*, there were a couple operations specialists from Division, a signals man who spoke English and implored Butler to call him Bo, and a roly-poly combat engineer who wore a hand-knitted yarmulke under his helmet while crawling through German minefields. So far, Butler thought, they'd heard nothing that everyone present did not already know.

"There are two possibilities," Seryoshka went on. "One, we can probe for a weak spot in the enemy line. This would entail reconnaissance-in-force. Or two, and more simply, we could force the hinge."

He paused to let his audience think it over. It was clear to Butler that his friend preferred the second alternative. Forcing the hinge meant striking at the point where two opposing formations intersect, the small gap between two divisions, or corps, or armies—the higher up, the better. It was a risky ploy: in effect, you were doubling the number of units that stood against you. What you hoped to achieve was an interlude of uncertainty, a temporary breakdown in the enemy's tactical coordination. Whenever two military staffs are confronted by the same problem, there is likely to be a delay during which things are sorted out, intelligence shared, boundaries set, responses calibrated. By the time the dust settles, with any luck, you've accomplished your objectives—in this case, to rip the seam apart and hold it open long enough to push a motorized regiment through. If not, you're fucked from both sides.

"One argument in favor of going for the hinge is the enemy's order of battle. Facing us in this sector, we have the 21 SS, one of the so-called foreign divisions, in this case mainly Bulgarians. On its left flank stands the 345 Infantry, a regular Wehrmacht formation dredged up this summer from what's left of Franconia. Old men, boys, desk-murderers."

The chubby engineer grunted. This last was a term for Germans of fighting age who, until now, had passed the war on the home front, mostly in office jobs. The popular epitome of such people, given currency by the likes of Ehrenburg, was the nameless Berlin bureaucrat signing orders for mass deportations.

"So, you've got an SS division with German commanders, decent supplies and foreign troops flanked by a green Wehrmacht division with a core of veteran staff officers and NCOs. On the face of it, a textbook opportunity for exploitation."

"What textbook would that be?" wondered one of the Division men.

Butler hoped Seryoshka was prepared for this. Red Army doctrine was essentially conservative—designed by geniuses, so the joke went, to be carried out by idiots. It favored the broad frontal assault, prepared by heavy artillery fire and conducted by an overwhelming mass of politically motivated foot soldiers. Such innovations as the Blitzkrieg were scorned as inherently Fascistic. Which did not, however, prevent Soviet officers from admiring a man like Patton—this despite the general's widely reputed anti-Communism. More than one Red Army tank commander had confided to Butler that he hoped to fight against Patton someday.

"That book," Seryoshka said coolly, "would be Voroshilov's account of the Civil War. He writes of a cavalry tactic known as *probing for the fault*. 'The enemy's weakness lay not in lack of arms or men, but in lack of proletarian unity. We taught ourselves to exploit this.'"

They all stared at him. The yurt went quiet except for the sizzle of green wood in the tiny *burzhuika* stove. Without warning, Bo, the signals man, threw back his head and laughed. Then they were all laughing.

"Voroshilov!" Bo declared, toasting with an imaginary cup.

Meaning, Butler guessed, they'd decided Seryoshka was lying. Had Voroshilov, that old fool, even *written* a book? If so, who would want to read it! But never mind. It might be a lie, but it was a grand lie—a Russian lie. The kind of thing a Red Army man prefers, most days, to the truth.

"So we strike the hinge," said the senior ops specialist, once things had settled down. It had the resonance of a ruling. "For that we need current intelligence. Not many line-crossers lately. Anyone want to go over there and grab a tongue?"

They all became serious again. Probably because they understood what a tongue was, and what grabbing one entailed. Butler did not. But he liked the phrase, he jotted it down in his notebook.

"Not a Bulgarian," said the signals man.

"No. A German."

"That means an officer," the engineer said thoughtfully. "At least a sergeant."

Ops nodded. "It will be difficult."

"I'll go." Seryoshka slapped Butler on the shoulder. "You come, too. This will make, what do you say? Good material."

It sounded like one of those plans that cannot possibly succeed. But to hear Seryoshka tell it, such operations were commonplace.

The first task was to cross the death strip, the two-to-three-hundred-meter gap between the forward positions of the opposing armies. This area, a narrow open valley with woods on either side, had been mined by the Germans, employing a variety of explosive devices triggered unpredictably; they were very clever about such things. On moonlit nights, Russian sappers would sneak out and clear paths through the minefield, marking them with strips of cloth. On other nights, and often the same nights, German engineers would sneak out and move the cloth strips around, bury new mines and sometimes engage in sharp, hand-to-hand engagements with their Russian counterparts. It was a dangerous game but it passed the time between offensives. And it was necessary, from the Soviet point of view, because to take the pressure off, to just leave the mines lying there, would be as good as telling the Germans, We are not coming yet, you can relax for a while.

The chubby Russian engineer was called Lyubov. He insisted on joining them, though Seryoshka tried to talk him out of it. There was a fourth man, a Chechen, whom Seryoshka had known in Stalingrad. *Light on his feet, you can never hear him coming—he moves like a ghost.*

They waited until ten o'clock and then headed out, first in a crouch and then down on all fours. It wasn't dark; it was never dark with all that snow. The Chechen went first with Lyubov whispering at his heels: "That way— no, to your right. Stay away from that bush there. Now straight through." Butler expected at every instant to hear the hiss of bullets; he could practically feel them whipping through his jacket, burning channels in his skin.

Until you do something like this, you don't think much about the precise location of each of your extremities, or how far up in the air your backside might be at any given moment. In that respect, it was educational.

Seryoshka's breathing came from somewhere close behind him. Butler had expected to be assigned the last position himself. *No. If there is an ambush, it will likely come from the rear. They let you go by, then shoot you in the back.*

The crossing took forever, then suddenly it was over. Now they were on the German side, in sparse woodland which qualitatively was no different from the woods across the valley, but which felt alien, witchy, crawling with monsters. Any one of these shadows . . .

What you need to understand, Seryoshka had explained, is the nature of a front line. This isn't the Great War, we're not talking about trenches with cannon fodder lined up in neat little rows. These units are spread out along a wide sector, the leading edge is lightly manned—it's a web of forward observation posts and dug-in sentry positions, with patrols moving between them. If it were tighter than that, we could open up with mortar fire and, boom, there goes the opposition. The other thing is, what is on a sentry's mind? Imagine: it's the middle of the night, it's cold, you're awake while everyone else is sleeping, you're assigned to a certain area, after a few watches it becomes as familiar as your old schoolyard. You keep your eyes and ears open, but the truth is, you don't expect anyone to be out there. Not really. You know if you hear a noise in the forest, it's probably some animal. Or it's the sergeant, coming to check on you. If you catch a glimpse of something, flickering among the trees—well, soldiers are always seeing phantoms. Every battlefield is haunted. You've seen them, haven't you, Sammy, the phantoms?

Butler was surprised. But yes. Yes in fact, he had seen them. Figures with no particular features, yet as insistently present as the people in a dream.

So: there you are. It's no great difficulty to grab a tongue. The trick is picking the right one. You want a tongue with something to flap about.

Advancing at a crouch through the German-held woods, Seryoshka pulled the cover off his sniper rifle. If such a thing could be an object of beauty, then this Czech-made Moisan Nagant with its big-eyed scope, its oiled ashwood stock and burnished barrel was beautiful. Gently he loosened the sling and looped it around his neck. He unclasped the bayonet and handed this, hilt first, to Butler. One edge of its blade was a row of shiny teeth.

The Chechen moved silently into the darkness. Lyubov followed, not so silently. Butler's limbs began to tremble and his breath took on a rattling sound; he prayed it wasn't as loud as it seemed to be. A minute passed, and another. He lost all sense of direction; stars glimmered through the leafless canopy. While Butler was looking up, one of his feet got tangled in something, a vine maybe. He bent to work it loose. A muffled sound came from not far away, as though someone were trying to speak. This was followed a few moments later by a soft thump and some crunching of undergrowth. Then it was quiet.

Breaking free, his heart pounding, Butler moved to where he thought the sound had come from. He found his three companions kneeling around something. He didn't want to look. No, he needed to—it was, as Seryoshka had said, material. The man lying in a gray uniform jacket, bulked out with layers beneath, was obviously dead. The Chechen wiped his knife clean on the man's sleeve.

"The CP is over there," he whispered. "Maybe three, four hundred meters. That's what he said."

"Do you think he was telling the truth?" said Lyubov. There was a look of childish amazement in his dark little eyes.

"It's a little late to ask now." The Chechen shrugged. "Anyway, he was trying to call out. I didn't have any choice."

What followed seemed endless. They crept from one tree to the next, kept still for a while, moved again. Twice, they came upon sentry posts. Each time they retraced their steps, moved sideways for a distance, then forward again in a new direction, orienting themselves by compass. Butler got the feeling the night was slipping away from them, any minute the sun would start to rise. At last they came in sight of their goal: a dugout with a slanting roof, camouflaged with leaves and netting, whose lower purlin ran flush with the forest floor. There was light enough, by a waning moon, to make out a thin stream of smoke curling from a pipe bored through the timbers.

There was no need for talking; this was what they had planned for, everyone's role was already assigned. Butler's was to stay put and keep watch. Lyubov likewise, a distance away. The two of them, at this crucial stage, were extra bodies; the delicate work was best left to experts. Seryoshka pressed his rifle into Butler's hands, trading it for the bayonet. Then he was gone, one shadow among many. Butler peered around. *Keep your eyes moving and your body still.*

Experimentally, he raised the rifle to his shoulders, admiring the way its mass was balanced. He swept it in an arc, sighting through the scope. At high magnification, the woods looked brighter. He caught a glimpse, he thought, of Lyubov, half hidden behind a tree.

No. Not Lyubov. The uniform was wrong. The figure, approaching Butler at an oblique angle, seemed very close, but that was an illusion, an artifact of sniper's optics. He lowered the weapon and now could see both men, Lyubov and the other one. Lyubov was looking in the wrong direction; the enemy was coming up behind him.

Butler felt something he took for panic. Only it couldn't be panic because at its center was an unnatural calm. What it was, he realized, was simple confusion.

This very situation had been covered in their plans. Butler knew exactly what was expected of him: he must do *nothing*—and that was an order—except stay where he was and keep quiet. If Lyubov were sniffed out, that was for Lyubov alone to deal with. Let him kill the enemy soldier, if he could, or be killed himself. Even let the enemy soldier sound an alarm. The vital thing was, let the problem stay where it was; do not spread it any further, do not involve other members of the team, do not get involved yourself. We will each have to manage as best we can, if anything goes wrong—*our only advantage, and it is little enough, will be the enemy's uncertainty.* The plans were explicit; there was no questioning their terrible logic.

But now, confronted by the reality of the thing, Butler wasn't sure he could do what he needed to. It had never been his way to merely watch—perhaps that was why he'd never soared to great heights as a journalist. He pressed his eye to the scope again. With his thumb he found the safety.

Through the lens, he watched the sentry freeze—he must have sighted Lyubov—and then slowly reach for his Mauser. But the rifle was strapped to his back, the sentry had to grope for it, there was a dry sound of leather rubbing against cloth. Lyubov turned. The other man had a grip on his rifle now and was drawing the bolt. A queer noise came from Lyubov's throat, like a scream he almost managed to choke off. The enemy took aim but Lyubov pulled the trigger first—a single shot from the pistol Butler hadn't noticed in his hand. The blast was like thunder in the sleeping forest.

If every second that followed was the frame of a motion picture, then it seemed to Butler he was moving in slow motion through a full-length Hollywood epic. In some frames there were shouts, flashing lights, rapid-fire concussions. In others, the screen filled with a close-up of one of his comrades. There wasn't much dialogue, mostly curses and orders bellowed in Russian, German, Bulgarian or some mongrel soldier's argot. One memorable sequence featured Seryoshka charging like a madman across the mined valley floor with a bundle slung over his shoulder like a sack of laundry, the scene lit by flare bursts overhead and machine-gun tracer rounds. Most of it, though, was a chaotic montage, a Dadaist plunge into the fractured madness of modern war, like Picasso's *Guernica* reworked as an *avant-garde* horror show.

It seemed no more realistic, no more believable, when the scene changed to the *politruk*'s yurt, lit now in a blue-gray wash that stood for dawn. Lyubov lay on a cot, bleeding from a gunshot in the upper thigh: the wound of Anfortas, lord of the Waste Land. Seryoshka sat at the table smoking *papirosi* that were said to come from the ops chief's personal stock. The Chechen was unaccounted for. *Dead, if he's fortunate.*

Butler was scarcely aware of his own position in the yurt, nor of how long he'd been there. His thoughts were disordered. It was worse than seeing phantoms. For six years now he had been writing the story of this war, starting with the dress rehearsal in Spain. Suddenly he was part of the story himself, a character. From here, every word he'd written seemed untrue. Not a grand Russian lie, like *War and Peace.* Just off the mark, somehow. Too dry, too weak. Too rational.

Propped beside the stove, a glass of vodka in his trembling hand, sat a young blond man in a Waffen-SS uniform, his collar insignia identifying him as an Untersturmführer. His name tag read Knappe. But for everyone else—Seryoshka, the *politruk*, Lyubov, or the soft-spoken intelligence officer who sat very close to the prisoner, from time to time refilling his glass—this man's name and rank, all the details of his individual identity, were irrelevant.

To them, this was only a tongue. And it was talking.

DISPUTED TERRITORY

The Varian Fry Brigade—its numbers reduced, provisions exhausted, maps destroyed, plans out the window, leadership divided and training irrelevant—nonetheless crossed from Czechoslovakia into Poland in better shape than when it had touched down a week and a half before.

Item. Eddie's Polish had sharpened. He practiced in sporadic, occasionally useful chats with the partisan Petra. *What are those small buildings, in that field?* That is a peasant's hut with a chicken coop. Say this: *Peasant's hut. Chicken coop.* We will go there now and ask for food. Say this: *Give us eggs, please, or we will shoot you.*

Item. Tamara had grown proficient with her weapon, a Simonov automatic rifle cribbed from a dead partisan. Once, on the single-fire setting, she shot a rabbit. Then she wept over it.

Item. Martina had gone from shock at Timo's act of unprovoked brutality to a state of chronic, low-level anger. It was progress.

Item. Bloom had recused himself from quarrels over the Brigade's next course of action and settled down to the business of soldiering. Which narrowed the contest to Grabsteen versus Martina.

Item. There were days when Stu would keep his mouth shut for several hours at a stretch.

On the debit side, however: if Martina didn't get a bath soon, she was going to die of bodily self-loathing.

Just across the border, an obstacle—an elevated railbed. The line had been cut through a pine forest, the cleared space perhaps seventy meters wide, the embankment five or six meters above the surrounding ground level.

Getting across was no problem, except that while clambering up one side and down the other you would be clearly visible, even by starlight.

The Germans patrol these tracks constantly, Petra warned. They've built little lean-tos, like hunters' blinds, just inside the tree line, where they have wide, unbroken fields of fire. You never know you're being watched until the shooting starts. "A German machine gun," she said, her voice that of a tour guide repeating a line that never fails to interest schoolchildren, "makes a sound like ripping canvas."

So they paused there for a while, on a hill with a partly obstructed view of the railbed, thinking things over.

"We're down to two cans of Spam," Stu announced. "Shall we have ourselves a little feast? Or save it for the other side?"

"If you wait," said Timo, "you might not have to split it so many ways."

Martina stood beside Petra, long past caring about things like dinner. Furtively, she glanced at Harvey Grabsteen, who stood not far away staring down the shadowed hill toward the glimmer of silver iron amid yellow grass. As though sensing her attention, he turned to catch Martina's eye. Here it comes, she thought.

"That's one of them," he said. "Right down there."

When she didn't get it, he spelled it out: "A feeder track. They run north and south over the mountains, between the big east–west trunk lines. These are the tracks they bring the Jews on, from Hungary, Macedonia— the few places they haven't cleared out. The junction is up around Ostrava, and from there the main line runs east all the way to Lwów. Birkenau has a feeder of its own, like this one."

For some reason, she looked down at her feet—the forest litter, *the very ground I'm standing on.* It was hard to believe she was here, so close, so infinitely powerless. "We *wanted* to bomb them," she said. "The Secretary himself signed the memo—the planes could've made it here from Trieste. It got as far as Marshall's office. Then McCloy squashed it."

"I heard." Grabsteen's voice was soft, by his standards; his stare lacked its usual antagonism. "What else could you have done? At least you tried."

"Something, maybe. Talked to Eleanor. Written to the papers."

"Believe me, there's been no shortage of people writing to the papers. Rabbi Silver has seen to that."

"You know Rabbi Silver?"

His expression soured. Back to the old Grabsteen. "We've crossed swords with the AJC on many occasions. A bunch of timid old aunts, scared to death of offending anybody. They might as well be Episcopalian."

"I don't know—I've known some pretty offensive Episcopalians. Did you ever go to one of their weddings? Twenty minutes from the *Book of Common Prayer* followed by eight hours of heavy drinking. Then the cuff links come off."

Grabsteen laughed. He seemed to surprise himself by doing so. Martina guessed he hadn't laughed for a while, no more than she had.

"So what now, Miss Panich?" he asked, in a tone that seemed almost a self-parody, ostentatiously goading her. "What do you recommend at this juncture?"

"I'd say the usual. Yell at each other for a while, then shoot ourselves in the foot. Then, a break for processed meat."

Anyhow, it was obvious enough. They would wait for dark, then go over the tracks. The waning moon wouldn't rise until after midnight. Wisps of cloud were moving swiftly off the Northern European plain. Good Blitzkrieg country, up there: a thousand kilometers of open, sandy ground for panzers to race across. Down here, south of Kraców, the land was better suited to mules, wood grouse, ravens prowling for carcasses, the rarely spotted but persistently rumored lynx. And partisans, of course, and SS Jäger, and other creatures of the night.

It was eerie, stepping out of the black woods into dimensionless half-light. The embankment was very near yet crossing the narrow strip of cleared ground seemed to take forever. It felt like a dream of swimming, the night air as dense as water, as dangerous to fill your lungs with. The slope was unexpectedly steep—out of everything, you hadn't expected *that* to be a problem. Martina repeatedly lost her footing, gravel came loose and fell with a sound like rain, somebody was saying *Shh, shh*— annoying, and ineffective—then a rough hand grabbed her by the sleeve, hoisting her up.

She crouched for a few moments at the top, the shining rail an arm's length away, a faint smell of pine tar, staring at Timo's dark eyes. Not into them; they were hard and reflective, obsidian. She would not forgive him. Yet in another part of her mind, a separate filing tray, lay the knowledge that a man like this, who could kill without thinking, pull a trigger as easily as scratch his nose, was useful to have along.

My God, she thought. *Look where I am, look what I'm doing.*

To prove it to herself, she placed a hand on the cold iron. She expected to feel something like an electric shock—an instant of contact with all the souls that had passed over this spot on their coal-fired passage into hell.

There was nothing. Emptiness, the night, whispers of her comrades, the voice going *Shh, shh.*

Nothing: a void. Something you fall into. That was the worst thing of all.

Down the opposite slope, west of the tracks now. A different territory, from the feel of it, the ground marshy where it wasn't frozen. They waited inside the tree line for the moon to rise behind them.

Not far into the woods they heard rustling sounds, first in one direction, then another. There was no time even to be frightened. They were already surrounded; they had walked into a trap.

Martina grabbed at her tommy gun, expecting to be shot. But no shots came. Only footsteps, and then faces—swarthy, shadowed by hat brims, wrapped in scarves, too many to count. So close you could hear them breathing. The gun breeches were tiny black holes in your peripheral vision.

One of the dark figures stepped forward. He removed his hat so they could look at him. Fearless, a narrow face with dark hair thrust sideways off the brow. He spoke loudly in Polish, the words terse and formal-sounding. Then he stopped and peered at them, his eyes moving from face to face—trying, Martina guessed, to pick out the leader. Good luck, she thought.

From behind her Eddie murmured, "He says we're trespassing. He says this place is controlled by the AK, whatever that is."

"Armija Krajowa," said Petra.

Martina racked her memory. All these Polish factions—London Poles, Lublin Poles, the Committee of Polish National Liberation, she'd read all about them, briefing papers by the dozen, but the names were a blur of strangely placed consonants.

"English?" said the narrow-faced man. His turn to be surprised now. Something about Martina attracted his notice; he addressed her in a heavily accented voice. "By authority of General Bór, I order you to identify yourselves and to state your reason for coming here."

Armija Krajowa—she had it now. Largest of the non-Communist resistance groups. Ties to the British. Big noise in Warsaw. Probably friendly. "Tell him we're the good guys," she said to Eddie. "Tell him we're Americans."

"*American?*" The man stared at her. "This is a lie. No Americans are here. Also, you do not look like Americans. You look like Zhidy. Like the

ZOB, only more . . . more flesh on you. The Russians must be feeding you good." He turned to a man standing nearby and said something in Polish.

Eddie translated: "He thought we were all dead."

"Not quite," said Martina. "Not yet."

Apparently a decision was required, but the man's authority, conferred by General Bór, was not so great as to enable him to make it. Martina could empathize.

Please, he said, would the Varianoviks follow in this direction? (For some reason, learning the Brigade's name gave him a certain satisfaction.) Also please, to keep their hands off the weapons, otherwise there will be unhappiness.

Not even Harvey Grabsteen wanted to argue. No more unhappiness, not just now. Martina was tired but traipsed along in reasonably good spirits. She doubted anything really bad was going to happen. Whatever the Armija Krajowa might be, it was not the SS.

They crossed half-frozen swampland where stretches of broken reeds and cattails alternated with stands of river birch. As the moon floated higher it began to pale in the approaching sunrise. At the center of the swamp, the land rose into a stony hillock overgrown with twisted, needled, spiny scrub like a witch's pincushion. If you stepped off the path, a hundred thorns would snag your clothing and hair until you were effectively immobilized. The only way through was a kind of tunnel, low enough to make you crouch, with a machine gun staring back at you from about thirty meters in. Beyond that, the real defenses began.

Martina couldn't make out what kind of fort it was. Certainly the guerrillas hadn't built it; the stonework was too massive, too enduring. It might have stood here for centuries, slowly subsiding into the wetland. Yet it had none of the scale, the towers, the high walls of a traditional fortress.

As they walked by, the long-faced man patted a stone. It was squarish, half a meter to a side, crusted with mustard-colored lichen. "These were cut for the Teutonic Knights," he said. "They rounded up Slavs to do the work, in exchange for their families' lives. A big man, some *aristo,* built a keep out here, but he could not defend it. So it was empty for a long while and the local headmen carried off what they could. The ruins lay under all this puszcza—jungle, I think?—until a Hungarian artillery officer rode by. He saw these big rocks and thought, Why don't we hide some guns in here? The Russian hordes, you see"—pointing into the trees—"were expected to come swarming through the Moravian Gap up there, making for Prague. It didn't happen like that, but still, the Austrian engineers rebuilt the place. And now it belongs to the AK."

A tidy summary, Martina thought, of centuries of bloody warfare. Of which the outcome remained in doubt. "Don't the Germans know you're here?" she said.

"They bombed us, once or twice, when they still had petrol for their aircraft. And they send their thugs out—though not so much these days, with the problems they've got. We can see them coming, we've pre-sighted mortars to cover the approaches. As for the bombs, they don't do much, only shift a few rocks around. It was a ruin to start with."

They turned a corner, then another. The place was built like a maze, each twist providing a new sight line for defensive gunners. At last they entered a sort of courtyard, at one end of which stood a concrete blockhouse the size of a very heavily built two-car garage. A doorway was cut into this, and through it stepped a man in formal military garb, complete with gold epaulets. In a curt voice he gave what sounded like an order.

The long-faced man saluted, then turned around. "Captain Borojsza will speak to the leaders, one at a time."

Grabsteen stepped forward. Martina cleared her throat.

But the Pole pointed to Petra. "First, you."

Petra hesitated, giving Martina a look that blended resentment and resignation. *This is all your fault—but what does it matter?* Then she allowed herself to be led into the blockhouse. Martina surveyed the courtyard, trying to gauge whether she and her comrades were guests or prisoners here. *Is that what Captain Borojsza was about to determine?* They had not been asked to give up their weapons—that was good. But overlooking the courtyard were sentries in pillboxes built into the walls—you could just see their heads, sometimes the tip of a weapon. Not so good.

After several minutes, from the blockhouse, came a woman's sharp cry, an outburst of pain. Not good at all.

It was another half-hour before Petra emerged. One side of her face was puffy, and a stream of blood ran down from her temple. Yet she didn't appear to be in pain, and a worm of doubt tickled at Martina—perhaps it was a little *too* obvious. A scream, a trickle of blood. *Between us Poles, let's put one over on the Yanks, what do you say?*

The uniformed man stepped smartly through the door. He barked out a question, two syllables.

Petra pointed to Grabsteen. Two syllables in reply. *That one.*

The long-faced man said, "Now you, please."

*   *   *

By the time Martina's turn came around, Captain Borojsza was in a benevolent mood. He sat behind a map table made of heavy wood that looked like a relic of the Franz-Josef regime. The blockhouse was lit by tiny windows high in the wall and a brace of tallow-burning lamps mounted in such a way that Martina's face was illuminated while his remained in shadow. On the table, Grabsteen's canvas bag lay with its seam sliced open, a considerable pile of Swiss-denominated currency spilling out. The captain pointed a sausage-shaped finger at Martina and said something in jovial-sounding Polish. He looked like a man who would be fat if only he could get enough to eat.

"So you truly are Americans," the long-faced man translated, mumbling from a stool drawn close to Martina's. "American Jews."

"What if we are?" Good manners, she judged, would be wasted on this brute.

Her attitude did not appear to trouble Captain Borojsza. He spoke at some length, his manner philosophical.

"The captain says, This is not something we expected, that the Jews should return. We were planning for the Bolsheviks. Yes, and perhaps the British— we have gotten ourselves in their debt, they never forget such things. But the Jews? We thought they were done for. And on top of that, Jews from America? A most curious thing. Yet there must be a reason. What can it be?"

Martina sat there, stony-faced. "Well? Has he figured it out?"

"He has. It is obvious, the captain says, this is a Bolshevik stunt. All along, they were planning to use the Jews to spread their revolution—just as they used Trotsky in the old days, and now they use Grossmann and Ehrenburg. Because the Jews, with their cleverness, they can convince you of anything. They could sell you your grandmother's old underwear, and make you believe you were buying the wedding gown of the Tsarina! Only the Bolsheviks were not counting on Hitler. They thought, three million Jews in Poland, we have plenty there to work with. But now comes Hitler, and suddenly in Poland are no Jews. Incredible! Now we must start from the beginning, what shall we do? Ah—Jews from America! Millions of them, all Bolsheviks at heart, and loaded with money!" The long-faced man cast an eye at the table, Grabsteen's bag of Swiss francs.

Captain Borojsza smiled. He spoke briefly, gesturing with one hand.

"The captain asks if you will join him in a drink. A glass of our fine Polish vodka?"

Martina did not know what possessed her to say yes. She was spitting mad and felt like having a shot, was probably what it came down to.

The captain drew a bottle and some glasses from a filing cabinet that seemed to hold many bottles and no files. He spoke while pouring. "Our Polish vodka is much better than the Russian, the captain says. No one is sure why. Vodka is an ordinary thing, and yet there is mystery about it. For example—you make it, as everyone knows, by mixing water with alcohol, at an ideal ratio of three-to-two. But if you mix twelve parts water with eight parts alcohol, you get only nineteen parts vodka. Do you know this? It is unexplained. What happens to the twentieth part?"

Martina gave the captain what she hoped was an icy stare. Then she tilted her head back and drained the two jiggers of fine Polish vodka from her dirty glass. It tasted like cat piss.

"It's because of the molecular structure of the two liquids," she sputtered. Was this true? she wondered. Something she dimly recalled from a hated Chemistry class—or was she just making it up on the spot? Judging by the men's expressions, they couldn't decide either. "The water blends with the alcohol in such a way as to economize on intermolecular space. To be exact, you'd get nineteen-*point-one-three* parts of this shitty Polish swill."

Captain Borojsza listened with narrowed eyes while this was translated. He stared at Martina, then leaned back in his chair and brayed with laughter.

"The captain says, You see what I mean? These Jews, they are the clever ones."

She guessed that in this context, it was not a compliment. "Does the captain want anything else?"

A quick exchange. "No, the captain says we are finished here. He says now you must go." The long-faced man paused, glanced at his superior, then added, "He means all of you, out of AK territory. I am to escort you. However, in consideration of this . . . generous contribution, you will be allowed to remain here for a day, to rest. And you may choose which direction you are expelled in."

"That's mighty big of him. What are the choices?"

The man looked chagrined. "Back to Czechoslovakia. Or the other direction, into the German Reich."

That day in the AK compound was the longest the Varianoviks had known. To Martina it felt as though they were becalmed on a flat, gray sea. Nothing moved around them except for the bored, aimless pacing of the sentries on the wall and the rare overflight of a predatory bird, coasting under the clouds in majestic desperation.

There was to be, evidently, no mingling between the Americans and their grudging hosts. You might have thought ordinary human curiosity would draw them together—especially when the Yanks lit up their delicious-smelling cigarettes—but evidently the war had worked a deep change in how these Poles regarded outsiders. Or was it only how they regarded Jews? An unloved people who were supposed—weren't they?—to be dead.

They took turns dozing through the afternoon. But by the time twilight fell, everyone came fully awake. There was a fraught, menaced feeling in the air, like a hushed woodland once the hunter has set up his blind, the night creatures committed suddenly to stealth. As if by instinct, the Varianoviks drew more closely together, close enough for a quiet murmur to suffice for all of them. Having done so, they found nothing to talk about. They sat dumbly like a family huddled around a dead radio, staring past one another at a world that grew stranger, less Earth-like, from one moment to the next.

"What the hell are we doing this for?" Stu said suddenly.

They all turned to look at him. He had not spoken loudly—you couldn't, with the AK men out there—yet his words rang out like a *cri de coeur.*

"I mean, really." He stared at his hands as though a moment ago he'd been holding something precious. "Why did we come all this way? What do we think we're going to accomplish, besides getting ourselves killed? All for a damn scrap of paper."

His eyes were full of tears—of grief and disappointment, Martina supposed. Tears for their dead comrades, for a million vanished strangers, for the doomed few who remained.

The Varianoviks waited, as if unsure whose duty it was to answer him. The big Moe's, maybe—*Pull yourself together, soldier.* Or Tamara's, a gentler touch, stroke his brow and promise that it would all be better in the morning. Instead, after a silence that lasted long enough you couldn't tell whether the two events were connected or not, Harvey Grabsteen—the *last* person Martina wanted to hear from just now—spoke in a wistful voice.

"I used to have this old teacher. A German, as it happens—he must've been ninety, but still he could act the clown. And he said once, Boys, there's a thing or two they don't tell you about this Creation business."

Oh, shut up, Martina felt like telling him. But she realized dimly that Grabsteen was speaking in his rabbinical capacity, a side of him she'd always found implausible and somewhat unseemly. At this moment, though, his grating, high-pitched voice had a certain heft.

"This old fellow said, You know, there really were *two* Creations. The first one, that's when the world was made. But the second one is when the world became *real.*

"You know how it starts—first there's only the Word. The Word is the *ain sof,* the breath of God, it moves over the waters of Eternity, it calls forth Being from the depths, it's like a big cosmic burp. I'm sorry, that's how the old fellow talked—he'd have been much happier if they made him a wedding jester instead of sending him off to study in Vilna. Anyhow. *But,* he says, the Word alone is not enough. The Word counts for nothing, because already it holds everything within it. All possibility, all time, every makeable form, every thinkable thought, it's all in there already—so, now what? What's the point of it? It's just so much divine indigestion.

"Here is where the second Creation comes in. Because for the Word to matter, there must be an ear to receive it. Or let's make this sound more theological: the divine generative impulse must have a ground upon which to act. What good is the Seed of the Universe if there's no womb to plant it in? Pardon me, I'm only quoting my old teacher. And so now there must appear—from where, who knows?—a receiver, a vessel of some sort—let's call it the ear—into which the *ain sof* can be breathed.

"And now, boys, you've got something. God utters the Word, and the ear says, No need to shout, I can hear you! This is the first tick of time, it's the first instance in which one thing follows another.

"From there, as you know, it gets colorful. We hear about the Garden and the two trees and the wily serpent and, let's not forget, the naked man and woman. What do you expect, God should tell a boring story? The point is, finally the world is real. It's real to the mind, real to the touch. It's something we can believe in. The Word alone couldn't do this. Even the *speaking* of the Word wasn't enough. What was needed was the *hearing* of the Word. The world became real when it became part of a story, our own story.

"But here's a funny thing. There are parts of this story we know, and parts we don't. We know about the wily serpent, but where was the grinning chimpanzee? What do you hear from the noble stag or the long-suffering camel or the duckling with his Oedipal complex? Okay, there's the Tree of Life and the other one, with the forbidden fruit—but what about the Tree of Stout Lumber or the Tree That Drops Those Damn

Seeds All Over My Lawn? You could say, Oh, those things don't matter, they play no role, they're only set dressing. What blasphemy! To think *any* part of God's creation is not crucial or beautiful or lacking in purpose. No, what's happened is obvious. It's that ear again. The ear has gotten hold of the Word and is shaping it, trimming it, spicing it up. Certain parts are thrown in, others are left out, others still are, let's say, a wee bit overdramatized. But you see, boys, this is the Second Creation. And this is the one that sticks. It's the tune you leave the theater humming.

"We don't have to make a judgment about this. It's enough to say, the two things are different. Like *Hamlet* is different from *Webster's Dictionary.* Sure, God's first draft is comprehensive, it's magnificent, it's perfect. Believe me O Lord, you're the greatest, there's some terrific stuff here— love the scenery! and *dandruff,* how did you come up with that? But about these myriad beasts . . . I'm just wondering, do we really need a thousand kinds of ant? What, twenty thousand? Well, you're the boss. But as soon as God leaves the room, it's Get me rewrite."

Grabsteen paused. What her comrades were thinking Martina could only guess. They were listening, you could say that much—Stu perhaps most intently.

"We have in the world today"—suddenly, a shift in tone. Crisp, officerly, several shades more grim. "In the world today, we have a man who believes himself a god. He speaks, and the nations tremble. *Führer, command us, we shall obey.* But such a man requires an audience, an ear to receive the dark Word. Otherwise, how can his terrible plan, his anti-Creation, be carried out? And this, for us, so far, has been a problem. Because we know this man, we know who he is, what he has commanded, what has been done in his name. Yet all of it remains in some sense unreal. Or you might say unrealized, uncomprehended. The millions of dead Jews are like those creatures you never heard about in the Book of Genesis—the nameless ants that Adam crushed under his foot. Were they really there? Maybe yes, maybe no. Who's to say, since they never made it into the final draft? And here, friends, is the importance of our mission."

He paused, and again the mood was different. A thunderous silence, like the moments before a storm comes crashing down from Sinai.

"Until now, we thought none of this terrible story would ever be put in writing. No one could ever open a book and read, *And the Devil said, 'Let there be darkness.'* So the events of our lifetime—which, granted, are hard to believe—will never be fully real for those who come after us. Or so we thought until, a couple of months ago, our comrade Miss Panich received tidings of a certain document. Which, while not penned in the inky finger of Satan himself, is as close as we may ever come. 'The Führer has ordered me—' The key word here being 'me.' The Führer ordered *me*, not you, because I am his favorite, *der treue Heinrich*. Which, in turn, gives us reason to think the document is genuine, that it bears true witness. It is the dark Word, the breath of anti-Creation, made real. And it proves for all time that these were actual people, their lives every bit as real and true as their deaths."

He looked around as if expecting to see ghosts among his audience. "Unfortunately, until the paper is in our hands, we won't know what comes next. 'The Führer has ordered me to wipe out the Jews.' And then what—is there more? Obliterate their memory? Erase them from the history books? We don't know. Our man in Carpathia has not seen fit to enlighten us. Like any storyteller, no doubt, he wants to have a hand in the editing. So let us put his name above the credits. *Isaac Tadziewski presents.* . . . If we can do that, our mission will have succeeded."

Martina saw now that the Varianoviks had been joined by a couple of Poles—good Catholics, probably, whose religious sensibilities might not embrace the more intemperate flights of Grabsteen's *midrash*. Still, they seemed no worse for it.

"Well," said Stu, breaking the silence. "When you put it *that* way . . ."

Laughter. Relief.

Nightmares to follow.

When Bloom shook her awake an hour before sunrise, Martina was surprised how deeply she'd slept. For years she had suffered insomnia. Now all it took was a coffin-sized patch of ground and a reasonable assurance that she wouldn't be murdered in her sleep, and she was down for the count.

Their escort consisted of half a dozen AK men. They were already assembled, anxious to depart. The brigade was given a breakfast of dark, stale, all-but-flavorless bread. Martina thought of one of the briefing papers she'd read, a summary of intelligence reports from "sources in the Polish Underground." Her image of this Underground was based rather closely, she supposed, on Ingrid Bergman and Gary Cooper, living heroically in caves alongside noble peasants, blowing up bridges, wiping out whole German formations with Great War–vintage rifles and a bag of hand grenades. And Bergman, for all her wailing histrionics, with never so much as a lipstick smudge or a hair out of place.

The briefing paper, as she recalled, had detailed Nazi euphemisms for what was happening to the Jews. *Deported. Chosen for special action. Sent east. Presently employed draining swamps.* And one other that now came to mind: *The air has been cleansed.* Meaning the smells associated with Jewry—garlic, caraway, peppery chicken broth—would no longer offend sensitive Gentile nostrils.

She gobbled the tasteless bread anyway, as she had drunk the captain's vodka. Because she felt like it. And to hell with all of them.

"This is as far as I take you," said the horse-faced man.

It was mid-afternoon and they stood beside a narrow, quick-running river.

"There is a place you can cross, only a little farther. An old bridge. I would do it in daylight, if I were you. That way, you can tell whether the bridge is being guarded. Once it gets dark . . ." He shrugged.

"What's on the other side?" Grabsteen asked him.

The AK man looked at him as if this might be a trick question. "Over there is Silesia. It's Polish land, but the Nazis claim it as part of Greater Germany. They have concentrated their forces, building a line of defense against the Russians. Also, there are settlers, ethnic Germans from other countries—many of the native people have been expelled. We do not operate over there. The population is hostile, the whole atmosphere is . . . clouded."

"Let me get this straight," said Grabsteen. "You mean the opposite bank of this stream—*right over there*—that's the Third Reich?"

The AK man stared, apparently unable to provide an unequivocal answer. Borders, nations, thousand-year empires—such airy constructs might or might not apply to the reality on the ground. "We do not operate over there," he repeated. "AK territory ends where we stand."

"Who does operate there?" Martina asked.

He gave her a canny look; he must have detected something in her voice. "There are . . . isolated bands. Certain individuals working against the Germans, in their own fashion. All Poles are members of the resistance, it is said."

"Do you know anything about someone called the Fox?"

The man glanced quickly around at his AK comrades, none of whom gave any sign of comprehension.

"You're really not Bolsheviks, are you?" he said to her quietly. "I never believed it. Our captain . . . he is not so stupid as he might seem to you, that is mostly just a kind of performance. But I knew, these people, these

Americans . . . there is something more to this. Bolsheviks have their plots and cells and secret agendas. You do not seem that type. They are perhaps fools, I thought. Off on some fool's errand, trying to get themselves killed. But not Communists—something else, a thing we have not seen before. And now, the Fox!" His eyes gleamed.

Martina said, "The Fox what?"

"I don't know. It fits—only that. It is all crazy. And none of it belongs in AK territory. The captain was right—it is better you go across the river."

They spotted the bridge less than two kilometers farther on, a simple plank-and-beam affair laid across sagging timbers and stiffened by king posts with angled braces. Near the center, above water that churned white between ice-glazed rocks, sat a vehicle that resembled a wider, unlovable version of the jeep. The machine gun mounted in back, partly shielded by armor plates, was manned by a soldier in a gray uniform whose head was too small for his helmet. Two sentries stood at the far end, talking, glancing now and then up the road into the encroaching forest. There might have been more that the Varianoviks couldn't see; they had only a narrow vantage between old cedars some distance off, at a bend in the river.

"Welcome to the Grossdeutsches Reich," said Stu in a singsong voice. "We do hope you'll enjoy your stay."

No one laughed; no one did anything.

After a minute, Bloom stepped away from the river and looked up at the sky. Clouds had blown in, Wehrmacht gray. "It feels like snow," he said. "I'd rather not fight in a snowstorm. We're too likely to shoot each other."

"What should we do?" asked Eddie. Wide-eyed, trusting: The old veteran must know.

What impressed Martina was how much it felt like being back on the chicken farm. The same matter-of-factness, the same assurance in the big man's voice. Now, we want to make this realistic. We want you to feel like you're really over there, with real Germans shooting at you. Listen carefully, here's the plan. You don't have to like it, or even understand it—you just have to do your part.

They had called him M-1, and they all had been afraid of him. Now he held their fear at bay. It was going to work: he believed it; they believed him.

"All right," Bloom said. "Here's how I think this ought to go."

They drew in close. He made marks in the ground with a stick. Two of them—no, make it three—would head off inland, at an angle from the river. "There's a road that way someplace. Find it, then come back carefully toward the water. Keep as quiet as you can.

"Two more—we need somebody with a good arm—start moving down the riverbank. Take a couple grenades apiece. The vegetation's thick in there, so don't go too fast or you'll make noise. Be ready to move quickly once the shooting starts.

"Everyone else, stay with me. We'll move up closer to the bridge, but hang back in the woods and wait.

"In twenty minutes, you people on the road open fire. Don't worry about aiming, just put some lead in the air."

"Suppressing fire," said Stu.

"That's right. You lay down suppressing fire. And if they come after you—run.

"Now you people by the water move out. You need to get within thirty-five meters, closer is better. Your job is to take out the Kübelwagen.

"The rest of us will come right through the trees. We'll keep low and fan out and open up with everything we've got. With any luck, by the time we get there, the MG'll be out of action. We'll do the mopping up, then we all run like hell to the other side and we find someplace to lay low."

A pause. One last moment to think.

"Any questions?" Bloom said. He looked from one of them to another, meeting each pair of eyes. "All right, then. Check your watches. Twenty minutes. Starting now."

It went as planned, more or less. Tamara, clutching her Simonov, led two others through the woods, making for the road. Eddie and Timo kept to the river. Martina stayed with the main group, and very slowly Bloom led them forward. Too slowly, she thought—the fight was going to start without them. Yet when they halted, still a long sprint from the near end of the bridge, only seven minutes had gone by.

During the time that followed, Martina felt as though every war movie she'd ever seen went flickering through her head. Even the newsreels, big guns going off on battleships, the Führer shrieking at the Sportpalast, French citizens popping corks to celebrate the liberation of some town, GIs slogging through mud, their helmet straps loose, grinning blearily at the camera. Why do soldiers wear helmets and not partisans? How did

Chaplin do that Hitler speech in *The Great Dictator*—was it improvised on camera?

The first shots, when they came, sounded fake, *pop-pop-pop,* like a radio cowboy show.

"Go!" shouted Bloom.

Martina was caught off guard. Not ready yet, time out, I'll be there in a minute. This was her first confrontation with the strange truth about war that once it gets started, there's no way to make it stop; it roars down like an avalanche until all that deathly energy is exhausted. There were screams and explosions, and the terrible hot stink of cordite nearly set your nostrils on fire. There was running, falling, a sharp rock meeting her shin, somebody yanking her upright. It was Grabsteen. His expression was fierce. He took her shoulders and turned her in the right direction. Onward and upward. The stutter of ripping canvas. And then the bridge.

Some of the planks were burning, and there was a big hole near the *Kübelwagen.* One of the vehicle's tires had dropped through, and the front bumper rested on a beam. The gunner lay all over his weapon, limbs dangling, his body having lost all solidity. Two other Germans lay unmoving nearby and a fourth was sitting with his back propped against the king post, hands in the air and a shinbone visible through the mess of his trousers. He looked weirdly calm, as if this were all happening in his imagination. Martina could empathize.

Cautiously, the Americans emerged from the cover of the trees and moved out onto the bridge decking. The blood of the dead men and of the lone survivor was a more vivid red than Martina had expected. Also, there was more of it, whole sticky puddles. She felt light-headed, like she'd stood up too quickly. She took a couple steps, unsteady, her feet disconnected— at any moment she would collapse.

Someone was there, an arm slipping under hers and around her back, taking her weight. She turned to look into Timo's dark eyes, his unshaven cheeks, narrow and wolflike. "Thanks," she said.

He nodded. He held her until she regained her equilibrium. Other people moved around them; Bloom was demanding to know whether everyone had made it.

"So, you're alive," said Martina, taking a step away. "I guess you've got a good arm. Where's Eddie?"

Timo looked at her. He shook his head, slightly.

She thought he hadn't heard. "I said, where's Eddie?"

Bloom shouted, "I'm only counting twelve. Who's missing?"

"Lubovich," said Timo. His voice sounded far-off, indifferent. "Eddie

Lubovich didn't make it. They spotted him just as he was tossing the stick. He didn't have time to duck. But the grenade, it was a perfect shot."

Silence, then. Broken by a choking sound from Stu, who began to cry unabashedly. Tamara tried to comfort him. Everybody doing their jobs.

"Where is he?" Bloom demanded.

Timo pointed.

Martina didn't look.

In war, this counts as victory.

And so, victorious, the Varian Fry Brigade buried its latest dead and administered first aid to the prisoner—Bloom having overruled a popular motion to finish him off. The German was regular Wehrmacht, not SS, and by the look of him—a stocky *Bürger* about Bloom's age—had probably been called up in a latch-ditch conscription. First aid amounted to tying off his ruined leg in a bloody tourniquet, and he looked on in seeming wonderment while Stu attended to this.

"Danke," he said, almost blubbering—Martina couldn't tell if it was from pain or a pathetic sort of gratitude. "Danke, Herr Doktor."

He looked surprised when Bloom responded in brusque, interrogatory German, running through, she supposed, the standard POW catechism. What is your unit? How many men? Where does this road lead? Are there villages nearby? How often do patrols come through? The German, who answered readily, might or might not have been telling the truth, but he was too frightened to keep his mouth shut.

At last—Martina understood this well enough—the man said, "Sind Sie Juden?" Are you Jews?

Bloom just stared at him.

Grabsteen butted in. "Macht's nichts, wer wir sind." His German sounded more like Yiddish, and he turned back to Bloom. "Tell him it doesn't matter who we are. Just make sure he lets them know, when reinforcements come, what he's seen. Da wird eine Rechnung sein—there will be a reckoning. Die beginnt hier."

A low-pressure front had been moving down from Scandinavia, scooping up moisture from the Baltic Sea, and depositing this as cold rain and damp snow over the disputed lands between the rivers Oder and Dvina—places whose names and nationalities were uncertain—northern Poland, East Prussia, the Wartheland, the western Soviet Republics. As it approached the Tatry Mountains, this sodden air mass was thrust upward, into colder bands of the atmosphere, and the precipitating moisture turned to dry, feathery snow.

The Varianoviks followed a narrow road that unwound generally north-west. After a few kilometers they left this for an even narrower road that forked to the right, guessing it might be safer. What they could see of the countryside looked desolate: thin woods, low hills, many little streams and ponds, a good deal of marsh. The snow blew in their faces and the day grew dim, though Martina guessed they had an hour left before real dusk. Their hope was to find a barn to spend the night in.

A reordering of the landscape became gradually apparent. The streams were regimented into drainage ditches and irrigation canals. Former swampland had been reclaimed and tilled. A hillside was shorn of trees and instead sprouted the head-high poles used for stringing up grapevines. Along one shoulder of the dirt lane, hardwood saplings stood at regular intervals, steadied by stakes and ties.

As its level of organization increased, the land took on a quality of . . . well, not beauty, she thought, more like a determined sort of cheerfulness—the attitude of a modest flower bed doing its best in a bad part of town. You had to admire it for what it was.

Only—what was it?

Part of an estate, she guessed. Prosperous, with a large staff to manage the grounds. She kept a lookout, trudging onward, blinking snow out of her eyes, for a big house nestled on a rise somewhere. The picture was so clear in her mind that she failed to notice what was actually there, right ahead of her.

Bloom stopped walking. He thrust an arm out in front of Martina. The brigade came to a halt.

A short distance off, just discernible through swirling snow, stood a stockade fence, built of rough wooden planks and tall enough to conceal whatever lay behind it. You could just make out shingled rooftops, a few stone chimneys, here and there a wisp of smoke. The road led to a gate whose timbers were cut in the shape of a Gothic arch, surmounted by a sign unreadable at this distance. From there the wall ran perhaps fifty meters to either side, then jigged away out of sight. It seemed to describe a very large polygon, of which they could make out the nearest three faces. Martina had never seen anything like it before, except maybe the outer wall of the castle at Leuchtenburg. But that was a thirteenth-century fortress. This was, as best she could tell, a farming estate in Nazified Poland.

"What should we do now?" said Harvey Grabsteen—words Martina, for one, never expected to hear him utter.

"What choice do we have?" said Tamara. Her blood was still up from the battle. "It'll be dark soon. We're caught in a goddamn blizzard and we need a place to stay. This looks like it."

"What if—" somebody began.

"Then we deal with it." Tamara wagged the barrel of her gun.

Nobody argued. They moved forward cautiously, the sharp smell of wood smoke coming in gusts of cold air that played around the rooftops ahead, lifting the snow and carrying it over the wall.

Martina got it then. *Walled village*—another of those medieval conceits that seem to resonate with the German, what, folk-soul? If Ingo were here, he'd know the ten-syllable term for it: *Volk*-something-*ge*-something-*heit*. He'd tell you how it ran from Wagner right back to Jesus von Kreist. But before he could do that, Martina would interrupt: It's running *here*, that's the point. Right here to Nowheresdorf, Lower Silesia. Where the holy Teutonic farmers have built a wall to keep the heathen wood-hares at bay.

"So you are proposing," Grabsteen told rather than asked Tamara, "that we storm the gate and shoot anyone who tries to stop us."

She slapped a fresh magazine into her Simonov, a reply eloquent enough.

"Maybe we should take a look around first," Stu suggested.

"Maybe you could all keep your fucking voices down," growled Bloom.

Jews, Martina marveled. When only three of them were left in Europe, they'd still hold an election in which no candidate received a majority. Then split into at least four irreconcilable factions.

Alone, she ambled up the road. The gate was wide enough to accommodate a farm wagon—or a Mercedes staff car—and its heavy door had one of those little flaps for peeking out, just like the gate to the Emerald City, at the end of the Yellow Brick Road. Indeed, at closer range, this whole place had a fantastical air about it. The cast-iron latch was needlessly massive and ornate. Above the arch, carved in old Fraktur lettering and burned into the wood, summer-camp-style, a sign read

ARNDTHEIM
Gegr. 1924

Somehow, she'd known it would. Some specter of memory, a stirring in her *Ur*-something-*geist*. She tried the latch but it was secured from inside. So she took the butt of her rifle and began pounding on the thick planks.

"What the hell are you doing?" Grabsteen yelled.

Relax, Rabbi.

Before long the others had caught up to her, and there was a complementary clamor from the other side of the wall.

"Wer is da?" a man's voice shouted, muffled by wind and snow.

Martina figured childish English was preferable to pig-German. "We are friends of Ernst Moritz Arndt," she called. "You have to let us in."

After that, it seemed, the people on both sides of the wooden barrier were too surprised to say anything. The next sound was a clunk of metal as the latch was unfastened. The heavy gate swung back on impeccably oiled hinges.

By this time Martina's mind was swimming with names, faces, slogans, tastes—a vanished world that would never change and never die. The wall had no place in it. Neither did the little man with the felt cap who stood just inside, peering at Martina with a mix of curiosity and fear. But the village behind him, opening like a stage set as the curtains slide apart—yes, she knew that well enough.

"Who the hell is Ernst Moritz Arndt?" Grabsteen was stupid enough to ask.

Tamara shoved past him, past Martina and the man in the felt cap, into the tiny village of Arndtheim. The sight of it brought even her to a halt: the covered well, the immaculate little green, the half-timbered cottages with their empty window boxes and second-story balconies; the well-tooled dream of a perfect, pocket-sized Germany. "What the hell is this place?" she demanded.

"Exactly what it looks like," said Martina. "Fairy-tale Land."

MÄRCHENLAND

This blue flower, then. You imagine some ethereal, blushing, feathery sort of thing, insubstantial as a song, pure as the storm-cleansed sky. It consorts with ferns, shuns toadstools and earthworms. It is the well-loved familiar of rare butterflies, who visit only at certain hours of a summer afternoon, borne on the gentlest puffs of nectar-scented air. It winks demurely from the mossy clefts between old oaks' toes. It beckons blushingly and then, at the last heartbeat, fairylike, flickers bashfully from view. Which is what makes it so hard to find. What makes it the perfect emblem of Romantic longing. At least that's what you think.

Admit it, Ingo—that's *exactly* what you thought, until the past week or so. Clutching your little red poetry book, mooning over this haunting image, pining for that impossible object of desire. *I am searching for the blue flower,* you've told yourself. *It is a sacred quest, through a God-haunted country. And if I should fail, even if I should perish in the attempt, my death will be a blessed thing, a release from the holy torment of a martyr.*

Ingo, what an idiot you've been.

Worse than that: you've been a sucker. You've bought into the oldest spiel in the book. So be it—now you know the truth. About this blue flower, and a few other things as well. Too bad you had to learn it the hard way. But really, isn't it about time?

The sad thing is, it wasn't that much of a secret. Novalis himself, who thought up the *blaue Blume* in the first place, fairly spells it out.

> *I live through the day*
> *Full of courage and trust,*
> *And die every night,*
> *Seared by soul-burning lust.*

Which pretty much explains what kind of metaphor you're messing around with.

Emblem of poetic longing—what a laugh. It's an emblem, all right. It's an emblem because it pops up at the least expected times and the most unwelcome places. It unfurls and stands proudly and declines to wilt. It may not be the biggest thing in the forest but it sure calls attention to itself. My, what a striking color!—and you'll turn blue yourself if you try to ignore it. No use hoping it will go away: like the rankest weed, the blue flower needs to be . . . plucked. And plucked. And plucked again. Before you know it, you've got pollen all over the place. Any moment now somebody will notice, and you'll die of shame. Your death will come not as a blessed release but as a stupid and vulgar joke.

Lately he'd not been sleeping well, what with one thing and another. He lay open-eyed much of the night, reviewing certain scenes, imagining others, while a thousand more swam darkly in the shadows of his mind. He thought sometimes—thought quite hard, actually—about an archery contest and naked swimmers and two boys kissing in a meadow. He thought about a particular blond body that lay in a condition of despicable inviolacy only a few steps away. More than anything he thought about Anton. Sometimes his thoughts resembled ordinary memories (though what does "ordinary" mean, in this context?), but often they were more vividly colored, strangely paced, racing and slowing and occasionally locking on a single frame until the film caught fire. Images and sounds and textures and other unnameable sensations teemed so thickly in his mind that he experienced a sort of mental suffocation. It was like being caught, swarmed-over, in an especially violent dream, a dream that arose not in the mind but in the body itself. And Ingo would languish on whatever that night's bed might be—the forest floor, a stiff cot at a youth hostel or, once only, a decent mattress at a wayside inn, it made no difference to his transfigured flesh—damp with sweat, cool in the night air, burning with need, unable to keep still or to move, to think clearly or to surrender himself to oblivion. He had found the blue flower, he had devoured its seed, and now it was growing inside him, drawing nourishment from his gut.

He was a horrid, sticky mess. Everything, every feeling and mood and memory, clung to him. *Nevermore will you come out of this wood*—they had tried to warn him about that, too.

On the other hand . . . did he really want to leave? Ever, ever again?

*   *   *

The odd thing about these thoughts, or dreams, or agonized visions, where Anton was concerned, was their incompleteness. They resembled some modern school of painting—Cubism or the *Blaue Reiter,* Ingo knew little about such things—in which the central image is distorted or broken into pieces, changed from a three-dimensional object into a purely intuitive representation, as though you were being shown not the thing itself but a certain *feeling* about that thing. If the artist hated what he was painting, it would look one way; if he loved it, another. When Ingo thought of Anton, or tried to, he succeeded only in calling up certain aspects, isolated impressions: a flashing smile; a long leg, and how it flexed at the knee; the specific temperature of breath moving across his stomach; a string of words that played and replayed itself with no particular meaning, serving simply as a medium for that wonderful, throaty voice.

Where had he gone—the actual, warm, breathing, fully formed Anton? How had Ingo lost hold of him? And why could he not bring him back now, alive and whole, if only for a sliver of a second?

They had had so little time together. That was one thing. But even so— those days had been the most intensely felt, the most deeply experienced of Ingo's life. Of course they had ended, but did that mean, of necessity, that they were just . . . *gone?* Beyond his grasp, sliding deeper into the past at every moment? Is that how it worked? So much for comforting nostrums like *I'll always be with you,* or *You'll live in my heart forever.*

Another thing, though. What exactly *had* it been? Ingo had assumed it was love—and if it wasn't, for God's sake, what more was required? But he wasn't sure. He knew there'd been more to it than you could measure by just tallying up the things they'd done, the physical things. (Even now, in his fallen and gooey state, Ingo shied from the frank language of sexuality.) Yet how *much* more? More in what way? For all he knew, anyone who'd ever done such things with another person felt like this. But no—he didn't believe that either.

The fact remained, irreducibly: he could not remember Anton as he felt he ought to. Somehow, in more than just a literal sense, they had parted. Some crucial aspect of Anton, the person he had been, the things he had meant, now had dropped into the past. In one respect this was a blessing; it marginally decreased Ingo's nightly torment. But on the whole it made him feel more miserably alone than ever.

*   *   *

Then the sun would rise and the nighttime ordeal would seem stranger still, because it would have no place in the glaring world of daytime. Here people would move and talk and laugh and quarrel as though Ingo were simply one of them, not a broken, half-ghostly being, disfigured by the fires of lust and never made whole again. And he would pass among them like a visitor from another realm of being, scarcely able to understand the native tongue, let alone grasp the finer points of social comportment. *I feel the breeze of another planet*—Stefan George, as usual, getting here before him. And the queer thing was, nobody seemed to notice.

Now and then Martina threw him a certain kind of look: inquisitive, perhaps concerned or sympathetic. God forbid, not pitying, please. But she never pressed it further than that—she had, mind you, her own wild garden to tend—and for the most part Ingo was content simply to be left alone.

The journey east did not require much of his attention; it proceeded and it carried him along and on a certain level he even took an active role in it. He joined in with Hagen's hiking songs, and gathered firewood, and hefted his share of the supplies. He tossed in his two cents on the question of which path to take—the nature of woodland trails is such that you never can really be sure. He ate and drank and relieved himself behind bushes and bathed in cold mountain streams and even tried once to scrub the dirt out of his clothes. But that was less than a success and he found, rather to his surprise, that he still felt embarrassed undressing in front of others.

Ingo, he thought, you are a fool. But a singular fool, at least, *ein eigener Narr:* a fool of your own creation.

And then, once upon a time . . .

Es war einmal, that had been the Grimms' formula. A ritual phrase, an incantation to blur the boundaries of time and cast the listener back—or perhaps sideways—into another world with its own strictures and possibilities. At any moment along the path you might encounter a giant, a wolf, a crone, a tricky fellow dressed in rags—but whether woman or youth, elf or ogre, it surely would not be who or what it seemed at a hasty glance. You need to bear this in mind, because in this world—as perhaps in others—when opportunity presents itself, you have but a single chance to grasp it. Likewise when danger arises you have only an instant to step clear. Hesitate too long, or misjudge the situation, and you are lost.

Once upon a time, then, Ingo woke at an indefinite hour in a wood that was not quite silent and not quite dark. A pale glow seemed to emanate from rocks and leaves and moss, and tree trunks stood flat as shadows, and the sky held a memory of moonlight but no moon. From somewhere— neither far nor near—came a soft rustling amid the undergrowth, maybe tiny creatures venturing abroad, maybe restless spirits trudging on their endless journey. Maybe a monster closing in. Maybe a lithe-limbed, pretty sprite with mischief in his eyes.

Ingo could not guess what time it was. He remembered tossing on his bedroll until quite late, but after that he must have dropped into a deep, if not necessarily long, slumber. His thoughts were dulled as though by a sleeping draught, and his limbs felt so heavy they might have been para-lyzed. He tried to recall his last dream but found only unconnected impres-sions that ran together like watery paint. More of the usual, he supposed. Lurid fantasies, memories spun into fantastic lies, emotions he had no name for. The insanity of sleep meets the panic of waking. He lay on his cushion of fallen needles like a man trapped between the last world and the next, a citizen of neither.

Suddenly, Isaac loomed above him—as if he were floating there, weight-less and ghostly pale. Ingo's heart slammed a couple of times, then calmed with recognition. Only Isaac.

"Shh," the boy admonished him, "get up," though he seemed to make no sound. He motioned with a flick of the head or the casting of an eye; for some reason the precise gesture was hard to focus on, yet its meaning was clear. *Come on—let's get out of here before anyone else wakes up.*

Ingo could find no reason to refuse. In his bleary state the idea made good sense. He sat up and rubbed his eyes and soon was stumbling away from the camp, which that night had been pitched on a broad ledge in the foothills of northwest Carpathia: he wasn't entirely sure which country they were in. Ahead of him, Isaac ducked through a scrim of black-leaved laurel that edged the old forest road, and they stepped out onto a north-facing slope formed mostly of naked, rain-smoothed rock and hence easy to walk on, even in semi-darkness. They proceeded obliquely downhill. Ingo tried to catch up with the smaller, more quick-footed boy, but he could not.

By increments, like a ticking watch, the landscape grew brighter: dawn could not be far away. Now all the questions Ingo ought to have asked pressed down on him. What was Isaac up to? Where he was taking them; why did Ingo have to come along? As if overhearing, Isaac looked back across one scrawny shoulder. You might, had you been so disposed, have read his quirky, corner-of-the-mouth smile any number of ways.

The ground leveled off and the sky took on a faint blush of magenta. A sound of moving water came from someplace ahead. In crevices between rocks appeared tufts of blue-eyed grass, *Sisyrinchium,* a dwarfish cousin of the lily clan, whose lavender six-pointed flowers wilt in the evening but open again in the warmth of afternoon. Ingo would not have recognized it, would never even have seen it, a couple of weeks ago. To have loved, he thought—even for an hour, imperfectly—is to have glimpsed the world through a different set of eyes. And through those eyes, to have perceived a whole new dimension, a secret plane of reality, hidden from ordinary sight. So much he had learned from Anton, so much. He lurched onward dumbly, feeling something like bereavement. His feet met the rugged concavity of a draw with the easy familiarity of old neighbors whom time has turned into friends. The air smelled of mountains, of autumn, of heartbreak.

Isaac at last stopped, but Ingo, overfilled with his own thoughts, didn't notice in time and the two nearly collided. Isaac laughed, intercepting him with a stiff, sinewy arm. There was no guile in his laughter or in the clear, faceted sparkle of his eyes.

"I've got something to show you," he said—practically the first words either of them had spoken all morning. "Only we're a little early, we've got to wait till just the right time. Okay?"

His voice, his entire outward manner, had a surface impenetrable as concrete. Ingo couldn't fathom what, if anything, lay underneath. He supposed this was a useful survival trait for an undersized kid in tough surroundings. Isaac squatted down on the irregular ground and he followed suit. There seemed no need to talk about anything. The day came on rapidly now; the sky lost its rosy flush, and a rope of gray cloud stretched across the eastern horizon, backlit in yellow. Ingo rubbed his hands together, anticipating the pleasure of sunrise.

"Okay, let's go," Isaac said suddenly. Quickly he was up and moving away, lower into the mouth of the gully. The footing was difficult here, and sharp-pointed rocks, having tumbled from someplace above, lay all around; it would be quite easy to trip and land on one. Nonetheless Ingo struggled to keep pace, steadying himself by using scrappy little fir trees as handholds. Soon his fingers were black with resin and smelled of Christmas. Ahead, the hill reared up in a promontory, deeply cleft down the center and dark except for a thin silvery line, like a spider thread, that ran down its face and disappeared among a jumble of boulders. The sound of water grew more distinct.

"It's a waterfall!" Ingo said, understanding at last. "Wait, I want to look at this."

Isaac shook his head. "Not from here. Come on. The sun's almost up."

He led them on a roundabout path, deeper into the draw and through a copse of quivering birch. A narrow stream darted along a groove in the rock, making quiet, somewhat musical noises almost like giggling. The first rays of dawn—pink-tinged gold, like amber with a smidgen of blood inside—struck the slope above them. Then they stepped clear of the trees and the waterfall stood before them, tumbling perhaps three stories into a little chasm it seemed to have churned out for itself. Numerous protrusions from the cliff face shattered the silver column and sent water jetting and splashing and streaming in every possible direction, in patterns that altered continually. Glittering skeins dangled and waved like gonfalons, and through them, at just this instant, blazed the sunrise—the light breaking into a thousand colors, each droplet becoming a minuscule prism, and the water in turn dissolving the sun into its molten essence.

Ingo drew his breath. It was one of the most beautiful things he had ever seen, and he was no stranger to beauty. He stared for a minute or two—the vision never ceased changing, like a highly advanced type of kaleidoscope—until after a while he became aware that Isaac was looking at him. Bemused, he looked back.

"I knew you'd like it," said Isaac, sounding pleased with himself. "I'm not much for nature, myself. But I thought, you know—I bet Ingo would go for it."

"But . . ."

But why—the question was too obvious to ask.

"I owe you," the kid said with a shrug. "Like I told you. I owe you one bigger than this, actually. But hey. It's pretty, right?"

"That it is."

They stood and admired it a while longer, though the magical effect diminished rapidly with the onset of full daylight. A particular combination of circumstances seemed to be required for the full effect: sun, water, season, observer, each needed to be in precise alignment. Ingo had no intention of upsetting it by asking how the hell Isaac had known about this place. Certain things are best regarded as eternal mysteries, and he was quite sure this was one of them.

Afterward, there was no thought of going straight back to the campsite. Something must have come loose in Ingo's brain, like a broken electrical coupling, because all he wanted to do was lie on the rock in the morning sun. He wasn't really drowsy; to the contrary he felt unusually alive and alert, though in a languid, catlike fashion. He was worn out from days of hiking; just to sit still was an indescribable pleasure. More profoundly, he was exhausted from the nightly onslaught of *The Sorrows of Young Ingo*—insomnia, doubt, aloneness, desire—which were not lessened by the knowledge that they were not his alone. He was hardly the only citizen of Secret Germany, after all. There was a whole underground nation of people like himself, unconfined by borders or language. That realization had been thrilling at first, but after a while the strain of it began to wear at you. You hankered for normality. You wished things could get boring again, if only for a day or two.

That morning, sprawled in the sunlight, Ingo felt bored in the nicest possible way. The chortle of water slipping invisibly among the rocks seemed to poke gentle fun at his self-absorption, his Gothic melancholia. Had the others been around—Butler, Hagen, Martina—he might have found it difficult to just let go, to lie there unself-consciously, doing nothing, planning nothing, regretting nothing. With Isaac, somehow, it was different. With Isaac, you could just say to hell with it all.

Speaking of Isaac, though—where was he, what was he doing, while Ingo lay there enjoying his short-lived truce with the world? Was he okay? Happy, angry, apathetic, impatient to grow up, nostalgic for his childhood? Was he thinking of his family, his lost home across the sea? Or cooking up some fresh scheme to torment Hagen and thwart the frowning fates?

It would be as useful to ask, What do foxes dream of? Where does the fire go when you blow out a candle? The only thing Ingo cared to know was that when he turned his head sometime around mid-morning, Isaac was perched next to him on the rock, upright and frisky, red hair lying in tufts around his elf-ears, raring to go. Which was more or less exactly how he would always remember him.

Isaac declared he was starving to death, and Ingo—despite having left his appetite somewhere around the Leuchtenburg, and shedding a few pounds to prove it—decided he must be starving, too. Maybe the idea of food touched some nostalgic chord in him: Remember the good old days when we used to *eat*? Life was so much simpler then.

Again, the campsite would never do. No, our food must be cooked up in a proper kitchen, served on proper plates at a proper table. We must on the side have a satisfying beverage—thank you, but no more of Frau Möhring's dandelion-root "coffee." Above all we must have only pleasant company, which means present company, because things become complicated if we toss in any one of our trailmates, don't they? There would then be debates, differences, misunderstandings. Whereas with just the two of us, old comrades from the Battle of Frau-Holle-Quell, everything's right out in the open—right, pal?

And so they walked a while, but not the Wandervogel sort of walking, determined and vigorous and good for you. More like playing hooky and getting away with it. The land was their co-conspirator, deflating below the foothills into a lumpy plain, easy on the feet and undemanding of the eye. None of the grandeur of the Iron Mountains here, nor the evocative, quasi-medieval *Landschaft* of Thuringia. The place was actually rather boring—it made Ingo think of Maryland, the remote stretches south of Annapolis where colored people lived. The fields were cramped and less than impeccably tended, though extraordinarily green. The woods, tidy and safe-looking, lacked the impressive antiquity of German forests and those deep, alluring shadows where nameless danger abides. Fuck all that, as Isaac might have said. This was good, ordinary country, pleasant enough to amble through, but nothing to write home about.

In due course—about two minutes before Ingo would have insisted on a break—they came through a stand of poplars, the highest leaves faintly blushing with the first kiss of fall, to find themselves at the edge of a village, if "village" wasn't putting it too grandly. A couple dozen houses slumped beside the road, their yards and sheds and outhouses and livestock pens drawn up around them like an old woman's skirts. The principal buildings looked as though they might once have been taller and more gracefully proportioned, but over the decades had fattened and sagged, while creepers and roses and gooseberries and lilac bushes had filled in the gaps between them, and the surrounding woods and meadows had crept in, so that whatever sharp, right-angled lines had once divided the domestic from the wild, the pasture from the garden, the wall from its copious mantle of ivy, were now scarcely even a memory.

At the center was a dusty common, more or less rectangular, cropped by sheep and edged by a row of thorny shrubs sporting festive scarlet berries. An old pump house, apparently still in use, was ringed by a well-kept bed of flowers Ingo couldn't begin to name: humble domestic varieties, their colors at the brink of open war—scarcely Anton's cup of tea. Small children, alike only in their drab, hard-worn clothes, were running around on the grass but stopped to watch the newcomers in undisguised fascination. A young mother, her attention roused by the silence, looked up from her knitting and stared just as brazenly. Nobody waved hello or even nodded in their general direction.

Ingo murmured, "I guess they don't get too many visitors around here."

"What's to visit?" said Isaac.

At the far end of the green stood a small *Wirtshaus,* probably the only public accommodation for miles and miles. Though hardly distinguishable from its neighbors—the smithy two doors down could have been its twin, with the front wall torn open and an extra chimney thrown in—it called attention to itself by the scarlet geraniums (even Ingo knew a geranium when he saw one) that tumbled from boxes under a pair of wide front windows, veiled from the inside by panels of white lace. Tacked up by the door was a hand-painted sign on which an oversized yellow chicken bathed cheerfully in a stewpot; naïve and whimsical, it might have been the work of someone's talented daughter.

The room behind the lace curtains was furnished in three corners with heavy wooden tables and a muster of chairs sufficiently sturdy to withstand a drunken brawl. In the fourth stood a small iron stove and an empty woodbin; autumn was still a few weeks off and these people clearly weren't rushing it. The place was otherwise empty.

Isaac made for the table farthest from the windows. A bench was set into the wall and Ingo chose this for its protective attributes. Isaac sat blithely with his back turned to the door. The landlord entered from a back hallway looking slightly flushed, wearing suspenders over his white shirt and a bright blue yarmulke. If anything about the advent of this pair surprised him, he didn't let it show. Dark, avuncular and not at all portly, he addressed them in a language so exotic, so rife with unusually situated consonants, that Ingo guessed it was Polish. Isaac responded in Yiddish, barely glancing up. The innkeeper again showed no surprise. He replied briefly, shaking his head, then his tone changed and he seemed to offer a suggestion, to which Isaac assented with a shrug.

"Nice place here," Ingo ventured sometime after the man had gone, because it felt odd to sit there facing each other without saying anything.

Isaac offered no opinion. He fiddled with the table's only adornment, a fistful of pink blossoms in a stoneware jar. His nose was thrust into these when the landlord swept back in and gave him a little smile, tolerant and amused. He set down two glasses, a murky green bottle, half a loaf of coarse bread and a bowl of something squishy, black and redolent of vinegar. Ingo waited until he'd gone before giving this a worried once-over.

Isaac said, "My aunt calls that stuff eggplant caviar." He had lined up the glasses and was sloshing tawny liquid into them—thicker than wine, more clouded than any sort of liquor Ingo was familiar with. "For folks too poor to get the real thing, I guess. Here you go: the local poison, it's all they've got."

Ingo risked an experimental sip and was jolted by warring sensations, the hot tang of alcohol juxtaposed with a tongue-coating sweetness that faded in time to a vague fruity aftertaste.

"It's supposed to be cherry," said Isaac. "That's what the guy said. And today's stew is supposed to be veal. But in places like this, who knows? The cherry's probably apple—you know, the little green kind with holes in them. And the veal's probably last week's beef. But like my Aunt Rachel says, it's all in the preparation. She says, Give me a deep dish and some seasonings and any old kind of bird, and I'll make you a duck paprikash you'll be dreaming about for months." He raised his glass. "To friends."

"Friends." Even then, the word had taken on complicated shadings. Martina had applied it to him and Anton. He'd applied it to her and Butler. Nothing was simple anymore.

The eggplant caviar, which one ate by spreading it over chunks of caraway-seasoned bread, was surprisingly good, though it resembled nothing Ingo had ever eaten before. And the stew, when it came at last— after a good part of the bottle had been put away—was rich and brothy, fleshed out with beans and leeks and peppers; and by the time you got to wondering about the provenance of those little cubes of meat, the question was basically moot.

A handful of other patrons straggled in for lunch. Ingo guessed them to be farmers or laborers on their midday break. Whatever they were, they showed little overt interest in the two boys at the corner table. Now and then Ingo felt someone's glance straying over him, but by now he must have shed the more obvious signs of Americanness, of being anything besides just another wandering *Junge*, dusty from the road, overdue for his twice-weekly shave, spending his papa's money on food and drink. Isaac, of course, looked like nothing but himself: a semi-feral teenager who gave the distinct impression of being, in the new parlance, "rootless." On this day, none of the locals took exception to that.

Not that Ingo would have noticed, or cared. Just now, all that mattered was the feeling of supernal well-being that had descended upon him. The sun had dropped a bit and moved around the corner of the building so that warm yellow light came streaming through the nearest window to spread like a magic carpet across the floor. By its diffracted radiance everything in the room took on a revelatory glow—not at all blurry or hazy, rather a deepening of luminosity, such as one sees, for instance, in Rembrandt. Faces, flowers, half-filled glasses (they were on their second bottle by now) all seemed to possess an inner radiance. Every object, every being had become more wondrously itself. The glowing surface of the table spoke of a craftsman's honest, painstaking toil, subsequently burnished by years of hospitality. The pink blossoms winkled so beautifully from their jar that you could understand, just then, what kept the bees going all day long. Isaac's arm, laid uncaringly beside his plate, was a marvel of intricate design, from its endearingly awkward elbow down the length of the slender forearm to the wide, strong and somewhat clumsy-fingered hand. And all these things somehow were intertangled—the warmth, the food, the beauty of natural things, the *gemütlich* little pub, the freckle-faced boy—though Ingo might have been the only one to notice. Ingo the constant observer.

Watching the innkeeper go about his daily chores—truly, the man was a paragon of competence, quietly attentive to his patrons' every wish—Ingo experienced what he felt then was an epiphany, and might well have been so. Here was a good life, he realized. Here was an honorable way to live and a worthy thing to be. To provide for all and sundry a haven, albeit temporary, from the tempests of the world outside, a place of comfort and nourishment and fellowship . . . well, you could do worse, couldn't you? He topped up his glass and stared contentedly into its blood-tinted depths.

It was around this time that Isaac found his tongue.

Not that he hadn't kept up an off-and-on background chatter—on the food, the townies, the Polish language, the kind of shit the Socialists make you eat, how this place reminded him of the town where Eli and Rachel lived, a nice enough place if you're a fucking cow. Ingo attended to all this in an absentminded way, as you half hear a radio droning quietly in the background. Suddenly, after an interval of daydreaming, it struck him that the boy's tone of voice had changed. When or why, he couldn't have said. But Isaac was speaking now in a quiet and steady voice—not at all like himself, yet paradoxically more like himself than Ingo could remember. Which was not to say that he had any real idea who Isaac was—but then, who did?

"Running away," Isaac was saying just then, "that's what they called it. But I wasn't running, and I didn't really go anywhere, so how could it be running away? It was just . . . picking someplace different to sleep for a while. Maybe they should call it 'lying away.' What do you think?"

Ingo scarcely knew how to respond. Fortunately, Isaac didn't appear to want an answer.

"I mean, what did they expect? For me to spend my whole life sitting in school doing lousy and getting laughed at? Forget about it. Fucking school. Me and books, we never . . ."

Ingo believed this was the first time he had ever heard Isaac talk about himself, his past, the sort of thing most people consider important. "You and books?" he prompted.

Isaac looked across the table at him. Really looked. There was something unsettling about that stare. The green eyes were glazed with drink— as Ingo assumed his own were—but that was a surface phenomenon, a bodily thing. Burning through them, like sun through the waterfall, shone a clarity and intensity of awareness rather uncanny in a kid who was usually so blithe, so nonchalant. The eyes seemed to actually *see* you. It reminded Ingo of Halloween, when certain people can stare right through the mask and figure out who you are. Those eyes locked on him for a second or two, long enough for Isaac to come to a decision.

"It's not like I'm stupid," he said. "I always know what's going on. I can multiply and remember names and dates and all that shit. I just don't read." He paused. "I *can* read. I know all the fucking words, I've got the rules of grammar down. I can talk fine. But when something's on paper, forget about it. I look down, I see what it says, but somehow, it doesn't *mean* anything. You open a book, maybe it's *Treasure Island*. There's pirates and gold doubloons and all. Okay. But does it make sense, or is it some idiotic kid thing? As long as it's just on paper, I don't know. But if I could *go* to the fucking island and meet the pirates myself, then I could tell you in two seconds: this one's an asshole, that one's all right, take the treasure and run. Or maybe, this whole thing's a load of crap, it's even worse than *Peter Pan*." He shrugged. "I guess that's just how my head works. The point is, sitting in school was nothing but a waste of time. I needed to be, you know . . ." He waved his glass hazardously. "Out here. Seeing it for myself."

Ingo started to reply—that words on paper to him had always seemed *more* real, more nuanced and colored, than the humdrum business that passed for daily life—but Isaac signaled with the least perceptible twitch of the jaw that he wasn't quite through.

"So anyway, I just sort of left. I didn't 'run away,' that's bullshit, too. But it's not like I had a lot of choices. They were sending letters home to my folks, and my pop was going bananas, and all over what? Nothing but shit on paper. So one thing led to another, and these guys who I thought were my friends turned out not to be friends after all. But see, I figured that out pretty fast, once I got out there. Because even though they said one thing, it was just words—you could take one look and see what the real story was. They had this thing they wanted somebody to do for them, and I was the first sucker that came along. I was, like, convenient. And when the whole business blew apart, well, I was convenient then, too. I looked exactly right on paper. Just the kind of troubled and misguided youth, quote unquote, the bulls needed to track down. The rest of them, my old buddies, they were all-American kids. Just like, if you look at those Jungdo assholes, I guarantee they're all a bunch of straight-A, good-mannered, pious Lutheran flag-waving patriots. They could slice my balls off tomorrow and it would be *my* fault—I corrupted *them* somehow, what a shame that bad elements like me are ruining decent deutsche Jugend. If you think I'm exaggerating, it's time to get your nose out of the fucking book."

Ingo wasn't sure what he thought, only what he felt. And that was growing more fraught by the minute. The least of it was, he wanted to reach across the few inches of empty table and take Isaac's hand, which seemed suddenly childlike and vulnerable, into his own. Because, behind the anger, the street talk, the knowingness, the whole tough-kid shtick, there was an Isaac quite different from the one he thought he knew. And this secret Isaac was maybe not so diametric to himself as Ingo had supposed. This Isaac felt things with a dangerous intensity; his whole being, like Ingo's, was a single raw nerve—he merely chose a different means of shielding it. Safety in brazenness. But even then, so late in the game, Ingo might have been selling him short.

Isaac focused his eyes on Ingo with surprising steadiness, given the probable level of alcohol in his blood, as if he were calibrating the change in emotional climate. Then he said calmly, with grown-up *gravitas,* "That's not what I wanted to say, though."

Meaning, as Ingo later would surmise, that he'd wanted to say *something,* some definite thing. And perhaps—though this might be pressing it—that's what the whole day had been about, from the predawn wake-up to the two bottles of local poison.

"The thing is"—Isaac spoke quietly, bringing his face close enough for Ingo to map the changeable contours of its topography, the small lines that formed and vanished around his mouth, his pale temples, his guileless eyes—"like I said before, I always know what's going on, if I can see things for myself. Like with you. That night back there at the Jugendtag—I was getting my ass kicked, but I knew what the story was and what it had to do with me. And then when you showed up, the story changed, but I got that, too. I saw how you fit into it. Maybe you didn't get it yourself, not right away. I think you're sometimes, maybe, a little slow. I don't mean dumb or anything."

He flashed a smile, a magical yet somehow heartbreaking smile, which seemed older and sadder than the rest of him.

"I know you're smart, anybody can see that. I just think you don't always pick up on certain things that are kind of obvious. But that's all right, it doesn't matter. You've got . . . my aunt would say, He's got a good heart, that boy. I used to think that was hilarious—you mean he's not going to *die* anytime soon, Aunt Rachel? But I guess maybe I've never known a lot of good people before. Really good, deep down. Like that stuff the fucking Germans go on about, Ehre und Treue, honor and loyalty, except the people who won't shut up about all that wouldn't know Ehre if it bit their putz off. And then there's people like you, who never talk about anything at all. You probably think you're totally different, like nobody would like you if they really knew you. Which proves you're smart, because mostly you're right. Most guys, if they think you're a Schwuler, they'll kick the shit out of you, worse than if you're only a Jew. Imagine being a Jewish faggot!" He laughed but his eyes didn't change. He seemed anxious not to be misunderstood.

Ingo felt trembly inside. This was a territory that remained foreign to him and rather forbidding. He'd done a few things and thought about many others, but never had he talked about them. Only a little with Anton, but that was an exceptional case, and anyway, the talking part had been superfluous. With Isaac it was different. Everything was, almost.

"I just thought," said Isaac, clenching and unclenching one hand, as getting a grip on something, "that somebody ought to tell you . . ."

And as quickly as that, the focus blurred—as though Isaac had picked up one foot and then, in mid-stride, forgotten exactly where he meant to put it down. Ingo later would learn to recognize the pattern, to track it minutely through all its stages of progression. People drink differently and respond to it differently, but in a certain type of person you can discern quite clearly an upward arc leading to a point of daring, preternatural clarity, like the view from the edge of a cliff. And then, the fall. Several years hence, when the potted palms began to wilt in his *Bierskeller,* Ingo could gauge, practically to the minute, when it was time to call the cab. But on this summer's day, Isaac's sudden loss of concentration alarmed him. He supposed, not getting the obvious, that his friend needed some air. So he paid the proprietor, adding a liberal gratuity, and the two boys stumbled together—it was Isaac who lost his footing, but with his grip on Ingo's shoulder they shared the disequilibrium—out the door into the green, sun-drenched afternoon.

He would remember certain subsequent details—what he'd thought, how he'd felt, what the two of them had talked about—but not others. He would remember thinking that this was becoming a regular thing with them: Isaac lurching along, weak at the knees, while Ingo half dragged him toward some destination of which he himself was unaware. He would remember how Isaac's thin body felt pressed to his side, an arm draped around his neck. The voice in his ear. Sudden bursts of laughter. Silences, broken by hummed, half-forgotten childhood tunes. The wildness of a grin, the pink cheek flushed with sun and warmth and overindulgence.

He would forget other, more vital things. Where the hell they thought they were going. What time of day it was. And whose bright idea it had been to cross someone's soggy meadow and clamber up onto that huge pile of hay, a whole field's worth heaped together in the only dry spot, so it seemed, amid acres of empty bottomland.

The hay he did remember. How it smelled—nutty and earthy and sweet—and how it sagged under your weight but only so far, then it lifted you again, and you felt as though you were floating up in the air. You could sway, you could bounce, you could roll around luxuriously; the hay both held and hid you, and you were absolutely safe. He remembered how it trapped the sun, the warmth seeming to radiate not just down from the sky but upward from the golden mound itself—as if these wild grasses and flowers had been storing up sunlight all summer long, and now that they'd been cut, their stems and blades and flower heads carefully laid, layer upon layer, to make a bed for two boys tired of walking and drowsy from lunch, all that patiently husbanded warmth was gently seeping out, around and over them like a blanket. He remembered how hot it was, the two of them sweating, their skin gleaming wet. Isaac pulling his shirt off.

He did not remember the exact order in which things happened next, nor was he certain there was anything much to remember—only certain details that clung to his mind with singular tenacity.

He had closed his eyes, then opened them, but it must have taken longer than the instant or two it seemed, because in the interval a number of things had rearranged themselves. Ingo's clothes lay folded beneath his head, a makeshift pillow. Isaac's were strewn all over the place, and he was sprawled on his back, apparently asleep, like a marionette whose strings had been cut. His head pinned one of Ingo's arms against the hay, and Ingo left it like that. Not that he cared about waking Isaac—he'd have to do that, sooner or later. Only not just now.

There wasn't much he could do from that position except look around, and so he looked. There wasn't much to see except Isaac, and so he studied him in fine detail, bringing to his subject the passionate interest of a naturalist examining some rare and striking specimen, discovered by chance in its natural state in the wild. He followed the red hair as it marginally darkened and trailed down behind the ears onto the narrow neck. He traced out the bone structure around the upper chest. Counted the wispy, orange-blond hairs that had gained a tentative hold in the cleft of the chest. He considered the matter of skin tone, the darker regions, tinted raw umber and freckled heavily by the sun, bordering so closely on the lighter zones, according to the whims of anatomy. Thus the skin around the shoulders was mottled tan and brown, while centimeters away, in the tender hollow of the armpit, it was pale as chalk and the sparse hairs looked quite dark by contrast. And so, downward.

In the course of his examination the budding naturalist made a number of observations, fodder for later reflection in the laboratory. In no special order:

- That the body, though indeed trim, looked less skinny when unclothed. Under these field conditions one notes areas of fleshy softness and others of distinct muscularity. Surprisingly often, one finds both present at once, as for instance in the belly (long, warm, rising gently at each breath) or the buttocks (partially obscured, but more clearly linked to the straplike sinews of the thigh than one had previously supposed).

- That the evident disproportion in size of various body parts— hands, head, legs, torso—becomes less striking when viewed in a more comprehensive context. It is as though the body in its entirety possesses an organizational logic that is not apparent until the subject is fully revealed. (This point merits further inquiry.)

- In contrast, certain unexpected features appear. Who knew that the hipbone extends so far upward, relative to the plunge of the abdomen below the navel? How carefully was this knee design tested? Will it hold up under stress? What on earth could cause hair to grow so thickly *here,* while elsewhere it is either very sparse or absent altogether?

- One last item of note—of unique interest in itself, but also in contrast with other recently examined specimens—appears to bear out the snowflake principle: No two are the same.

By this time it was only too obvious why Ingo had taken up the humanities instead of the natural sciences. He found himself in what might be called his blue-flower state. But this was somehow different, less hopeless or thwarted, indeed almost enjoyable in an excruciating sort of way. To lie next to Isaac was, almost, like being with a lover. He could feel the heat of the body beside him, the softness of the skin against his own. He could hear the air moving in and out as the pale chest swelled and contracted. Could smell the strange but not disagreeable mix of odors—cookies fresh out of the oven, a puppy after rolling around in the yard—of healthy young bodies that could use a bath. That was about all he could do without waking the boy. But for the moment—maybe because he was half drunk and half dreaming, maybe because it was the best deal on offer, or maybe because in this instance, contrasted again with that of Anton, anything more was superfluous—it was enough.

Then, it appears, he slept. Or maybe he slept before and after. Or else he dreamed the whole damn thing.

The boys woke up late in the afternoon. The nearly sunset chill awakened them: night and autumn sneaking down from the mountains, putting out feelers across the summer plain. Groggily they pulled on their clothes and headed back to the camp in the foothills by the last light of day and the first pale limning of moonlight. Isaac, leading at a surefooted pace, could as easily have found his way in the dark.

Ingo trailed along feeling confused but strangely content, among other incompatible things. He felt as though he had made love and that he would never make love again. He felt dejected and alone, yet for the first time in his life recognized and understood. He felt lost in an unfamiliar world, on the very border of his true homeland. He felt ordinary and powerless, singular and omnipotent. And beneath it all, like the undebatable number written below the line in an arithmetic problem, he felt something bald and unexpected. He didn't understand where any of this had come from. From within or without? Why here, why now? Why him? Why Isaac?

Years later, in a wholly different world, he was no closer to knowing. But at least he knew this. All those things he could not, no matter how hard he tried, remember about Anton—big and small, trivial and crucially important—he could never get out of his head where Isaac was concerned. Isaac, who had never been his lover. Who, unlike Ingo, was able to flit between the two worlds at will, the real and the imagined, the dreamlike past and the nightmarish present. Who doesn't read, whose clothes don't fit, who is to blame for absolutely everything.

Isaac the trickster, the wild card, the fool.

Isaac, my destiny.

Isaac.

CHANGING SCENES

From Butler's journal.

2. SEPT

The journey of a thousand miles begins with a hangover.

3. SEPT

I think the story has changed—not Innocents Abroad now. That was wrong anyway. The Old/New World scheme doesn't fit, the fault lines lie elsewhere.

Something sharper, a biting edge, Tucholskyish. Chronicle of bourgeois kids doing, as Berliners say, their Wandervogel. Borrow that wonderful line from Joseph Roth—"They have a sort of loden-jacket relationship with Nature."

Perhaps hard to sell that, however.

Or Waugh. Comedy of class and type. Heart of Greenness, in which with neither fear nor toilet paper our heroes plunge into darkest Germania, the land that swallowed Roman legions, inhabited by tribes of brutish guitar-strumming boy scouts clad like heathens in sandals and short pants. As calamity is heaped upon misadventure—my god, wails the Hysterical Brunette, I have lost my comb!!—suspense mounts to an unbearable pitch. Will the Jew succeed in his plot to drive the German mad via insolence and incorrect adjective endings? Will the Catholic Lass shag the Expatriate till his schwanz falls off (and if so, will she be properly contrite next morning)?

Later p.m. note to self: Take the gown off, dear fellow. Don't make it too literary. No one will read it.

5. SEPT

What a day! Wax poetic in scene-laying. Sweet shorn grass carpeting meadows gentled by grazing. Sunshine butter yellow, its warmth enfolding one. Lying there, we five, under a boundless Bohemian sky. Overhead, weightless, majestic, Heine's Greek-god clouds—imagine how the characters see them.

Isaac: an outfielder stretching to make a catch? The ball's trajectory sketched in cirrus.

Hagen, god only knows. Thor that would be, or Wotan—or who was the beautiful young thing, slain by Loki's trickery? Baldur? [LOOK UP] A castle . . . perhaps too obvious. Clash of warriors. Siegfried and namesake. Dragon!

Marty? The female point of view is not, as critics have noted, our author's strong suit. Always the danger of trivializing. 'A puffy hairdo, how unstylish.' Keep it neutral, if unimaginative—a ship, an elephant, an apple tree.

Ingo: a land in the heavens, dreamy and perfect, fields to roam in, flowers to pluck, cozy grottoes for one's intimate rendezvous. A pathos about this character that grows on you.

Expatriate: Clouds.

6. SEPT

Summer returns. Rather nice the way these hills roll out, how many hundreds of years have peasants lived off them? The earth so soft and black you could stew it right up, no need running it through a cabbage.

At midday discover a pond isolated from view. Therefore: man muß schwimmen! Now the delicious drama—will this play in America?—of everyone taking their clothes off.

Catholic Girl contests with Fearless Flapper, a match that goes three rounds. 1. Demure, locate a bush to undress behind, the absurdity of this no obstacle. Clothing removed in a definite order, hung out daintily on branches. 2. The line is crossed with the unclasping of the bra. Linger here a paragraph. Conflict of emotions plays out in the eyes. Why not? Go ahead. I can't. This isn't the Victorian Age—it is 1929. I can't help it. Plus, look, I'm the only girl! So what? You've been to the Meissner. It's nothing,

it's natural. All right then. Ooo, yummy! I feel so free! 3. Out from behind
the bush, breasts white and pertly upturned, pubis bared, legs in brazen
mid-stride, three steps toward the water—then freeze. They are staring at
me. Ingo, who has known me all his life. And Hagen, Isaac, I barely know
them at all. Aaaaa!!!!

Same stage, separate drama. The Blond Godling is perfect and knows it.
Quite pleased to suffer one's admiration. The Scrawny Urchin more than a
match for him in brazenness, which only makes the contrast even more
telling—a Kollwitz puppet, all joints and limbs, beside a Michelangelo casting of muscle and sinew. Neither can spare much body hair. Each feigns
indifference—unawareness—of the other.

Not so Ingo. Blatantly gawking. The only question being, where to
look. Phaedrus or Pinocchio. [GOOD. Use this.] Embarrassment of riches—
though in a currency of limited circulation.

Expatriate swoops in, hefts Frozen Flapper on a shoulder, splash, in we
go, shrieks and laughter, fists on one's back. Put me down! With pleasure,
my darling. Let loose, she flails, submerges, down then up, spluttering.
You bastard! Rising like a naiad naked from the quivering depths. Wetness
like molten silver streaming down her tits, her slender belly, proud hips,
mons veneris. A Venus indeed.

All this, before lunch. Then more miles behind us.

7. SEPT

Lovely bit of Carpathian folklore: There are bodies of water here—the
knowledge of which is a great secret, only certain old women possess it—
where, if you swim in there, confer upon you the ability to pass unseen
through walls.

'Old wives' tales.' Why attribute such stories to women only? One
does, however. The Grimms even put that superannuated nanny on their
frontispiece—imprimatur of folkishness. Yet so many of the stories (this
one, a case in point) project clearly a male sort of fantasizing. Slip unseen
through the neighbors' wall, spy on their pretty daughter in her bath.
Or disguise yourself in an old frock so you can ravish delectable Red
Käppchen.

Perhaps the old dame functions as a Geheimnisträger, bearer of secrets.
I may be aged and ugly, but I know where the tiny bodies are buried, I
know a spell to make you a werewolf, I know a root that will keep you
alive.

—Further thought. Is there something about a landscape that gives rise to a folklore of atrocity? Children baked alive, devoured by wolves, left to die in the forest. The shiny apple is poisoned. The smiling lady is a witch. You don't find such tales everywhere, do you? Can a place then be a natural home to wickedness, a nexus of dark energies? I bet the Steiner people would say so. If not, somebody. The Thule Society, the Rune Guild, the Armanenschaft—we suffer no shortage of pagans with Ph.D.'s.

Idea for a dissertation. (What field, anthro, lit, philology?) Geographical survey of folktale motifs, ranked by degree of relative ghastliness. Scale runs from cannibalism down to social impropriety (sore spot with the Japanese). Results to be presented in narrative and cartographic form. The question: at what point on earth is the well of consciousness most fatally—Platen's word is best—verziechend?

8. SEPT

Behold, a new prospect. North and east from these mountains, we see the marches of Northern Europe. It looks like a muchness of nothing. A desert, from which the lights of Prague and Vienna—the lights of fucking Düsseldorf—must shimmer like an oasis. Go South, young man! Go West!

Why then does the German soul pine for the unpopulous East?

9. SEPT

An evening's break from the rigors of the open road—modest inn at a crossroads in the Moravian Pass whose charm, though marked, will be hard to convey to an American readership inclined to view the private indoor bathroom as a matter of birthright. Here one finds a sturdy built-on bathhouse equipped with a magnificent oaken tub. For a few coins the landlord supplies heated water, a mound of towels, and a block of soap smelling of unknown local herbage. This fine vessel would accommodate all of us, but you know the Brunette. (One hopes by now the reader will at any rate.)

Thus, while the water cools and the lady ablutes adjacently, a grumbling male contingent seeks consolation in a pitcher or two of the local beer which is not too many kilometers removed from being a true Bohemian Pilsner. More exactly such consolation is sought by Ingo, Isaac, and the Transparent Narrator only, as drinking of alcohol is one of 3 mortal prohibitions of the Jugendbewegung, as writ in the Gospel of Hagen. The others—one perforce enquires—are in order of ascending deadliness: Smoking of tobacco. Visiting of prostitutes.

This far, one might hope to carry at least the more sophisticated type of American reader. But even this audience is lost (and given up for dead) when the Narrator poses the natural follow-up: 'So, you're allowed to have a steady girlfriend, are you?'

To which Hagen, in behalf seemingly of German maidenhood, takes immoderate offense. We then must suffer one of his periodic lectures— this one concerning the sacrosanct nature of the marital bond, the dangers to normal healthy development posed by 'a premature and morbid type of conjugality,' and of course, the obligation to defend one's own sisters from defilement.

But wait: lest the reader feel that he has heard this sermon before, we rush to assure him he has not. For when Isaac makes some feckless inter- jection or other—one does not often jot these things down, nearly all are unprintable—to the effect that German Youth in this case ought to find itself some baggier hiking shorts, because its balls are going to swell up, Hagen surprisingly takes no offense. Natural sexual yearning (geschlecht- liche Sehnsucht) must have a healthy outlet: so he informs us, his manner straightforward, instructional. On which account, masturbation is encour- aged and may be practiced quite frankly, as one attends to other bodily needs. Indeed one ought not to be furtive in such matters, as this might indicate, or be symptomatic of, some sexual incorrectness.

At which astonishing point, the female of the species appears, demurely sheathed. Hagen does not terminate his lecture but turns his attention to certain dietary practices recommended in such cases. What with one thing and another, the details have been lost.

10. SEPT

Enough.

One has had enough. Walking, sweating, fornicating on terra ardua, communing with the genius loci.

One misses Leipzig. Better: Berlin. Waking at ten, an intelligent news- paper. Rudeness of pedestrians, ugliness of streets—waiting at the corner for the tram to pass—then out of nowhere, an apotheosis. A violin sighs from an upper window. You imagine the beauty up there, she is sixteen next month, waif-waisted, practicing her recital piece. You stare upward as an elderly linden fans yellow leaves against the coal-smeared sky.

[*Long descriptive passage crossed out.*]

Enough of this landscape. Sum it in a sentence. If you should ever want to lose a thing, to let it drop, then stroll away and think of it nevermore—do it here.

Enough of cows!

Of the Brunette however. Toothsome, musky, mischievous, untiring. The eyes that blaze then slowly close—eclipse of passion. The arms, enveloping. The mouth, hot, hungry, generous with laughter, lair of the sharp tongue. The body, sweet and bountiful as a soft fruit plucked hot in the sun; you seek to taste it but it, instead, consumes you. Her voice, her hair, her elbows, small feet, trivial complaints, shallow breathing in the night, moments of zany, girlish abandon. By no means ever enough.

11. SEPT—ARNDTHEIM.

What, wondered the Expatriate, would Tucholsky make of <u>this</u>?

12. SEPT

Finally catch one's breath. Nothing I've ever seen before. Whole new world here, but (the usual rub) likely of zero interest to New World readers.

They do not like 'commune'—the term sounds too Parisian, I suppose. We are a voluntary community, they say, freiwillige Gemeindshaft, and we choose to share the labors and the rewards. And by the way, we don't like talking about this, actually (while never ceasing to blather), so why don't you put down that expensive writing instrument and come join us for a mug of applemint tea?

It is not much Marx. It is rather very Morris—though no one fesses to having read News from Nowhere, so there must be some intermediary, a vector. They place great value here upon handcraft, the thing well made, no more complicated than it needs to be. The perfect emblem of Arndtheim is the honey-dipper: a curious curvaceous elongated knob, carefully lathed and grooved, that emerges from the pot impregnated with oozing sweetness. Thus Arndtheim: a well-earned bounty, an earthly abundance, with just that twist of oddity, those funny grooves running right through the grain. An essential stickiness.

I don't know what it is about these people that annoys me so.

They dress as they imagine good German peasants might dress, or ought to dress, or dressed once upon a time, in some golden agrarian age: loose-fitting smocks, wide britches, leather moccasins, wide-brimmed hats, all made by themselves.

They labor together, that is true. Whether they labor equally or not? Not only the cynic suspects an unacknowledged hierarchy.

They plant their herbs and food crops in keeping with the cycles of moon and planets, using complicated charts marked up with astrologic formulae. Further, there are mysterious preparations to vitalize the soil, draw the appropriate cosmic energies, or deflect negative influences back to the Underworld—don't enquire too closely about this unless you have an afternoon to spare. It's all very Madame Blavatsky, I think, though they make it out to be scientific.

They do not like squares. For them, it must be the circle, the conic section, the hexagon (shape of a honeycomb—and yes, of course, they keep bees, great wood-framed enclaves of this earnest and Socialist-minded insect). The village is laid out in alignment with the poles and with the exact directions in which the sun rises and sets on the summer and winter solstices. This gives six bearings—hence, six lanes webbing out from a central green or common. The innermost structures are workshops, a mule-powered grain mill, a smithy, and a pleasant timbered edifice that should very much like to be a village inn or pub but is obliged to call itself the Community House, a library–cum–school–cum–dining hall. Second ring out, cottages of the permanent residents or, as they call themselves, 'settlers,' as though this were Jamestown 1609, or Erewhon 1890. Subsequent rings house the less permanently situated (hard to tell who lives here, actually, even the residents themselves don't seem to know). The living is rustic but comfy enough. Marty and I have got a little cabin in which one hears a stream lapping pleasantly through the night.

13. SEPT

Chilly, these last mornings.

Book shelves, don't you find, are mercilessly revealing. In the Gemeindehaus (loitering, shirking our kitchen duty) we discover Kant and Hegel and Schopenhauer: well enough. Freud of course. Spengler in successive editions. The usual moderns, Kästner, Hesse, Rilke, Hofmannsthal, the Manns. Wyneken, Blüher, Baden-Powell (in translation), canon of the Youth Movement. Waist-high stacks of magazines, pamphlets, journals, broadsheets, most badly written, execrably designed, amateurish in every way. Others less so.

Then, the odd things. Last, the worrisome things.

Among the former, highly colored romances by Guido List, a Walter

Scott of the Ring Cycle set. Wise chieftains, fearless warriors, 'runic magi.' And of course a stable of blond Frauen of fulsome breast, ready and happy to (as the saying goes) throw the babies.

Among the latter—who is Raoul Francé? He would seem to be a Monist. (Whatever that is.) His Discovery of the Homeland, 1914, entreats men of German blood to quit the cities, those dens of filth and 'cosmopolitanism'—i.e., Jewry—and return to the fields, the forests, the good rich earth of their ancestors.

And who, pray, is Ernst Haeckel? A biologist of some kind, one gathers, though what kind one cannot guess. He is all over the shelf, some of his writings quite dusty indeed. From 1866, 'Oekologie,' a term I don't recognize, a monograph having to do with Nature and the intricate relationships therein. Relationships chiefly fratricidal. The fellow seems to take fiendish glee in the prospect that certain organisms shall surely exterminate their fellows, and that (if one reads him correctly) the same applies to certain races. One looks in vain for a clear definition of 'race.' Is he talking about the hated French? The Lapps, trespassers on Nordic ground? No, one suspects one knows whom he is talking about.

From Haeckel, a short hop to Wilhelm Heinrich Riehl. Who at least comes right out with it. 'We must save the sacred forest, not only so that our ovens do not become cold in winter, but also so that the pulse of life of the people continues to beat warm and joyfully, so that Germany remains German.' This in 1853! Right-wing tree-worshippers espousing the 'rights of wilderness.' How could this possibly be understood in America?

Finally, the namesake, Ernst Moritz Arndt—hence 'Arndtheim.' Queerest of a queer lot. A treatise from 1815, Darwin barely out of diapers, sounds radical even today. On the Care and Conservation of Forests: 'When one sees nature in a necessary connectedness and interrelationship, then all things are equally important—shrub, worm, plant, human, stone, nothing first or last, but all one single unity.'

Sounds cozy and warm, for those who enjoy their panentheism. Yet a paragraph down, one chokes upon dire warnings against miscegenation and, a few pages later, scurrilous diatribes against the usual villains: Slavs, Mediterraneans, and . . . need it be said?

The message, ringing and clear: We belong to this world, our natural place is here, like the stag, the eagle, the oak. Our bodies are meant to thrive on this hard continent, our souls shaped by this climate, these mountains, a quality of sunlight, a sharp scent of tannin in the air. And so it is our sacred duty to defend this place, this German soil, this German water, these German trees, against all that is alien, corrupting, industrial, 'civilized'—not for our own sake, for we are merely part of the whole, but for the sake of that greater, unified thing, the living body of Germania.

A stirring vision, and so very dangerous. Over a century old yet very much alive here, evolving, ramifying, in this 'model hamlet.'

Oh, and did you know, this Arndt man wrote also fairy tales. There is a book of them and they appear very common indeed.

14. SEPT

Talk of leaving. Talk of staying. Talk of politics. Talk.

Last night late—too late to record, now half forgotten—a disputation over Hesse, whose recent novels are enjoyed in Leipzig arguably to excess. Minds here divided. These people approve the author's mystical aspect, likewise his iconoclasm. His focus, however, upon the singular man, the lone wolf, emphatically they do not. Hesse lacks völlig social consciousness, they say. At which point, roughly, the Demian was adduced. This slight auto-Bildungsroman is taken by these credulous folks (in such matters more conventional than they suppose) at face value: Max Demian, mini-Übermensch, meets sensitive but unenlightened narrator and shows him the Way.

Here the Expat, mildly intoxicated, essayed an alternative exegesis: the Demian as daring (though botched) attempt at homosexual confessional. Admittedly, one hoped to shock. One hoped also, however, to make a gesture of goodwill toward Marty's old friend, whom we have here unkindly called the Invert, who does not, for all one's chumminess, show signs of warming toward ourselves. And so, with muddled intent, we began ticking off the points (which, need it be noted, have the striking feature of correctness).

In the throes of Pubertät, whilst his comrades speak coarsely of women, pseudonymous young Emil thinks only of his friend Max Demian. Consistently, through all his changing moods, he employs the term Sehnsucht (yearning, desire) to characterize his feelings—though the word never appears in the text when Max is more than two sentences away. The friend's striking looks are (redundantly) detailed—variously called 'womanly,' or weiblich, and androgynous. In a stuffy classroom, Emil stares fixedly at the back of Max's neck, rapturously inhaling the 'soft smell' there. Max gives as good as he gets, referring pointedly to the ancient Greeks, who held in honor certain (unspecified) things now felt to be abominable. He confesses himself to be 'interested in' the younger boy

for no obvious reason—or rather, one obvious reason that is nowhere
openly acknowledged. He quivers once at the edge of a great declaration,
only to retreat as, indeed, does Hesse himself, into silence and misdirec-
tion. The only female character of note (Max's mom!) enters late and
serves merely as a double and stand-in for her son, whom she looks
and talks exactly like. Once, yes, it is true (we were obliged to respond to
a predictable objection), Emil glimpses in a public park a Real Girl, and
thereupon fixates implausibly upon her slender, small-breasted, and suspiciously boylike image. But this flimsy narrative ploy serves two purposes.
First, Emil's chaste daydreaming about this girl, whom he never tries to
meet in the flesh, excuses him from the opposite-sex involvements of his
schoolmates, which he finds crude, dissolute, and unappealing. Second, it
impels him to create art, starting with a portrait of his comely Muse—
which, when it is done, depicts not the nameless Mädchen but the mäd-
chenhaft Max, right down to his full, sensuous mouth. And of course the
story closes with a boy-to-boy, lip-to-lip kiss, concerning which the author,
in his haste to explain it away, makes his feeblest and most craven showing
to date.

—All of which, one had hoped and rather expected, might have earned
at least a friendly nod from Ingo. To the contrary! Said Kerl avoided one's
eye from 'homo-' onward and slunk from the common room during the
ensuing spirited discussion. Thus was the Expat left to defend an unpopu-
lar (but honestly unassailable) position with no one to hand him ammunition. So much for gratitude. So much for wearing one's tolerance upon
one's sleeve.

We shall carry on, though. We shall not be so easily blinked out of this
fellow's eye. Where the Brunette goes, we mean to follow. And thus far,
she seems devoutly disinclined to go anyplace without our Ingo tagging
along.

16. SEPT

The evening meal here is the high point of the day, communally speaking. People are done with their labors in the garden and the vineyard and
the workshops and the mill (my own day's assignment: shepherding!
which gives one time to think and write), and everyone has a pent-up
impulse to socialize. Usually there is something on for the evening—a
topic for discussion, lessons in folk dance, a musical recital—so dinner is,
you might say, the last open slot of the day. 'The boys,' as Marty calls them,
are not present, unaccounted for since midday, their movements lately

hard to keep track of. Quite the oddest trio imaginable, but there you have it.

The big hall where we eat is a curious mix, Arts & Crafts with a touch of barrier-free Gropius functionalism. Socialist interior design: no rugs on the pale wood floors, but a superfluity of wall posters, Blue Rider prints, portrait of Rosa Luxembourg, her coiffure in itself a form of torture.

At our table is one of the Big Men About Arndtheim (which pretends to be a pure democracy, but strikes one as more an ideocracy, led by those with the strongest opinions)—a fellow named Alwin. Tall, bright-eyed, articulate though given to talking in slogans, his distinguishing affectation is dark hair worn long and straight, past his shoulders, and a deerskin waistcoat. Rousseau's homme sauvage, or his German cousin. Who falls to discoursing, this night, on the calamity soon to befall Western civilization. The nature thereof, unspecified. The signs, the auguries, however, unmistakable. One hears this kind of thing everywhere, of course, but Alwin gives it a twist. He sees cracks in the cultural edifice where other observers—Yanks above all—might see breadth and novelty.

Look, says Alwin, at the chaos of art. There is no true subject matter, no world-vision, not since the Pre-Raphaelites. Today's artist seeks only that which is instantaneous, effortless, which relates to nothing and means nothing, which lacks both antecedent and consequence. The topic of art is art itself, nothing more.

While he speaks, a young girl pops up beside him, flaxen hair in two long braids, just big enough to clamber onto his lap. Alwin steadies her with a hand but otherwise pays her no heed. His mind is on higher things.

Observe, likewise, the decadent state into which literature has fallen. The writers of our age have nothing to offer beyond the most minute self-absorption. This Irishman with his huge novel about a Jew who leaves his house, walks around Dublin, and returns home again. Or the Frenchman with his seven volumes about eating dinner and falling asleep. Even our own Professor Mann, feeding us sickly tales of a stage magician or a pervert by the sea.

The girl says, Daddy, please, we are so bored, there is nothing to do, will you tell us a story?

And God in heaven, says the Big Man, do not speak of music! Shush now, Hildi. Without doubt, we bear witness today to the death of composition. Better the degraded mewling of Berlin cabarets than the tuneless fiddle-scratching of Schoenberg!

Onward in this vein he goes, quite vividly. The girl twirls fingers in his long hair. He speaks once to her, in annoyance. Come, Hildi, calls a woman across the room, leave your father in peace.

Is this the mother? Wife, mistress, brood mare, we are not sure what categories exist here in the Great Experiment.

'Perhaps then' (when at last the Ideocrat pauses, the Expat ventures to suggest) 'what is wanted is a unifying theory, a sense of where we stand in history, what is required of us. For instance, Marx suggests—'

One is permitted nothing further.

'We need no more ideology!' the fellow shouts, or rather, shrieks. Somehow one senses: he is quoting somebody. 'Spengler tells us' (of course, one knew Spengler was coming, sooner or later) 'we need hardness. We need fearless skepticism. We need, above all, a new class of socialist overlords!' Actually, for overlords, Herrenvolk, a word the Hitler party takes pleasure in.

The Expatriate finds no words to suit the occasion. Across the room little Hildi laughs, entertained by some antic of Isaac's. The woman— wife, mother, martyr, none of the above?—sighs, brushing hair out of her eyes. Already a few strands of silver there.

Thus the state of progressive Germany, in these last months of the decade.

17. SEPT

A night of lovemaking and faraway dreams (a dance hall; shouting at père de famille) yields to 'morning-red,' the fiery dawn.

There are fists on the door. Then, in the room, the German boy. I am not awake, not really, and the boy is shouting. Where did all that stony self-possession go? Marty clicks on like a switch. She asks him: What's the matter?—in English of course, and he answers in German, but by now we understand each other as well as we ever shall.

'You must get out quickly,' he says, in which tongue I do not recall. 'They have come. Look, they are just there.'

Who, where—always a headache when there hasn't been enough sleep.

Marty a swirl of motion, whipping a sheet around her nakedness, crossing the room. 'Hagen—you're bleeding.'

At this one's eyes do rather pop. Blood it is: a long cut down one arm, a double-slash, elbow to wrist, as though he'd yanked it from a dragon's teeth. No tasty Blöndchen today, Herr Drache—but a close-run thing.

'My god, you're dripping all over. Butler, come here, do something!'
Such as?

Something, that is all. Here is a problem, a débâcle, it can perhaps be fixed, perhaps not, but for god's sake don't just sit there. The essence of Marty. One loves her for it, even at such times.

Young Siegfried does not care to be fussed over. 'You must go, quickly. I will be all right, it is not serious.'

You feel he has been practicing all his life to say this. Meanwhile dripping like a Polish faucet all over the cabin floor. The Expat, upright finally, finds his clothing in the still half-dark cabin, a gauze of muslin floating at the window in dawn's cool breeze. Some kind of ruckus outside, toward the center of the Dorf. Doors bang open, or shut—voices not quite raised to a shout but urgent, agitated, charged with adrenaline, you can feel the rawness of fear and anger as clearly as in a shortwave broadcast.

'The Jungdo!'

At last the Expat understands.

Nod from the boy.

'How many?'

'I could not tell. A dozen, perhaps. Enough.'

Marty's eyes flare. 'What about Isaac and Ingo?'

The boy sets his mouth. He will not answer. But you see it there, the unsaid thing, in his eyes.

'I'll find them.' Sic, Expatrius. 'You two go down to the stream, I'll meet you by the footbridge.'

One does not, please understand, wish to be heroic. So what is one doing, then? Maybe not much. Maybe one is just curious—one does not wish to leave the theater while the third reel is snapping before one's eyes.

Ingo and Isaac and Hagen share a cabin that sits off some way to itself, near a line of poplar trees. Getting there unseen should not be too difficult, if one moves with suitable speed and stealth.

From the village center, a woman's scream, the watery splatter of glass breaking, a lot of it at once. You picture the large windows in the Gemeindehaus. Sturdy wooden chairs—a table even—lifted and hurled. Now more of it, crashing, wood cracking, children's wails, dull thumps. DO NOT think of chair legs pounding into flesh.

Reaching the poplars—fluttering leaves like a thousand tiny pennants, pea-green brightening to yellow in the upper branches—and suddenly here is Hagen again, puffing, a hand to his side, pressing the ribs. Injured there as well? Seemingly so, a rip down his shirt. In this light he looks half murdered. But the face is weirdly calm, the eyes fixed. Resolution in that face. Age-old strength, a warrior nation. Yet a child's flesh, easily mangled. You think of all those schoolboys memorizing the 'Death Song' and imagining themselves in that burning castle, last stronghold of the Burgundians, glorious stench of smoke and blood in their nostrils, their little fingers strumming the fucking minstrel's harp, croaking out a ballad of vengeance and honor. Then 'destiny's footsteps,' and Dietrich, NOT you, is the last man standing: so mote it be. Die for the joy of it.

'What are you doing here?' the Expat honestly wonders.

The boy does not reply, he does not even look. You would not understand. No, well, all right then. We step quickly forward and gain the nearest wall of the cabin, shielded from the village—safe so far. Nothing to be seen through the window. Creep around the corner—motion in the distance, a disturbance, is that fire? Then in through the door.

They have already been here and torn the place apart. Blankets shredded, a knife's work. Contents of knapsacks dumped out, kicked around, pawed through. Pages ripped from a book, flung widely. Lift one at random—a love poem—then let it fall.

The Expat feels he has been here before, picked his way through the same cloud-lit aftermath. Except the last time was in Berlin, or maybe Leipzig, the bloody wake of street fights, tavern brawls, raids upon bookstores and the 'nests' of enemy student groups. It's been going on for a decade now, getting more violent every year, so people say. This year mainly it's the Communists, variously titled, versus the Hitler mob. Worse in the south, they say—you should see Munich!

In the doorway a shadow. Hulking there like Frankenstein's monster, a hyperthyroidal bullyboy twirling a Freikorps bayonet between his fingers as one would a toothpick. He looks from one of us to the other, brutishly incurious. The Expat realizes: We have seen this one before, the fellow with the bandage on his nose. Salt of the Boden and pillar of the Reichstag's largest voting bloc. Look around for something to fend him off with. A hunk of unleavened Socialist bread? A tent pole? The monster lurches forward into the room.

And then . . . his knees wobble, he loses his balance. Someone has clipped him from behind. Winding it backward, you catch the CLUMP of something hard striking something padded with clothing. As the brute staggers, Ingo is revealed—battered and bleeding, it seems, from a wound in his side, but puffed up in anger, one arm raised, a good-sized rock in it like an oversized fist. Fist = Faust. The rock meets the big fellow's head—

no padding there. The sound this makes will be hard to describe in a fashion not off-putting to the average American editor. The next sound is easier, a floor-shaking thud.

'Well done!' This from the Expat, or some tantamount banality.

But Ingo is not done and is in no humor to be congratulated. He steps past the body—is it breathing still?—and rounds upon young Hagen. 'What did you do to Isaac?' he says.

In the German boy's face, in his eyes, his firmly shut mouth, all is as before. There is a thing that will not be said, a page that will never be written.

'Damn you,' says Ingo, and he is the warrior Ingo yet, possessed by some angel of rage. 'First Isaac, now this. I'm going to kill you.'

Yes, he would have, I believe it still. The rock had blood on it. The Expat stepped in front of him but this, from Ingo's point of view, must not have presented a credible impediment.

'That is not true,' said the German boy. (At any rate, he said something that conveyed less alarm than was warranted. Perhaps 'That was not my doing,' or even a question, 'Why would I have done that?')

Ingo was past such fine points of dialectic. He meant to smash the little Burgundian with his rock und das wäre das. If Hagen would not panic, the Expat would do it for him. Ingo stepped closer while frantically the point-of-view character calculated angles, the chances of tripping him up, the odds of making a run for it.

Never believe, however bad things may seem, they cannot get worse. At that moment outside the cabin appeared a whole gang of the marauding toughs, five or six or more. Chanting, perhaps very badly singing, some piece of Schweinerei—one could recall, later, a single line, 'when Jew blood runs from my knife.' Before Ingo could react, Hagen was out the door. You heard his voice, a clear tenor descant. You saw him pointing—over there, comrades. You neither could tell what he was up to (showing where Marty had gone?) nor take the time to puzzle it out.

'Let's go,' the Expat said.

How then to account for Ingo's hesitation? What thoughts stormed through his mind, what feelings pressed outward from his breast? For immeasurable moments he lingered there, the Jungdo thugs only paces away. Hagen talked rapidly, gesturing, blood congealing on his arm whilst the bigger toughs watched him dumbly.

'Now!' the Expat hissed, and in time, barely, Ingo came unstuck.

They climbed out the back window and were quickly lost among whis-

pering poplars. The day turned golden, sunlight everywhere, Marty waiting beside the little brook. A beautiful dawn spread itself across the eastern
marches of old Germania.

In the air, an alarum of birdcalls, an early chill—it would soon be
autumn, 1929—and a smell of burning.

WILDERNESS

Ankle-deep in snow at the edge of the Greater German Reich, wearing a dead man's uniform, Ingo trooped grudgingly onward, eyes on the boot-marks left by the soldier ahead, the one he thought of as the Defrocked Priest. Ingo did not, he guessed, look so out of place himself in this curious hunting party, a rabble of foreign SS volunteers representing most of the nations of Eastern Europe. Like him, on the whole, they were overaged and unsoldierly. Their joints ached from the sudden cold and they were not slow to complain about it, in the degraded Deutsch that was their only common tongue. Eight now altogether—all on foot for this outing—they followed a road too narrow for automobiles and too rough, too broken, even for horses, through a land that seemed to belong to no one. A sign they passed half a day ago had reminded them this was a "nature protection territory." Meaning, it seemed, you could shoot people here, but you couldn't poach the game.

Escape, he figured, was not impossible. He had taken to lagging behind and nobody cared. Now and then the Priest glanced around to give him a nod or a weary flick of the hand like a desultory benediction, but then looked away; you couldn't afford to take your eyes off the path for long.

There was, of course, the problem of footprints. Once the others noticed he was missing they would turn around and retrace their steps, then his, in the snow. Ingo did not fancy being hunted by these men. Sure, he was armed, he could take a few with him—but then what? It would be a messy business. And maybe he was still Catholic enough to have thoughts about dying with blood on his hands, even the blood of the guilty.

There were opportunties, though. Here and there along the trail, especially on slopes, big rocks jutted from the ground, their surfaces blown free

of snow. You could get a foothold there, heave yourself over and land on
the downslope. Pick a spot where the evergreens are small, use low-hanging
limbs for cover. It was a chance. How badly would these men care? They
were going for king's meat—*living Jews*. Why waste time or bullets on
lesser quarry?

He nonetheless trudged onward, holding his place in the column and
watching shadows lengthen around him. He shifted the weight on his
back, moved the Schmeisser's strap from one shoulder to the other. He
couldn't have said why.

Well, okay, he could.

Somewhere up there, ahead of the column, unseen for hours now, was
a man in a black uniform, an SS officer. He was the pathfinder, blazing a
trail for the others. And he was Master of the Hunt, all his senses honed,
his intuition acute. *He had a mysterious affinity with the game*—where had
Ingo read that? A Karl May novel? And somehow, beneath those things, he
was a blond boy Ingo had known, or at least thought he had, in a different
world, an end-of-summer version of this same countryside.

Maybe there is mystery everywhere. Maybe nobody's motives are clear,
everyone's feelings are chaotic, their yearnings unnameable. Maybe any
given person, in unforeseen circumstances, is capable of acting in any con-
ceivable manner. I caress you, I murder you, I bind your wounds.

Maybe.

Only it seemed to Ingo—it always had—that Hagen was harder to deci-
pher than most people. Qualitatively harder; a different sort of nut to
crack. After a dozen years behind the bar at the Rusty Ring, chatting up
every odd duck that waddled in off Connecticut Avenue, he still thought
so. So maybe that's what bound him to the hunting party; maybe he hadn't
given up on untangling that particular knot.

Also, there were the tracks in the snow. Ingo had expected them, in a
way. The snow had stopped falling night before last, and since then all the
game in the forest seemed to have been on the move, scrounging for food
or searching for a nice place to bed down for the winter. Or, who knows,
looking for a date. In the Boy Scouts Ingo had done the customary thing,
plodding through the woods with a fold-out guide to animal tracks, trying
to identify the little furry and feathered creatures who had preceded him.
You hoped for a bear, a fox, but what you got were raccoons and skunks
and the occasional bunny.

Without thinking much about it, he was back at it now, out of the corner of his eye. Still hoping for a fox. And getting, again, something different. This time, human footprints. He paused to consider them, and after a

few moments the Priest ambled back to join him. The tracks were not fresh; the edges had blurred from snowmelt. There appeared to be two sets, one falling mostly in the indentations made by the other, and there was something odd about the shape of the shoes, a boxiness. The prints followed the trail for a while, then turned off on what might have been a deer path, narrow and steep.

"Not bandits," the Priest said judiciously. His jaw was bony, black with stubble, and served as a pointer for his eyes. "Escapees, I'd say."

"From one of the camps?" said Ingo, perhaps rashly. "Like the one at Auschwitz?" He hoped this was not pressing it too far. Hölderlin cautioned against the mortal error of *Wortschuld*—the sin of uttering, of all unspeakable things, the most unspeakable.

The Priest shook his head. "They're in better shape than that. See how far apart the footsteps are? They're moving along pretty quickly. People who come out of the big camp there—and I tell you, there aren't many— they stagger. And they'd be barefoot, or near to it. These ones, see, they've got shoes of a sort, something homemade, maybe a strip of old tire with cloth sewn around it. Slave workers, I'd say, off a farm somewhere. Folks like us—foreigners, right? Except they waited for an invitation."

It was sometime after they had overtaken the others, while listening to the latest in a limitless repertoire of filthy stories from Janocz the giant—this one involved a nun, a bar of soap, and a chicken—that Ingo experienced a revelation.

Warfare, he realized, is a team sport. It is not really so different—well, okay, rather more extreme—than any of those activities he'd sought to avoid in high school. The likeness between war and, say, varsity football went deeper than Darwinian group dynamics, locker-room crudeness, the playing-field pecking order and the fact that Ingo had no aptitude for either. It went deeper even than the familiar and, by now, boring requirement to prove one's manhood. Deeper than the prospect, never far from mind, of physical violence.

The most telling sameness, to Ingo's mind, lay in that transcendent entity, the *team:* a fraternity, a brotherhood, a shoulder-to-shoulder, thick-and-thin union—a true *Bund.* To belong to a team, to really belong, is to feel a profound identification with your teammates, a dissolving of the boundaries between you and them. We are Cardinals; we are *Kamaraden;* we are all in this together . . . none of which had ever applied to Ingo, vis-à-vis any given sampling of his male brethren. Not in Boy Scouts. Not in high school, or at Catholic U. And how much more so, not here, not now.

If all men were like me, he thought, it would be hard to get much of a war going, wouldn't it? On the other hand, if all men were like me, there wouldn't be much of a world. Would there?

The hunters were in no hurry. Whatever might be ahead of them would still be there tomorrow; that's how Ingo read their attitude. Tomorrow, maybe next week. If it's a boar, then let it fatten up a while. If it's a Jew, let it starve. If it's a slant-eyed Russian with one of those little submachine guns, the kind that never jams—well, just you wait, Ivan. I'll see you when the time comes.

Hagen—the other men called him *der Chef*—did not join them at their campfire.

"He keeps to himself, that one," said the man Ingo knew as Eyebrows. From his accent, maybe Lithuanian. He was a chatty sort, and it disturbed Ingo very much to think that, had this man walked into the Ring one day, wearing ordinary clothes, smoking an American cigarette, he probably would've found him an engaging fellow.

"They're all like that," the Priest said. "Think their shit is honey."

All who? Ingo wondered. Germans? Officers? The regular SS?

"No, this one . . ." Eyebrows nodded rhythmically, as if hearing a private song. "I've been with him over a year now. We've been out on, what, maybe thirty, forty operations. Big sweeps, some of them, two hundred men, artillery support, once even spotters in airplanes. Other times, only a few of us, like now. And I tell you, all those times . . . hell, I can't think of a word the fucker's ever said to me. Not one bleeding word, not Attention or Forward or Eat shit. It's odd, wouldn't you say? Goes against the book— a good National Socialist is supposed to be one of the men—maybe a bigger man, maybe more powerful, but still a comrade."

"Where'd they teach you that—Rovno?"

"They didn't send me to Rovno, I went to Lublin. This was in forty-one."

"Forty-one. Been at this awhile, eh?"

Eyebrows nodded absently, the inaudible tune still playing for him. Then he sighed. "Long enough. I was a Party member before the war. An agitator, you might say. Fifth column, right? Volga Germans, my family were—over there for five generations, still spoke German at the dinner table. Not the proper sort, mind you. First thing they told me in Lublin was my German's no good, I'd never make rank talking that gibberish. Well, they weren't lying."

The campsite was in a hollow, crowded by rock faces and hulking pines. Straight overhead, Ingo could see white stars like holes in the papery darkness. The fire cast little warmth but its glow was comforting. The hunters had spread out their bedrolls and were done eating, waiting now for weariness to carry them off.

"How can you be a Volga *German*," mumbled Janocz the giant, as though talking to himself, not caring about an answer. "That's like being a Danube *Russian*. Or a—"

"Just wait," the Priest said tartly. "You'll be seeing Danube Russians soon enough. Rhine Russians, too, if the Yanks don't get a move on."

A couple others chuckled, a rueful noise. It struck Ingo as odd they should view the Reich's looming defeat with such equanimity, like something that didn't affect them personally. *We're not Germans, are we?* Or maybe it was something different. Fatalism, in its unvarnished form. The native mind-set of Central Europe, crawling ineluctably westward. Someday, it might reach America.

"I guess that's what the Reds wondered, too," Eyebrows said. "Five generations over there, then one day Comrade Molotov signs a piece of paper, him and Ribbentrop, divvying up Poland. You take that part, we'll take this. Not long after, they told us to leave. Like that—go back home to Germany. Your Führer is expecting you. Five generations, so what? You're still German, it's in the blood.

"Next thing we knew, a flat in Wedding. A real shithole. Then a farm in fucking Galicia, where not even a Polack would want to live. You're building the New Germany, they said. Didn't look like Germany to me. Hell, I barely knew what Germany looked like. I was starting to miss the Old Country, I wished the Bolsheviks hadn't thrown us out. Then the invasion came—'Kick the Russian door in,' remember that, 'and the whole rotten house will crumble'? So I figured, you know, this was my way back. Free ride home on a troop transport, and a chance to square things with the commissars."

Nobody asked how his plan had worked out. It was obvious: here he was with the rest of them. A hunter tonight; but soon enough, the hunted.

Ingo had half dozed off when Eyebrows said, in the darkness, "I never even made it to Russia. Vilna, that's as far as we got. Shooting the Chosen People in a ditch. It was better in Galicia. Shit, it was better in Wedding. But out here, you know, in the woods, the wilderness . . . this isn't so bad."

*   *   *

Afterward he fell into something that was not quite sleep, not quite dreaming: a silent but agitated realm like the first few inches under the water of a swimming pool. In this state he was able to think rather clearly—clearly enough to suspect that, by daylight, none of these thoughts would make sense—and one particular idea seemed to hang there, waiting for him to seize it: a memory that glittered just out of reach, like a ring falling slowly to the bottom. He strained for it, his chest aching with need.

I've been here before. This very path. The same mountain—only it was summer then.

This might have been true. Equally it might've been a wholly unreasonable fancy he could not, in his half-dreaming state, dispel. The thought excited him; but paradoxically it did not cause him to awaken, rather to enter more vividly into this state of semi-awareness.

Okay, maybe he *had* been here. Under what circumstances, though? The long hike east from the Leuchtenburg? The longer, sadder journey back? Each question summoned its own stream of possibilities; they bobbed up around him, too many to choose among. Frustrated, he rolled over on the hard ground. Twigs jabbed his cheek—*this* was real, if nothing else. An insect buzzed noisily near his head. He gave it a couple of swats but the damn thing wouldn't leave him alone. In the end he gave up, he rolled onto his back and blinked languidly in the honey-colored sunlight. The insect— an enormous dragonfly—hovered like a fixed object above one eye. If he were a frog, or an enchanted prince, he could've flicked his tongue at it. Instead he let out a languorous sigh.

"Glad to hear you're alive over there," Martina noted acerbically from her nesting spot among ostrich ferns a few steps way. He propped his head up to give her a baleful glare.

She was so full of herself these days. Ever since she and that *Schwärmer* . . . Ingo didn't want to think about it. At the same time, how could he not? They had made the crossing, he and his old friend Marty, albeit by different bridges. They were grown up now, physically and otherwise. And they were free—weren't they?—*to shape their lives,* as the Meissner Formula had it, *by their own choice, responsible only to themselves, following their own inner truth.* For them, anything was possible, nothing was forbidden. It was almost 1930, for God's sake.

Still and all . . . it was hard for him to think of Marty like that. The girl next door. A girl, period. Girls in general. Their odd shapes, the bulges and squishiness, the smells. How much luckier to love boys, who were pure and hard and clean.

All right: I give up.

Ingo pulled himself to a sitting position, fully aroused now. Aroused as in awakened and in that other sense as well. But then he always was, wasn't he? Even while sleeping. All his dreams were about the same thing. He lived in a state that was evidently well known to a certain breed of poet: Goethe called it *seliger Sehnsucht*, blessed desire; Novalis, *heiliger Glut*, sacred lust. Quite common, apparently. To be expected and, indeed, commended. But just now, damned inconvenient.

Butler was talking. Ingo could not hear—or, more likely, chose not to waste his attention on—what he was saying. The tone was the thing: knowing, long-winded, didactic, above all pleased with itself. Blah blah blah, *ineluctable historic process*, blah blah, *enfeeblement brought on by* blah blah blah. Hagen took exception to this and while he had nothing interesting to say about it, he at least had the grace to say it in clear, well-formulated Deutsch. Isaac was patently bored, which seemed an eminently sane response. With a glance in Ingo's direction, he stood up, stretched like a tawny cat and ambled away, with no apparent destination in mind.

From the campsite a little winding path, the staple of all good *Märchen*, twisted through an obligatory jumble of greenery that Ingo, without Anton, could not name, skirting rocks, ducking beneath ancient limbs, dipping into glades where unseen water whispered mysteriously, creeping up and up onto stony ledges suitable for flinging oneself off in a paroxysm of unconsummated longing.

He found himself following this path, though oddly unaware of having decided to do so; he could remember none of the preliminaries, such as walking out of the camp. How far he had wandered was anybody's guess. Isaac was somewhere ahead of him—he knew that much. The sun fell through the trembling leaves in fat, oozy globs that ran down your limbs like melted butter. You wanted to drink it in. To toss your clothes away and writhe in it. The thrilling notion of being naked transformed itself with magical ease into the feeling of cool air moving between his legs, moss cushioning his bare footfalls, damp fronds tickling his knees. A curtain of drooping willow hung before him, a thousand leaves shot through with yellow-green light. He parted the branches—they were downy to the touch—and stepped into a shady, hemmed-in, isolated glade.

Isaac was sitting on an old fallen log like a sprite perched on its toadstool. His head, rather large for the waifish body, turned toward Ingo, his smile wider than his jawbone should have allowed. On his back and limbs, freckles now claimed more territory than his plain pale skin. He was not willowy like Anton nor beautiful like Hagen. Ingo could not get him out of his mind. Sleeping or waking, he heard the droll boyish voice. The eyes' emerald sparkle held him spellbound.

Is this real? he wondered. Do I really feel this way? He could not remember. It seemed so, and yet not. It was as though he had leapt ahead, somehow, and these feelings had cropped up in a time of their own, without his having gotten around to feeling them. Ah, the impatience of youth. Everything that is imaginable—and what is not?—must happen right here, right now. Because I want it, I breathe it, I yearn for it. And yearning is holy. *I praise all who long for death by fire.*

Isaac was talking, or not talking. He was making a joke. He was acting the fool. He was laughing, always laughing. In some dreams the laughter is everywhere at once and in others it comes only at the end, a fulfillment, a joyous release.

But this was no dream, was it? No dream had ever been so real. No leaves had ever whispered so gently. No flesh had ever felt so warm.

"How come you never took a swing at it?" Isaac said.

Ingo did not remember. He could only shrug.

"The thing is," Isaac said, with a finger raised, as if giving a signal, "you miss out on a lot. There's a lot of stuff you'll never know, because you don't like to take chances. I'm not saying that's bad—it's just how you are, that's all. With you, nothing's only for grins. Everything's a big deal. And I mean, a *big* deal. You look at some picture on the wall and think you're seeing God, when it's only a pal from school you've got a crush on."

Oh, come now. Isaac had never read a word of Hesse—Ingo would've bet his life on it.

"But I *like* you," said Isaac with a foxy grin, brushing off this flagrant improbability. "You're a decent guy. In fact you're the only guy I actually trust. I mean, the Socialists, they're okay. But they're all a bunch of fucking Kräuter. One minute they love you, the next"—shrug—"hey."

Ingo glanced down, conscious suddenly of his exposed and completely defenseless state. No secrets between them anymore.

"Still," said Isaac, "after all this time, who's to say what really happened?"

Nothing, you think, miserably.

"Are you sure?" Isaac laid a hand on his arm. It burned there sweetly like mountain sun. *Selige Sehnsucht.* Infinity in an afternoon. Love in death, ecstasy in pain, passion in solitude. Things that might have happened. Things you will never know. Passions, and sorrows, and losses irrecoverable, and, finally, sleep.

*   *   *

A hand on his shoulder woke him sometime before dawn. The sky, now a soft rosy gray, looked very close, rubbing the black treetops. Hagen's face peered down at him. Tense, urgent, expressionless. The eyes flashed coldly, *Stay quiet.*

Around the camp, every second man lay dead. Every other one—like a macabre, inexplicable game. Choosing up sides on the nightmare playground. *Eenie, meenie, miney, moe.* Ingo was alive. Eyebrows had his throat slit open, blood splashed generously over his mouth, his neck, his chest. The Defrocked Priest was sitting up, stuffing things into his knapsack. The next man over had a knife hilt protruding at an angle from his heart (his own knife, they would discover). Janocz stirred sluggishly, like a bear overdue for hibernation.

And so forth.

Wordlessly, Hagen organized the survivors—all four of them—and they moved around the camp's perimeter. There was no shortage of tracks. In fact, there were too many, a wanton trampling. How could this have happened without waking anyone? Why hadn't they posted a night watch? And where had Hagen been all that time? Ingo guessed it was a little late for questions, yet there they were, waiting to be asked, as glaring as the heartless sunrise.

It was some while later—they had moved out by then, their weapons in their hands, safety catches off—before anyone spoke. Hagen had gotten some distance ahead. Ingo watched him move through the woods with effortless grace, like an angel with gray woolen wings. His legs flexed, then straightened; his body seemed to float from the path to a hump of stone, then onto a long, bulging hemlock root. His cape flowed around him. In half a minute, he was only a *feldgrau* flutter, another shadow in the woods. Then he was gone.

Janocz said, "Why did they do that?"

He meant, Ingo supposed, why kill only half?

The Priest slowed to look at him, perhaps debating whether it was worth his trouble to answer this stupid man. Then he looked at Ingo and their fourth comrade, Zim, a thin-framed former gangster—so he boasted—from the alleys of Odessa. For their benefit, the Priest said, "It was the Fox, obviously. Why does the Fox do anything?"

Janocz shook his head. "Why?"

The Priest gave them all a canny look. His stock-in-trade, these looks.

"The Little Fox," he said, in the melodramatic voice of a radio-play narrator, "just likes to have a bit of fun. That's all."

Ingo could not grasp any of it. He felt dizzy, like a kid at a loud party, too many things going on, running and laughter, the house made strange with decorations, a clown plucking quarters out of your ear. If it truly was the Fox who had done those things—yes, and if the Fox was truly Isaac—and if Hagen had picked up his trail, if they had not waited too long to get started . . . but that was too many ifs, like too many panes of glass, reflections playing between them, the view warped and pale, impossible to focus on.

Still: if.

The morning turned that stubborn gray that refuses to brighten past a certain point. On a day like this at home Ingo might not have stepped outside until evening, when the sky disappeared and the lights came on, the avenue crowded, taxis honking, a radio blaring from a window upstairs, the chill and gloom shrinking to minor inconveniences like that curb you don't want to trip over. But here you were stuck, with no door inside, and the chill went right to your heart; there had never been brightness or warmth, and never would be. You moved, you breathed, you endured—it wasn't much, but what was the alternative?

Fatalism, endemic to this landscape, especially virulent in winter—now Ingo had caught it. If, by some ludicrous whim of the gods, he should live through all this, he was doomed to be a carrier. Anyone who looked at him might be infected. They would have to quarantine him, perhaps on a chicken farm, with a supply of cognac and a large collection of German poetry. Also a phonograph, so he could listen to Mahler's *Kindertotenlieder*. Songs on the death of children. He'd have to smuggle the damn thing into the sunny U.S. of A., but it could be done.

With such thoughts, and others no more reasonable, Ingo passed the day, or rather the day moved around him. They came down from the hills into a countryside flatter and—who could've imagined it—more desolate than the one they'd left. It was swampy and shrouded in mist so faint you could barely see it. The occasional stand of trees on higher ground—short-needled pines with some alder and scrubby willow—offered little consolation. Only a botanist, Ingo thought, would find anything of interest here. This curled and dried-up frond, what was that? Or these barbed seed heads that clung to your trousers? Maybe in spring, should it ever come, they would pop open and tiny black seeds would sprinkle down—not here, but wherever you'd carried them—and from the tiniest one would issue a stalk, a leaf, a flower. Something, if not exactly to hope for, at least to bear in mind.

He couldn't tell if Hagen was following a trail or proceeding by instinct alone. There were footprints in the snow, but Ingo could make no sense of them; he wasn't even sure if they'd been made by human beings. Something was wrong with the shape, yet what sort of animal made a track like that? Actually, what sort of creature would live in these deathly marshes? Something, perhaps. Negroes in Washington lived in alleys, whole families of them. They built shacks out of packing crates and tar paper and tacked up a picture of Franklin Roosevelt, torn from a newspaper, on what they pretended was a wall. The point being, living creatures are adaptable, and unwilling, generally, just to sit down and die.

Sometime in mid-afternoon, though it felt like dusk, *der Chef* stepped out from behind a tangle of stunted, black-stemmed willow and signaled them to halt. They squatted down among broken reeds—there really was no place to sit—and Hagen pulled a pack of cigarettes from his cloak and passed it around.

The good National Socialist, Ingo thought. Still a comrade, despite his unquestioned superiority. Despite that aristocratic pallor and the ruins of beauty in that narrow, lupine and hungry-looking face.

Hagen caught Ingo staring but did not react, just looked back for a moment, then elsewhere. Was Ingo only imagining that he had recognized him? Did Hagen remember anything about that summer? Had it—had *they*—meant anything to him at all?

"These cigarettes are French," the Priest murmured reverentially, turning one with loving care in his fingers. It was rolled in an oval shape and longer than customary. "Where'd you get French cigarettes?"

At first it seemed Hagen was not going to answer. Ingo recalled what Eyebrows had said—dead Eyebrows, who would never walk into the Ring, never be mistaken for an engaging fellow—about Hagen never talking to common *Soldaten*. But to Ingo's surprise, to everyone's, *der Chef* was in an expansive mood just now.

"The old man has a cellarful of them," he said. His manner was informal, and his tone, though correct, had lost much of its former stiffness, like leather smoothed and worn-in by long use. In the face, though, something . . . not quite regret, nor wistfulness—a certain, maybe, disconnection. "You should see all the things down there. French cigarettes, French cognac, Alsatian beer, red wine from somewhere south, tins of fish. Parisian perfume."

He waited for the men's reaction—bawdy chortling, *ooo la la*—but made no pretense of joining in. A comrade, but made of finer stuff.

"I asked him, as you asked me, where it had all come from. And he said, From everywhere. All over Europe. And he told me a story, something that happened in Prague back in Heydrich's day. Heydrich was living up at the palace, and the old man was teaching at the university—the oldest in the German-speaking world, so he told me. Quite proud of that. He had just learned, that day, that a famous scholar was coming to town, the leading expert on something or other—Fellow of the Reich Academy of Science, personal chum of Goebbels, table reserved for him at Horcher's. The sort of fellow who's hard to impress. Still, of course, the old boys in Prague, the faculty there, wanted to make an impression. Perhaps they thought, Here's our chance."

Ingo was interested to watch the expressions that moved, like screen images, across the soldiers' faces as they listened. To them, names like Horcher's and Goebbels—*Heydrich, up at the palace*—must conjure a world that was fabulous, far-off and now all but vanished, a rapidly fading dream. They had never glimpsed this glittering world with their own eyes, but they had believed in it, the Thousand Year Reich at the height of its glory. Some reflection of that glory, however faint, may have bounced off this and that shiny surface, a collar pin here, a lightning rune there, until it found them, lending an illusion of majesty to their wretched, anonymous lives. They had been, in their crisp Waffen-SS uniforms, citizens of the New Europe, in a war that was for them a great, dark, irresistible romance.

Like the professors in Prague: *Here's our chance.*

"So they came to Cheruski," Hagen went on, "perhaps, I don't know, because he was a German, not a Sudeten Czech. And he was a Brigade-führer by that time, too. Look, they said, here is the menu—we're going to start with a pâté of smoked trout and dill, do you think he'll like that? And Cheruski said, Yes, he will like that. And they said, For the second course, sautéed wild mushrooms, *sauce madère*. What will he think of that? Yes, very good, the old man told them, he will like that very much. And for the main course, they said, duck—there are plenty of nice fat ducks there on the Donau, old women feed them scraps of bread. We'll send the caretaker down to shoot some, he's a peasant, he knows how."

The other men chuckled. Imagine, not knowing how to shoot a duck!

"So the Professor said, Yes, duck, that's good, that's something out of

the ordinary. But then they asked him, What shall we do about the wine?
We have these Czech wines, they're quite good, really, but . . . And the
Professor told me, *You should have seen them.* Like little boys, afraid
Mommy will be disappointed by their school report."

The men nodded, puffing their French cigarettes, their faces rapt. It was
amazing: they cared, actually, about this ridiculous story, a dinner in Prague,
a bunch of tame Nazi scholars toadying up to some VIP from imperial Berlin.

Hagen seemed to have forgotten his own cigarette, but he lit it now,
scraping a match with a thumbnail in a quick, practiced motion, the flame
spurting magically from his hand. He took a deep draw, let it out audibly,
like a sigh.

"The Professor said, The wine? That is no problem. Do you have an
automobile? Yes, there was a car, but not much gasoline. That is no problem either. Hand me that telephone. So the Professor makes a call, somebody he knows who works for the Protectorate. Then he says, Jaekl, come
here, would you?"

The men exchanged glances. They knew Jaekl; they didn't much care
for him. Here was a part of the story they could understand.

"Jaekl, take these car keys, and this menu, and drive down to Paris,
that's a good lad. Go to a shop in the Ninth Arrondissement—here, I am
writing down the address—and show them the menu, then tell them to
select the wines. And for God's sake, be courteous about it. These French
are touchy. Tell them it shall be dinner for twelve, night after next, you
must have the wine right away. Here is some money. Now, *go.*"

He nodded, a signal that the story was over. He took another slow pull
at his cigarette.

The hunters broke into laughter. "Now, *go,*" they repeated. "Just like
that. Now, *go.* Imagine it! All the way to Paris!"

Even Janocz laughed. Ingo doubted that he knew what he was laughing
at—something to do with Jaekl, or gasoline—but he laughed loud and
heartily, just the same. As though the story had dwelt longer on one of the
wine bottles, and there had been a nun.

Later Ingo surmised—no, he was certain—that the break had been calculated, that Hagen had kept an eye on his watch and the fading daylight.
They had not stopped there in order to rest (*Who needs rest,* the big Moe
had said, back on the Eastern Shore, *you can rest when you're dead;* they'd
thought he was joking), but in order to kill a couple hours until darkness
began to fall.

The story, too, was probably calculated. Not so much to put them in mind of happier days, when a certain kind of man could send a driver halfway across Europe to fetch wine for a certain kind of meal. Rather, to distract them, to send their thoughts elsewhere, anywhere. Away from this ghastly place and whatever lay ahead of them.

What that was, they found out soon enough. By the last light of day— curious, how these days that never got bright were so slow turning dark— Hagen led them along a narrow trail that could not be seen but that must have been there, for he followed it unerringly. Straight on, then off here, over there, down then up, through this pine grove, between those cattail-crowded bogs, down this tiny isthmus of packed and frozen mud. Maybe he'd memorized the route; maybe he oriented himself by some ancestral sensitivity most present-day men had lost.

He had a mysterious affinity with the game. Yes, Karl May, Ingo was sure. May had taken one trip to America, he had gone out West, stayed a few weeks, breathed the air of the open prairie—and made a whole career out of it. Fantasies of the Wild West, Saturday-matinee stuff, gobbled up by generations of German schoolboys. Hagen would have read them. The allure of the wilderness, a wonderful place where you didn't have to take a bath or memorize your verb declensions, and there were no girls to tease you, none at all. Perhaps the occasional Indian maiden but that was different, more like a kind of pretty horse. Long black hair you could stroke. And the Indian boys, naked except for their loincloths. Something for everybody, Karl May. Guns, too, and shooting.

The writer himself, Ingo gathered, had been a committed pacifist.

Now . . . was he hallucinating? Or was there, just ahead, a little cowboy's vision of Fort Apache? The high wooden stockade, rising out of the waste. No entrance that he could see. At the center, some kind of . . . watchtower? Too dark to tell.

Hagen signaled them to halt.

"We'll wait here," he murmured.

Wait for what?

They shared some bread, a heavy dark loaf Magda had made, dry but welcome. The Priest stuck a canteen in Ingo's hand. The liquid that met his tongue had a burning sweetness; one of those horrible Balkan fruit brandies—also welcome. And the evening ticked on.

There was no particular time at which Hagen told them to move. For a while they busied themselves checking their weapons, making sure the clips for the MPs had been filled, Janocz setting the bayonet on his Mauser, Zim the gangster organizing his stock of ammunition and hand grenades according to a unique system he had developed and no one else understood; perhaps it was just something to do, a private battle ritual. Ingo had noticed that everyone seemed to have a ritual of some kind. Usually simple, kiss your crucifix, button your jacket right to the top, unsnap the field knife at your belt. Uli, the yellow-haired partisan chief, had had a way of becoming absolutely still and staring into nothingness—it looked like a form of prayer or open-eyed meditation. Suddenly he would snap out of it, then be up and moving. Janocz the giant went off to empty his bowels—"Otherwise," he told them afterward, "I shit myself. Every time, it happens."

Ingo groped for some ritual of his own, absentmindedly running a hand over his backpack. Yes, the talisman, the book of poetry, was still there.

They went single-file until they were close to the wall. As defenses go, it wasn't much. Ingo had seen more formidable barricades in Brookland, neighbors with tiny backyards who liked their privacy. Still, it was too high to scramble over, and from the look of it too heavily built for even Janocz simply to smash through. What was Hagen's plan? A rope and grappling hook? A grenade taped to the boards?

He led them, counterclockwise, into a little patch of woods that grew right up to the wall. Or rather, the wall had been built so that it zigged into the woods, then made a turn, an angle of perhaps sixty degrees, and zagged out again. Curious. It was quite dark now, no moon yet. When they reached the trees, Hagen switched on a hand lamp.

Ingo's instinct was to flinch, to peer around and see who might be watching. But they were practically touching the wooden planks and could've been spotted only by someone hanging over the top.

As they moved between thin, pale trunks—birches he thought, maybe poplars—he made out the sound of moving water. Not loud, probably just a stream, something you could get across. But when they reached the water he understood that getting across was not what Hagen intended.

The wall had been built in such a way that the stream passed right under it. The beam of Hagen's lamp played across silver-white gleaming water that darted fishlike between ice-covered rocks, then vanished into something like a cave or tunnel. It was neither, really; just an arbitrary point where the builder's excellent plan had come up against a certain unaccommodating reality: *This stream runs right where I want my wall to go.* The builder hadn't yielded an inch, which struck Ingo as very German, though he supposed the French had done much the same with their Maginot Line. The upshot was, if you scrunched down low enough, and didn't mind getting wet, you could slip under the wall by wading up the streambed—you might have to crawl, just at the end—and then pop out the other side.

It made him shiver to think about. Not only because of the cold. Something tingled within him. He did not believe in premonitions. This was more like a bat's trick of sensing how sound waves bounce off obstacles, only without the bat's clever faculty for interpreting the signals that came back. Eventually, the picture would become clear to him—by then, though, too late.

Meanwhile: the tingle.

When they were close enough, Hagen turned off the hand lamp. They waited awhile, letting their eyes get reaccustomed to the darkness. After half a minute Ingo could not *quite* see the shivering pallor of water in front of him.

Hagen tapped the Priest on an arm. *You first.* Then Zim, then Janocz. Saving Ingo for next to last.

A flash of insanity. *He is sending us in there to die.* But that was impossible, there could be no motive for that.

Still, it was the only time Ingo could think of—ever—that Hagen had chosen not to take the lead. That must mean something, but there was no time to wonder what. He heard a quiet splash, the Priest sucking air through his teeth, a muffled clank of weaponry—the remnants of the partisan-hunting squad moving in for the kill. And behind him, Hagen's breathing, quick and ragged, as though he'd been running a long time and had just a little bit farther to go.

MODEL HAMLET

"**Y**ou may not shoot us," said the red-faced man in the felt cap as the Varianoviks brushed past him, through the gate and up the principal
street of Arndtheim. "It is forbidden to harm anyone here. We are under
special protection."

"Oh yeah?" said Tamara. "Protection by who?"

The man started to answer but someone else nearby—a woman,
though you could hardly tell under all the wool—made a sound in her
throat, not much more than an audible breath, and he shut up. Two other
figures stood behind them, indistinct through the veil of falling snow. One
was small enough to be a child.

"Well, come then," said the woman—in English, to Martina's surprise.
"Let's go someplace warm."

Her voice was gruff but not, Martina thought, unkind—the voice of a
farm wife long accustomed to riding herd on a complicated household.

She led them past houses that looked deserted and a large, barnlike
structure that stood partly complete, snow swirling through its rib cage of
rafters. Darkness was setting in quickly now. From what Martina could
see, the place had not changed in any fundamental way. A new building
here and there, a windmill on the green. The biggest surprise was the community hall, which once had served as everything from a school to a public
dining room. It had been expanded in the most thoughtless manner—
doubled in size and divested of architectural distinction, like the work of
some provincial Albert Speer. You could imagine what Ingo would say.

The woman pointed them up a smaller lane toward a rambling, two-
story building of the traditional sort. It must have been here during Martina's earlier visit, but in the interim it had grown, spreading from the
middle outward like a maturing *Hausfrau*. A sign up front, swinging in the

wind, depicted a fat man holding a stein in one fist and a platter of *Wurst* in the other—an image at once banal and irresistible.

Inside was more of the same. A low ceiling, smoky fire in a wide hearth, tables and chairs of simple design built of chunky blond wood. The walls were made colorful by a collection of paintings, mostly impressions of generic German scenery by so-so artists, though a couple showed flair. And there were posters, which featured not heroic workers and Socialist slogans—the reigning motifs of 1929—but soldiers and farmers, defenders of Europe against a nameless menace symbolized in one instance by what appeared to be a bucktoothed, sickle-wielding Mongolian. The most appealing of the lot, graphically speaking, done in muted greens and earth tones, showed a man plowing his rich brown field while in the background, ghostlike, was a fainter image of the same man in a Wehrmacht uniform, holding a rifle. While Martina could not read the bold Gothic slogan, the image spoke clearly enough: Someday this war will be merely a fading memory, and your reward will be a piece of our newly conquered land.

It was all strange. The electric light was strange, oozing out of parchment shades and small, twinkly bulbs above a mirrored sideboard stocked with bottles and plates and glassware. Strange, too, how the room filled up, going from empty to crowded with no stages in between—people coming through the door, emerging from the shadow of a hallway, seeming to pop up, like gnomes, at all the little tables: Americans, Germans, a couple of kids, a lady who might have been their grandmother. Who knew what anybody was? The red-faced man—breathing in huffs, looking frightened—threw his coat on a hook and assumed the role of innkeeper with the deliberate ease of an actor finding his chalk mark on the stage.

And strangest of all, the illusion of sanity. As though everything here, the comfortable room, the make-believe village, was somehow part of the normal course of affairs. A group of wanderers appears at the village gate—nothing odd there. They happen to be armed to the gonads and speaking a foreign tongue, but never mind that, let them enter, let them warm themselves by our hearth. They are welcome among us, for we are decent German country folk—never mind that we are living in Poland, behind a wooden barricade in a mostly deserted little town that never seemed altogether real in the first place. Never mind that we are surrounded by people who would happily murder us, or that to the east, closer now than a few weeks ago, the Red Army stands in all its bloody, glorious, teeming chaos. Forget all of that, because here, at our little inn, by the reassuring glow of our log fire and our filament bulbs, everything is in order, *alles ist gemütlich.*

Martina was not fully mindful of having sat down until the woman, the farm wife, shedding layers of wool, dropped into a chair across the table from her. Grabsteen—suspicious as ever—came to join them. On the varnished wood of the tabletop, mischievous little hands had scratched words and initials Martina couldn't interpret and a crude drawing she could. We are on a set, she thought—but a damn good one, well dressed, every detail thought out. The work of a Lubitsch, a Wilder, an Ophuls, one of those Jewish masters who fled the Nazis and wound up in Hollywood. Only this one had stayed behind, like Isaac. Stubborn, disbelieving, apolitical . . . it didn't matter. Suddenly history lurched, and it was too late for Hollywood, too late for anything. The trap had closed.

Bloom's voice rang through the room, "I need vol-un-*teers*"—climbing in volume and pitch on each syllable. "Teams of two, get flashlights, search every inch of this place. Go into every house, look behind every bush. I want to know exactly what we're dealing with here."

"I'll go," Tamara said. "Come on, Zilman."

"That is not necessary," the woman at the table said quietly. Her hair was silver; Martina got the idea it had turned prematurely and not so long ago. "We are but twelve, all counted, including the children. There used to be more—at one time, over two hundred—but the others . . ."

"I remember you," Martina said all at once, surprising herself. She strained to retrieve the memory, which had slipped almost out of reach: a tired-looking young woman, always half stooping, whether picking up discarded toys or gently scolding a small, flaxen-haired girl. "You were somebody's mother. Was it . . . Helga?"

"Hildi," said the woman, maybe confused, though not very much so, staring thoughtfully at Martina. "Hilda, really. I am somebody's mother still. Soon, God willing, shall I be somebody's grandmother. And you—you are American." She spoke as if this were perfectly logical. Americans? Yes, one had known they would come eventually.

"If you two don't mind," said Harvey Grabsteen, his voice honed to that cutting timbre that causes people around the world to glance over their shoulders, thinking rude thoughts in a hundred languages, "maybe you could save Old Home Week for some other time. It's urgent, first of all, that we obtain provisions. Food, in particular. And second"—this to the German woman—"we need to know whatever you can tell us about partisan activity in this area. There's a certain Underground leader we need to contact. The matter is of historical importance, and you've got to help us."

He did not need to add, *or else.* Martina was embarrassed by him, his presence, his attitude, though at bottom she felt no differently. She was as anxious to find Isaac as anyone, and fully understood what was at stake. It was why she had come here and why she'd dragged Ingo along. *Ingo,* she thought with a pang. Poor Ingo.

The woman at the table studied Grabsteen through clear gray eyes that struck Martina as intelligent, troubled and unnaturally detached. Hanna, was that her name? You got the feeling she was not fully present, that this pushy Yank didn't seem entirely real to her. Well, who could argue with that? Yet something else was going on, Martina was sure. A subplot, and hardly a comic one.

The red-faced innkeeper moved among the tables handing out earthen-ware mugs from a large, wobbling tray. Close behind him a boy of eleven or twelve, elfin-eared, grinning widely because nothing *this* interesting had happened for some time, struggled to balance an armload of bread, wheels of cheese, and crude-looking knives maybe the work of a local blacksmith.

"There ya go, pal," said Martina, giving Grabsteen a hard smack on the shoulder, "provisions. In particular, food."

"We have always been willing to share what we have," the woman said defensively. "We share with the Poles, with the soldiers . . ."

It was not Martina's imagination, the pause here. From the woman's intonation, the sentence was meant to continue, the list meant to go on. "And you share with the partisans," she said, "right?" When the woman didn't meet her eyes, she went on quickly, in what she hoped was a reassuring voice, "Listen, I've been here before. Some friends and I. People called me Marty back then. It was years ago—before the Nazis."

"Yes," said the woman. "I know who you are."

The look she gave Martina sent a chill up her spine. Not the wondering look of someone who remembers you, dimly, from some far-off time—more the frank gaze of someone who knows you well, who was just talking about you the other day. What's Marty been up to? Be sure to tell her I said hi.

"I am Anna," the woman said. "I am—"

From somewhere in the building—a different room, an upper story—came a woman's cry. It began as a yelp of surprise, but as it drew itself out, it became something else. Though not really loud, muffled by walls and floorboards, it possessed some quality that brought every conversation to a halt. Toward the end, before tapering into silence, the cry became a wail of protracted agony, a sound not recognizably human.

"Come," said the woman Anna, rising from the table. "Please, Marty, come with me. Not you, sir. I need a woman only, thank you."

★   ★   ★

Martina had known, more or less, what she would find in the cheerful room at the top of the narrow staircase. Not the little stove in the corner or the geraniums in pots on the windowsill, nor the pretty lace curtains and the stenciled leaves that twined across white plaster walls. Those things didn't surprise her, now that she was remembering Anna, remembering the good-natured domesticity that had prevailed here, but they were not what she had dreaded to find as she hurried up the stairs hearing the other woman's nervous breath and the tentative murmur of voices down below.

The girl lay with her head and shoulders propped up and her flaxen hair splayed against an assortment of plush down pillows. She looked too small for the high bed with its four stout corner posts. An attractive quilt with a Tree of Life pattern, bright red apples on green limbs, picked up the livid, blood-pink coloration of her cheeks. At its center, the quilt swelled over the enormous mound of her belly. Her hands and her forehead were chalk-white. She was maybe nineteen years old, and you wouldn't have bet on her seeing twenty.

Martina's first, demented thought—it must seem cynical, but it didn't feel like that—was, *So this is how they did it in the good old days.* No doctor, no hospital, no painkillers. A girl on a bed. Blood-soaked blankets. A steaming pot on the stove. A sharp-eyed crone in a chair in the corner, an utterly miserable grandmother-to-be and, if you were lucky, the local midwife. If not, some woman recruited at random, with no qualifications other than the shared misfortune of their sex.

"Hildi," Anna said, as though speaking to a small child, "here is someone to help us. An old friend . . ." Now a glance, a wordless question, before the secret finally exploded: ". . . a good friend of Isaac's. A friend of us all. This is Marty, and she has come a great distance to help."

"How long has this been going on?" asked Martina, out in the hall.

"Two days now. It is not genuine labor. She has terrible cramps, but they are not real contractions. I don't know what to do. There is no one to ask. None of us has been able to sleep. There used to be someone here who knew about herbs—but she left, everyone left, and she took all the books that might be helpful."

They walked down the hall, just to be moving. Left and right, doors stained chestnut brown stood closed, conserving heat. A small window at the end of the hall framed a view of an empty lane. Snow floated through the glowing sphere around a Dickensian street lamp.

"What *happened* here?" Martina said. The question fell out of her mouth, as so many things did, before she had time to consider it.

Anna nodded. Meaning, perhaps, she didn't object to the change of subject. "Nothing happened quickly. But everything became different over time. Those terrible right-wing people destroyed a few things, not really so much. In those days, we did not have so very much to destroy. Then they went away, and we fixed everything up, and life went on. Some of the residents would leave and others would come to take their place. There was always a certain"—groping for the English—"permanent basis."

"I remember a man. Long hair. Good-looking."

"Ah—that was Alwin. Hildi's father."

Her expression was hard to read. Martina ventured, "So you and he were—"

"Not married, no. We were hardly even a couple, really. Alwin believed . . . well, we all believed things then. So many things we believed in! Great and foolish and in between. Each of us with our own philosophy of life, our own religion. 'Every worker his own boss, every peasant his own lord, every Dorf its own Reich!' Such fine slogans we had." She shook her head. "And you—did you marry? You had a . . . man friend, with you, I believe? A writer?"

"That's right—a friend. The writer part I don't know about. He never got around to that great novel, I don't think. After a while we just fell out of touch." Having gotten, she thought, what we wanted from each other. "But you decided to stay. Here in Arndtheim, I mean. Even after the Nazis?"

"Well, what better place? So many of our comrades back home were being arrested. Others went abroad, to Geneva, to Paris, to Lisbon. To New York, even, or Barcelona. But we were already abroad, do you see? In those days we were. We had our little bit of Germany here—a better Germany, a Germany of the future—and it had always been part of the plan, Alwin's plan, that we should be entirely self-sufficient. Thank God for that. It is true, sometimes we laughed about it. At the windmill, especially! But now . . . thank God."

"What happened to Alwin? He gave up finally?"

"Oh, no." Anna looked surprised; Marty had not understood at all. "No, they came here, the SS, after the invasion, when this place became part of the Reich. We were terribly afraid. We expected them to burn the village and send us to one of their camps. Hildi led the smaller children into the forest, to hide there. I thought I would never see her again.

"They strutted around, these mighty SS men, and they looked at the cottages and the workshops, and they looked at us as well—up and down, as though it were all some kind of . . . exhibition, and we were simply part of it. One of the officers had been here before and he acted as their guide. See the model German hamlet. See how they grind their own meal. See how they weave fabric for their clothing. It is like the days before the awful French came with their Enlightenment, and the English with their factories. This is the real Heimat here. The soil, the woods, the sunshine. Hardworking villagers. Just how we like it."

She sighed. "So they left the place standing. It fit nicely, don't you see, into their great plans. They wanted to turn this part of Poland into a new German homeland, and we had shown how to do this. Of course, a few things needed to be straightened out. The streets must run just so, north–south, east–west. There must be certain new buildings, important for our culture. And certain elements that have no place in the new Germany—these foreign books, these degenerate paintings, these Bolsheviks, these Jews—they must be gotten rid of. The SS men made no big fuss about it. They were actually rather courteous, people later remarked upon that. We regret, dear lady, that we must take your Tolstoy novels and burn them. We regret having to slash up your picture here, but why does this woman appear to have six arms? We regret that we must take your man out to the woods and shoot him in the head, but this is what happens when one chooses to sleep with a parasite. We regret—"

There were tears in her eyes, though she seemed to have decided, by an act of will, not to cry. As if she did not want some phantom in a black uniform to have that satisfaction.

"Alwin and I had not been . . . together for some while. But you know, one does not stop loving someone, just because . . . and he was Hildi's father." Unexpectedly she took Martina's hand, her eyes glowed, and she forced a kind of smile onto her face. "But Isaac," she said, her voice becoming a stage whisper, "he always seemed to know when danger was coming. He was gone that day, and stayed gone for some time. We were afraid they'd gotten him—"

"Wait a minute. You're saying, Isaac was *here* then? That he *stayed* here? Even after the war started?"

Anna gave her, once more, that look of surprise. Marty has not understood. "Of course he stayed here. Where else? He was one of the family by then. Our poor little family, if you could call it that. He was so terribly clever, and he got on well with the Poles. And of course Hildi by that time was completely in love with him. Had been, really, since she was a young girl."

Martina shook her head. This was too much to deal with all at once. Like a flood of paperwork, reports on dozens of subjects, dropping on your desk faster than you can read them, much less respond appropriately. "Isaac was *here*," she said, feeling dull-witted, groping for the obvious. "Which means, he's been here all along. Which means, he's *still* around here someplace. Hiding in the woods or something. Is that right?"

Anna gave her hand a little squeeze, then let it go and turned to look out the window. At what? Swirling snow, empty cottages, abandoned dreams. Southern Poland, winter of 1944.

"Isaac," she said, "is the father of my grandchild. He had better be around here someplace. And he had better come soon."

"Something isn't right," said Bloom, shaking his head. "The place is almost empty, and we haven't found anything suspicious. No weapons caches, no secret rooms. But there's something wrong. I've just got a feeling." He paused, waiting for the inevitable objection from either Grabsteen or Martina. Hearing none, he shoved his chair back, straightened his legs beneath the table and groaned in exhaustion.

"I've got a feeling, too," Harvey said after a while. "I've got a feeling that if we sit here long enough, the Nazis are going to come and kill us."

"If we sit here *long* enough," Martina said, just for the fleeting pleasure of contradicting him, "the Red Army will come and liberate us, and we can march off in solidarity with our comrades from the East."

"Remind me to tell you sometime," said Grabsteen—with a little smile, as though he, too, enjoyed the game, even if he was too tired to play it just now—"about Stalin's policy on immigration to Palestine. And about the official announcement of the liberation of Majdanek, which curiously made no mention of Jews."

"The problem *now* is," Bloom said loudly, "we all need to rest, but we can't afford to relax. What I think I'm going to do is put everyone on two-hour watches, one on and two off. We'll have four people out on the perimeter, while everybody else is inside getting some shut-eye. Then there's the problem of whether to trust the natives. They're a little *too* friendly, if you ask me."

"They're Socialists," explained Martina.

That seemed to cut no ice with Bloom, who gave her a blank look. Nor should it, she supposed. What had Captain Aristotle said? One never really knows who anybody is.

"Why don't you take the first watch," Bloom told her, not a question at all. "Go find Stu, he's upstairs someplace."

"Not Stu. He needs to stay with Hildi."

"Not Morrie either," said Grabsteen. "His leg got hurt back at the bridge."

"Well, then"—Bloom swept his arms in exasperation, a slapstick gesture that almost knocked a mug off the table—"how in hell am I supposed to put together a watch list?"

"You'll figure something out," Martina said, patting his knee.

"We know you will," seconded Grabsteen. "We have every confidence."

Sunlight returned the next morning. For some reason, this made things even harder to believe. The view from the front window was motionless and sentimental: timbered cottages, fallen snow, scarcely a reminder of the present century. Martina amused herself for a while, sipping hot liquid she chose to pretend was coffee, by trying to imagine what this movie-set village might be good for. Something between *Alexander Nevsky* and *Holiday Inn*. Rita Hayworth dying beautifully in childbirth. Crosby crooning the love theme in full combat gear. And Fred Astaire—born Frederic Austerlitz—doing a nifty turn as a Jewish partisan, miraculously eluding his pursuers, leaping from rooftop to rooftop in the show-stopping dance number.

From a cupboard somewhere, a radio materialized. The red-faced innkeeper, as a courtesy to his guests, ran through the dial until he found the VOA. They listened to Benny Goodman and a news broadcast. That was the first Martina had heard about Roosevelt's reelection. A fourth term—unprecedented!

She didn't have to guess what Ingo would say.

0800. The offgoing watchstanders reported various discoveries. One, you can climb the windmill tower and get a decent view of the countryside. Two, these people have everything—there's a cold room under the barn where they've got the whole carcass of, we think it's a deer, a *big* deer, all cleaned and strung up on a rope. And three, wait'll you see the Hitler Youth Hall.

"I have no desire," snapped Martina, feeling crabby and still cold from her 0400–0600 stint, "to see the Hitler Youth Hall."

"We could use a CP," Bloom pointed out. "Someplace to meet in private. Stash our gear and whatnot." He glanced meaningfully around the common room, where villagers and Varianoviks sat elbow-to-elbow. Weapons and backpacks were scattered haphazardly. The elfin-eared boy, called Michi, as in Mouse, under the guise of wiping down a table, was fondling somebody's machine pistol.

Martina guessed Bloom was right about a command post. Things were getting a little too comfy in here. "All right," she conceded, "let's take a look."

Bloom was gracious in his moment of victory. "I guess we could make do with two per watch," he said. "That way everybody gets more sleep."

They pulled on their coats. "Come on, sport," Martina called to Michi. "You look like you could use some exercise."

The boy understood only that he had been summoned. Perhaps he expected a scolding for his forwardness with firearms; his face lit up when it became clear that an expedition was intended. He tugged on a pair of oversized fur-topped boots that, by rights, should've been on the feet of some soldier awaiting his doom in an open trench, whistling "Lili Marlene" through frostbitten lips. They followed a path tramped in the snow by last night's ceaseless patrolling, out to the village green and then crosswise to the large wooden building whose only feature was a squat belltower, devoid of bell.

Michi saw her looking up there and provided some explanation in rapid, matter-of-fact Deutsch.

"I think," ventured Bloom, "he says they gave the bell for the final victory." When Martina didn't get it, he added, "The brass—you know, for shell casings."

"Ah," she said.

Michi nodded proudly.

Wait'll you see the Hitler Youth Hall—just that, no further hints. Now Martina understood why. What could you possibly have said to convey any notion of this? The entire floor of the large, open room was taken up with . . . what? A display, a construction, an over-the-top and distinctly boyish fantasy. She scoured her memory but only two comparisons—both remote—came to mind. The first was an eccentric museum-style exhibit at an equally eccentric Masonic monument called the George Washington Memorial, across the Potomac in Arlington, depicting in all its quaint, harmless insanity a miniature Shriners Day Parade. At the press of a

button, Sousa squawked through tinny speakers and some kind of con-
veyor-belt mechanism propelled thousands of tiny figures, miniature
vehicles, marching bands, floats, regiments of war heroes, fire trucks,
open Cadillacs full of waving dignitaries and, as Martina recalled, even a
troupe of dancing bears, around and around and around until the bizarre
became monotonous.

The second and more telling comparison was the model-train set on
which her cousin Abie had been working since he was nine years old. The
project had been launched on his bedroom floor with a standard Lionel
kit and a few imitation trees. From there it moved to a special table in
the basement, where the railway line sprouted branch tracks, tunnels and
switching yards, and the landscape complexified to include hills, a river,
grazing sheep, a whistle-stop platform complete with passengers and—
as adolescence expanded Abie's worldview—a village that soon became
a medium-sized town, featuring such enterprises as an auto dealer, a
haberdasher and—in what might have been a very quiet protest against
Prohibition—a Chicago-style saloon. Abie would be about thirty now. As
far as Martina knew, the model railroad was still growing at a steady rate.
And if her cousin lived to be one hundred and three, he possibly could
achieve something on the order of what lay before her in the Hitler
Youth Hall.

She stared at it—over it, through it, around its periphery, across its
immeasurable expanse—for quite some time, as did Bloom. What else
could you do, really? She stared at the tiny cottages with their honest-
to-God thatched rooflets. At yellow-brown fields where teams of oxen
tugged perfect little plows along furrows of—she tested this with her
finger—actual dirt. She stared at the roads winding over hills and along
stretches of reclaimed swampland—yes, with real water, held in black
earthenware ponds and channeled through pebbly drainage canals. At the
orchard, its hundreds of well-pruned limbs heavy with their crop of tiny
red fruit. At the stable, the kennel, the chicken yard. The meadow through
which a party of hunters, traditionally attired, trailed a pack of brown-
and-white hounds. You could practically hear the treble squeal of the *Jägerhorn*. Martina did not doubt that somewhere, if you peeked behind every
shard of rock and lifted the dainty boughs of every bush, you would find
the wily fox, no bigger than a hangnail.

"Da ist Arndtheim," Michi informed them.

No fooling. The Lilliputian village nestled near one corner of the intricate panorama. Everything was there: the spiky windmill, the inn with its
wagging sign, the wooden barricade, even the boxy *Hitlerjugendhall* in

which they stood. You half expected to see a tiny Tamara waving her Simonov and shouting unrepeatable oaths in a voice like a cricket. And a teensy Grabsteen, being a weensy pain in the ass.

Martina then realized that if Arndtheim was real—that is, if the model village matched the original—the rest of it must be real, too. This was not just a panorama but a map. For some reason this gave her a creepy feeling, as if she'd been granted a vision she did not care to see: the thousand-year paradise, a land whose milk flowed as white as Aryan skin and whose honey ran as gold as the hair of a fecund *Mädlein*. It was high summer in the Reich, and though there couldn't be a sky, obviously, you knew it was blue and cloudless. So, too, the countryside was without blemish. Swamps had been drained, underbrush cleared, cottages emptied of dirty Polacks and—just a morbid guess here—a nearby shtetl, in the interest of hygiene, burned to the ground. The place where it had stood was now a hunters' meadow. As for the Jews . . . well, what else should be done with vermin? We shall have no weevils in our flour, no weeds in our rye field, no unwholesome ideas festering in the minds of our children; and just so—for the principle is precisely the same, *meine Herren*—no Jews breeding like bacilli among us, contaminating healthy German blood.

Michi was chattering now, pointing out this and that. Martina experienced a momentary urge to walk over and strangle the boy. Or at least pick him up by his foolish ears and spit in his little Teutonic face. The wave of anger passed through her and then out, over the imaginary landscape. It left her feeling shaken, upset with herself. *One never really knows who anybody is.* Including—perhaps especially—oneself.

"Wo fährt dieser Zug?" she asked, in her crude but usually effective tourist-guidebook Deutsch. She pointed toward the farthest edge of the landscape, where a narrow-gauge rail line snaked between ponds and sedge fields and patches of dark evergreens. In a corner, just before the track ended abruptly by the wall, stood a cluster of red-brick buildings as stately and stern as military barracks.

Michi replied earnestly and at length, an expression of manlike seriousness on his face, proud of his detailed knowledge.

"I'm missing a lot of it," Bloom confessed. "Something about the Austrian cavalry. Won it back from the Poles. Now the SS . . . something about a temporary, um, installation. Factories, very important, artificial rubber. Very bad stink. After the war, better. For now, don't go there."

"No danger of that. But what I asked was, Where does the train go?"

"He's telling you," said Bloom, looking away, something in his voice like helplessness. "The train goes to Auschwitz. That's the nearest market town, it's where the farmers around here sell their produce. If the room was any bigger, you could see it from here."

Harvey Grabsteen, not one to quail, led a couple of Varianoviks laden with ammunition through the snow to the Hitler Youth Hall. He paused barely a moment before striding across the beautifully rendered countryside, crunching trees, fences, neatly tended homes and domestic livestock blithely underfoot. He may, perhaps, have put on a bit of a show, kicking bits of paradise out of his path. It was, in its way, horrifying. It was, in its way, hilarious. A fart at a funeral.

"We'll need something to block these windows," he said, "if we're going to defend this place."

So now he was an expert on fortifications? Martina said, "Defend it against what?"

Wide shrug, *beats me,* like a Borscht Belt comic. "Against *whatever.*"

Martina shook her head. In another crazy mood swing, she took pity on the model-makers. Just when you think you've got everything in order, the Jews come back.

So: a day, then a second night, then a second day. Clouds as heavy as smoke. Smells of greasy cooking—the nervous innkeeper threw open his larder, and out came platters of schnitzel and sausages and potatoes in their myriad constellations. From the kitchen, laughter. From the bedroom at the top of the stairs, intermittent wails.

The worst part for Martina was just waiting around. For Isaac, for Isaac's baby, for the Germans, for peace, for *Götterdämmerung*—any one of which, or some diabolic combination, might come at any moment, though many moments passed, then many more, and nothing changed.

She went on watch in mid-afternoon. For two hours she tracked round and round in the snow beside a tall, slender man from Chicago named Arthur whom she understood to be an accountant, or perhaps an economist, something to do with money, which might be why she had tended to avoid him. Also, he reminded her somewhat of Eddie, or the kind of man Eddie might've grown into, easygoing and gently humorous. They talked about Henry Morgenthau, a safe topic. Arthur felt Morgenthau was wasted at Treasury—he would've been so much more effective at State. With half her mind, Martina hummed Cole Porter's "Just One of Those Things," a wordless commentary that went down well at Washington parties but which, to Arthur, was just a tune. With the other half, she watched Timo climb the windmill tower. *A decent view of the countryside.* Unusual initiative on his part, she thought. But what did she know about Timo? The same thing anyone knew about anybody: zilch.

At four she went off watch. Around five it got dark. Sometime after that, the shooting started.

It might, Ingo thought, have been a form of baptism, horribly botched. The water was so cold you didn't believe you were feeling it. Perhaps you weren't actually feeling it, your nerves had switched off. Which meant later, back on. Another thing to dread.

The wall came down a lot lower than he expected; the builder had made concessions to topography after all. There was justifiable doubt whether Janocz would fit, and in the event it required concerted tugging from the other end—you could imagine Zim and the Priest over there, teeth chattering, trying to get a handhold on the blubbery giant—but they managed it. Then it was Ingo's turn, and after the spectacle of Janocz his own efforts to scoot through, which ended in writhing like a damned eel, didn't seem so pathetic. Afterward, maybe, they would all share a laugh, passing the Priest's canteen around.

Hagen was under and out in a heartbeat and a half. No time for laughing now.

They stood among the trees, just inside the walled enclosure. Hagen gave them a few moments to catch their breath. Then, cautiously, they moved forward until the vegetation thinned out and they could see, at last, what they'd gotten themselves into.

After the close darkness of the woods, this place seemed almost glaringly bright. There were actual streetlamps—among the few, surely, burning that night in all of Europe. Feeble things, each casting no more than a puddle of faint, moon-yellow pallor; but the impression of brightness here was less a question of being able to see clearly than a feeling of having space around you, the world opening up. By degrees Ingo was able to make sense of the dark shapes looming before him, some in silhouette, others mere bodies of deeper shadow.

For instance. The tall thing at the center that looked like a watchtower—that was a windmill. He could make out an indistinct motion up there, blades swirling invisibly, and hear a faint whizzing, immaculately oiled gears transferring energy to some mechanism below. Electricity for the streetlamps. Out of chaos—the unruly wind off the steppe, with its scent of Bolshevism—purpose, order, utility. From what once had been unfruitful Polish soil, behold: a transformation, amazing as a fairy tale. Now it is Germany.

What made Ingo think he'd been here before?

The Wild West. Four bad guys and their native guide, a brooding and dangerous renegade, creep into the dusty little village under cover of darkness. They make for the saloon first, saving the bank for later, but something thwarts them—a barking dog, a sheriff making his rounds or, most likely, a sharp-eared youngster, banished upstairs while the grown-ups talked and laughed down in the parlor. His window's open and he's looking dreamily at that big prairie sky when from the street below . . . was it a clank of spurs? A horse rattling its bridle? And what are those shadows moving stealthily past the dry goods store?

No, not the Wild West. The heathen East, never thoroughly conquered. A land where monsters roam and people vanish in night and fog. *They've all been sent East, haven't you heard?* The village lay clean and tidy under its cap of snow, snugly buttoned behind mullioned windows. The tingle came again but Ingo could only acknowledge it; they were on the move, cottage to cottage, one empty lane to the next. A carpet of yellow light lay in front of a larger building that Ingo tried to place, but he could only come up with odd, utilitarian things: a Lions Club, a school annex, one of those places in the country—a single large room under a tin roof—that Negroes worship in. Nothing quite fit.

They moved up a narrow road, Ingo and the Priest on one side and the rest on the other. The structures they passed all appeared to be empty. Toward the center of the village they grew larger, and a few had lights on. At a traverse street, the hunters paused. Then slipped across, one at a time.

What was Hagen's plan?

Now the large building loomed straight ahead. Its pitched roof rose to a cupola, perhaps a small belltower. Schoolhouse? Closer to the mark. They moved sideways around it, keeping their distance. In places there were neatly clipped shrubs to hide behind; street trees as well, but these were no more than adolescent-sized. At last they gained an angle from which Ingo could make out a signboard in front of the building, its carved lettering discernible by reflected light.

HITLERJUGENDHALL

Across the road, the village opened onto a sort of common. The windmill was there, and a smaller structure that looked like a gazebo. Ingo's tingling amped up. *Everything is different, and yet . . .*

He knew, but didn't. He wasn't quite ready for the journey to end, the old Ford to roll to a stop near Olney, Maryland. For a thirty-two-year-old Isaac to emerge from behind the well house.

Those footsteps, he figured, must be Janocz or Zim crossing the street. They clattered heedlessly; he turned to shush them.

It was not Janocz or Zim. Right up the middle of the lane, weapons slung indifferently at their sides, came Tamara, Marty's friend, and a guy Ingo didn't know too well, a band teacher from somewhere.

Here?

Ingo opened his mouth—too slowly. The burst of a German machine pistol ripped the night apart like a wolf's teeth tearing its prey. The American man—Bobby Zilman was his name—went down on one knee. It was too dark to read his face; Ingo only imagined a look of amazement. Then Bobby seemed to vanish in a second burst of gunfire that knocked him backward into the shadows.

At approximately the same time, though the sequence wasn't clear to him, Ingo killed the Defrocked Priest. It happened quickly, his hands moving as if under someone else's control. Next moment, he was standing there with the feeling of having been punched in the side. He hadn't gotten a proper grip on the Schmeisser, and it had bucked against him.

Tamara went down. Ingo figured she was dead, leaving him alone against the other three. But from the darkness in the lane, a series of small flashes: Tamara's automatic rifle, noisy chatter like a string of small fireworks going off. Zim shot back, though Ingo could see he was scarcely aiming, just making short sweeps with his MP. Ingo raised his own weapon and squeezed the trigger until the clip was spent. Then he dropped behind some bushes and groped for the ammunition pouch on his belt.

For a moment, all was quiet.

Across the road, a long, deep groan. It came from Janocz, and somehow, just from the sound of it, you could tell he was mortally wounded. A dying mammoth. Different noises came from somewhere around the corner—a door banging open, footsteps crunching rapidly through the snow. Ingo looked up to see Hagen standing above him.

Just standing there. He glanced down once, long enough for Ingo to feel foolish for having been caught like this, an ammo clip dangling futilely in his hand. Then Hagen looked away, up the street, where the footsteps were coming from. He had drawn his pistol, a Walther automatic, but for some reason, or no reason, he chose not to use it. There were shouts—among them, Tamara's—and another burst of fire, followed by a blaze of return fire that lasted for a while. That would do for Zim, Ingo supposed.

"There's another one, over there!" Tamara shouted.

Hagen still did not move. He neither raised nor dropped the Walther. He seemed to have accepted, in advance, whatever fate might befall him.

Ingo scrambled to his feet, slipping in the snow. A death wish, he thought grimly, though he had no truck with such Freudian claptrap. He stood there in his SS uniform with an empty machine pistol in his hands; and there stood Tamara not a dozen paces away, pointing her Simonov right at his face.

"Don't do anything you'll regret," he said.

That must have surprised her. She lowered the rifle a little, squinting at him through the darkness. Other people were coming up behind her. Perhaps she felt safety in numbers. Her body seemed to relax. "Oh, it's you," she said finally. The gun twitched over toward Hagen. "Who's this one, then?"

Hagen let the pistol drop from his fingers.

"Funny you should ask," Ingo told her. "I've been wondering that myself."

Martina was upstairs, sitting with Hildi. The girl looked drained of something vital, one of the humors, a medieval essence that nowadays applied only to Central European physiognomies. From Bratislava to Danzig, people still died of an incorrect ratio of phlegm to black bile. Hildi's cheeks glowed with a fever you couldn't feel by touching her forehead; she was being consumed from within by a cold, wasting fire.

The little body in her belly remained absolutely still. Lying low, awaiting its chance. *Come soon,* Martina nearly prayed. Toward God, fate, doom, chance, the futures market and the four planes of the Sephiroth, she felt identically ambivalent. For Martina, life was possibility, not certainty; so was whatever might or might not lie beyond it.

Between bouts of excruciating pain, Hildi pushed herself up by the elbows on an ever-growing mound of pillows; dozens of geese must have given their entire breasts to fill them. Sometimes she rallied her dwindling energies to attain a state bordering on conversational normality. This seemed to happen especially in early evening—could that be when she expected Isaac to arrive?—and it was happening now, while Stu grabbed an early dinner and Martina was standing what she thought of as the Hildi watch.

"I can barely remember," the girl said, speaking English out of politeness, smiling at her own hesitations, "before the Nazi time. It must have been so . . . pretty."

Nazizeit, the term they used here. As though talking about the Ice Age, the Lower Cretaceous, some rough patch of natural history that was beyond human agency, no question of interrupting it—and to prove the point, Anna had quoted Rilke: *Who talks of victory? To endure is all.*

"It was okay," said Martina. "It wasn't the Golden Age."

"But people call it the Golden Twenty-Years?"

"Twenties. Yeah, they do. They're kidding themselves. Didn't anybody ever tell you—" She should have kept going, blathered something, because the sudden pause caught Hildi's attention.

The girl's eyes froze on her, black beads suspended in blue ice. Still young enough to sense, instantly and with one hundred percent accuracy, when a grown-up is about to dissemble. "Tell me what?" she said in her sweetest voice.

"How Isaac got here in the first place." Because it wasn't as though, Martina thought, she didn't have a right to know.

"No . . . I am not sure."

"He came here—we all came here, but it was on account of him— because some big nasty guys were planning to kill him. Because he'd played a trick on them, stolen some documents, I don't know, I barely understood it at the time. But that's your Golden Twenties. Gangs of bullies marching around singing battle songs and beating each other to death. Even the good parts . . ."

. . . were a lie, she intended to say, thinking of the economic boom, drunken Fitzgerald and crazy Zelda, Hoover and his gang of pious crooks. But that was remembering backward. "Actually, the good parts were really good."

"That is what Isaac says."

"You see a lot of him?" This breaking a little promise to herself not to interrogate the poor girl. Wait till she's better, *then* give her the third degree.

Hildi sat further upright. She seemed unsure whether to answer, or how. Martina guessed she'd made her own promises, not so little and not only to herself. The strain in her face made you want to hug her, to reassure her—but what sort of reassurance, under these circumstances, wouldn't be another lie?

"Everything is a secret," Hildi said at last. "For years has it been so. Before the war—ever since I remember. From the Poles must we keep secret what we have, how much food, how many animals, or they will feel,

I don't know—neidisch. From the Nazis must we keep our politics. Since the war, is it even harder. The partisans must not learn this, the army must not know that. Even Isaac must—"

Her eyes grew momentarily wild; she had almost spoken the unspeakable, let slip the greatest secret of all. *Even Isaac must not know . . . what?* Martina was beside herself.

"So, we built the wall," said Hildi, recovering nicely, only a little flushed around the ears. "That made everything easier. Our whole world now is hidden, so within it we are safe. My papa said, Socialists are no good at lying anyway. Lying is the province of the Right, people who live behind locked gates, making plans, counting profits. We live in the fields, the factories, apartment blocks—for us, talking is pleasure, sharing is necessity. We are truth-tellers. After the wall, our truth is locked inside. The lies out."

Martina thought you could argue that the opposite was true. But she kept that to herself.

"We see Isaac if he wants to be seen"—the answer to Martina's question, catching her by surprise. "When he needs food. When he is hurt. When he . . . when he wants—"

Suddenly she was sobbing. It was a relief, almost. The girl did not object to Martina's arms closing around her, and as her crying spell continued, the first soft trickle burgeoning to a steady stream, Martina found herself supporting Hildi's weight from the waist up. And so she felt very plainly, as though her own body were involved, the sharp jolt from all the muscles around the girl's abdomen.

Hildi's crying stopped. For an instant, she didn't breathe. Then she gave a yelp of more astonishment than pain. "O mein Gott," she whispered.

Martina eased her back down onto the pillows. Hildi's eyes were wide; her hands were shaking on either side of her belly, like she was afraid to touch it.

"Is it the same as before?" Martina asked softly, once she thought Hildi was able to speak.

The girl only shook her head. Then she shook it again, more emphatically, and closed her eyes.

Martina stood up. *I'll get Stu*, is what she was going to say. But it was in that moment, precisely, that the first spray of gunshot, like a fistful of little rocks thrown hard against a piece of wood, came from somewhere inside the village wall. Insanely, Martina welcomed them.

At last, she thought. No more waiting.

LAIR OF THE BEAST

Butler had been afraid many times but the experience of pure, unreasoning terror had thus far eluded him. His Satanic baptism, when it came, was not by fire but by water—the cold waters of the River San, not so much as rivers go, typical of the winding tributaries of the Ukraine and southern Poland, meandering like a royal bloodline and quietly gathering strength before allying downstream, in the north, to create the mighty, half-frozen barriers behind which the Wehrmacht was preparing without hope to make its next-to-last stand.

The Red Army, for reasons Butler could not determine, had a particular dislike of rivers. Therefore the Soviets had devised any number of ingenious methods to get men and vehicles across them, each more fiendishly difficult, fraught with risk and effective than the last. To deal with the minor obstacle of the River San, Comrade General Krivon had dispatched a platoon of engineers wearing thick goat-wool vests, some new type of undergarment designed to retain warmth even when immersed in water and jaunty black caps that came to a little peak and gave them the look of Dark Elves out of a Scandinavian nightmare. These men spent several days smoking Butler's cigarettes and readying the components of a special pontoon bridge—the Fascists have nothing like it—while taking turns reading aloud from the latest inflammatory screed by Ilya Ehrenburg, the most colorful of the propagandists and a writer whose knack for the bloody-minded metaphor Butler could not help admiring, however hard he tried. Had Ehrenburg been reared on the Capitalist side, he by now would have made a bundle in Hollywood and be spending his leisure hours in printed silk shirts beside swimming pools, instead of commuting between Moscow and the vilest reaches of the Eastern Front, chatting up field marshals and common foot soldiers, daily adding new species to the Nazi bestiary and generally outdoing Butler at his own game. Envy is a frightful bore as well as a deadly sin, but there you have it.

The order to cross came on a night that began with a fattening moon but by 0200 or so had turned moonless. It was seasonally cold, with a light wind that got heavier when it found the open run of river, along which it could work up a nice north-to-south velocity. The pontoon bridge resembled nothing Butler had seen before and so did the engineers, after they crushed out their last Camels and pulled the caps over their faces and got down to earning their rubles. The bridge rolled forward on specially built runners, its sections stacked three tiers high. At water's edge the engineers engaged a sort of hand brake that stopped the runners cold, then undid a latch that released the pieces of the bridge, which slid on greased skids down the natural declivity of the terrain and landed in the water, one after another, *plop plop plop*. They thereupon sank to a depth of between thirty and forty centimeters, where the Germans could not see them, nor the Soviets either, though the latter knew where to find them. More or less.

All very well—except, of course, that in the actual event everything went a great deal more slowly, with an incredible amount of heavy mechanical clacking and grinding, pieces getting stuck or else coming loose prematurely, bridge sections hitting the water and floating away downstream. Before long, even if the Germans had been sleeping like Red-Beard under his mountain, they would've begun to suspect something was afoot. But the Germans were not sleeping; they were awake and launching flares and sighting in their MG-42s. And at that moment, when the excitement seemed to have reached an ungodly peak, Seryoshka shouted *"Now, comrades!"* and they all went into the water.

The engineers had been in there for some time already, up to their necks, clamping the bridge together and keeping it properly aligned, and quite a few of them were dead. The others were dying as fast as could reasonably be expected, but meantime they managed to hold the incredible sinking-floating Bridge to Hell in one piece long enough for an entire motorized reconnaissance regiment to hurl itself from the Soviet side of the river, and a better-than-company-sized remnant to arrive intact on the opposite shore. From there it was a dash into the woods, through the blazing line and into the German rear—a classic Red Army set-piece of this latter phase of the Great Patriotic War.

Butler had been briefed endlessly and well; he understood the plan and anticipated the high rate of casualties. What he had not expected was the terror. How could he have, when he had not known terror before, except as a category of human experience that many of his favorite writers liked to spill ink over? Hemingway had written about it, as had Dostoyevsky, Remarque and even, in his pungent way, Ehrenburg. For Butler's money, they were all a pack of liars.

This terror, real terror, was not a trial of the soul or a contest of will against mortality. There was nothing heroic about it, scarcely anything human. It was reptilian and vulgar and crude—a thing of the body, an eruption, like some gland bursting open inside, flooding all your inner structures of maturity and self-control, reducing you to infantilism. It began with crapping in your pants without being aware of it. From there it got worse—much worse—and entailed involuntary moaning and wailing and shameful whimpering. It extended, in certain cases, to losing consciousness, though Butler was not to be so lucky.

No, Butler was fully conscious, hyperconscious, as though his mind had freed itself of the inconvenience of having to control this soiled and quaking body. He was alert to every sound, all the mortar explosions and chattery gun bursts, the thrashing of bodies in water and the grinding of vehicle treads, the sergeant shouting at you to get out of the way unless you wanted to be crushed, the astonished bellows of men being crushed a moment thereafter—right down to the bubbles that came from men's mouths in diminishing chains as they sank beneath the surface. He saw every muzzle flash, the thrilling trajectory of every tracer round, the dimensionless glare of every phosphorus charge igniting overhead and descending in perfect slow motion, the shadows rearranging themselves to receive it, the river spitting like a momentary fountain upon its impact. And he registered with distant satisfaction, almost pleasure, like a spectator at a boxing match, the artillery opening up on the Soviet side, shots called in by an observer at the water's edge, ripping holes in the line ahead, blowing the German defenders back to Franconia.

Beyond frenzy, a transcendent stillness lies. Hundreds of men trained to kill and persuaded to hate were doing their level best to obliterate one another. Some were better at this than others but all had been provided with the latest tools of the killer's trade and most were making a creditable showing. Butler was aware of each one of them, as you might become aware, by staring long enough, that a thunderstorm is not a monolithic downpour but rather an intricate matrix of single raindrops. If you blink, you can almost catch a wave of droplets in mid-flight, frozen in your visual memory. Butler flinched at a salvo from a Katyusha rocket battery—they called these things Stalin organs, after their cluster of shrieking pipes—and in the moment that his eyes were closed he believed he had glimpsed the ethereal web of bullet trajectories woven in the air above the river.

He was aware, too, of Seryoshka beside him, in the very moment that a shell from a Panzerfaust met the forward plate of their armored personnel carrier. The hot light and the hand yanking at his sleeve and the backward thrust of the blast wave and the instantaneous deafness came as a series of discrete events that spun themselves wonderfully into a single, unbroken experience, flowing without effort into the icy embrace of the River San, the utter darkness, the end of breathing, the unheralded and somehow anticlimactic arrival of Butler's own death, like a snap decision to join a party that you had earlier decided to pass on.

He closed his eyes. He would die, then, thirty to forty centimeters beneath the surface of the River San—and that's all she wrote.

Seryoshka persuaded him to reconsider. The suddenly ferocious Cossack grabbed him by his decadent, Western-style haircut and tugged him out of the water, where everything was peaceful, where neither enemies nor editors could get at you, back into the raging battle, the horror and violence all around. What are friends for?

To his unhappy surprise, Butler returned to himself. His body and mind were one again. He was shaken but he was now ready to ignore that. He had done the *rite de passage* and was still alive, at least for the next few moments. Thus it seemed the better part of valor to make a dash for the German side of the river. Before long he was safely through, and very cold, and it occurred to him that somewhere along the line he had lost the old Remington.

He was not ashamed, afterward, to have been afraid. But he was disappointed that so little, spiritually speaking, had come of it.

He felt himself in no respect different from the man he'd been before. Perhaps, to a minor degree, he had learned something about what kind of man that was. Perhaps, to be honest with himself, he wasn't a writer at all, just an ordinary person. Because in the wake of that river crossing—a trifling instant, really, in the life of that great beast the Red Army—he discovered that the last thing he wanted to do was commit any part of the experience to paper. Which was just as well, for there was no paper, and nothing to write with. He felt, in fact, that he had no more stories to tell, and no one to tell them to anyway. He had lost—some time ago, now that he came to think of it—any sense of there being an audience out there. What might be out there, or even what *out there* might signify, he neither knew nor cared any longer.

All he cared about was right here, in the few square meters around him: a huddle of comrades, a clean rifle, a pair of good Finnish boots drying on the hood of an American jeep in the woods of occupied Poland. Fire had been ruled out as too dangerous; the Germans, frantic at the penetration of their line, had even put a couple planes in the air, though most of their fuel was being hoarded for some mischief in the West. No fire meant that the soaking, shivering invaders would just have to warm up as best they could—but these were Russians, warming up as best they could was a national pastime.

Granted, it was a strange life. It was not the life that had been dealt to Samuel Butler Randolph III some thirty-eight years ago on the West End of Richmond, Virginia. And what with one thing and another, it wasn't likely to drag on much longer. But for all that, it was his life, the one he had made for himself. And here on this side of the River San—in what Ilya Ehrenburg, a real writer, liked to call "the lair of the Fascist beast"—that was really all that mattered.

"We've had a message from the other end."

The voice belonged to the signals officer, Boris Yosefovich, the jolly fellow who'd been posted to Washington and wanted to be called Bo. Butler liked him well enough but couldn't fathom why the fellow was talking while everybody was trying to sleep. Then, groggily, he realized Bo was speaking in English.

"Where is he, then?" Seryoshka replied, his rounded Oxbridge diction a contrast to Bo's American-style choppiness.

Butler heaved himself upright. The two men were huddled over a map which they were scrutinizing in the beam of a tiny flashlight. Dawn was in the wings, but the curtain had not yet begun to rise.

English . . . what in God's name was that about? Two things, Butler reckoned, forcing his brain to work. One, they didn't care if he overheard them. But two, as far as everyone else was concerned, this conversation was secret.

"What's the other end?" he mumbled. "Who are you talking about?"

Bo looked up anxiously.

Seryoshka gave him a nod: *You explain.*

"In an operation of this type," said Bo, "you can't just charge in blindly. You want some guidance. We've got a man over there with a radio. A good fellow, a Slav."

Butler tried to think this through. In fact he'd thought it through a hundred times already, from any number of angles. "You're Puak's man, aren't you," he told Seryoshka. "You have been all along."

"Who is Puak?" Seryoshka blithely wondered, back to Russian now. He had that twinkling Georgian smile down cold.

Bo concerned himself with the map.

Butler nodded. He *had* thought it through, and what he'd concluded was that it didn't matter. It didn't matter if Puak was using him for some inscrutable purpose, a pawn in a brain-racking chess game. It didn't matter if his best friend in the world, these days, was in on the plot. What mattered was history, and how it would be told by generations yet unborn. About that, Puak was dead right—which meant Puak was justified in whatever methods he adopted and whatever tools he chose, including Butler himself, to get the job done. Being a good Communist meant, among other things, coming to terms with the idea that you're nothing special, just one among the millions, and your life is of value only to the extent that it can be consumed like fuel to drive the Revolution.

So, "Who's Puak?" Seryoshka had said, and as far as Butler was concerned, that was swell. He knew that game and didn't mind playing it. Gesturing toward the map, he said, "Your Slav with the radio—where is he, do you know?"

Seryoshka raised an eyebrow, just perceptibly, which Bo understood as permission to reply.

"Right about here—some kind of village, must be a tiny place, there's no mark for it. Shouldn't be hard to reach, but we'll have to travel mostly by daylight. The terrain is difficult—see all this water? The Germans patrol the rail line, up here, and this is the main road, heading to Kraków. If we stay well south of that, we should be all right. The biggest danger, at this point, may not be the SS so much as the Armija Krajowa. The London Poles," he explained for Butler's benefit. "We think they're well armed, and we know they're anti-Soviet. They see the Germans falling back, so already they're looking ahead to the next battle. And the next enemy is us."

Who can blame them? Butler thought. And he saw from the other men's eyes that they didn't blame them either, but also that if these Poles were a problem, then they'd deal with it.

"How much farther?" he asked. Meaning, of course, How long will it take? *You see, my son, here time becomes space.*

Bo gave him a Washington grin, that can-do attitude, praise Lenin and pass the ammunition. "If we're alive this time tomorrow," he said, "we'll be cooking breakfast in Arndtheim."

SCHLOSS BURGUND

In Hagen's face, Ingo thought, you could read an entire history. Not the history made up of dates and names, noteworthy events, laws enacted, wars waged; the fellow who built a machine that changed how we live, or the one who wrote a book that changed how we think. The Gospel of Hagen was more like a poem, the kind meant to be sung, not recited. And in the pregnant immanence of the moment, with the blood of the Defrocked Priest spattered over his boots, Ingo could well imagine he was hearing the damn thing, scored as a full-blown oratorio: the *Hagenlied*, all its movements playing at once but broken into uncompleted phrases, no theme occurring alone or intact. He remembered a piece of music, American, not German, meant to convey the effect of a passing parade, a gay patriotic affair, only with too many bands marching too close together, this one coming and that one going, trumpets slightly out of tune, drummers a bit too excitable, as drummers will be. It was clever and awful, the sort of show-off art Ingo detested even when it succeeds in making its point, perhaps especially then.

Thus Hagen's face: lit partly by cool northern light from the Carpathians, partly by the flaring of a log fire someone had kindled too early, before the wood was dry, and dominated by the blood-black effulgence of those eyes, now gleaming, now dark again. Across that face a hundred expressions played, none lingering long, as though he were very quickly donning and discarding a large collection of masks.

"You've been a member of the SS for how long?" Grabsteen demanded, facing him across the ruined slopes of what had been a perfect miniature vineyard.

Hagen did not reply. He seemed not to comprehend the question.

"He would have signed up early on," Ingo suggested. "As soon as he was eligible, right out of Gymnasium. Gone through the usual brainwashing at Wewelsburg, got his commission in time for the war."

"Thank you *so* much," Grabsteen snapped. "I wonder if you'd be kind enough to let the prisoner answer for himself."

Hagen might as well have been someplace else, sitting placidly by a window in an empty room, not bound tightly to a straight-backed chair in the *Hitlerjugendhall* at the vertex of an arc formed by half a dozen Americans. It was just past breakfast time. They had brought him a rump of bread and a cup of ersatz coffee, but both lay untouched near his feet, dwarfing a tiny wooden cow.

"Have you *personally*," Grabsteen resumed, with an angry glance at Ingo, "participated in crimes against Jews?"

"Oh, come on," said Bloom. "Of course he has. They all have, one way or another. They're all gears in the same engine."

Grabsteen was unmollified. "Were you a member of an Einsatzgruppe? Were you ever posted to a concentration camp? Did you assist in the forced removal of Jews from their place of residence? Were you charged with enforcing the terms of Nazi racial policies, for example the Nuremberg Laws of 1935? Did you ever command a subordinate to harm or kill any Jewish man, woman or child?"

When he paused for breath, Martina said quietly, "Did you shoot Alwin?"

Hagen turned slightly in his chair to look at her. Unemotively, he shook his head.

"It was you, though, wasn't it? Who brought them here."

Again, no answer, unless one were coded into the set of his jaw, his sad silvered eyes.

Ingo nosed in; he had a few questions of his own. More than a few. "You thought Isaac would be here, didn't you? And if he wasn't, you were going to set a trap for him. Right? That's why you came—you weren't following a trail. You just *knew*."

No denial, no shake of the head. No confession either. Only the shifting expressions, the secret oratorio.

"This is pointless," Bloom practically shouted. "If you guys want to kill him, then take him out and do it. Or hell, I'll do it myself. But don't expect him to break down and confess to being Adolf Hitler's illegitimate son, who's done everything from running the gas chambers to sucking Rommel's cock. Pardon me, Marty. Because that's not going to happen. Anyway, what difference would it make? You can see he's a Nazi. What does it matter what *kind* of Nazi?"

"It matters," said Grabsteen.

For once, neither Martina nor Ingo disagreed.

After a while they got tired of asking questions, tired of Hagen's resolute silence and tiredest of all, probably, of how he seemed barely to register their presence, as if they were no more than ghosts. They might be doing their best to haunt him, but this was a man accustomed to being haunted; he'd seen his share of ghosts more gruesome and terrifying than these could ever be.

It was time for Bloom to go on watch. That was their stated reason for breaking off the interrogation. A more honest reason might have been that this German officer in his black uniform, in some manner none of them could pin down, was starting to unnerve them. His proximity was oppressive. We won't kill him, they decided, not just yet. We'll stick him in a room somewhere, back at the inn, maybe, where we can keep an eye on him.

So they prodded him at gunpoint—the whole pack of them, safety in numbers—across the green and up the narrow staircase. They chose a room at the very end of the hall and lashed his wrists together and tethered his ankles to a bedpost. They kicked a chamber pot in his direction. Finally they stood looking down at him, while Hagen sat on a corner of the bed looking at who knows what. His own private horror show. Or maybe a comedy, a bit of fluff to amuse our boys on leave from the front. Sing along with Zarah Leander now, lads; in the morning it's back to hell.

"Somebody ought to stand guard," Bloom said, though he didn't stick around to argue the point. He had saddled himself with coat and rifle and was already lumbering to the door. "I don't think he can wiggle loose. But you never know."

"I'll stay," Ingo said—too readily, perhaps. Martina gave him a look, but it was only a look, he thought. She doesn't suspect anything.

What might she have suspected, though?

There was a time.

All those years ago, the very thought *alone with Hagen* would've shot through him like an electric charge. A complex charge, positive and negative at once. In which respect, was anything different now?

Alone with Hagen. In a room at a cozy inn, somewhere near the end of the world, in a storybook version of Germany.

There was a time: it was true. Incredible as it now seemed, Ingo knew those days had really happened; they had dawned as punctually as this one and set as surely this must, too. Yet they seemed infinitely long ago, before winter and war and loss had even been thought of. A different Ingo had lived in a different body then.

I feel the breeze of another planet. Hardly a stranger one, though. A different Ingo, but not a greater fool. And a different Hagen . . . but still the same enigma.

Who are you? Ingo wanted to ask. But he did not speak, and neither for a while did he look at Hagen directly. He moved from corner to corner in the room, paused to glance out the window at Arndtheim, a paradoxical place that was dying and gaining new residents at the same time. He walked to the door and closed it, unable to bear the sounds of Hildi's pain on top of everyone else's. Then he crossed the room again to the only chair, near the window, and sat down. The light fell starkly on Hagen's prematurely aged face.

Now, at last, you dare to look at him. And quickly away, for he is looking straight back at you. Muster your resolve; raise your eyes to meet his.

Hagen said: "I would never have wished that harm should come to him."

Precisely that, for the German construction admitted no ambiguity. Much will be lost in precision, poorly recompensed in snap and color, when English muscles in as the international language of scholarship. "When?" Ingo asked—meaning, as Hagen must have understood, in which world? This one or that, ersatz or authentic?

Hagen shifted on the bed. He did not intend, perhaps, to draw attention to the bonds at his wrists. Ingo's hand almost, *almost,* moved to the knife on his belt—as if for an instant it was controlled by a will other than his own. More likely, his own will was not the firm, dependable thing he might have wished. A very old problem.

"You are blind," said Hagen. "Always, you were blind. You look at a thing and see . . . I don't know. Not what is there, truly. Also with a person—you look at him and you see a character from a story. The role, not the actor."

"I don't think so," said Ingo, which was honest enough. He could see what Hagen meant, though.

"Na ja. So, tell me, who then is Isaac? Who then am I? Not, what part do we play."

Ingo considered. Remembered. He kept quiet a long time. Hagen kept quiet as well, though note that he does not take his eyes off you. He is making a point: he is stronger in captivity than you in freedom.

Well, fuck that. He's just a prisoner. He counts for nothing now, if he ever did. As far as you're concerned, he is faceless and nameless. You will conduct your interrogation, and once you're satisfied with his responses, you will leave.

"Here's what *I* think," said Ingo, somewhat fortified. "For starters, I think you set us all up back then. Isaac especially. I think you tracked us to the Leuchtenburg and pretended to warn us that your Jungdo buddies were looking to kick our ass. But the whole thing was a con. Your plan was to tip your pals off, first chance you got, as to where they could find us. And that's exactly what you did, because that's how it all played out."

You sit back, awaiting his reaction. It comes in his own good time.

"Tell me what you remember, exactly," the prisoner said. "Not at the Leuchtenburg. After that, here, in Silesia. Tell me the story. Of this"—now a measured pause, holding at arm's length the fatal word—"betrayal."

"No," said Ingo. "I don't have to do that."

"That is true."

"I don't owe you anything."

"Of course not."

"You know, you're lucky I didn't kill you. Because I could have. I ought to have. Back in the woods."

"Which woods?"—pinning you with his glance.

You understand, too well, that he is asking not *where* but *when*. The frozen woods of 1944? Or the enchanted forest of 1929? *I don't know,* you say, perhaps too quickly, and only to yourself.

Of course you're lying.

Es war einmal, that's how they begin. Once upon a time. *Es war einmal,* three boys went into the forest. It was a beautiful warm day. One boy was very pale, with hair as white as summer clouds and eyes as blue as the sky. The second boy had red hair and a comical face with freckles and a mouth that was too wide and a nose as big as Pinocchio's. And the third boy, though he must have been there, was invisible.

These boys walked for what might have been hours, or it might have been only minutes, for in the forest, in those days, time behaved differently than it does now. After a while they came to a river. The river was full of quick-moving water that sparkled like diamonds and tickled your skin like a thousand shivering elvers, because it had flowed down all the way from the land of werewolves and it still held the cold of snowy peaks and also a certain mysterious power, the magic of transformation: it could change truth into fantasy, happy dreams into nightmares.

The boys took off their shoes and stuck their feet into the water, but it was too shallow for swimming and the rocks too slippery to wade out on. Then the pale boy said, There's a place where the water is deeper, where we can jump in and swim. Swell, the red-haired boy said. And the other boy said nothing, because in addition to being invisible he had no voice.

Now you may ask how the pale one knew about the place where the water was deep. But you will never learn the answer, even if you think hard about it for fifteen years.

The boys followed the river downstream and finally came to an old wooden bridge, the sort of bridge trolls like to live under. But under this bridge there was only water, clear and deep and blue and cold, though not so cold you didn't want to swim in it. By now, the day had grown quite warm and the boys were tired from all that walking.

The pale boy said, I am going to dive in from up there, and pointed up at the old wooden bridge. And the red-haired boy said, You think it's deep enough? And the invisible boy thought, *No, it isn't,* but he could not say so.

So the pale boy began taking off his clothes, and so did the red-haired boy. As to the third boy, who can say?

Now, the pale boy's body was beautiful. Yet even so, you feared to touch it, on account of its hardness, and also because of a dangerous power it seemed to possess.

The red-haired boy was not beautiful, but really quite odd. His limbs were gangly and his neck too thin, his ears altogether too large. Yet you did not fear to touch this unlovely body, and in fact you would have enjoyed touching it, on account of its warmth, and also because of an attracting energy it seemed to possess.

As to the third boy, who can say whether he was fat or thin, handsome or hideous? Perhaps he had no body at all—only a pair of invisible eyes that watched the other two boys clamber onto the old wooden bridge, and a secret heart that swelled with envy and longing.

They climbed and dove and came up spluttering, and they dunked each other and floated on their backs and kicked themselves leisurely to shore. And so the hours passed or perhaps only an instant, for time was behaving so strangely that it might have stopped running entirely. At last they hauled themselves onto a big rock that was warm from the afternoon sunshine. But by then the sun was falling low, and the rock was mostly in shadow, and as the naked boys lay there they began to feel cold.

We ought to put our clothes on, the invisible boy wanted to say, though he had no voice to say it.

We ought to light a fire, the pale boy said, in a voice clear and strong.

All right! said the red-haired boy, who had no intention of putting his clothes on, even though goose bumps were forming on his unlovely but magically attracting skin. You got matches?

We don't need matches, the pale boy said. He dug into the pack he carried everywhere and drew out of it a magnifying glass such as a young naturalist might carry into the woods. All we need, he said, is kindling. And he looked at the invisible boy, whom he seemed to be able to see just then, and said, Go look for some dry leaves, and some little twigs, and some bigger branches for when it gets going.

The invisible boy did not think to ask why he should gather kindling while they just lounged on the rock. It might have been that he had no mouth to ask such a question, only a pair of eyes and a heart that caused him mainly sorrow. So he did as he was bidden and returned in no time at all, for time had stopped running. But while he was gone, a terrible change had occurred.

On the rocks before him, lower down than before, just at the edge of the water, the red-haired boy lay as one who is dead. His eyes were closed, and blood was all over his unlovely skin.

The pale boy was kneeling over him and the backpack he carried everywhere was open with its contents spilled about. In one hand the pale boy held a long strip of cloth such as a young assassin might use to strangle his victims. In the other, a knife of fearsome length and sharpness. Hearing footsteps, he froze like a statue, his face as cold as a snow-topped mountain, his eyes as blue and empty as the sky.

Now the third boy, who must not have been invisible any longer, did not give thought to the awful scene that lay before him. It might have been that his actions were guided only by a heart that pumped with horror and rage. But at least his voice had returned to him, and he let out a frightful bellow. Then he set upon the pale boy, heedless of his assassin's tools, and it seemed likely that one or the other must presently die.

Suddenly, the third boy felt a terrible sharp pain in his side and looked down to find that his body was visible once more, with a long and fearsome knife sticking into it. And he froze like a statue, if a statue that was magically bleeding.

At this, the pale boy leapt up and grabbed his clothes from the rock, then ran off into the forest.

The now-visible boy stood looking at the knife dangling from one side of his belly. And though it caused him pain and there was an alarming amount of blood, it seemed to him that the knife had not actually stuck in very deep. Certainly it had not penetrated to his vital organs, owing in part to the thickness with which these organs were girded with flesh around the boy's middle. And when he put a hand to the knife, it fell with a clang to the rock.

The boy made a bandage for himself, using a length of the assassin's cloth he cut to size with the murderous blade. It might have been that, by now, his brain had started to work again. And it is certain that time was running once more, because the sun dropped ever lower behind the trees. And still the red-haired boy lay on the rocks, as still as death.

Yet he was alive. His thin chest rose and fell, the heart beat strongly beneath his unlovely skin. The now-visible boy lifted him up like a child and laid him on a softer patch of ground, away from the water. Then he took his own shirt and dipped it in the stream and began to clean the other's wounds. As he wiped the blood away he saw that the wounds were mainly on the knees and the hands and the forehead, and that of these the one on the forehead was worst. It lay just under the thick red hair at the front, as if an assailant had bashed him with a rock. Though as the third boy's brain continued slowly to work, indeed as it worked without stopping for the next fifteen years, he began to see that there could be another explanation.

There was no question of moving the red-haired boy that night. Hours went by, and he lay there as one who has fallen into an enchanted sleep. Making a fire was now impossible, for the young naturalist's magnifying glass was useless without the sun. So the third boy did the best he could; he pulled the injured boy's clothes back onto the unlovely body and lay down beside him, holding the other boy close, sharing his own body's warmth. Thus they spent the night, and all that while the now-visible boy's heart was filled with strong feelings of many kinds. He felt confusion and fright. He felt anger. He felt hope. Despair warred with determination in his breast. Hatred for the one boy wrestled with a feeling for the other that he could not name, or perhaps chose not to.

Finally, at the first light of morning, the third boy stirred himself from the rock. He looked down one last time at his friend lying there in an enchanted sleep, then bent low and kissed him very lightly beside the mouth that was too wide. But whatever magic that may have had, it was not the sort needed to break the enchantment, or maybe he was not the right sort of person to attempt it. So he stood up and said, I am going to get help. Then he set off through the forest.

He never saw the red-haired boy again. Never, ever. Because when he returned later that day, with two companions, having fled the village where a gang of assassins had arrived, the boy was gone. And though they looked and looked, and called his name in the woods, he appeared simply to have vanished, like the morning mist.

It might have been that as he slept, the red-haired boy transformed into a kind of animal, a wild stealthy creature of the forest, and that he arose and slipped away to live among his kind in the woods. Which is a thing that happened in that part of the world, in those days, and perhaps it happens still.

"To begin with," says the prisoner, having heard this story, or those parts of it that were any of his damn business, "you nearly frightened me to death. You were bigger than I was. Older as well. Already I had seen you break the nose of one of my comrades. What did you expect me to do? Stand there while you murdered me? You were going to, I believed. You believe so yourself, don't you?"

Don't answer him. Listen maybe, don't speak. You're confused just now. The shrieking of that poor girl down the hall doesn't make you any more clearheaded.

"One more swim, we decided. One last dive, before the Schwuler gets back. I am sorry, we were cruel to you at times, I know we were. We . . . left you out. But again I ask you, what did you expect? We were boys, not angels. You may have had certain . . . ideals, certain illusions. About Isaac, especially. Don't say anything please, there is no need. I do not know or care, anymore, what you felt. What you wanted, or what held you back. I would like to say I do not care what you think of me now. Very much I would like not to care. But for some reason I cannot help it. I feel a need to . . . explain myself. To you."

Not to Isaac?

The prisoner looks at you as if you'd spoken out loud. His eyes are bright but you have a sense, looking into them, there's something unhealthy about that brightness.

"Isaac and I . . ." Shaking his head, smiling; the smile as always defies interpretation. "Isaac and I have always had, from the start, an understanding. I mean this in no shallow sense. I do not mean a convenient mutual arrangement, though perhaps it began like that. When we met, you know, he was seeking information for his Communist friends."

Socialist, you think. Though who could believe a good Republican would draw such fine distinctions?

"And I wanted . . . shall I tell you what I wanted? Perhaps not. Nothing more than the novel experience, at first. To be friends with a Jew, the most forbidden thing. To conspire together. Yes, I say conspire. You did not suspect this, I think. Isaac stole the papers and my comrades in the Jungdo vowed revenge on him—so went the story, and everyone believed it. Why should they not? Yet it seems funny to me that *you* fell for it. I would have expected . . . after all, you and I have certain things in common, have we not?"

No, you think, *we have not.*

You tell him: "Go on. Conspired to do what?"

"I had the access and it was natural that I should obtain the papers. Poor Cheruski, always the dotty professor. I so despised him! I thought him the summation of every filthy-minded schoolmaster I ever had known. Perhaps I despise him still. Yet I also have come to pity him, and over the years it is the pity that has weighed most heavily. So long, so wretchedly, did he wait for the call from Berlin! But there they would have eaten him alive. He never knows when to shut his mouth, he would have ended up at Oranienburg—you know, they say Stalin's son is locked up there. And *that's* only if he was fortunate. So I kept him in Prague, under wraps you might say, for as long as I could. Had my old classmate not been transferred out of Assignments, I might have gotten him safely to the West. Let the British figure out what to make of him, or you Amis.

"I'm drifting off subject, you say? No, you didn't, thank you, but so I am. I took the papers and gave them to Isaac, and I was so kind as to let him receive the credit as well as the blame for that. It might be, also, that he slipped a page or two from the other side into my hands, I do not remember.

"No—I shall lie to you no longer. I remember it perfectly. I remember everything. The truth is, it pains me, even now, to take from you your illusions. We all need our illusions, don't you think? God knows, I wish still to have some of mine. It would be a . . . a blessing to believe once more, to believe in anything. But you know what I mean. You of all people."

Go on.

The prisoner smiles, an expression no more natural than the glow in his eyes. "Do you recall how we met? Do you recall where? It was Frau-Holle-Quell, mein Kamarad. You remember surely Frau-Holle-Quell. For myself, I will never forget it. Nor should I wish to. Many things that have happened since then I would happily forget, but not that. You were there, and I was there, and that tall fellow was with you, he was rather nice, what was his name? He came to the Leuchtenburg. And of course Cheruski was there with his little pack of disciples, and the impressive Count von Stauffenberg, about whom I could tell you a few stories. But Isaac—how did *he* happen to turn up there, do you suppose? Just in time to bump into our swinish Gruppenführer and get himself quite nearly killed. Might that have been a planned encounter gone wrong? Two little spies, conspiring to trade secrets, betraying their comrades, having their bit of fun? Playing— you have a wonderful term for this—*playing both ends against the middle,* isn't that right? Ah, but not so skilled at it, not quite yet."

No.

"You don't believe me? Or is my English wrong? Believe me, my friend. Believe me, if for no other reason, because I am too weary to lie, I haven't the necessary concentration. Your friends will come soon and shoot me, if you don't shoot me yourself. But even were I to walk out of here alive— well, what would that mean? Five million Russians are waiting on the other side of the hill. And were I to run the other way, your Mr. Roosevelt has promised to bring whom he calls *war criminals* to what he calls *justice,* which is to say he plans to line the SS up in front of a wall somewhere. If there is a wall left standing at that point.

"But I am not afraid of death. I do not seek it, yet it holds no fear for me. We are too closely acquainted, death and I. Not friends. One might say, neighbors."

I can imagine.

"I don't know what you think of me—as I have told you, I would prefer not to care—but you cannot possibly know the kind of war we have fought over here, on this side. You Amis landed in France five months ago, in a few months you will be riding your jeeps around Berlin, and history will record that the war was fought and won by you. But over here, my friend, we have been fighting for *five years,* we have lost entire generations— and surely not all our dead were war criminals. Count yourself lucky, you don't have time to hear *that* story. You may yet hope to fall asleep without dreading the nightmares that must come. You may hope to hold a child in your arms without thinking of other children . . . but perhaps we should simply leave it: *You may hope.* It is wonderful to hope. Another blessing."

Don't give me that, Ingo thinks. You launch a war on three continents, and after it turns out badly you start looking for *pity*? You can do better than that.

"Tell me," he says, "you've got nothing to lose. Tell me in plain language what you've done. How many of those 'other children' have you killed? Why does a bleeding heart like FDR want to stand you in front of a wall?"

A mask falls over the prisoner's face—a mask that never stops changing, one expression shifting into another. His hands have begun to tremble. He draws his lips inward, as if to moisten them. Then, without warning, the eyes twitch up and catch you by surprise. A queer little nod, like the look on your face has given something away. Damn him. And damn yourself, for remaining here, for listening to this.

"I was a cavalry officer, did you know that? How could you. Yes, an old-fashioned horseman, on account of my well-attested riding skills. We opened an SS riding school, I was among the first instructors. That would have been 1936. I wonder, what was Isaac doing then? During the Polish campaign we managed to field an entire company. By the time of the Russian invasion, it had grown to a brigade. We didn't see much action in the early stages—that was a tankman's game. But when winter came and the engine blocks froze up, we were the only German formation, I think, that remained fully mobile. The Russians launched their counteroffensive around Moscow, and we were thrown in to check their advance. Twenty thousand Siberian horsemen on those rugged little ponies, and about five hundred of us alive by then, on animals that were cold and half starved and poorly shod. But we made them pay for every inch. We bled them. And most of us got killed, of course, and those who didn't . . . well, you come out of something like that, I can tell you, a different man. Things that mattered once don't matter anymore, while other things . . .

"I wish you could know what I mean. But I can never explain it. Still, if you should happen to find yourself alive one day when around you is only death—all your comrades under the ground and you walking above them, hammering little birchwood crosses into the earth—at such a time you might find your view of life wondrously simplified. A man thinks, This is the only thing I love, the one thing that matters to me. All the rest, the devil can take it."

You watch the prisoner with rekindled interest. You guess he's leaving a good deal out. But you sense nonetheless that he is making, if not a confession, at least a sort of final testimony. Saying the last things that need to be said.

"The trouble with war is that you cannot just walk away, even when you grow sick of it. You wish to, but you cannot. So you do the best you can manage, which is to create your own small peace, somewhere. You would think it foolish, my friend, the things men will do. They will take any animal and make a pet of it. Or they will find some kid wandering around, half crazed, his whole family dead, and they'll turn him into a mascot. I knew a man who carved a chess set out of roots. We were living down in a hole. It was called a bunker but really it was just a hole with some canvas pulled over the top, and when you leaned against the walls you felt roots digging into your back. So my comrade, he would cut these roots out, and after a while he had a collection, so he began to carve them into chess pieces. A waste of time, no? But it kept him sane for the rest of his life, which as I recall was long enough to get the black pieces finished and half of the white.

"For myself, I wanted more than that. I wanted a . . . more comprehensive sort of peace. So I wrote to my friend in Berlin and asked to be transferred out of the cavalry. I volunteered for partisan-hunting duty, which had been popular for a while, until people realized you could get killed doing it. In fact this was quite likely, it could happen at any time, no need to wait for the next offensive. Therefore such duty became less popular and they were employing mainly foreign regiments—Romanians to hunt Czechs, Slovaks to hunt Poles, and so forth. Everybody to hunt Jews. My request was ignored for several months but then—you know how things happen in the army—one day, out of nowhere, my orders arrived. I believe Cheruski might have intervened somehow, because my assignment was to this sector, which was more than I had hoped for. By then, you see, I was no longer in the business of hoping. Yet here I was. And I was happy it was so. For it brought me back to Arndtheim. Also to Isaac."

You stare at him. You shoot X-rays through his skull, but they reveal no obvious malignancy. During this examination the prisoner watches you, almost piteously. He cares what you think. The next moment, disconcertingly, he laughs.

"Don't you see? It was the old game again, the old conspiracy. Both ends against the middle. Here was my greatest enemy, the notorious partisan, der Fuchs. The only Jew left in Silesia who wasn't counting his final hours in a camp somewhere. And here was I, his nemesis, the terrible Partisanjäger, wearing a Death's Head and riding a big white horse. What could have been more perfect? It was within our power, more than ever, for each to give the other what he most desired. For Isaac, protection. He had his own little band by that time, people who depended on him for survival—including, I was to learn, this ridiculous family here, crack-brained people left over from the Twenties who hadn't enough sense to get out. And for me, peace. A separate peace, on a secret front. Which turned out, however, not to be so simple to arrange, when one considers what I had been sent here to do."

No kidding. When one considers.

"In the army, you know, always there is someone watching you. They watch from above, but even more so from below. They expect you to do your job. If your job is to cook porridge, they want it thick and steamy in time for breakfast. If your job is to kill partisans, they want, at the end of the day, to see a bit of blood on your hands. The more blood the better. So the problem becomes, whose blood shall it be? Also, how do we extract it in sufficient quantity to satisfy everyone, above and below, yet manage also to keep certain people, secret people, absolutely safe?"

"I'll bite. How?"

The prisoner's smile saddens. "Both ends against the middle, remember? Protection in exchange for peace. For Isaac—to give you one example—I rounded up enough lumber to build the wall here, to turn this place into a little Schloss. Otherwise, these foolish people would have been murdered long ago. The Poles would have done it, or my men, or the foul spirits of the water, in revenge for all that swamp draining. There were many things I did of this kind—not least turning a blind eye to the reports coming in about this bandit, the Fox. As for Isaac, I can say he paid me in full. If anything, he was too generous. Each time we met he would hand me a little square of paper, no bigger than a ration card. And on this paper I would find a list—each item neatly written out. As you know, he hates to write, so he does it carefully."

Yes. I know.

"Everything was there: names, dates, hiding places. Enemies of the Reich, you see—bandits, saboteurs, rival guerrillas. Peasants known to shelter fugitives. You could never be certain who anybody was, not really. You only knew, here is an inventory of human lives. Take what you need, but don't be too greedy, you've got to make the supply last out the war."

"That's ridiculous. Obscene. Isaac would never—"

"No? Then what else would Isaac have done? Tell me that. I'm not asking what *you* would have done, or some other person. We're talking about Isaac, and we're talking about myself. Two natural traitors. He got his start long ago by betraying his family, his friends. I began by betraying my Volk. We simply carried on from there. It has been for us an ideal partnership, a perfect balance. More than that. More than you can know. Or perhaps it might be that *only* you can know."

No. I can't. I won't.

The prisoner sighs. "Or perhaps not. It doesn't matter, I suppose. Though I might add, if you are looking for proof . . ."

"I'm not."

"Nonetheless. I have not wholly lost my knack for picking up the odd document here and there. I seldom get my hands on anything of great value—just a few things for Isaac to send up through resistance channels, to maintain his good standing among his peers. Such peers as remain. But there was one time, a dinner party Cheruski threw—you know, the poor fellow tries so hard to weasel into the Reichsführer's inner circle—and there were some big shots there, including that fellow Hoess, who runs the camp. Another cavalry man, as it happens. Well, Hoess had this memorandum, a duplicate off a message pad, and he was showing it discreetly around, only not *so* discreetly after his ninth or tenth cognac. And it seemed to go astray, because later he was looking for it, quite pale actually, but I don't believe he found it again."

"I know what you're talking about. Why should I believe you?"

A shrug. "Well, you know Isaac got the damned thing from somewhere."

"Sure—if it exists."

"That's right. But then, you'll know soon enough, won't you?"

"Soon? Why's that?"

The head cocked, words not needed: Listen.

From the room down the hall, an aria of agony. The soprano's voice ascending, reaching a peak, holding there, then trailing into a low, agonized groan.

The prisoner nods. "Isaac may be a slippery little Kerl, but he's loyal when he chooses to be. He's not going to hide in his hole at a time like this."

Out in the corridor, Ingo just stood there, his brain boiling. He watched as though from the wrong end of a telescope, so that everything seemed very far away, Martina hurrying up the stairs and crossing the hall with no more than a glance in his direction, then disappearing into Hildi's room. The door bumped shut behind her.

He took a step to follow her, but the second step wouldn't come; some hidden power resisted him.

End of the corridor. Top of the stairs. Symbols fraught with terminality. *Women,* he grimly thought. Guardians of the final mysteries; high priestesses of beginnings and ends.

Opposites attract—well, sometimes they do, when they don't repel. Look at Ingo and Marty. Look at Ingo and women generally. Or look—the next thought, lying in ambush, now pounced—look at Hagen and Isaac.

He is back in the room, facing the prisoner while the prisoner observes him blankly.

"Where did Isaac disappear to, then?" Ingo demands. By this time, there is no need to spell it out. The terrible image, *blood on the rocks*, is sufficiently clear in both their minds.

"Where does the Little Fox ever go? Never very far. He regained consciousness and found himself alone—he was frightened, no doubt. Disoriented, possibly. A blow to the head. You were right, the water was too shallow. I suppose he went into the woods and waited there. Until everyone was gone. It is what he does. It has kept him alive for a remarkably long time."

"So . . . where did *you* run off to?"

"I ran, that's all. I was sixteen years old, for God's sake. I thought I had just seen a person die. I thought I was about to be killed myself. I was . . . in no ordinary state of mind. As soon as it grew light, I headed back here. On the way, I almost ran into the Jungdo boys. They were marching down the road in formation, left-two-three-four, as they did everything else. I took a shorter path and reached the village ahead of them, but by that time . . . *ach*, everything happened so quickly."

"So you just ran into them. They just happened to be there. At the ass end of Silesia."

The prisoner makes a thrusting motion that would've been alarming were his wrists not securely tied. "People like that," he says hotly, "they find you. Eventually they do. You think you've left them behind, outsmarted them, and perhaps you have, for a while. But they keep coming. Such men, it is in their nature. This is what *they* do, just as the Fox slips away and hides."

Now the prisoner falls quiet, and Ingo sits there brooding. A piece is missing. Not a minor one.

"It still doesn't quite explain . . ." Thinking aloud, but also inviting the prisoner to help, should he care to. "All along, you and Isaac, even before Frau-Holle-Quell—well, maybe it *was* a game to him. That would make sense, wouldn't it? Sort of make-believe, switching roles, like cowboys and Indians, then Indians and cowboys. But you . . ."

You aren't really one for games, are you?—addressing in his mind not the haggard SS officer before him but the boy in his clean blue uniform, sixteen years old, self-possessed, untouchable. "What were *you* up to back then? For that matter, what are you up to now? If you're not here to set a trap, then for God's sake, why *are* you here?"

The prisoner's ever-changing mask freezes now into a single face, and Ingo bodily draws back, because it is a face he knows.

"Are you completely unfamiliar," the prisoner says, in that moment Hagen again, Hagen the beautiful, "a man like you, a Romantic, with the concept of unrequited love?"

Then the face crumbles, the years rush back. The prisoner lowers his head until it rests on both of his hands, lashed together and clenched into a single fist. "I was only a boy," he says, so quietly you can barely hear him. "And you know, boys do fall in love."

Snap, Ingo thought. It was not a minor piece. And it fit perfectly.

Somewhere, in a different world perhaps, or a series of interlocking and strongly similar worlds, the late-autumn sun drifted across the sky, birds took wing, little girls cried and hugged their dollies, young men laid down their lives for the Mother- or Fatherland, a blue-haired widow toddled from her apartment in Adams-Morgan to take tea at the Rusty Ring, a painter tried to convey the essence of his complicated lover by giving her six arms, and an army led by Communists raced an army led by Christians to a river that flowed like an artery through the heart of their common foe.

There is only one question left to ask—a small, overlooked, seemingly unnecessary one—in order to finish the picture.

"Where," you need to know, "do I come into this? Why would Isaac drag me back over here? There must have been a hundred other ways of doing it."

"Oh, well . . . that."

The prisoner shifts uncomfortably on the bed, bound there still. But you cut him free a while ago. This poor fellow will never escape; he is powerless, and always has been.

"I suppose, really, that was an idea I might have, you know, slipped into his head. He liked it very much. It . . . I believe it amused him."

Amused him?

Well, it would have. "But"—the missing piece is close by, your fingers tingle, groping for it—"why, though, Hagen? Why me?"

The prisoner shrugs. He is beyond help now, and you pity him.

"Certain things in common?" he murmurs tentatively. Then he answers in that abrupt German manner that still manages to surprise you. "I suppose after so much time, so much loss"—at the end, an almost bashful smile—"I needed someone to talk to. And so did you, Kamarad. So did you."

"That's crazy. Verrückt. I was perfectly okay, thanks, right where I was. I didn't need anything. Especially from you."

Hagen had the grace not to respond directly. "I knew you once," he said after a measured pause. "I knew you, not in detail—what town did you grow up in, what is your favorite color—but more generally, the sort of person you were. And I see now the sort of person you have become. I do not say one is better, one is worse. Only that the two are different."

"No joke. The whole damn world is different."

"Just so. Exactly so. Es war einmal, the world was wide and green and beautiful. Is that what you mean? And in that world all things were possible. One could live freely and honestly then, with no need of make-believe. One could be simply oneself. You, Ingo—you felt that way once upon a time, didn't you? You were a Schwuler who read poetry and didn't care for swimming and fell in love rather too easily, I think. This was the Ingo I knew. And this Ingo—I remember quite clearly—was brave enough, and truthful enough, to be exactly that. I would say he was quite courageous. More so than I.

"But that world is lost, is it not? Something happened that took all that warmth and beauty and possibility away. This new world is a cold, dangerous, unforgiving place, and within it one can no longer live as one lived then. You cannot; I cannot. We have drawn into our shells. We no longer permit ourselves to yearn or dream—above all, not to reveal our love. We have come down from the Magic Mountain to live in exile on a desolate plain.

"Ah, but Isaac. Our Isaac, by some miracle, has continued to live in that other world. He is still up there on that mountain. Still follows the *Meissner-Formel.* 'We will shape our lives by our own choice, following our own inner truth.' You remember? A naïve attitude, I'm sure you'll agree. Unreasonable. A bit mad, even. Yet that was Isaac then, and it is Isaac even today.

"God knows, he was far from perfect. He was not handsome, or noble, or especially virtuous. He was nothing other than himself. He could be kind, sometimes, and there was laughter always behind those eyes. One came to love him for that. I did, and you did also. And so we must love him still, because however different we ourselves have become—you a recluse, like Eichendorff's hermit, myself a 'war criminal'—Isaac remains simply Isaac. The world has changed unimaginably. But he, alone of all of us, has never shrunk from it. It is not a matter of courage, I think, nor of tenacity, nothing of that sort. It is a matter of sheer wonder. A singular being, bestowed upon the world."

"Ein Eigene."

"Pardon me?" said Hagen, for Ingo had not meant to speak out loud and the word was barely a mumble.

"Get some rest, Kamarad," Ingo advised him. "You look terrible."

Hagen lowered his eyes. He could not rest; they both knew that. Like a starving beast of prey, he could only wait in some fading imitation of hope.

Down the hall the girl roared in agony, grunted in rage—you never would have believed such sounds could come out of that frail and nearly bloodless body. Ingo supposed there was a lesson here. But he was too tired to draw it.

Such females as were still in Arndtheim—Marty, Anna, Tamara, an ancient *Oma*, a dark-haired teenager whose complexion and comportment were in open revolt—hurried in and out of the room like agents on an urgent mission that could not be spoken of.

Ingo stepped down the stairs with elaborate care, because they were steep and his feet unsteady. No, his feet were fine, his mind was the problem. The innkeeper signaled him in some imperceptible manner—one tap-puller to another—and when Ingo sat down near the fire he slid a plate of potato hotcakes and a tankard of black beer in front of him. He remained standing until Ingo signaled back in the same occult fashion, as he would've Bernie or Vernon. Then the man lowered himself into a chair across the table. His face was not so red now. He looked oddly at ease.

"Your friend over there," the man said quietly, in perfectly neutral German. Shall we talk about that soccer match? His eyes did not move. Never before had he spoken a word to Ingo, yet Ingo understood perfectly. He leaned down to tighten a boot lace and, in the process, casually glanced toward the front of the inn. Timo was sitting alone there at a table by the door. Ingo looked away, took his time with the boot, and finally sat up. The innkeeper was munching one of the hotcakes.

"He's been sitting there all morning," the man said pleasantly. Nice weather we're having, ja? "I believe he is waiting for something. I should keep an eye on him, if I were you. My name is Alex. I am Michi's father."

"I'm Ingo. You have a fine son. This is very good beer."

The two men shook hands.

"What do you put in these?" said Ingo, admiring a bit of hotcake speared on a fork. "They're quite delicious. Waiting for what, I wonder?"

"He looks like a Slav to me—is that right?" Then, more loudly: "Buttermilk, with a dash of sharp cheese and just a bit of green onion."

"Yes, I noticed the onion. He's Serbian, I think—but so what? These might go over nicely in Washington. Perhaps a bit more salt, and a touch of sugar."

"Already there's sugar."

"Not enough for Washington."

"You know how it is with Slavs. They have a bond among themselves. You don't look like an American."

Ingo rolled his eyes. Yes, FC-Bayern should've taken that match easily. "I don't feel like one, not lately. If they have such a bond, what are all those purges about?"

"Family squabbles. You know how it is. We make the beer ourselves, right here."

"I like it very much."

"Thank you."

It was midnight, plus or minus, when Martina stumbled down those same stairs. Ingo was still sitting in the common room, and by that time most of the Varianoviks not on duty were there also, along with most of the Arndtheimers. They were engaged in a vigil that no one had planned and no one acknowledged. They sat and waited and listened with averted eyes to every sound from the room at the top of the stairs. During the interludes, the difficult silences, they conversed in muted voices about nothing much, finally nothing at all. After the conversation ran out, they merely sat. Some appeared to be dozing but nobody really slept. The BBC was playing Viennese schmaltz. There was news of fighting in Italy, heavy losses on both sides. The war, it appeared, would not be over by Christmas.

Alex, the innkeeper, kept the stove lit and the pantry open, and young Michi, thrilled at being allowed to stay up so late, ran a continuous shuttle between the kitchen and the common room, fetching beer and food and, as the hours stretched on, water and brandy. It was one of those nights when you could not get drunk, no matter how much you put down your throat. Ingo considered going upstairs to check on the prisoner—no one had done so lately—but then a door creaked up there and a moment later, one clunky footfall at a time, Martina stumbled down. Reaching the bottom, she announced in a hoarse whisper: "It's a girl."

At this, a happy clamor, shouts for Michi to top up the glasses, toasts to the newborn, the mother, the landlord, the absent dad, until somebody—maybe Tamara, no one later could be sure—thought to ask, "How's Hildi?"

To which Martina, sprawled in a chair no more than an arm's reach from Harvey Grabsteen, made no reply at all.

The baby resting in Anna's arms looked peaceable. Anna looked peaceable as well, a contented grandma for now, walking slowly back and forth across the room, letting the natural motion of her body rock the baby against her breast.

Ingo stood for a while in the doorway, hesitant to go any farther. But no one shooed him away or shot him admonitory female glances; in fact, he seemed to have reacquired the trick of invisibility. So after a while he stepped inside and gazed down at the tiny creature—hard to think of it as a girl, or as anything else—and then at the new mother, who did not look dead to him. Not quite. The pink was gone from her cheeks, that is true. Her eyes were shut and you could not be sure, without staring a long time, if she was breathing. She was. As Ingo watched, her lips opened slightly and her eyelids fluttered in some unimaginable dream. What might one dream about at such a time? Something ordinary, he guessed. Brushing your hair, closing a window—in the dream these would be astonishing, unprecedented.

Stu sat in a chair pulled close to the bed. You got the feeling he'd been there all night and that he was keeping a vigil of his own. Wearily he raised his eyes to acknowledge Ingo. He shook his head very slightly.

The baby, then. Ingo looked close, then closer yet. He was searching—who could doubt it?—for Isaac in there, concealed among those improbably small features. He found nothing of the sort—rather, a sleepy godlet from a more refined, less odorous plane of being, tired from its journey, gathered cozily into itself and taking its ease among hushed, awe-filled worshippers. Look at it: a deity with no hair, its mouth a sublime pout, blithely cuddled beyond all care and strife—ready, however, at a moment's notice, to assume the task of ruling its tiny, all-important realm.

A tear came to Ingo's eye. He wanted to kiss the curious, shriveled being.

So much, he thought, for the great mysteries. And now I shall take myself to bed.

★   ★   ★

There remain gaps in the narrative that a thousand twilights will not close. How did Ingo happen to wake up in the prisoner's room? Where had the prisoner himself gotten off to?

The village of Arndtheim was lost in its collective slumber, or so you might have thought. And Ingo was walking in his sleep; that is practically certain. He bumped through the empty common room, upsetting chairs, then stood alone in the upstairs hallway; he shivered in the snow and wondered why his boots were not on his feet; he peeked into the birthing chamber to find it empty—no, not quite. On the bed, a slender lump lay covered by a sheet.

Not in that order, necessarily.

The night was past, but morning hadn't yet come. It was the *Zwischenstufe,* the in-between stage, when shadowy beings, spies, inverts, partisans, creatures of the *Dämmerung,* traitors disguised as heroes, bartenders as SS men, emerge from the nether realm and for a brief but sometimes epochal moment take the center of the stage. Infantry assaults are launched at this hour, and their success may hang on neither the whim of the war gods nor the relative might of the armies but on an ephemeral thing Clausewitz called the *Schwerpunkt.* To armor-plated military minds, the term has come to signify the literal "heavy point" of an attack; but Clausewitz was a classicist, not a Lutheran, and he borrowed *Schwerpunkt* from his study of Grecian wrestling. Two naked athletes square off, maneuver, feint, pivot, prowl the mat—and all the while the heavy point shifts between them, unseen, immaterial, yet ineluctably decisive. At an unforeseen moment, one of the wrestlers, deeming the balance to have swung in his favor, will leap to the next stage, the gross and terminal business of physical conflict. So with armies; so with battle. "Bloodshed in war," sniffed Clausewitz, "is like the occasional cash transaction in a business normally run on credit."

Hagen knew that. He was gone from the bed, out on the battle plain, maneuvering, while Ingo lay dreaming, no doubt, some grossly physical dream. Now, out in the village, the dream had changed, but it was still no more believable.

The predawn hush was a con. Beneath it lay furtive rustlings Ingo couldn't quite hear, etheric messages he could almost decode, flickering shadows that might have been wandering phantoms but more probably were hunters, tracking you, waiting to get you in the open, lining up the shot. All this Ingo knew at once and it sent a chill right up his spine, rousing him at last to complete and terrible wakefulness. That's when he realized he was not wearing his boots.

It seemed foolish—therefore fitting—that he should die barefoot, as he had been born. Having socks on spoiled it. Ingo half turned to go back inside, but then, around the corner, came a wooden *clunk:* the village gate closing. *There,* he thought with a kind of relief. Surely he hadn't imagined *that.*

He moved up the street in a series of low bounds, like a large and grace-less rabbit, trying to land in spots where the snow had been worn clear. Reaching the gate, he yanked open the view port and stuck his face into it. He saw nothing of interest. Whoever had slipped out was gone.

At places along the wall, shaky platforms had been built with ladders to reach them, so you could climb up and look over the top and perhaps, in some Karl May fantasy, get off a few shots with your trusty Winchester. Bloom had scoffed at these improvisations: too high, too narrow, too far between. Nonetheless Ingo made for the nearest of them, not so much out of interest in what was happening outside the village wall as from a desire to get his feet out of the snow.

From the top, he stared out over the bumpy, unbeautiful countryside of Lower Silesia. It lay unmoving, loosely bandaged in a gauze of mist, as though the land itself had become a casualty. He waited for any motion, an involuntary spasm of leaf or branch; he listened hard for the hillside beneath the naked orchard to heave a great, slow, racking breath.

Nothing: the air was still. The mist somehow obscured both distance and direction; you couldn't even tell where the sunrise would come. An identical half-light lay on all sides and left little to choose between bright-ness and shadow, for neither was complete.

Ingo watched for what seemed a long time, probably just a couple of min-utes. He seemed to have passed through the cold to whatever lay beyond it. His head felt wobbly from fatigue broken by too little sleep; he might have done better not sleeping at all. Maybe that's what Hagen had done.

At this thought, some movement caught his eye. He snapped his head around but saw nothing—just the cloudy void of a meadow veined with a silver stream, and a scattering of black, tapered conifers like bottles left standing on a table.

There—movement again. Only it seemed to Ingo that what he'd glimpsed this time—no more than a flickering shadow—had come from a different place than before. So maybe there were two things moving out there. Predator and prey? A pair of lovers? No, a stranger dyad still, resis-tant to definition.

Yes. See, right there: a shaking of boughs not far from the village wall. Then a few seconds later, farther out, a dark form shifting in the meadow. Not a tree at all. A silent and nearly motionless human body.

Ingo drew a breath so sharp it nearly became a gasp. Foolishly, he slapped a hand over his mouth and for several heartbeats didn't breathe at all.

Not fifty paces away, slightly below Ingo and off to one side, Hagen stepped out of his hiding place. It would not have counted as such in ordinary daylight, just a gap between bare-limbed larches. He slipped forward now, quickly and boldly, away from the village. He was holding his arms out from his sides, not swinging them but simply letting them show, as if to demonstrate that he carried no weapon.

A separate peace, thought Ingo.

At the edge of the meadow, Hagen halted and raised one hand—not a wave, a signal.

Across the clearing, the dark, still form unfroze: Pinocchio jerking to life. Ingo strained his eyes, willing all the light in Poland to gather itself in that one spot. For a crazed instant, the spell seemed to work. It must have been Ingo's imagination, or perhaps something less easy to explain away: a genuine vision. In that flash of time he saw everything with perfect clarity.

The loose-jointed stride. The mismatched and ill-fitting costume. The red hair, partly hidden beneath a peasant's cap—the cap set back at a jaunty angle and the hair receding, laying bare an old scar. The eyes, bright as ever. A cunning in them you'd noticed before but perhaps not given sufficient thought to. Or else the cunning had grown more acute and dangerous over the years, honed to a death's edge from living in the wild.

Nose, mouth, comical ears—all the features emphatically present, if anything exaggerated. Yet the effect of them, taken together, was different now. The skin sagged a bit; lines sketched by grinning had deepened into crevices; the mouth was off-center and stubborn; the nose jutted defiantly, a challenge thrust at the world.

Yet it was Isaac. Even from this range, so far removed in years as well as distance, he was recognizably the same person as before. A man, but hardly bigger than he'd been as a boy—his frame now bony from hunger, not adolescence.

Isaac. A miracle.

In that moment of luminous clarity, you noticed other things as well. Everything. The trembling of Hagen's shoulders. The single halting step he took, tightening the gap. The mist like dragon's breath, a poisonous vapor on the land. A dark bird circling distantly; now a second—Odin's ravens, Memory and Thought.

And just before the vision ended, before the colors faded to gray, you glimpsed the strangest thing of all—a scene that might have been bor-

rowed from the Scottish play, Birnam Wood inexplicably arriving outside the castle. But it wasn't trees moving out there, it was something
among them, something substantial, and in that last fraction of an instant
you got the fleeting impression that a host of knights, their armor dulled
by rust and mud, their lances thick as cannons, had assembled at the edge
of the woods beyond the meadow, awaiting the shrill blast of a battle horn.

End of vision. The long Mitteleuropan nightmare resumes.

You see Hagen moving forward. Down there in the mist he must not
share your broad field of view, because his progress is tentative, halting.
He seems to stumble like an athlete off balance.

Isaac's view is no better, but he has an instinct. He moves unerringly
toward Hagen, and it seems to Ingo that he is reaching into a pocket. His
feet do not slow; the hand knows what it's looking for. There, a scrap of
paper, white and limp, that he raises like a tiny truce flag.

You might wish to linger here.

You might wish to savor, a few moments more, that separate peace, a
remarkable silence in the swirling storm of war, a respite, if only provi-
sional, as all things are in the black center of Europe. You might wish for
time to oblige you by pausing, as it has done before.

Now: Suspended like statues in mid-step, the two friends, or enemies,
opposites, conspirators, lovers, wrestlers, mutual predators, fellow prey—
whatever the truth might be, or all the tangled truths at once—stand perhaps five paces apart. The *Schwerpunkt* hangs between them, perfectly
balanced despite their asymmetry, German to Jew. They are near enough
to speak in quiet voices, to hear each other's breathing. They are as close,
just now, as they will ever get.

Sadly, you can work no magic. You cannot stop time, nor avert what
must happen. If you survive, the next moment will haunt you every time
you close your eyes. So perhaps you will not wish to survive, after that last
bit of innocence is lost, after dawn arrives and the mist of unknowing
burns away.

All right, you think, or some war god thinks, or the Earth itself.

All right—go on.

ON THE RAVEN'S BEAK

The boy Shlomo opened his eyes as usual in the hour before dawn. As usual he lay for a time quite still, wondering if he actually were awake or in some strange dream mocking wakefulness. In the half-light he could not be certain. The guerrilla base was quiet around him, though he knew the sentries were out there and, just now, especially vigilant. For at this uncertain hour, neither day nor night, wild creatures would be scurrying back to their lairs, and vampires crawling into their *Grüfte,* and enemies moving in to attack. Unless you were quite alert you could not be certain which was which. You might waste bullets on some ghost—that would be foolish. People would be angry and someone would say *He's only a boy,* and that would shame you.

Shlomo was no boy any longer. His papi had told him so.

He rose from his bed of fir needles and stepped out of the little hut that he shared with some of the children. He had not wanted this—he belonged with the men, the warriors—but had made no objection when they put him there. Nor when they placed clothes on him, layer upon layer as the summer changed to fall and now to winter. But at shoes, he drew the line. He had loved to go barefoot when he lived with his family, and had gone barefoot in the big camp even when snow covered the ground, as it did now.

Be glad of the snow, Papi had told him. *You feel the snow and you think: This means I am alive.*

His papi had no longer been alive when he said that. He could not come along when Shlomo marched out in the morning on work details. He could not lie with him at night, holding him close and keeping him warm. So: Be glad of the cold, because it tells you that you are alive, and Papi is not. And that is why Papi comes to visit only at the in-between time, neither night nor day, neither dark nor light. For this is where Papi lives now, in the world you cannot find on any map but is quite real nonetheless, that lies not in space but in time.

Du siehst, mein Sohn, zum Raum wird hier die Zeit.

The boy walked through the silent camp and out onto a spine of rock that jutted like a crow's bill from the face of the mountain. He passed one of the sentries but the man made no effort to talk to him, having learned over these months that Shlomo would not answer. Shlomo spoke to Papi and Mama and they warned him to be careful of strangers. *In these times,* Papi gravely said, *one can never be sure whom to trust.*

The boy remembered standing in the big camp one day, barefoot in the spring mud, and when the sun broke the horizon he had looked up and there, just there, were the mountains. They seemed so close. And yet he had never noticed them before. He had never looked up, he supposed. One mountain in particular—this one, where he now sat—had stood out from the others, on account of this spine like a great dark beak, its sharp profile catching the easterly sunlight.

"You see that mountain there?" his papi told him later, after the sun went down. "It's called Vysoká today, but once upon a time it was Krkavec, the Raven. Only they don't say *which* raven, eh?"

And Papi had laughed, gently and sadly. So much, so much, the laughter said, none of us will ever understand.

Shlomo—who was not called Shlomo then—had resolved that he would come here. And so he had come, though he could not remember just how. He believed he might have learned some tricks from Papi, such as how to become invisible at certain times, and how to tell SS men from vampires, though they look very much alike. He wondered if he himself—the one to whom they gave shoes he wouldn't wear—might be already a citizen of Papi's world, even while his body ate and slept in this one.

The boy gazed out from the mountain with his wide, empty eyes. He watched the sentry light a cigarette, warming his fingers for a few seconds in the flame. He watched an eagle circle slowly half a mile away, a deity of the skies. He watched shadows move across a land that once had been called Poland. *Names,* he thought—peculiar, how they always changed. The great fighter himself—so Shlomo had heard one partisan tell another—had not always been called the Fox. He had once had a different name, that of an ordinary boy.

"Isaac," the great fighter told him. He was sitting near Shlomo on the rock, though the sentry had not seen him arrive. "My name was Isaac."

Izaak, Shlomo repeated. The word tasted funny on his tongue—sharp, like a knife edge. But sweet as well, like green pepper.

"And you were Tzadik," the great fighter said, in his gentlest voice, the one he used with the children.

The boy gasped. No one remembered that name. Even he himself had almost forgotten it. The delight of hearing it again surged through him and he stood up straight, his bare toes clutching the rock, and he laughed like a little boy being tickled.

The sentry looked around but only for a moment—he had gotten used to this sort of thing. Everyone knew that the boy saw things other people could not; he heard voices to which everyone else was deaf. You came to accept it, as you accept almost anything, even death, after a while. After a while, it seems natural. Every shtetl has its jester, its *opnarer,* so why should a guerrilla base not have a holy fool? There is a place for everyone in this world and also, we may hope, in the next one.

"The thing is," said the great fighter, whose secret name was Isaac, "it was the right thing, what you did. You were right to go hide there at the edge of the woods. It's what your mama wanted. She wanted you to stay alive."

Yes, I know. It was true, his papi had told him. Even so, the boy found it strange that anyone else should understand.

"Only I guess it's made you a little crazy," said Isaac with a shrug. "That's all right, too, I think. I knew some people who weren't crazy at all—or only for a little while, when they were young—and it always seemed like they were missing out on something. But you—you don't miss much, do you?"

The boy had no idea. He had begun to tremble. Which was quite odd, because he scarcely felt the cold.

"Don't worry." The great man touched him on the arm—his hand burned there with a welcome kind of warmth, a living fire. "It's kind of a question of balance. It's like you're in some narrow place, you might fall off on either side. So you lean a little this way, a little that—you want to stay up there for as long as you can. Eventually, you fall off. That's how it goes. You lean a little too far one way, and—" He made a sound like what happens when an egg hits the floor.

The boy laughed. The sentry did not turn his head.

"The thing is, it happens to everybody. As far as I know it does. It happens to whole countries, even. Look down there, what's that? Silesia? The Grail Kingdom? It could be anything. It could be America."

Into the boy's eyes came a sudden sparkle. *Amerika!* That magical land.

"Yeah, well, you wait. Just stay on your feet, that's all I'm saying."

The great fighter, who once upon a time had been a boy called Isaac, began walking away. He moved easily although the path, here at the edge of the cliff, was treacherous. After several steps he paused and looked back at the boy.

"See you next time," he said.

Solemnly, Tzadik raised his hand.

And the great fighter passed into the *Dämmerung*.

ANOTHER GREEN WORLD

Out of the dawn, out of the woods, came a single clap. It was not loud. There was no second clap, and the land was too flat to produce an echo. Just one sound, then a return of silence.

One shot, that's all a good sniper needs. The best snipers in the world, by the winter of 1944, were serving in the Red Army. They were veterans of Stalingrad, Sebastopol, Kharkov, Odessa, the most gruesome battles ever fought. Seryoshka had killed already, by his own tally, one hundred and twenty-two men, Germans, Bulgarians, Romanians, Croats, Italians, Lithuanians, every sort of Fascist and counterrevolutionary and running dog he had managed to center in his scope. A single shot for each.

Now, one hundred and twenty-three. To the list, add one American.

The bullet must have passed through the thin body and out again before Isaac heard the shot. He did not die immediately. High-velocity rounds often penetrate their targets without inflicting major trauma at the point of impact. So you had this further and deepening horror, of watching the look change on his face, realization spreading across his unlovely features even as the tiny spot at his throat grew larger, like a flower opening. You watched him lift a hand, slowly, still disbelieving. *What the hell is this?* Then, that little stagger.

All the rest happens quickly—the eyes go wide and white, the paper slips from his fingers, flutters like a falling leaf, and Isaac dies. You feel his presence ebbing out of the world. You close your eyes so as not to see him fall.

You died also, then, in a way. The Ingo that you had always been, who could fall asleep without dread, who could awaken in hope. But another Ingo was there, smoothly taking control of your body, or perhaps the other had been living inside you all along—the Ingo that broke a Gruppenführer's nose and almost killed Hagen and surely killed the Defrocked Priest. Now he wanted to kill again. But first you needed a weapon, a target and, while you're at it, some fucking boots wouldn't hurt.

So: Race up the lane, screaming bloody hell, shutters popping open and people yelling down. All of it a blur. You grabbed the Schmeisser but threw it down—worthless at long range. In the common room, a Mauser stood propped against a wall. Take that. Take the innkeeper's coat as well, to cover this damn uniform.

By this time, you had managed to rouse the whole village; even women worn out from the childbirth and its awful aftermath were poking their heads out. You caught Marty's eye or she caught yours. She saw the difference right away, and you saw the surprise, the nonrecognition. Meet the new Ingo, how do you do? No time for a handshake just now. The bloodlust was upon you.

At what point did Bloom catch up? You remember a big hand grabbing your shoulder, some kind of question barked in your face. You must have answered. Perhaps intelligibly. Somehow or other, the Varian Fry Brigade got its act together, with an unknown adversary at the gate, those bastards that killed Isaac and were about to pay for it. You fell in with the others— marching side by side, a team player at last—and together you climbed the ramparts and readied your weapons, still quaking yourself with battle rage. Yet at the same time you were icy-calm inside, operationally calm; your hand steady, your eye sharp, your goal to murder the first thing that moved.

But you had gotten there too late.

By the time Ingo reached the top of the wall, across the meadow in full battle array stood what looked like the entire Red Army. He didn't realize at first it was the Russians, only that it was not what he expected. He had imagined bad guys, evil Nazis, a field of gray uniforms, a cavalry charge. Instead, this unbelievable sight: the whole meadow lined with American jeeps and Studebakers, half-tracks, armored personnel carriers and an honest-to-God tank, a T-34 that was noisy as hell and sat there swiveling its short-muzzled gun back and forth like it wanted to end the war right then and there by itself.

Between the Americans in the village and the Soviets near the tree line, Hagen stood at the center of the open space over Isaac's sprawled body. He was staring down, ignoring the growl of approaching engines, the hundred weapons sighted in on him. His head hung low, and even from this distance you could see his shoulders quaking.

The Red Army commander must have signaled a halt. The vehicles sat with their motors idling. Through hatches and windows and firing slits you could make out round-topped, dark green helmets, sometimes a face, sometimes enough of a body to draw a bead on. Ingo looked down the long barrel of the Mauser from one to another. It was a bit like staring down a roller coaster. You could practically hear the screams. But his finger held steady at the trigger. He did not plan to kill randomly. He wanted to find the right target. He wanted to be sure.

The door of a truck opened with a metal squawk and a man got out waving a white piece of cloth, apparently someone's undershirt. A second, taller man stepped out from the driver's side, and together they moved across the meadow toward the village. The man with the flag glanced at Hagen, then away. Clearly this broken and surrounded German, whoever he was, presented no danger. The man kept walking, drawing closer until you could make out his dark mustache and the sheen of his rifle stock. You noticed also that the rifle was equipped with a large telescopic sight.

The second man—for a few moments you'd taken your eyes off him— was meanwhile walking over to where Isaac lay with Hagen tilting over him. The tall newcomer ignored both of them, his head moving slowly from side to side as if he had dropped something there. Then he saw what he was looking for. He bent over, and when he straightened again he was holding a piece of paper. How big is a ration coupon? Something about like that, maybe. In the same moment, his other hand dipped into a pocket and came out with a small silver object. As he flicked it, you saw that it was an American-style lighter. The flame leapt quickly to the paper, and for a second or two the man's face was lit by the glow of fire.

What was it, the expression on that face? Triumph, fulfillment, a touch of smugness, a liberal dose of self-regard: that's how Ingo read it. And it was funny that his own instantaneous reaction, a surge of hatred, and not the expression itself, or the face on which it appeared, was how he recognized Marty's old pal Samuel Butler Randolph, the Third and very last.

The Mauser is an accurate weapon, if your eye is good and your grip is firm, and as he raised this one, the new Ingo thought, *I've wanted to do this for a long, long time.*

But the shot, when it came, was not yours.

Everyone had forgotten Hagen. By that time he was little more than a ghost, so perhaps he had temporarily vanished. When he reappeared he was holding his Walther, a classic German officer's handgun. You need a strong hand to fire one properly, and Ingo supposed that Hagen's final reserve of strength must have passed straight through that little barrel, for every bullet found its mark.

The first two were for Butler. They were placed just so, *thump*, the first in the head, then *thump*, the second in the heart. Hagen pivoted easily, master of the *Schwerpunkt*, and ran off a series of four shots into Seryoshka, who was in the middle of a slow-motion turn, the bullets tracing an arc around his back, his upper arm, his chest, then his chest again, straight-on. A fifth bullet, delayed by half a second while Hagen adjusted his aim, seemed to pass right through an eye.

That was the end, for the hundred weapons that were sighted in on him began firing all at once, and pieces of Hagen flew in all directions like red confetti tossed gaily at a parade. It was astonishing: he simply blew apart. Ingo, the new Ingo, saw this as an almost enviable sort of death, a splashy exit.

When you climbed down from the wall, when you opened the gate and stepped through it, out onto the battle plain, were you perhaps seeking an end like that for yourself? If you were, no one blames you.

One of the Americans began shooting. God knows why, or at what, or even who it was, though Ingo's money was on Harvey Grabsteen. Especially in respect to timing, for the shooter waited until you were beyond the protection of the wall, with the hundred Soviet marksmen hastily scrubbing Hagen's name off their barrels and chalking in that of yours truly. But then Bloom was yelling, and the shooting dried up.

After that, nobody fired from either side. Ingo was a perfect target, big and slow, but he might as well have been carrying the Hammer and Sickle in one arm and the Stars and Stripes in the other. He crossed the meadow in an unbroken march, the longest of his Wandervogel existence. Something about the heedlessness with which he did it, as if no one were left in the world save himself and a few scattered corpses, must have flipped some switch in the collective Soviet-American mind. By the time he reached . . .

No, not yet. Take a breath, slow down, let the world catch up. Russians were crawling out of their vehicles. Americans were climbing down from the wall. He heard Marty's voice, somewhere behind him. *Wait up, damn it.* He heard the gate swinging wider, then more voices. Now a Russian was coming up from the other side—cautious but friendly, holding out his hand. *You are American? Call me Bo.*

All right. Go on.

★   ★   ★

Isaac lay on his back. It was a terrible thing to look at, but you had died already, so what was the threat? You were kneeling beside him. You were touching his unlovely but still loved skin.

Regrets, dreams, sorrows, laughter. Memory and thought. His crooked smile, jokes you learned from him, questions you would never ask, then, now or ever. The warmth of his mouth. The danger in his sideways glance. Whom had he betrayed, how many, why? Sun on the water. Blood on the rock. A night sky, the mountains—adoration, yearning, stars overhead. His freckles. The smell of warm hay in the sunshine. His green marble eyes.

People have gathered around you but now stand back, or maybe they simply cannot come this far. You and Isaac are alone, away from winter, far from 1944.

Only one person can follow you here. Only one is able to brush past you and reach Isaac, touching his dead face with its tiny fingers. But when you look down, you see it is no person at all. It is a tiny god, a being who belongs in this frozen world no more than Isaac, no more than you. The godlet moves in someone's arms, but then the arms withdraw and you're holding the magical being yourself, as one might hold a small planet. The incredible limbs move and the dark eyes flash; the mouth opens, round as a button, to speak in a language only you can interpret.

Yes, you tell the little god, for you have understood its question. You feel its life squirming in your hands, its densely concentrated holiness.

Yes, you say—and that answer becomes a promise, a sacred vow. Yes, I will save you. Yes, I will protect you. Yes, I will tell you stories someday, funny stories about your daddy, each with a happy end. Yes, I will make your daddy live for you. I will live for you myself, to make it all come true.

Yes. I will take you away, to a place where nothing can hurt you, no one can threaten you. And you will be free there, you will have everything, you will know love and your love will be returned. And never will winter come again, and never loss, and never sadness. And there you will live forever, as we too still live—far, far away, in that magical country.

Another green world.

ACKNOWLEDGMENTS

Heartfelt thanks to Ed Shindle, my
friend and German teacher, for his kindness,
patience and steely resolve.

A NOTE ON THE TYPE

This book was set in Monotype Dante, a typeface designed by Giovanni Mardersteig (1892–1977). Conceived as a private type for the Officina Bodoni in Verona, Italy, Dante was originally cut only for hand composition by Charles Malin, the famous Parisian punch cutter, between 1946 and 1952. Its first use was in an edition of Boccaccio's *Trattatello in laude di Dante* that appeared in 1954. The Monotype Corporation's version of Dante followed in 1957. Although modeled on the Aldine type used for Pietro Cardinal Bembo's treatise *De Aetna* in 1495, Dante is a thoroughly modern interpretation of the venerable face.

Composed by Stratford Publishing Services, Brattleboro, Vermont
Printed and bound by Berryville Graphics, Berryville, Virginia
Map by David Lindroth
Designed by Wesley Gott